TIJUANA NIGHTS

OTHER BOOKS BY LEIGH K. HUNT

The Nights Series

Tijuana Nights

Venice Nights

Paris Nights (Releasing 2016)

London Nights (Releasing 2017)

The Dawn to Dusk Novella Series

London Dusk

Standalone Novels

The Mediterranean Source (Coming soon)

Find out more on Leigh K. Hunt's website:
www.leighkhunt.com

TIJUANA NIGHTS

BOOK I

THE NIGHTS SERIES

LEIGH K. HUNT

This is a work of fiction. Names, characters, places or incidents are either the product of the author's imagination or are used fictitiously, and any resemblance to actual persons living or dead, business establishments, events or locales is entirely coincidental.

Cover art and copyright © by Dwell Design & Press
Editor: J.C. Hart

ISBN-13: 978-0473291945
ISBN-10: 0473291940

AUTHOR FOREWORD

After some time of both London Dusk and Tijuana Nights being on the market separately, I have made the decision to combine both books together, mainly because London Dusk is Mack's story of how she met the team. I felt that if you just read London Dusk alone, you wouldn't get the full story, and the same theory went with Tijuana Nights. Although Tijuana Nights is written to be a stand-alone novel, I did have some concerns that readers may feel as though they didn't know Mack's full story.

So, now they are combined! Enjoy.

If you've already read London Dusk, please turn to **Page 111** to read Tijuana Nights.

Desperate times end in close calls...

London Dusk

Leigh K. Hunt

This is a work of fiction. Names, characters, places or incidents are either the product of the author's imagination or are used fictitiously, and any resemblance to actual persons living or dead, business establishments, events or locales is entirely coincidental.

Cover art and copyright © by Dwell Design & Press
Editor: J.C. Hart

DEDICATION

For my Mother, Ceals

You have been one of my biggest writing supporters from the word 'go'. Thank you for always reading... thank you for always being there.

xx

ACKNOWLEDGEMENTS

I really owe the writing of this book to Cassie Hart, my amazing editor. When she was editing Tijuana Nights, she basically held a literary gun to my head and told me to write Mack's story from the beginning. The Zombie high-heels are for her.

Michael and Abigail - you two are my grounding in all parts of my life. I love you both more than anything else in the world.

Melissa Pearl, T.G. Ayer, J.C Hart, and Richard Parry, my team of Inklings who always need acknowledgement for their continued and unwavering support in my life. Some days I just wouldn't know what to do without you all.

A big shout out to my proof-reader, Erin Travers, and my formatter, Tee Ayer, and of course - my lovely team of beta-readers! Your feedback on this novella was fantastic, and you helped make the book stronger. I couldn't do it without your sage advice.

And finally - the biggest acknowledgement is to my family. Thank you for believing in me. Thank you for always being there. And thank you for always encouraging me to pursue my dreams.

1

Drum and Bass pounded the air in my Mini, as I wove my way through the London streets. Friday's rush hour traffic wasn't due to hit for another few hours, and I couldn't wait to get home to start wrapping up my latest history project.

I had just spent the day at the London Library, tucked away in their writer's room, enjoying the focused atmosphere while doing research. The London Library is one of the places I have come to seriously love while doing my job. While most days I work from home, I've been known to just go to the Library for no apparent reason whenever I'm in the city centre.

Today was an excellent day in terms of productivity. I wasn't far away from wrapping up this research report and sending it to my client. There is nothing quite like the high of finishing something you're really proud of.

The heavens opened just as I pulled into my street. In my head I had already walked in to the house, started the fire, changed into my slippers, and pulled something out of the freezer for dinner for Luke and me, before starting my work in front of the roaring fire.

I pulled into the driveway of my house and a smile lit my face as my eyes fell upon Luke's car parked in the garage.

He was home early. I grinned.

He worked so hard, all of the time. I often found that because he was so drained whenever he got home from work, or being away on the multiple business trips that he had to take all of the time, there was never much time for just him and I. He'd supported me so much in my career as a Historian, and I loved it when he took a little time out just for himself. It made for a happier him, and a happier relationship between us.

I pulled my car in beside his, and walked inside, dumping my keys on the bench and kicking off my shoes. A flash of irritation went through me momentarily when I realised the fire wasn't lit yet, so I spent a minute preparing that. Luke still hadn't come to greet me, which wasn't like him. In fact... I usually found him watching sport in front of the TV if he ever came home early.

I went through to my office and grabbed a few papers and my laptop, taking them back to the living room to my favourite armchair where, later, I would park myself for the night and write. The fire was starting to crackle, and I forgot my irritation with Luke. He was probably exhausted and had gone up to bed for a nap or something after his trip.

I took the steps two at a time as I made my way upstairs. The bedroom door was closed when I reached the landing. I paused, wondering if I should wake him up or not. As I pondered my decision, my eyes fell on a photo taken of me and Aunt Elsie down on the Dover Coast a few years back. My Aunt had signed this house over to us when she went into a care unit providing we pay for her care costs. She'd spent so much on my education, that I thought it was a very fair trade.

Elsie was my mother in almost every sense. Nearly twenty years ago, my parents were taking me to Wales for the weekend. While we were on the road, my dad fell asleep at the wheel, and we had a horrific head on collision. I survived it with minimal injuries. But they didn't. Elsie took me in and raised me as her own. She's a beautiful woman with a heart of gold. She's now in her sixties, and has had early onset of dementia for a few years. She's not that bad yet, but she can be a bit doddery sometimes, which makes her feel older to me.

A noise bought me back to the present and I looked to the door with confusion. I took a step towards the bedroom and paused again, my hand resting on the door handle. Distinct sounds met my senses, and my breath hitched. I silently turned the knob and pushed the door open.

I swallowed, my heart raced. Luke was in bed all right. A woman was facing away from the door, her pert arse pointed right at Luke's bulging cock, and she was tied up to the headboard of my bed.

"Come on bitch - tell me how you like it." Luke grunted as he pushed himself into her roughly before slowly withdrawing, causing her to moan in appreciation.

"Harder", she moaned into the pillow. Disbelief washed over me. I would recognise that voice anywhere. It was my best friend, Nicole.

"What? I didn't hear you," Luke commented, as he slapped her arse hard.

"HARDER!" she screamed. That seemed to appeal to him, and he pummelled himself even harder into her.

My heart raced, and I had the biggest moment of 'I don't know how to approach this' I'd ever had in my life. I just stood there, watching them, disgusted. I was never going to sleep in this room again. Or in that bed.

Clothing was scattered about the floor, so I started picking it up. They still had no idea I was in the room. But I quietly and calmly picked it all up, and silently walked over to the window. I unlatched the window, and threw it out on my front lawn. Then I turned to Luke, my heart felt like it was going to beat out of my chest, and I could feel the blood pumping in full force around my system.

I reached out, and grabbed his sweat-slicked shoulder, and wrenched him off her, with all my might. "WHAT THE FUCK!?" I screamed, fury finally ripping through me.

Luke's wild eyes swung toward me in confusion. "McKenna." He just stood there, his eyes flicking between me and Nicole. Guilt was written all over his features as I searched his face. "Wh...what... what are you doing here?"

I put my hands on my hips and drew in a deep breath, "What do you mean what am I doing here? I LIVE here. This is my house. What are you doing with her?" I pointed at Nicole who was still tied to the headboard; she visibly shrank under my accusing glare. I turned back to Luke. "Get out."

"Mack." His eyes pleaded with me. "Please."

"PLEASE WHAT?" I sneered. "Please Mack let me stay after I've been caught fucking your best friend?" I turned to Nicole, "What the hell were you thinking?"

"I..." she said quietly, and then shut her mouth. She was speechless. I was furious.

"How could you? How could you do this to me? You're my best friend! I trusted you with EVERYTHING." I could tell she was about to cry, but I no longer cared. I wanted to throttle her. Instead I clenched my hands as I turned back to Luke. I saw him trying to cover himself up with the sheet. "Take your shit, and go. And don't fucking come back."

"Mack..." he repeated. "Please don't do this."

I rolled my eyes and snorted with disbelief. "Do what, Luke? I haven't done anything here. NOTHING. You have done this. You did this to us." I pointed towards the door. "Now go." I waved my hand to dismiss him, and gave him a cold smile.

"I'm..." Nicole said, jiggling her arms. She was stuck. She couldn't go anywhere of her own free will right now, no matter what she wanted.

"For fuck's sake," I said darkly as I crossed over to her to help untie her.

"McKenna," she whispered to me, tears rolling down her face. "I'm so sorry."

I shook my head, and gave a disbelieving laugh. "You're sorry? You've got to be kidding me, right? You're sorry you're caught," I spat as I worked on the ropes, anger simmering within every tug.

"I never meant to hurt you."

With a final pull the rope came free, and her arms dropped. I turned to her, my stomach rolling with contempt. "Then you should never have done it." I swallowed, and I knew I was close to crying. "Now go."

She got up off the bed, and went to look for her clothes. When she couldn't see them, she turned to me in confusion. "I don't know where my clothes are." Luke walked over to her, wrapping her in the sheet from the bed. He was dressed, and ready to walk out the door. Obviously he'd found some other clothes to put on.

I pointed to the window. "They're on the front lawn. Now GO!"

"McKenna, stop," Luke said, holding his hand up. "We don't need to do this."

I blinked, tears threatening to fall. "Yes we do. I don't want you in my house. I want you to go right now."

"Mack..."

"JUST GIVE ME SOME FUCKING SPACE, LUKE!" I screamed at him, "GET OUT. NOW!"

He visibly swallowed, and turned Nicole towards the door, throwing me a look of regret. When I heard their footfalls on the staircase, I stood there in a stunned silence, still staring at the bedroom door. The front door banged shut downstairs, and I crossed to the window, my arms folded across my chest as if they could stop my heart from breaking, and watched Nicole run around the lawn, picking up her various items.

I sniffed, and my lip wobbled. I watched her run towards the garage, and moments later, Luke's car reversed out, turned around on the driveway, and I watched them disappear down the street. Tears openly flowed as grief consumed me and I sank to my knees.

"How could you," I whispered. "How could you." I curled up in the foetal position on the floor, staring at the ribs in the carpet feeling numb, tears pouring down my face.

I stayed on the floor like that for hours, getting colder and colder as the night closed in around London. I simply couldn't believe the betrayal of both Luke and Nicole. Two people I infinitely trusted with all my heart had broken me.

I had never once considered the possibility that there could ever be something between them. My brain replayed multiple dinner parties, coffee dates, and drinks, and not once had they ever given me cause to second guess the relationship between them. It made me seriously question my powers of observation. It was either me with a lack of perception, or they were just that good at deceiving me.

Eventually I came to the conclusion that I needed to move. Stiffly, I began to get up. I was cold, and when I moved, shivers ran through me. I knew I couldn't stay on the bedroom floor for the rest of my days. My nose was clogged up from crying. My eyes felt hot and puffy. To be quite frank, I was a bloody mess. I stood in the dark room, leaning against my reflection in the mirror, and questioned where the hell I had gone wrong. How could I have judged two people that badly and got myself into this situation. I was exhausted. Drained. And I didn't know what to do.

Eventually, I managed to find the liquor cabinet, and stare blankly at the bottles in front of me. My body was numb, but my mind wasn't. They had betrayed me. I needed to quieten my thoughts. Another shiver bought me back to reality, and I picked up a bottle of whiskey, my common sense telling me that would warm me up.

Tipping a good measure into a tumbler, I crossed the room to the now cold fireplace. I knelt down, my knees aching, and heaved a sigh as I bunched up more paper, stuffing it in, and laying the kindling. I took my time, concentrating on the task at hand, and lit it carefully. It helped me lose the immediate and invasive thoughts of Nicole being tied to the headboard and Luke enjoying her.

I swallowed back more of the whiskey as I absently watched the flames spread in the hearth.

I was tired. I didn't want to sleep upstairs by myself... not tonight. I wanted to be down here with the warmth of the fire for company. I walked to the linen cupboard, and pulled the winter featherweight duvet from its storage place, dragging it over to my favourite armchair.

I thought that Luke and I would be together forever. We'd never had the hottest or steamiest whirlwind romance - not like the ones you read in books. But it had been comfortable. He supported me in living my dreams, and in return, he got a wife-like figure to share his life with. Obviously that wasn't enough for him. We had discussed marriage once or twice, but I really didn't see the point in getting married. It was more his thing, based on his upbringing with a happy family.

When I thought about it more, we had never really even discussed having children. Children were not something I could see myself having in any foreseeable future with Luke, or ever really. Tears slipped down my face as I retrieved the whiskey bottle from the cabinet, taking it over to my chair. I glanced down at the research paperwork on my side table, and dismissed it. The happy thoughts I'd had earlier about writing my way through the night were long gone. There was no way I could possibly focus on work now.

But work was something I would have to turn my attention to at some point in the very near future. Without Luke's income supporting me, I sincerely doubted that I would be able to survive for long. "You bastard," I muttered, once again draining my whiskey glass. Emotions welled up inside me, swirling around. "YOU BASTARD!"

I smiled, feeling a tad better. But not for long. I didn't know what to do. I had to pay for Elsie's care costs, as well as live myself. I didn't have a mortgage to pay, but I did have an energy bill, plus the phone and internet, as well as for another load of firewood to be delivered. I knew I didn't have much in my accounts, but I wondered if Luke would mind me accessing our joint account to cover those things - fuck him, he owed me after what I'd seen tonight.

I pulled the brand new iPhone out of my pocket and turned it over in my hands. I had completely forgotten about it. I'd bought it that day as a special treat to myself, and because my old phone had finally bitten the dust after five years. I had no idea how to really work the iPhone, but the people in the shop had transferred everything over so apparently it was just like my old one. I unlocked it and opened my contacts. I scrolled through until I reached Jax's number and dialled.

Jax is my other best friend. She's straightforward, French, and very loving. A lot of people, if they're not used to her, think that she's over the top 'touchy-feely' but that's just how she's always been. When I first met her I almost thought she was a lesbian, but she's most definitely not. She would know what to do.

But the phone rang and rang, so I left a quick message asking her to phone me back.

I sat there watching the fire crackle in the hearth, and snuggled under my duvet, waiting for the phone to ring. My mind kept replaying the look on both Luke's and Nicole's faces. I could tell that Luke didn't expect me to be so ballsy with them. What did he expect? Me to roll over and take it? Be meek about the situation? No. And the cheek of them desecrating my house like that! Elsie would be absolutely appalled by that sort of carry on.

I wasn't going to sleep in that room anymore. Tomorrow I was going to move my stuff back into my old room, the one I grew up in. I didn't care that it wasn't the largest room in the house. I didn't want to ever sleep in that room ever again. And I was going to buy a new bed with new linen on our joint account. Luke could suck that one up.

2

Two Months Later

Finding a park on the street is near impossible in London, especially when you're in a rush. Already I had driven through three parking buildings and had yet to strike gold. Nothing pissed me off more than being late.

"Just one more loop ..." I muttered, "and then I'm just going to double park."

The cafe Luke had chosen drawing closer. And then I saw one. It was a small park, but since I had a Mini, I was pretty sure I could get into it.

It took a fifty-point turn to eventually get the car into the spot. When I turned the engine off, I rubbed my sweaty hands down my pants. I spritzed some perfume over me. I hardly ever wore the stuff, but I was so nervous and I didn't want Luke to smell my fear.

I bit my lip as I grabbed my handbag from the passenger seat, and ran across the road.

I opened the door to the warm, bright cafe, immediately noting how well-dressed everyone was. Mellow French café tunes sounded across the room, drowned out occasionally with bouts of laughter from the patrons. I gritted my teeth in determination, scanning the room for Luke.

"Can I help you?" Someone asked, pulling my attention from the crowd.

I shook my head. "I don't think so. I'm just meeting my boy-" I stopped and cleared my throat. "Err, friend here. My friend."

The waitress smiled at me. "That's fine. If he's not here already, just find yourself a spot. We're quite full today, but a table has just cleared over there, so that's probably your best bet. I'll come and take your order when he gets here."

I thanked her and wove my way between tables towards the empty table I wanted to find an 'out of the way' place, so that Luke and I could actually have a good, honest discussion, but the only table free was placed right in the middle of the room. Grimacing, I hung my handbag over the back on the chair and sat down. I rubbed the back of my neck as I checked my phone for messages, but there was nothing. I watched the people in the room. They were all dressed rather well, and the atmosphere of the place gave me the impression that this was a very swanky joint.

I hoped like hell Luke would arrive. I didn't want to pay for anything as I was still completely skint. I had tried to get a job, anything that would help keep me afloat, but I'd had no such luck. No one wanted to employ a historian with no practical work experience, like serving in shops or cafes. The bank had given me a small loan to help me keep Elsie's care costs at bay, and I had been mainly living off my credit card over the last two months. I was in debt up to my eyeballs, and something was going to give sooner or later. Luckily for me, I had managed to throw myself into my work and I finished off that report, and had been paid for it. That had definitely helped, but it was by no means lucrative. It just meant I didn't rack up the bills as quickly as I could have.

There was talk in the wind of another report coming my way, but nothing had been confirmed yet. This was the biggest issue I was having. I had nothing secure and no stable income. Writing that report after Luke had left helped me get through. It had been a brilliant distraction from facing my own demons. Now I didn't have anything.

Where the hell was Luke? I crossed my legs, but couldn't stop my foot from tapping away, and I found myself wiping the sweat from my hands again. I didn't want to see him. I had received a few messages from him since I threw him out, and he'd been around to pick up a few things and some clothing while I wasn't there, but other than that - there had been nothing. Not even an apology. I'd been through the blues over this, I'd been through anger. Now I was just numb. But that didn't stop me being nervous about seeing him again.

Around me, plates clattered, glasses tinkled as they were carried, people laughed, and there was a constant level of chatter.

And then I saw his sandy-blonde, over styled hair as he walked into the café. Luke wasn't bad looking, but he was definitely no super model. He had a good figure, probably from the hours that he spent at the gym each week. Now that I thought about it though, I wondered if he'd ever really been to the gym. I closed my eyes, and took a deep calming breath. "It's going to be fine," I whispered. I looked down at my chipped and very imperfect nails and started picking at the rough edges of them again.

"McKenna," Luke said with a small smile as he reached the table, his hazel eyes giving me a once over. He looked as though he was about to lean down and kiss me on the cheek, but then he changed his mind. He shrugged off his suit jacket, and hung it over the back of the chair. "Can I get you a coffee or something?"

"Yes, please." My voice came out with a slight

pitch.

He waved the waitress over, who took our order. "So ... I wanted to meet with you so that we could go over some of our mutually acquired assets, and the division of those."

He looked uncomfortable. Good. It didn't stop me from feeling slightly nauseous.

"What assets?"

He cleared his throat and ran his hand through his hair. "Well ... you know. There are a lot of my things still at the house that I would like to get back."

I nodded. "Yes, I agree with that. There are. I've already put most of your things in boxes in the garage. You're more than welcome to come any time to get them, just don't bring 'her' with you."

Luke refused to look at me, choosing to watch other people instead. "You know ..." He paused, and loosened his collar. "She's a good person. And she really misses you."

I stared at him, unable to believe what I was hearing. "You have got to be joking. Luke," I said, dangerously quiet. "You cheated on me with my best friend, and then have the gall to defend her?"

He avoided my gaze. "Nicole was always there for me, Mack. Always. She actually understood. When you were working, you were so caught up in whatever project you had at the time, and you hardly ever spent any time with me, or any of us. Sometimes this would go on for months! What did you really expect,

McKenna? That I was going to wait around while you finished the next report, and then the next? It was a never ending cycle of poorly paying, all-consuming reports, which cost us money. And our relationship."

"You're blaming this on me?" The people at the next table stopped talking, and a couple of them began eying us up.

Luke reached out and patted my hand, which I quickly withdrew from his reach. "Settle down, please." His voice and eyes pleading with me. "I don't want us to have a scene."

"Well then you chose the wrong place, Luke," I spat. The waitress chose that moment to put our coffees down in front of us, diffusing the situation.

"Listen. I want all of this resolved, just as much as you do," he said after she left, looking resigned to the fact that I was pissed off at him.

I stirred my latte, waiting for him to say something else, and trying to think about what I wanted to say. Since the day I had walked into my house to find him shagging my best friend, it had been some of the worst months of my life.

"So, what do you want to resolve? You can come and pick up your stuff. I'm happy for you to do that."

"Uh yes, thanks." He looked uncomfortable again. "There's also the matter of everything else that we need to sort out."

I stared at him. "Like what, exactly?"

"Well ... your car." He cleared his throat. "I bought

that car for you, so ... I'd like to be paid back if you are going to keep it."

My eyes flew to the window, where I spotted my little red Mini Cooper across the road, parked between two massive SUVs. "Of course I want to keep it, it's my car! I know it was a gift, but you can't give someone something and then expect them to pay you back for it!" I turned my cold glare back to him. "What do you think I am? Some sort mistress you can keep for sex and housewifely duties, and then when it suits you - take everything away again? We were in a relationship, Luke."

"Well then, you know how much it cost, so I'd like at least the depreciated value of the Mini back. Also, we need to talk about Elsie's care costs that I have been forking out because you haven't been making any money. I have a spreadsheet I can send you regarding all those. I think I'm entitled to some sort of money back for all the years I've paid for her to be cared for."

"A spreadsheet...of course. Ever the accountant." I took in a deep breath. That was thousands of pounds right there for her care. "Where on earth am I going to find that sort of money, Luke? Where?"

He shrugged. "That's not really my problem. I paid for Elsie out of my income ... now you can pay me back."

I swallowed, heat rising to my cheeks. "We were in a relationship, Luke!" I repeated, my voice laced with anger. "You agreed that WE would pay for Elsie's care in return for the house. You AGREED."

Luke nodded. "I know I did. Which brings me to my next point. We have been in a de-facto relationship for seven years, so legally I'm entitled to half the house."

I leaned back and gave him a cold, measured look. He was serious. Heat flared in my cheeks. "You want my fucking house now, too? What, it's not enough that you already have my best friend... now you want half of the only home I have ever really known?"

He looked at me pointedly. "I think I'm entitled, McKenna. I supported you our entire relationship, it's only fair that I have half."

I crossed my arms over my chest, and my lip automatically curled. "You are a heartless prick, aren't you?" I couldn't believe it; I was actually seeing red as I stared at him. "My aunt signed that house over to me, Luke, me!" I put my palms down on the table and pushed my chair noisily back as I stood. "You are not going to take my family home out from under me." My voice was getting louder and louder, but I no longer cared. Luke just stared right back at me, infuriating me even more.

"Then I'll see you in court."

"Fuck off, Luke. Fuck off out of my life. You're an arsehole. If you want your shit from MY house, you'll find it on the lawn."

He shook his head, a smug smile on his face. "My

lawyer has already told me I have a case. If you won't settle this between us, it goes to court."

I flung my bag over my shoulder, and turned on my heel.

"I mean it, McKenna," Luke shouted at me across the café. People had stopped talking, and they stared at us in a stunned silence. "You owe me. Don't you ever forget that."

I kept walking. Tears pricked my eyes as I pushed the café door open and stepped out into the fresh air. I crossed the busy road, and reached my car. I couldn't stop the tears from falling now, and sobs threatened to wrack my body. I didn't want to cry in public though. I held my breath as I unlocked the car and climbed inside, slamming the door shut.

Shoving the key in the ignition, I practically launched the car out of the car park before I had to pull over a mile down the road, anger and remorse consuming me.

I raised my water bottle to my lips and slugged back, letting the water calm me down as I drank. "Luke!" I said to myself in a whisper. "How could you?"

A message tinkled on my phone, and I pulled it out of my bag to read it. It was Jax. How did coffee go?

Awful, I responded. I leaned my head back on the headrest and watched the traffic pass me by. I had to get home. I couldn't believe I had told Luke I would throw all his shit on the lawn. That was such a Desperate Housewives stunt to pull. Unfortunately though, the more I thought about it, Luke did actually have a case. He had supported me throughout, my career had only bought in a trickle of an income. He'd also supported Elsie. He had paid for the power, internet and the phone connection, as well as all the food. And to top it off, he had also bought me my lovely car.

If it had been the other way around, and I was in his shoes, I would want something as well.

My phone tinkled again, and another message from Jax flashed up on the screen. I'm coming round with wine as soon as I finish work. Despite everything, I smiled. She knew exactly what I needed: a good girly sob session over booze.

I blew my nose into a slightly crumpled tissue I found at the bottom of my bag, disgusted that I had been subconsciously wiping it on my jacket sleeve. Jax would be appalled if she saw me in a state like this.

Before I pulled out of my park, I sent a text to Luke, not knowing how on earth I was going to do this. *Luke... you'll get your money. But just give me some time.*

3

I'd had far too much to drink, and knew that I was well and truly past my capable limits. But I just didn't care, and Jax kept the wine flowing freely into my glass, which I kept freely pouring down my throat.

The fire was roaring as Jax put more wood on top of it, and when she finished, she sat down on the floor opposite me stretching out her legs.

"So ..." She looked at me with glazed eyes. "How are you going to make the money that Luke wants? What can you do?"

"I have no idea," I answered glumly. And I really didn't know. I had tried finding a job, and I'd already got a loan from the bank. "I'm stuck between a rock and a hard place with this ... but Luke will hopefully give me some time."

Jax shrugged. "He may. Or he could just be a prick about the whole thing and want it all now." She sighed. "I wouldn't put it past him."

She lit a cigarette from the fire's flames, and held the pack out towards me. I took one, not even thinking twice. I knew I probably shouldn't smoke, as I had given it up years ago, but I was beyond a state of caring. No one was here to look at me disapprovingly, and I no longer had to answer to anyone.

I lit the cigarette and took a deep draw on it. It felt good. Tasted good. I smiled, enjoying the moment.

"If Luke comes back to me saying he wants it now, he's just going to have to wait anyway. I don't have the money, and I'll be damned if he's going to bankrupt me."

Jax burst out laughing, and took a slug on her wine glass. She looked at me thoughtfully as she swallowed her mouthful. "There are plenty of ways to make money if you're willing and able."

"No doubt," I agreed. "But for a washed up old historian like me?"

Jax shook her head. "You're not 'washed up' or even that old. Stop talking negatively about yourself like that. You have plenty of qualities that you could utilise ... You just need to think outside the box a little."

I had another puff of the cigarette, enjoying it far

too much. "What box?"

She shrugged, and blew out an audible sigh. "The box you have yourself in, Mack. Do you know how I managed to buy my apartment freehold?"

I nodded. "Prostitution."

Jax looked momentarily offended, and then smiled. "Yes, essentially. Acting as a High Class Escort. You know, you could do the same. You don't even have to sleep with the clients to easily earn ten grand a night. You could look into it."

I snorted. "You have got to be joking!" I had a gulp of my wine, while still chuckling to myself. When I looked up at her, I instantly saw she was being deadly serious. "You're serious?!"

"I am. I made a lot of money that way, Mack - and you could do the same."

I shook my head. "No way. Just ... no. I can't have sex with people for money. It's just not in my DNA. You ... You're gorgeous, and you have this confidence and air about you that makes you sexy. Me? I have nothing like that ..." I trailed off, watching Jax as she watched me. I was actually kind of speechless. She meant it. I was way too pissed to be having this sort of conversation.

"You don't have to sleep with the clients. That's what I'm saying. For ten grand a night, they are literally just paying you to escort them somewhere or for your company. When I worked for Annalise, we were ... what would you call it. Extremely Upper to

High Class Escorts. If they want to sleep with you the client pays a lot more. Don't you think that's something worth thinking about?"

She had a point.

She leaned forward. "I was making thirty grand a week for three nights work. You could do the same, and still tinker around with your little history reports."

I stared at her. "Thirty grand?"

That was more money than I could possibly imagine thinking about right now. That was an insane amount of cash.

"Yes, at least. I worked three days a week for Annalise, and that was my base rate. I paid for my education, my apartment, my car, everything I needed came out of that. And I even managed to put some aside as a buffer when I stopped working for her. It was really a win-win situation."

I put my hand up to my face. "Look at this face?! Does this face look like someone who could sleep with other people for money?"

Jax burst out laughing. "Sure. Look, all you have to do is read a few sexy books, maybe loosen up your mind a little bit for when you're in the bedroom, and you'll be fine."

Just the thought of me reading smutty books had me giggling. I was the first to admit I was a bit of a literary prude when it came to my reading tastes. I slowly shook my head. "Oh, I don't know. I'm just not that confident."

Jax snorted. "That's because you've never been with the right men. You would know sexual confidence if you had been."

I shrugged. "You probably have a point."

Jax started giggling. "Look, if you wanted to, you could always imagine the position Nicole was in when you walked in. A bit of BDSM wouldn't lead you astray. In fact ... it might actually empower you."

I stared at her for a moment, realised she was serious, and drained my glass. "And on that note, I think I should go to bed," I said, realising that the room was spinning just a little too much.

Jax smiled, her eyes twinkling with mischief. "Okay. Just promise me you'll think about it. I'm still in contact with Annalise, and I'm sure she would help you out."

I went to stand up but lost my footing and had to grab the coffee table to stay upright. "Okay," I muttered. "I'll have a think about it."

4

I was never drinking again. I could feel my heartbeat pounding through my head as soon as I woke from a very groggy sleep. I felt as though I'd hardly slept at all. I reached for the water glass on the bedside table, only to find it was empty. Morning sunlight streamed through the gaps in the bedroom curtains, hurting my eyes. I blinked a few times trying to clear my head, but it wasn't going to happen without some sort of medical assistance.

Swinging my legs out of the bed, I groaned. Hangovers were honestly the worst side effect of drinking alcohol. I ran my tongue over my teeth, only to encounter nasty morning fuzziness, even worse than normal since I failed to brush my teeth before climbing into bed last night. Stumbling to the bathroom with my water glass, I turned on the tap, and filled it. My reflection caught my eye, and I leaned closer to look at myself. "McKenna Carmichael, you are losing it," I muttered.

I was a wreck. My long blonde hair was still up in its standard ponytail, but it looked as though it had been attacked by a bunch of birds. My eyes were bloodshot, especially since my contacts were still in, and they now felt scratchy as well. I pulled the contacts out of my eyes, and sighed at my blurry reflection. My skin felt clammy and yuck. I filled the sink with hot water, and reached for a facecloth to dip. As the wet cloth met my skin, relief swept through me.

Yesterday had been one of the worst days of my life. I had no idea how on earth I was going to find the money to pay Luke. If I had gone and worked for Oxford University when I was offered a position there, I would have made a very good income. But Luke had persuaded me to stay private, saying that he would support me. He said he liked having someone at home... reminded me him of his mother staying at home and keeping house, with cooked meals, clean washing, and warmth.

I should have walked then.

While it was great having Luke support me to do one of the things I loved the most, it also took some extreme focus to write. So in all honesty, clean washing and cooked meals weren't exactly a priority for me during those times. I just never realised how neglected or lonely Luke felt. He had told me numerous times that he wanted to support my passion for writing and studying history. That he liked how obsessive I became over details, and that he liked that it made me happy. We had always spent plenty of time together, even when I was working. We saw a lot of movies, went out for dinner, and spent time with friends or just each other. I never ever thought that I had neglected him or our relationship because of my work. Or was it that he was just a dog, and using my work as an excuse for developing a relationship with Nicole?

I'm the first to admit that I'm addicted to my work, and hiding myself away in the archives when I can. More than the archives, I loved the travel. There is nothing quite as magical as travelling around Europe and delving into the history behind it.

But regardless of how much I loved my job, it didn't change the fact that I had absolutely no money to pay Luke.

It was good having Jax here to listen to my sob story for the millionth time. Thank god I didn't lose her as well during all of this. Jax made me feel like I didn't need either of them. In a way, I knew she was right, but it didn't stop me from missing them.

A knock on my bedroom door pulled me from my sombre thoughts. I wrapped my dressing gown around me, and opened the door.

Jax fell through it, passing me painkillers as she made her way past me to my bed. "God damn it, Mack, why the hell did we have to drink so much last night?"

I popped two painkillers and disappeared into the bathroom. I turned on the tap and shoved my face under the faucet and slurped at the water. Nothing had ever tasted more amazing.

"Your spare bed is bloody uncomfortable, by the way," Jax called out to me. Despite feeling like shit, I smiled. That was Luke's bed from his student days. Another thing to throw on the lawn when I got around to it.

I exited the bathroom, and cast my eyes to Jax's. "I'm a mess."

She looked amazing, even with a hangover. Long, dark, glossy hair fell around her chocolaty eyes. Jax was French, but she'd moved to England to study. I met her at a party once, and we had stuck together like glue ever since. Her full name was Jacqueline, spoken in that gorgeous and sophisticated French way, but ever since she'd arrived in London, she'd shortened it to Jax. When she met me, she started calling me Mack, even though most people knew me as McKenna.

"It was Luke's bed." I walked around to the other side of my bed, and climbed in beside her. "He'll be needing that now, I'm guessing."

Jax's eyes twinkled with mischief. "Perhaps we

could airlift it and drop it through the roof of Nicole's house as a 'free delivery'."

I shook my head, snorting with laughter. "If I had the money – I wouldn't hesitate. Instead, he can pick it up from the lawn with the rest of his crap."

"I would have burnt it as soon as he left." She pulled a packet of cigarettes out of her robe. "Shall we?"

My instincts screamed no, but I found myself nodding. The cigarette met my lips, and I lit it. Aunt Elsie would kick my arse if she knew I was smoking in her house. Luke would be disgusted, but I no longer gave a shit about what he thought. I got out of bed and opened one of the windows so that my bedroom wouldn't completely reek of smoke.

"Have you given any more thought to my proposition?" Jax asked.

I turned to her. "You're not serious?"

Jax shrugged at me. "Well, you can make a lot of money. It's entirely up to you."

"It's prostitution, Jax!"

She shrugged again, blowing out a lung full of smoke. "It's 'escorting', and a lot of the time you don't even sleep with the men, remember?" Her dark gaze met mine. "I made a lot of money. I just think you should consider it."

I reached down to the bedside drawer, and retrieved a pair of glasses. There was no way I could sleep with someone for money. Just the thought of it made me feel ill. I was nothing like Jax. She was beautiful and chic. People were drawn to her. I wasn't like that. Even if I was getting paid a load of money.

"I don't know if I can do it, Jax," I muttered. "I can't even read sex scenes in books - I skip over them. How am I supposed to perform the act with strangers? I'm not like you."

She laughed. "You are more like me that you know..." She stood up and made her way towards me. She dragged me over to the mirror, and tucked some lose strands behind my ear. "Look at yourself, Mack. You are not the prude you think you are." I lifted my eyes to meet her concerned ones in the mirrors reflection. "You are a stunningly beautiful woman. You have been burnt by people who don't deserve your love. But you need the money." She removed my glasses, and placed them on the windowsill, and let my hair loose from the rubber band I had tied around it.

My insides turned at her words. I did need the money. "But—"

She lifted her finger to her lips to stop me talking. "You have some of the bluest eyes I have ever seen." She spun me around and brushed my stringy hair out of my face a bit, loosely combing through it with her fingers. "And yes, your hair needs some work as you never look after it, but trust me - you have the base. I can turn you into a very desirable creature if you let me."

Her warm and comforting words wrapped themselves around me. "Do you really think so?"

She chuckled. "What, you think that because that dog cheated on you it means you're not beautiful, desirable?" She tutted with a shake of her head. "You are one of the most caring and wonderful women I know. You will find love again one day - but in the meantime, you need to pay that asshole back and get him out of your life." She lifted some lipstick and gently applied it, then turned me back to the mirror "You are beautiful, Mack. See? And if you let me help you, it won't be too much of a struggle."

Yikes. She saw me so differently to how I saw myself. Even with her playing with my hair and putting on lipstick, I could kind of see a difference. I turned away from her, crossed the room, and stared out the window nervously. Selling myself for money? It wasn't too different from what I already did. Each time I wrote a history report, a little piece of my soul was embedded into it... and people paid for that. But sleeping with a stranger? Having sexual prowess? I had absolutely no idea how I would do that. My mouth went dry just at the thought.

Jax was watching me patiently, waiting for a response. I looked back at her, giving her a brief smile. She had been there and done that - and there was nothing wrong with her. She wasn't scarred from the experience, or some sort of closet sexual deviant... that I knew of.

The more I thought about it, the more I realised what she was saying made sense. If I was earning ten grand a night, then I could pay for Elsie's care, pay Luke back in chunks, as well as still live. "Okay." I breathed.

"Okay what?"

"Okay, I'll let you help me."

She gave me a sharp nod. "Good. Just remember, this is not a lifelong commitment - just a way to make the money to pay Luke back. Then you can go back to doing what you do best - being a hermit." She grinned as she pulled out her phone and looked up a number. "I'm going to call my old manager before you change your mind."

I watched her leave the room, wondering what the hell I had just signed myself up for. Throwing my cigarette out the window, I felt the shower calling to me.

Half an hour later, I walked into the kitchen to the welcoming aroma of hot coffee brewing, a roaring fire in the living room, and Jax relaxing at the dining table looking a million pounds with her feet up on one of the dining chairs. "You have a few hours to mentally prep yourself before we have a meeting with Annalise."

"Annalise," I repeated slowly, my stomach dropping as I poured hot coffee into my waiting cup.

"Yes." Jax smiled. "She's on top of the London Escort scene. The same woman who recruited me. She'll look after you, Mack, you have nothing to worry about." Jax took a sip of her coffee. "She'll teach you everything you need to know."

"Today?"

Jax laughed. "No, probably not. Unless of course you want to. No, no, she just wants to meet you first."

Butterflies swept through me. I so wasn't ready for this. Prostitution was something that went against my moral high ground like you wouldn't believe, but yet here I was - desperate. I couldn't get a job. And the bank wasn't going to give me another loan, so I wasn't even going to bother asking. Desperate people do desperate things.

Jax was a real estate agent, and she made a lot of money. She had been one ever since I had first met her. She wasn't scared about putting herself out there and meeting people. I had always preferred my own company to large crowds. What on earth made her think I could do this I didn't know. I didn't even know what I would talk about with these men who would be paying for my company.

We sped through the wet, cobbled streets of London in Jax's Porsche, and pulled into an underground parking garage of a high rise. She ushered me into the elevator a few moments later, looping her arm through mine and stabbing her manicured finger at the highest floor.

She patted my hand. "Just be yourself."

More people got into the lift as we made our way

up the building, preventing me from asking Jax any more questions. The doors opened, revealing a beautiful reception area. 'The Agency' was titled in gilt letters above the reception desk. A young woman sat behind the desk with a headset, perfect hair, Prada glasses, and well-tailored suit.

"Jax," she exclaimed. She ran around the counter, and wrapped herself in Jax's arms. "It's so nice to see you!"

Jax chuckled. "You too, shortcake." She turned to me. "This is Mack. Mack - this is Annalise's daughter, Isla."

I automatically reached my hand out and shook hers.

"Welcome to the team." Isla grinned. She turned back to Jax. "I'll just go get Mum."

Jax guided me to a plush leather sofa. "Lovely kid," she whispered.

"She seems to know you rather well." I eyed up Jax. "You're not still working for them are you?"

"God, no. But I always kept in touch with Annalise. She's a gorgeous woman with a very shrewd mind for business. She often sends clients my way if they are looking for property or selling. I do the same for her if my clients need some form of entertainment."

"Darling!" A shout came across the room as one of the most striking women I had ever laid eyes on swept through the doors towards us. I was in awe. She had long, luscious, dark curls, vibrant green eyes, full lips, not a wrinkle on her face, and if I had to guess, she was probably about fifty. She was dressed head to toe in designer clothing, and she looked like a footballer's wife instead of a woman running a prostitution business. She air-kissed Jax, and turned her eyes to me. Suddenly I felt incredibly self-conscious.

I swallowed as she brushed her critical eyes over me. After a moment, she smiled and reached for my hand. "You must be McKenna."

I nodded. "And you must be Annalise." She looked nothing like a prostitute. It suddenly occurred to me that I had never asked Jax if she was still putting herself out there, or if she was just running the business.

She tinkled with laughter. "I am." She turned on her heel. "Come to my office, and we'll have a chat."

We trailed after her, passing multiple desks, filing cabinets, and coffee break areas with designer furniture and kitchenette units. Large floor to ceiling windows overlooked the distinctive London skyline. "Is all of this your Agency?" I asked as we got to her mahogany office door.

"Yes. Obviously, most people aren't here today as it's the weekend, but I do have a team coming in shortly to start work for the evening." She opened the door and we walked inside. It looked nothing like a standard corporate office. It was plush, with rich colouring, and had beautiful artwork lining the walls.

The only thing office-ish about the room was the large oak desk in front of the window. Annalise sat down on a leather sofa, kicked off her high-heels, and gestured for us to sit with her.

I bit my lip, waiting for her to say something. This was the strangest meeting I'd ever had.

"You have very good structure," she started, looking me carefully over. "Your height is a wonderful advantage in this business. How tall are you?"

"Five foot, eleven," I responded, unsure how it was an advantage.

"Can you remove your glasses for me?"

I pursed my lips together, and carefully took them off my face, letting them rest on my lap.

After a few awkward moments, she turned her eyes to Jax. "You're right... she has fabulous bone structure, even if she is a little shy. We can help her with that."

I felt like a prized idiot. This was the very last thing I expected to be doing. In fact, I would rather be doing anything else in the world than sitting here being critically analysed about whether or not I would be fit for hiring out as a sex object. I had to keep in mind that I was doing this to pay Luke back, and for my loving Aunt Elsie. This wasn't me, but it was a short term solution to a very big problem.

I had to admit that I could never have done this by myself. I never ever would have even dreamed about it. My career compass just didn't point in this direction. Jax was definitely hand-holding me throughout this, and if anything went wrong, she was going to get a stern word from me once this was over.

"Would you like to see how we operate?" Annalise asked me, her eyes turning kind and less critical.

"Yes please."

She laughed. "McKenna, you look exactly like all the other women who come to me for the first time. Scared out of their wits, and questioning whether or not they can actually do this." She sighed. "Well trust me, my dear, I have transformed even the most reclusive women into beautiful, poised peacocks. You have absolutely nothing to worry about."

I gave her a wobbly smile, and nodded. "I guess I don't want to lead you to thinking I'm fully committing to this as a career," I said clearing my throat. "This is only a short term thing for me. I'm in a bit of a financial bind that I need to get out of and Jax thought that this would be a good solution."

"You're in good hands," Jax commented as she stood. "Trust me."

Annalise clasped my hands within hers. "This is an established corporation with a very elite reputation. You will never have to do anything you don't want to. I have many women who work for me, some who have for years. This agency is nothing like working a street corner in the USA. This is a professional establishment."

I swallowed, nervous, yet somewhat comforted by

her words. "Okay."

"Now, come with me. I'll show you the place, and if at the end of the tour you still don't think you want to work for me, we can shake hands and you don't need to feel any obligation."

I looked at Jax, who in return winked at me. We followed Annalise out of the office. "This is the call centre part of the operation." She gestured out at the sea of desks. "My staff should be arriving shortly to start work for the day. We operate from 2pm through to 8am the next morning, seven days a week." She smiled. "Some clientele like company during the day of course, so we do have a skeleton staff on during the other hours." She sighed. "Half the call centre are dedicated to responding to client calls, and the other half responds to staff calls - whether they need a taxi, or if they just want to have a chat while waiting for their clients to arrive."

She turned, and walked down the hallway. "Down here we have our medical facility." She paused at a door. "All of our women have complete check-ups each week, and are monitored very closely. In today's environment, you just don't know what's out there - so we make sure all those working for us are in optimum health."

Yikes.

She opened the door to a sparse and sterile looking space, with a few comfortable looking chairs scatted about and a stack of magazines. A couple of doors led off the waiting area. "Through each door is a doctor's office. We have two female practitioners, and one male." She opened a door, and I peeked around, doing a quick scan of the room, before she closed it again.

"That's a lot of doctors," I commented.

Annalise smiled. "Yes. I have forty escorts who service our clientele, and with all the check-ups it's much cheaper to have our own doctors on staff. That way if anything happens it can be picked up immediately."

I had to admit, it all seemed incredibly professional.

We trailed after Annalise as she stepped back out of the medical area. "Down here is wardrobe and makeup." She turned to me as she walked. "If you like dressing up, you'll love this."

Dressing up? Was she kidding me? I didn't know how to respond. I would much rather slop around in my comfy clothes than actually get dressed up. Yes, I liked to see beautiful women on the pages of magazines, but if I was being honest, I preferred reading house and garden magazines, and dreaming of all the nice things I would do one day in the future if I ever had any money. Cripes, I had to change my mind-set. This was a completely different world.

We turned a corner into a brightly lit room lined with mirrors, stools, and makeup stations. "All makeup is done professionally, unless you're really good at applying your own. We have a number of staff here on rotation full-time. Whatever look you want, they can provide it. If you don't know, then they will sort you out with their professional eye." She walked through the makeup area and through a set of floor to ceiling double doors, and held one open for us. "And this is wardrobe."

I stepped through. Everything was brightly lit, and clothing hung in organised rows. There were mirrors placed every now and then. "Wow," I said quietly. "I have never seen anything like this."

"Incredible, isn't it?" Jax commented from beside me. "I loved working here. Mind you, it was in a different office back then, but it had the same set-up. Makeup artists and a wardrobe to die for."

I couldn't disagree. It was incredible. I felt as though I could be standing in the middle of Vogue Magazine headquarters, not an Escort Agency. I was completely out of place. "How do you do all this?" I asked Annalise.

She shrugged. "I saw that there was a need for upmarket company. Naturally I take a cut of what you make, and that helps fund this operation. But it all works rather well, lucrative for everyone."

I trailed my hand along some of the clothing in the nearest rack. The quality of the fabrics felt amazing. Nothing about this operation was cheap. And the fact that they didn't skimp on any costs, made me feel more and more confident. Actually...

something within me welled with excitement ... like I was going to be part of some secret organisation or something, as if I could be anyone I wanted to be. But I still had to talk money with her. Although Jax had told me I could make ten grand a night, I had to have some sort of confirmation.

"So... in terms of how much money I could make, what are your expectations?"

Annalise threw her head back with laughter. "Oh you are just darling!" She winked at Jax. "I think I could safely say that once we have you cleaned up and looking the part, you could definitely have an average of ten to twelve grand per date, if you wanted to."

I bit my lip. "Do I have to sleep with all of them for that sort of money?"

Annalise shook her head. "Definitely not. Ten grand is a base rate for simply being their date or companion. Some clients want genuine companionship, or a date for a function. You are there to accessorise them. If they change the terms of the contract, as in they want to take you to bed, they need to seek approval from us first as that changes the price." She patted my arm reassuringly. "You, my dear, would make a fine accessory. But if you do want to up your game and make more money, like say - twenty grand a night, you just let me know, and I can arrange for you to have clients with those needs."

I swallowed. She meant sleeping with them. If I was just someone's date, I could earn a lot of money.

But if I decided to sleep with them as well, I would get paid even more. And I really needed the money. I had come to the Agency expecting to provide sexual or companionship services. I was going to get in, do this, make the money, and get out. The sooner Luke was paid off, the better. "Do you mind if I up my game right from the start?"

Annalise shook her head. "No, not at all. I know you're in a bind. If you want—" She looked at Jax, lightly touching her arm. "Since you are coming to me via a very dear friend, I'll start you on some of our higher end clients. That way, you'll get out of this pickle you're in faster. Then afterwards, if you want to, you are more than welcome to drop any sexual services for just escorting services."

I don't know what made me do it, but for some reason I threw my arms around her neck. "Thank you!"

She patted my back awkwardly, but laughed at the same time.

Jax was right, I actually felt like I was going to be looked after at The Agency.

6

I thought that I would have more time to mentally prep myself, but apparently Annalise wanted me to start straight away. I still didn't know if I could actually go through with this, but as Jax said - I wouldn't know until I tried.

I looked at my blurry reflection in the mirror. I couldn't exactly see what this woman was doing to my face in terms of make-up, despite the awkwardness of getting poked and prodded, once I got used to it I found this part of the process actually felt quite relaxing. -

Jax was off with Annalise somewhere in the wardrobe area, no doubt finding something that I would never wear in a million years to stuff me into. I really wasn't used to this sort of critical attention. Yes,

I was blonde, and I had blue eyes, and yes, I was definitely taller than average. But I wasn't a model, or anything spectacular to look at, nor was I ever out to impress anyone. I always had Luke, and I thought that he loved me for who I was.

Even though it had been a couple of months, I just still couldn't believe that he'd chosen Nicole over me... Nicole had been my closest friend. We had met at University. She had been studying art history and the classics, so naturally we were like two peas in a pod. Nicole, while loving the arts, could never remember the right periods or dates, so I used to help her with that.

She was gorgeous. She always had been. She had jet black hair with light hazel eyes. Her mother was half Croatian, and had a dark, exotic look that she passed on to Nicole. Nicole's father was worth a lot of money as some sort of advertising business executive here in London.

She had previously only had relationships with super gorgeous, rich men that treated her terribly, which usually ended with Nicole in tears over one thing or another. She'd told me numerous times that she wanted to marry into money. That was one of the annoying things about her and Luke running off together. Luke had no money. He might have been an accountant, and yes, he earned a decent wage, but he was by no means rich. Not like the men she usually chased. I just couldn't quite believe that she would ever see anything in Luke, let alone throw away our friendship and screw him behind my back.

"You alright there, sweetheart?"

My make-up artist's voice drew me back into reality. I tried not to snort with laughter at the realisation she'd called me sweetheart, like some twelve year old, when I was probably a lot older than her. "Uh, yeah? Why?"

"You keep sighing, that's all." She laughed. "You ready for hair now?

"I guess so?"

"Just relax darling, and enjoy the process. When you work here, every day you get pampered. Enjoy it."

I tried to smile, but I think it came out more like a grimace instead.

"Oh, one more thing darling, you got contacts for those eyes of yours?"

I took a deep breath trying to remember if they were in my bag or not. "Yeah, I'm pretty sure I have some in my bag." Before I could even bend down to retrieve it, she'd passed it to me. I unzipped it, and started pulling things out and dumping them on the counter as I searched.

She started laughing. "Sweetheart, you're gonna have to vacuum out that bag one day. You have so much rubbish in there!"

"Don't I know it," I muttered. Finally I found the contact lens box, and undid the caps. I carefully put the lenses into my eyes, blinked a few times, and focused on my reflection. I gasped. My face looked completely different. I mean, I was still me, but somehow... I looked more defined. I looked up at the make-up girl, and gave her a slow smile.

She grabbed my shoulders. "You're beautiful, sweetheart," she said, her cockney accent wrapping itself around me. "And when we get your hair done, you're going to be even more amazin'."

I looked down at the messy pile of crap I had shoved all over their crisp white countertop, and winced. She was right. There was garbage all through my handbag. I reached out and swept the mess back into my handbag, wiping my hand over the surface area to brush off remaining debris, and crumbled parts of my handbag lining.

"See, told ya, you need to vacuum out that bag of yours." She chuckled.

"It's an old one," I said, trying to drop the embarrassment.

"Plenty of new ones here for ya, sweetheart. Ah... here she is. McKenna, this is Doreen, and she'll be your hair specialist for today." She grinned, and I saw the reflection of a chick who looked kind of gothic and steampunk, with loads of arm tattoos. She had a number of piercings in her ears, and no doubt in other places too, and she was dressed top to toe in leather; a leather waistcoat that she was wearing as a top, a black lacy bra, and tight leather pants. To finish off her look, she was wearing some serious looking black and red stilettos with zombies painted on them. "Doreen is the best we got here, so you're in good hands."

Oh boy. I watched my make-up artists retreating figure in the mirror's reflection and wondered what exactly I was in for with Doreen.

"Hiya." Doreen smiled at me. "So." She pulled the rubber band from my hair, and threw it in the bin beside us. "What have we got here?" She was chewing gum. I grimaced. The last thing I wanted was for any of that stuff to get anywhere near my hair. She ran her fingers through hair that I had, thankfully, managed to wash this morning in my hung-over state, and hummed to herself. There were a few moments silence before she finally spoke. "Despite what you have been doing to your hair by stretching it and pulling it up in a rubber band for what looks like...years, it's actually in relatively good condition." She pulled some scissors out of her tool belt and snipped off a little bit of the hair she was holding between her fingers and analysed it closely.

I was starting to panic. This woman did not look like my usual hairdresser. In fact, she looked so completely off the charts in terms of normality, I had to question if she was really someone I wanted to cut my hair let alone anything else. The last thing I wanted to do was start this job looking like David Bowie or Rod Stewart. My mouth was dry, but I refused to speak. I just let her continue doing her thing. I think I was too afraid to voice any opinions, just in case she pierced my ear with her scissors or something equally frightening.

"Yep." She nodded. "I think its fine. Definitely needs a good trim, which I'll do for you right now, and then I'll style it, and you'll be ready to go on your way to wardrobe."

I bit my lip and nodded. It wasn't like I had much of a choice. I had a feeling that if I jumped up and ran, chances were high that she would tackle me to the ground, zombie heels and all. Nerves streaked through me at the thought that I was embarking on this job very shortly.

Annalise had been quite clear that she had a client lined up already. She was going to show me his profile before I left to meet with him. I didn't know if that was going to make this situation any better. In fact, it could possibly make it a hell of a lot worse, especially if the client was unattractive... and if he was too good looking I would probably fumble and fart my way through the evening.

I looked at myself again in the reflection, and I had to admit that this chick was actually doing a good job on my hair. She was shaping my cut, which is something that I had never really had done before. Before I knew it, she was pulling straightening irons from her tool belt, and plugging them in beside me. And then she set to work.

Less than ten minutes later Doreen was finished.

She placed her hands on my shoulders and looked at me in the reflection. "Lovely, darling, just lovely."

I had to admit that she'd done a bloody good job. My hair was glossy, falling in all the right places, and for the first time in my life, with my make-up professionally done, and my hair styled, I actually felt kind of elegant. I guess I was seeing myself through new eyes.

Jax walked up behind me with a big smile. "You've done fantastic work with her, Doreen," she said. "You're almost ready to go now, honey. Just clothing and shoes."

I stood up, giving Doreen a shy nod of thanks, and fell into step beside Jax as we made our way through to the wardrobe area. "This is a pretty serious business, isn't it?"

"Yes, it is, but Annalise runs a tight ship here. She also has a couple of offices in other countries as well, you know. But this office is definitely her biggest."

"Wow," I muttered. "So how do you know everyone here? Like Doreen?"

Jax laughed. "Annalise throws a lot of parties, and I'm invited to them. Doreen has been knocking around here for quite a few years now. She's very good, and always a favourite hair-stylist among the staff." She steered me through a different door in the wardrobe area, and I found Annalise there, surrounded by an assortment of clothing.

"Ah, there you are." She smiled, standing up to

greet me. "And my, you're looking lovelier by the minute!"

I flushed, partly with embarrassment, and partly with pride.

"You're going to be perfect." She turned away from me, and selected a dark maroon dress, and held it up to me. "Hmmm, could be an option..." She put that one aside, and grabbed another dress, repeating the process. None of these outfits were items that I expected someone in this sort of business to wear.

"Now, Darren usually like his women to have a certain styled flair, a little quirkiness, and definitely all class. Thank god for you, my dear, that we don't need to do any accent training. I can tell that you are well bred and very intelligent, and that makes it a heck of a lot easier to work with you."

"Uh...thank you?" I mumbled. She was holding up a short white dress, with a cropped jacket. Something about it appealed to me.

"Yes, I think this one will work," Annalise said, handing it to me. "Go try it on." She pointed to a changing area.

I took the dress from her, and walked into the dressing room, closing the door behind me. Yikes, I was nervous. I was almost afraid to wear this dress just in case I perspired and wrecked it. But it was gorgeous. I looked at the label. Armani. I swallowed. I knew better than anyone that I had careless moments, and this dress cost a fortune. I stripped out of my clothes, and wiggled my way into the dress. It was tight, and I definitely couldn't zip it up by myself. I left the room, and walked out to the others.

"Belle," Jax whispered. "You look...stunning."

I turned my back to her, and she zipped me into the dress properly.

Annalise held out a thin silver belt, and wrapped it around my waist, quickly fastening it. "There you go. Outfit complete." She brushed her eyes over me critically.

"She needs new underwear," Jax stated.

I cringed. She was dead right. I couldn't go out in my cotton knickers and a ratty old bra.

"No problem," Annalise said, disappearing for a moment. She walked back in carrying two different sets, and held them out to me. "I think the white and grey would work better, instead of just dreary old white."

I swallowed and nodded. The underwear she was holding out was nothing like what I would normally wear. First of all, it had lace. Secondly, it didn't leave much to the imagination. At all. The G-string had hardly anything to it, and the bra looked uncomfortable. I pursed my lips together. I was in this for a good reason, and I just had to suck it up.

7

Ten minutes later, Annalise took a photo of me for my profile, I had my clients file loaded to my phone, and apparently I was ready to go. Jax was dropping me off. Saying I was nervous didn't even begin to cut it. Jax had even offered me something to relax, but I had a cigarette instead. Drugs, even prescription ones, had never really been my style. The most I ever took was paracetamol.

Smoking was something I never ever thought that I would take up again, but I dragged on the cigarette as I looked over the client file. His name was Darren Kennedy, and apparently he was some sort of entrepreneur in the steel industry. He wasn't bad looking. Kind of weedy, but definitely not ugly. The photo showed him dressed in a suit, with cunning eyes and a secretive smile on his face. As I analysed it, I wondered what this chap had that was so secretive that he was smiling about.

Was it the fact that he was going to get laid?

I flicked the remainder of the cigarette out the window and turned to Jax. "How did you even do this?"

She smiled, and grabbed my hand. "I just imagined someone else. That, and I was usually fairly intoxicated as well." She gave my hand a squeeze. "You'll be fine."

"Intoxicated huh?" I paused. "Guess that's always an option."

She laughed. "Look if you're worried about your performance in bed, don't be. There is no point. Just have a few drinks, and who knows - you might actually really like the guy. Think of it like a one night stand that you're getting paid for, and if you don't like him, just have a few more drinks until you do. It's as simple as that. Especially if you're not going to take anything to help you relax a bit."

I shook my head. "Alcohol will do."

She smiled. "Okay, well if you change your mind, I might just have something that will get you through." She opened up the car's centre console, and rifled around it there with her hand while keep her eyes firmly on the road ahead. She pulled out a small brown bottle with a rubber end and handed it to me. "It's rescue remedy - homeopathic. No bad stuff in it.

If you think you need to calm your nerves, take a few drops and it should help settle you down a little."

I turned the bottle over in my hand. "I can't overdose on it, right?"

"Nope, that's the beauty of that stuff." She chuckled. "I mean - everything in moderation, right? But no - you can't knock yourself out. So take some now, and then keep it in your handbag and just have a few drops every time you go to the bathroom or something."

I lifted the dropper to my mouth and squeezed. It tasted kind of yuck, but it wasn't unbearable. Did I feel the immediate effects of calmness wash over me? No, but as we drove closer to our destination, I did actually start to relax just a little. If anything, the rescue remedy had taken the edge off. Now I just needed a glass of wine or something to really help relax me. I hadn't thought I would be drinking so soon again after my night with Jax last night, but I was actually craving a little alcoholic relief.

The sight of the Thames greeted me, and my stomach rolled. We weren't far from the Savoy now, and I desperately wanted to lock the car doors and instruct Jax to drive me home. But my pleas were stuck in my throat. It wasn't going to happen. I just had to think about the fact that this was the quickest way for me to make the money I needed, not just for me, but for Elsie too. She'd done so much for me, it was time to return the favour. "It's just a one night stand," I muttered under my breath. I drew in a big lungful of air, and let it out slowly.

Jax pulled up to the brightly lit Savoy in the dusky London light. "Now, you're meeting at the American Bar inside. You know what he looks like, and he should have been sent a photo of you too. They have great cocktails." She winked. "Good luck."

I was about to say something along the lines of 'I don't want to do this' but someone opened my door and reached for my hand to assist me, and before I knew it, I was getting out of the car. Even though I desperately wanted to, I couldn't bring myself to wipe my sweaty palms on this white dress. Jax passed me my matching handbag, and gave me a small wave before she drove off.

"How may we assist you," the man who'd opened my door asked. He was suave looking in his full hotel uniform and glasses.

"I'm meeting someone," I said, trying to sound confident under his stare. "At the American Bar?"

He nodded. "Ah yes, right this way." He smiled politely, but his eyes didn't - causing me to instinctively tense. I never would have set foot in this place in my normal life. I knew from Luke and his constant work trips of how hotel staff could sometimes treat guests if they weren't dressed in the right way. He never took me away with him - I guess I never looked the part. I had to wonder how many other women he may have slept with at all those hotels, or if it was only Nicole. I followed the man inside. "Have you ever been here before?" he asked.

"No, not here," I responded. "It's lovely though."

He snickered. "Yes. The American bar is a very nice place to meet with people. It has a huge selection of cocktails to choose from, and they always have a pianist." Leading me down a wide corridor, he opened a door for me, and ushered me through. "And, here we are."

The melodic sound of the piano met my ears, as well as quiet chatter of the patrons currently enjoying the bars atmosphere. It was busy, but not rowdy. In fact, as I took in the beautiful black and white photographs of 1930s New York set in framed mirrors, I longed to have enough money to travel there.

I saw the sign for the bathrooms, and glancing at my watch, I noted that I was a few minutes early. I crossed the room, and found myself standing in front of the mirror, staring at my reflection. I was almost unrecognisable. I looked so completely different. I gripped the edge of the hand basin, and took a deep breath, my hair falling around my face.

"You can do this, Mack," I said with determination. It was in that moment, when I met my eyes in the reflection, that I wished I had taken one of Jax's magical pills. Instead I pulled out the rescue remedy, and squirted a decent amount on my tongue and swallowed. Then I took another hit of it for good measure.

Before I could start talking myself out of this, I straightened my dress, rearranged my jacket, brushed my hair, and reapplied my lipstick. My hair shone in the bathroom lighting, making me smile. It never ever did that at home, no matter how much I tried to get it to look good. I spritzed some Ralph Lauren perfume on my collarbone and at my wrists, and took another deep breath.

Now I was ready to face the world. Well... as ready as I was ever going to be anyway.

Before I knew it, I found myself standing at the bar. As I waited for the bartender to notice me, I took in my surrounding with more detail. The place was decked out in shiny chrome, plush seating, lots of wood, and in all honesty, it did actually remind me of New York a bit ... well what I had seen in the movies, anyway. Low lighting lit intimate areas, giving the bar the feeling of warmth. Combined with the man seated behind the white Steinway grand piano, playing soulful jazzy tunes that sounded as though they were from the 1930s period, I was starting to relax.

"Good evening, what can I get you?"

I turned to the young, surfer-looking American bartender and ordered a martini. I wasn't one for cocktails generally, and even though they had a selection of wines, I didn't really know what my 'date' had planned for us this evening. So a martini was made, and placed in front of me on a fabric napkin. I handed him my credit card, and winced at the price.

I shook the thought from my head. It didn't matter. What mattered was that my accounts would soon be flush with money and I could afford to splurge just a little for the sake of the greater good. I made myself comfortable at the bar and had a few sips of my drink, feeling the icy liquid slide through my insides, with the alcohol instantly hitting my nerves and relaxing me even more. Jax was right. Drinking helped.

A hand brushed my shoulder, and I looked up to see my client, Darren, standing there. "Oh, hello," I said shyly, letting him shake my hand as he leaned in and lightly brushed his lips across my cheek. He smelt good. Very good. And for some reason, it surprised me.

He smiled confidently back, his eyes sweeping appreciatively over me, and eventually resting on my face. "You look gorgeous," he said, his voice laced with an aristocratic edge. "Simply divine."

I smiled, and took a sip of my drink, my eye sliding towards the bartender who was watching the exchange with great interest. It's a date.... Just a date... I reminded myself. Darren was most definitely not the sort of man I would ever go out with. For one, he was short. Well, shorter than most men I met with anyway. A lot shorter than me. He was dressed in a smart steel-grey, silky shirt, expensive jeans, and casual shoes. Even though he wasn't my 'type', he wasn't bad looking, and I couldn't imagine why he would hire sex and entertainment, when I was sure there would be plenty of women attracted to his money and status.

I watched him assertively order himself a drink, and another for me. "Shall we go and sit where we don't have an audience?" he murmured to me once the bartender was busy.

I chuckled. "Of course," I agreed. We moved over to a seat, and settled in. For someone who I didn't know, it was peculiar that he sat right beside me, but I guess it was also appropriate since he was paying for my services. It was a very odd space to be in.

"So, McKenna, what is it that you do for a living... other than this?" He added with a wink.

I laughed. "Where do I start?"

He shrugged. "At the beginning, I suppose."

"I'm a historian, by trade. I deal mostly in cultural artefacts, dabble a bit in art history, but I'm also particularly interested in human migration and war motivation."

He looked taken aback. "You're serious aren't you?" He leaned back and looked me over, from head to toe, shaking his head. "Smart and beautiful... I would have thought you to be a runway model."

This time I really did laugh. "Me? God no. I'm far more interested in burying my nose in books than being a glorified clothes hanger." I took a few little sips from my drink, and eventually drained my glass while he continued to analyse me. It wasn't a pleasant experience being so scrutinised, but .the alcohol helped.

"Amazing," he murmured. "Simply amazing. Where on earth did Annalise find you?"

I pursed my lips as I picked up my next drink waiting for me on our table. "Mutual friend," I answered. I was not going to tell him about the reason why I now worked for Annalise, or even about Luke. That was far too much information. Jax said treat this like a first date, and I was going to do precisely that. "And what do you do, Darren?" I asked meeting his eyes.

He smiled, and sat back comfortably. "I started a business in scrap metal when I was sixteen, much to my father's annoyance, and then it grew from there. Even though I am now extremely successful, and I enjoy my life and the best it can offer–" He winked. "My father still doesn't approve."

Daddy issues. Great. This was what I had to deal with? "Well it's your life, not his," I said gently. "You need to live the life you love, and love the life you live. It's really as simple as that."

"Do you love your life?"

I looked away from him. "Not always. But I try my best." I don't know what compelled my honest answer, but he seemed satisfied by it.

"I love my life. Most of it. I am never lonely, I meet beautiful women, and I travel the world acquisitioning more scrap-metal yards and turning them into money making ventures. Something I have discovered over the years is that money always talks. You can buy just about anything you like... even love."

His gaze met mine, and I felt my mouth go dry. Oh boy. "But can you buy true love?"

He paused as he contemplated the question. "Doubtful. It probably doesn't help that I don't buy into true love, though. Real love, deep love, or true love as you put it has the power to hurt people. I don't have time for that drama. I have an empire to build. I have companionship, and plenty of money to throw at my companions. I don't have time to settle down, marry, or have children. Perhaps one day I'll get to that point, but I am having far too much fun right now to worry about any of that."

I swallowed. He was right - love had the power to hurt. I'd been hurt by Luke, as well as Nicole – two people that I loved. Two months it had taken me to numb myself from it all – but here was Darren and his comments, threatening to bring it all up again. Darren threw walls up around him because he didn't want to be hurt like that. Perhaps that was a good thing.

He rested his hand on my leg, his eyes dark. "You look as if you have been hurt by love before?"

I had to hand it to him and his powers of observation, and I shrugged. "Loved and lost."

He smiled. "When you're with me, you'll never have that problem. That's the beauty of these business arrangements." He was so sure of himself. Confidence simmered beneath the surface, but I had to really wonder what he was all about. He didn't want a meaningful relationship, let alone the possibility of having children, but yet he'd spent his life making a fortune. But for what, exactly? He gave my leg a squeeze that was actually more of a caress. "Shall we go have dinner?"

8

Hours later, I found myself with my arm looped through his as he led me back into the Savoy. He had taken me out on a super yacht that was docked in the Thames for a secluded business meeting meal. There were other associates of his and their wives and girlfriends there, and they had all sat around talking business. I was initially extremely nervous about getting on a strange boat with him, until I realised it was a business meeting and we weren't actually going anywhere.

After dinner, when the men continued to talk shop, I ended up getting rather tiddly with a couple of the girlfriends. They asked me how I knew Darren, and I ended up just saying that we'd met through a mutual friend. It was the easiest possible explanation.

Whenever I was apart from Darren, I would see him look me over from across the room, almost possessively. It was an interesting conflict, as I didn't ever want someone to ever have power over me ever gain... but there was something dominating about his gaze. It was thrilling, and in a good way. I wondered what this man had in store for me back at the hotel. That was when I realised I had probably reached that point of alcohol consumption where everyone looked gorgeous.

The women were dressed in a similar fashion to me. Utterly impeccable. I wondered if they had staff to help them look that amazing each time, but I didn't dare ask. There was no way I could look like this unless I had oodles of help. Nicole on the other hand was always very good at it. I wondered if that was one of the things Luke liked about her. He had always been image conscious - where as it was the last thing on my mind. If he was lucky, I would brush my hair before tying it up. If I wasn't going anywhere, he was fortunate if I got dressed or even showered.

But tonight, I looked like a rock star. Well, sort of. Maybe a rock star's wife. At one point in the night, I'd found myself in the bathroom, taking a selfie. Before I knew it, I had sent it off to Luke: Look at what you're missing out on, I texted vindictively. I knew I would probably regret that in the morning, but right now, I just didn't care.

Now that we were back at the hotel, my worries

were starting to run rampant with a mixture of ill-ease and nerves. I should have kept drinking. There was nothing thrilling about the way I was feeling now. I knew what came next. I knew that Darren would expect me to have sex with him. I also knew that if I wanted the money I would have to go through with it. It was not a thought that I cared much for. Weirdly, as we were standing in the mirrored foyer waiting for an elevator to arrive, I couldn't help but notice the drastic height difference between us. Made worse by the sizable heels I was wearing. It made for awkward moments, like when Darren's hand climbed up the back of my skirt and into my G-string so he could fondle me. Tension flooded my system, causing me to sober up even more.

When the elevator arrived a few other people got in with us, and Darren stabbed his finger at the highest floor and winked at me. The penthouse suite. That didn't surprise me. As people got in and out of the lift, I tried to calm my nerves by taking subtle deep breaths. The closer we got to the top of the building, the more the empty pit in my stomach turned into a great gaping chasm.

It didn't matter how much booze I had consumed earlier, I now felt stone-cold sober. We got out of the elevator and walked a short distance to a double set of heavy wooden doors. Darren unlocked the door with his card, and held it open for me. It was definitely a suite. In fact, the place felt larger than my whole house. It had high ceilings, ornate, heavy furniture; the place was vast. I crossed the room to the balcony doors, and stepped out into the night to take in the view. It was stunning. The Thames looked dark against the rest of London, which surrounded it with sparkling lights.

I looked down to see if the boat we'd been on was still there, but if it was, I couldn't identify it. Everything was starting to look the same. Darren stepped out behind me, and handed me a glass of Champagne, smiling.

"Lovely, isn't it?"

I nodded mutely, not daring to speak in case my nerves stuttered out.

"I always stay here when I'm in London. Not as often as I would like, but often enough. I used to stay at Claridge's, but this place suits me more... they're very discreet here. Unfortunately my business takes me all around the world. I find myself in Australia more often these days. Have you ever been there?"

I shook my head. "No," I said quietly. One syllable words were my limit right now. I just couldn't help but think of Darren naked now that we were up here at his room. This was going to happen whether I liked it or not. I just had to suck it up.

"It's an interesting country. They say it's full of criminals, but I have never seen much activity. They have stunningly hot weather depending on where you are, and the people seem to be rather pleasant. Most of my time is spent in Northern Australia. I have a boat there. It makes for good access out to the islands for business."

I drained my glass and gave him a tight smile. "I might just go use the bathroom."

He gave me a sly smirk. "By all means." It wasn't until I was walking away from him that I realised where I recognised that look from. His Agency file photo. Unease replaced the nerves inside me.

Just as I reached the bathroom and locked the door behind me, I heard club music start to quietly play from the suite's stereo system.

The bathroom's décor was just as opulent as the rest of suite with a rich velvet upholstered Louis chair, gold gilded framed mirrors, and black marble countertops. My hands started shaking, and I leaned against the vanity, taking deep breaths. I had no idea what I was in for, but there was something about that smile that had put me on edge. If I had to put my finger on it, I would almost say it was sadistic.

There had been nothing listed in the sexual preference area of his file. But something about the way he'd looked at me felt dangerous. I would just have to roll with it. I had come this far, and what's a little sexual variety in the greater scheme of things? After all, I would be paid a great sum of money, and I had been assured that he was a very valuable client.

I rifled through my handbag and retrieved the Rescue Remedy to squirt a whole lot more on my tongue. I was tempted to down the entire contents of the bottle, but knew that I could need more later. I straightened up and stripped off the jacket I was wearing. It was too hot in this stuffy bathroom. I gazed at myself in the mirror. "You can do this, Mack," I spoke quietly at my reflection. "You can totally do this. Millions have done this before you and for a lot less."

I turned on the faucet and filled up a glass with water and drank it back. An unfamiliar sound met my ears. A split second later, I heard a thud. I froze. "What the fuck?" I whispered. After a few moments of straining to hear, all I could distinguish was the sound of the music playing. I crept over to the bathroom door and inched it open.

There was a man standing in the room. Holding a gun.

My hand flew to my mouth. I could see Darren on the floor, unmoving. I swallowed, feeling every heartbeat, but containing myself. Seemed the higher dose of rescue remedy was actually working. I quietly closed the bathroom door, but not without hearing a slight click as the latch fell into place. I didn't dare turn the lock because that would make even more noise. Biting my bottom lip, I could hear my blood pumping through my system as I looked around the bathroom for some place to hide. I ran to the vanity, sweeping the handbag contents off the counter and back into my bag. The only place to hide in was the shower. I grabbed my white jacket, removed my shoes, and went and stood in the shower, pulling the opaque glass door closed as quietly as I could - hoping that he wouldn't be able to see me through it. I looked at the shower's white tiled walls and then down at my white dress, swallowing. I had to hope that either the killer wouldn't come in here, or I would blend in.

I was trying not to breathe too loudly. All I had to do was wait until the man had taken whatever he wanted and left. Then I could call in hotel security or whoever it was that dealt with these things. I swallowed. I should have turned off the bathroom light.

I wasn't cut out for this. I had seen my parents die, but my mind had blocked those memories as they were too traumatic. Other than them, I had never once seen a dead body. Even when my grandparents died, it was closed casket. I pursed my lips together. There had been a lot of blood around Darren. Adrenaline was ramping me up, making me want to run. I looked around the bathroom, but there were no windows anywhere. This was an internal bathroom that only had an extraction duct.

I did not want to die. I couldn't.

I wondered if he was gone yet. I reached for the shower door and was about to open it when I heard someone walk into the bathroom. I shrank away, with my back against the wall.

I could see a fuzzy silhouette of the man through

the opaque door. He was tall. Dark hair. Dark clothing. I didn't dare breathe as he got closer to the shower. I braced myself, slowly raising a shoe in one hand; it had a particularly nasty stiletto heel on it and was the only thing I had to defend myself if push came to shove.

Freezing water blasted out of the showerheads, drenching me. I screamed.

The door was suddenly thrown open, and I found myself staring into an amused face. With a gun pointed at me. He shut the water off. I couldn't believe I hadn't noticed the shower faucets were on the outside. I wanted to smack my head with stupidity, but instead, I stood there drenched, fury filling me as I stared right into the eyes of the man that had killed Darren.

"Stay right where you are," he said, his voice silky as his eyes assessed how waterlogged I was. I couldn't tell what nationality he was. He was almost African looking, but then he also looked Mediterranean, or even maybe from the Middle East somewhere. His accent was most definitely a Londoner's, though. His eyes weren't dark. They were golden. And they were entertained as they assessed me.

That pissed me off even more. "Honestly and truly, does it look like I'm going anywhere?"

He cocked a surprised eyebrow at me, his eyes never leaving my face. "Who are you?"

"That's none of your goddamn business." I threw

him my haughtiest look. When he smirked at me, it infuriated me even more. "Who the hell are you is more to the point!"

He shrugged, a dangerous grin spreading across his face. "I can be whoever you want me to be."

I glanced at the gun. "Are you going to shoot me with that thing?"

He looked like he was weighing up his options. That probably wasn't a good thing. "I haven't decided yet. I'll ask you again, who are you? Give me a reason not to shoot you."

"I can be whoever you want me to be." I threw the words back in his face. He barked with laughter, baffling me. I didn't know what was compelling me to be so defiant with him, but facing the barrel of a gun had instilled indignation in me that I'd never experienced before.

He sighed, still shaking with amusement. "Fine." He reached out and grabbed my arm and pulled me from the shower. "You can come with me, and we'll talk about this along the way." He held out a towel.

I shrugged his hands from me, snatched the towel, and got to work towelling my hair off, and semi-drying my soaking clothes. I was grateful he'd let me dry myself, maybe it meant he wasn't quite as barbaric as I originally thought. I bent down to put my shoes on. "What? You're not going to kill me?"

"Not yet," he muttered as he waited for me to get my shit together. He held the door open. "Don't even think about doing anything stupid, or you'll be dead in a split second."

I couldn't help it. I walked over to Darren... or what remained of Darren. I sighed deeply and swallowed hard. "Oh god," I murmured. It was odd, but a part of me was relieved. There had been something a bit off about him, and I was glad I didn't have to have sex with him. But seeing him dead on the floor was kind of a surreal experience.

His wallet was sticking partway out of his pocket, and I bent down to retrieve it. Opening it, I found a few thousand pounds enclosed. I knew I wasn't going to get paid for tonight, and I hesitated a little as I pulled the notes and shoved them into my handbag. Right now I was on the bones of my arse and I had to take what I could get. When I looked up, the guy was looking at me, eyebrows raised. "What?"

"You're stealing off a dead man."

I shrugged, pursing my lips as I looked down at Darren again. "I know."

I tried to remember what he looked like alive, but weirdly, I couldn't seem to find the memories. Seeing him lying there, slack, brain matter all over the sumptuous carpet - it didn't quite gross me out, but I didn't particularly like it either. If I didn't know any better, I would almost say I was sickly curious about it.

My research mind kicked into gear. My client had just died and I was analysing it? What the hell was that about? I took a step back from the body, disgusted with myself. I looked up at Darren's killer, a slither of fear running through me as I found him watching me.

"Your actions tell me two things. One, you are no friend of his, and two, you're not really fazed that he's dead." He eyed me with curiosity as I stared back at him wordless. "If it's money you need, I can help you get that from him."

I pursed my lips, watching him cautiously before answering. "Yeah? Are you going to let me go after that?"

He gave a small shake of his head. "Not likely." He pulled the clip from his weapon, pocketing it, before he handed me the gun. "Hold this, and I'll find you something worth your while."

I stared at him with complete and utter confusion, gun in my hand as he went to the bedroom and found a safe. I didn't see how he did it, but moments later, the safe was open. I didn't know if I was tangled up with some sort of master thief or not, but the whole situation was definitely bizarre. It made me wonder if there was something more in that rescue remedy than just Bach flowers, because I was not acting like a normal person. In fact... based on my actions so far, I would almost bank on the fact that Jax had laced that rescue remedy. I looked down at the gun in my hand, and wondered if I could perhaps clock this guy over the head with it.

"Come here," he instructed me. I jumped, the

sound of his voice snapping me back to the moment, and swallowed my thoughts. Jax was definitely going to get a bollocking from me when I got out of this. If I got out of this.

As I approached, I saw him pocket an external hard drive and a couple of other things. He gestured at the open safe door. "Help yourself."

I looked in. There was a lot of money there. Not enough to pay Luke out, but enough to make a good start. There were also a number of boring looking documents that I didn't bother touching. I grabbed some of the money, and quickly realised that it wasn't actually going to fit in my handbag. Silently, the man handed me an empty laptop bag, and helped me load the money inside.

This was crazy. I was stealing a boatload of cash off my dead client. Someone would find out. I knew someone would find out. Annalise was going to kill me when she discovered Darren was dead. This night was really not panning out as intended. "I can't believe I'm doing this," I muttered.

The man zipped up the laptop bag, and paused as he peered into the safe. There were a couple of slim-line black cases at the back. He paused, and slowly opened one of them. Something glittered from within, and I felt my breath catch. Before I even realised what I was doing, I had moved right up beside him to get a closer look. It was a stunning necklace. There were about ten rows of diamonds littering the choker.

"Wow," I whispered.

He snapped the case closed without looking at me, and pocketed them both without even opening the other one. "We need to go."

I paused. "Go where?"

"Well, we still haven't figured out who you are, and if you're not going to tell me – I have someone at my place who will."

"Who?" I asked, bafflement filling me. "Who on earth would know who I am?"

He winked, handing me the money-loaded laptop bag, "You'll find out soon enough." He closed the safe. "Come on, mystery girl. It's time for you to reveal all."

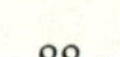

9

We left the room and rode the elevator down. There was an awkward silence, but I refused to talk. I looked for potential exit strategies the entire time we walked through the hotel, but whenever there were people, he wrapped an arm around me so I wouldn't make a run for it or cause a disturbance. Instead of walking through the reception foyer, he led me down a long corridor, and out an emergency exit at the back of the building. He beeped a large brand new black Mercedes SUV in the alleyway unlocked, and instructed me to get in.

I did as I was told. I didn't doubt that he would shoot me if I tried to run. There was something commanding about him. The worst thing was that I had no idea what was going to happen to me. After the shitty time I'd had recently with Luke, I was just too tired to even think about fighting this guy back. I was at the point of thinking that whatever happened... happened. It was out of my control. My entire life had been out of control recently, why should this be any different? And hey, at least if they killed me, Luke would never get a cent of his bloody money.

I rifled through my handbag, and found a packet of Marlboro Lights, breathing a sigh of relief that they weren't wet from our brief shower escapade. "Thank god," I said lighting one, and inhaling the smoke. I wound down the window, letting the cool night air touch my face. My hands kept shaking. I knew I was well and truly pumped full of adrenaline. The man started the car, and gave me a sidelong look of disapproval as he watched me.

"Smoking will kill you."

I shrugged. "So will you if I don't watch out. May as well have a little enjoyment along the way." I was being flippant, but I no longer cared. If I lived, I would have a good chunk of money to pay Luke with - if this guy let me keep it. If not, I was probably going to be dead anyway.

He drove quickly and confidently. The London streets still had a few people on them, more drunk than not, but for a Saturday night, it seemed relatively quiet. Every now and then we would pass a bobby car, and every time I saw one, my stomach turned. I didn't know if I should try and capture their attention or not.

Giving my abductor a sidelong glance told me that he was more than assured that I would do anything that stupid.

I flicked the cigarette butt out the window, and wound it up. We entered the more industrial part of London, and my nerves kicked in. I had heard a million stories about people being killed and buried in building sites and the like. I reached for my phone, to try and at least send out some sort of help signal, but I felt a hand clasp around my forearm.

"What are you doing?" he asked.

I shook my head. "Nothing. Just trying to... find my rescue remedy."

He looked at me in surprise. "Rescue remedy? As in the homeopathic stuff?"

"Yeah," I said quietly. He released my arm, and I found that I actually did want it. I pulled the bottle from my bag, unscrewed it, and lifted the dropper to my mouth.

"I wouldn't have thought that a party girl like you would have a need for it." I ignored him, and recapped the bottle before dropping it into my bag.

A few moments later he pulled the vehicle down a long narrow alleyway between two old brick factory buildings with enormous arched windows. They both looked abandoned, which didn't give me any hope. At least I was now mostly dry from the heating in the car. We pulled up to a garage, and he pressed a remote that opened the door wide. Lights flickered on as we pulled in, revealing a very clean, well maintained space. There was enough room for another three cars.

"Where are we?" My words came out small. In fact, I sounded afraid. I sucked in a deep breath to calm myself down. I had to pull it together.

"That's for me to know, and you to find out," he said gruffly. The garage door closed behind us. "Come on."

I grabbed the laptop case full of money and my handbag and got out of the car, following him over to an old metal gated elevator that rattled to a close behind me. It slowly ascended through the building, revealing a few musty and unused floors, until we reached the third floor. We stood in an enclosed foyer. He switched the lights on, and my mouth fell open in surprise.

The floors were polished wood, the walls painted a muted greyish green, and it actually had a beautiful hall table with a key bowl on it, of all things, and a huge abstract oil painting hanging above it. For a big tough guy, he seemed awfully domesticated.

I watched him throw the keys in the bowl, and step through the door that led out of the room. He turned and looked at me. "You coming?"

"Um..." I gave him a quizzical look. This situation was becoming weirder and weirder by the second. First he had killed my client, then he'd let me live, and helped me rob Darren. Now I was out in some remote warehouse, which so far resembled something out of a design magazine. Everything felt completely out of context. "Yeah... I guess." I trailed after him, only to find that my suspicions were confirmed.

It looked as though an interior designer had been well and truly over this place. High warehouse ceilings were littered with pendant halogen lighting. Enormous glass windows looked out at the night sky, and towards the roof line of the other buildings around us. To my left, I saw a kitchen with a huge stone island. And when I say huge, it was massive. I watched the man walk around and turn on more lights, revealing a very bachelor-like living area decked out in leather sofas and dark wooden furniture.

He looked up at me, and pointed at one of the chairs. "Sit."

I crossed the expansive room and did as I was told, watching him as he turned on heat pumps and emptied his pockets onto the coffee table between us. The case that held the diamond choker caught my eye, and I itched to pick it up. He put a smaller black case on top of it. There was also a hard drive, and a few USB drives that he'd also removed from the hotel suite. Finally, he sat down opposite me and pulled out a brand new iPhone from his pocket.

"I'm back," he said into the phone once someone had picked up his call. "Yeah, fine. I've picked up a little extra something though... I think you should come and have a look." His eyes cut to mine, and I sucked in my breath. My heart raced.

There were more of them. I pursed my lips, wondering if there was any way I could possibly get out of this place, and this mess that I was in. It seemed pretty damn unlikely.

My abductor finished up his phone call, and sat there watching me silently. I returned his gaze. He was very solidly built. He moved like someone from the military, but I couldn't be sure. No one from the military would just randomly kill someone in their hotel room, and then rob them. No... there was something else about him that I couldn't put my finger on.

His eyes carefully assessed me in the dim light. "Am I going to have to ask you again who you are?"

"Without a doubt," I retorted. "And again, I'm not going to tell you."

He shook his head with feigned annoyance. "Look around. There is no place to run. I am not restraining you. So far I have been more than hospitable towards you. Now, the least you could do is doing me the courtesy of telling me your name."

I silently shook my head, "I..." I didn't want to tell him my name. For all I knew, he could just kill me anyway. I looked around the apartment, refusing to meet his gaze. The more I looked, the more I realised that he probably hadn't bought me here to kill me. I swallowed and looked at the floor.

"Okay then. How about you tell me what you were

doing in that hotel suite tonight?"

I tapped my hand against my bare leg, considering the question. "No..." I didn't really want to tell anyone about my new occupation. He looked at me so earnestly, I almost felt ashamed to admit what I was doing there. Instead of saying anything, I just shook my head again.

I watched him, and he watched me. If he wasn't holding me captive, I would have thought he was extremely good looking, with his unusual colouring and eyes. But the mood I was in, the whole situation was just damn ugly.

We sat there in silence for about ten minutes before we heard a rattle at the back of the building. Fear sliced through me. Knowing my luck, I had probably just stumbled into some sort of illegal operation, and here were the henchmen to sort me out, once and for all. I itched to ask this guy who was coming, and what they wanted with me. Stubbornness had kicked in though, and I wasn't quite ready to show my curiosity just yet. A few moments later, two men walked into the room behind us.

My breath slightly hitched as my eyes drank in the new comers. My stomach lurched as I recognised them. One of them was the suave looking guy in glasses that had helped me out of Jax's car, and the younger surfer looking one was the barman. I swallowed. This whole thing felt like a set up. They didn't look particularly threatening, but then again, I had just had the realisation that my judge of character wasn't so great.

"Well, well, what do we have here?" asked the concierge. He had high cheekbones, aqua-coloured eyes surrounded by designer frames, and dark messily styled hair. I immediately felt tongue tied and a moment of unsettled nervousness developed under his gaze. I recalled that I'd felt uneasy when he helped me from the car as well. He was one of the best looking men I had ever laid eyed on. I desperately wanted to reach for my rescue remedy, but I didn't move.

"She was in the hotel room," my captive said. He shook his head. "I know I don't usually leave witnesses, but I saw something in her that could be potentially useful for us. So I bought her here. She could be a useful asset for that job we have coming up."

I gulped. "Asset?"

They ignored me and continued talking in hushed tones between them. I had absolutely no idea what their idea of 'useful asset' was, and I didn't know if I wanted to find out. I could hear snippets of them murmuring things like 'Tijuana', and 'distractions' and 'running interference'. None of it sounded good.

The American surfer bar-tender guy eventually disengaged from the conversation and sat down in the leather chair beside me, his eyes sparkling with mirth while he tried to keep a straight face. He looked out of place. He had longish unruly blond hair that curled slightly at the ends. "Well I think she would be perfect for the Mexico job. We've been looking for someone, haven't we? She's got the right look about her. I think we're all in agreement with that."

The other two stopped and stared at me. My captor had a calculating and assessing look upon his features, while the suave glasses guy looked almost bored. I had to get out of here. I didn't exactly know where 'here' was, but I had to try.

"Right, well." I sat forward and picked up my handbag, with my other hand resting on the money-loaded laptop case. "If that's all, I think I'll go now."

My original captor firmly put his hand on my shoulder and pushed me back into my seat, "We're not finished yet," he said quietly. He turned to the glasses guy. "Gabe's right. She would be perfect for Mexico, and that's precisely why I brought her back with me. Just look at her."

I sat deathly still as they watched me. Mexico? What the fuck were they talking about bloody Mexico for?

"She's a prostitute - Darren was her client."

I didn't know what I was more outraged about - the fact that he knew what I was doing there, or the assumption that I was 'just a prostitute'. "Hardly a fucking prostitute," I muttered.

My captive turned on me. "Well if you weren't there to shag Darren, what were you doing?"

I shrugged. He kind of had me there, but I still felt like I had to clarify the issue. "I have never, ever had sex with anyone for money. Darren was my first client, if you must know. And then you shot him. And I'm not a 'prostitute'. Had I actually managed to do my job tonight, I would have been a 'high class escort'."

He laughed. "Darling, call it what you like. I did you a favour."

"A favour? You call that a favour?" I huffed, and shook my head. "You've got to be joking. A hundred people saw me with Darren tonight, and now he's dead in his hotel room. And you call that a favour?"

"Yes, and now your fingerprints are all over the weapon that killed him, as well as the safe."

He was right. My thoughts went straight to when he asked me to hold his gun, and I silently berated myself for being so damn stupid. Instantly, I no longer cared about the money. I had to get out of there, preferably alive. These people were crazy. And I was in the middle of a nightmare. I should just go straight to the police and tell them everything, and clear my name. Annalise would back me up, I'm sure. And Jax.

But then again, maybe Annalise wouldn't. Doubt crept into my mind as I processed this. Darren was her businesses client, and the woman hardly knew me. She'd taken me in based on Jax's recommendation... and in all honesty, she didn't know me from a bar of soap. She could, in reality, hold me accountable for his death. I swallowed.

None of this, no matter which way I looked at it, looked good.

10

The surfer guy moved away from me and joined back in the conversation and I found my opportunity. I just had to make it through the door to the elevator, or perhaps there was some sort of fire escape on the outside of the building somewhere. I clasped my handbag tightly, making little movement as I lifted the strap up and over my shoulder.

I moved quietly forward, so that I was sitting on the edge of my seat and kept my eyes firmly on my captives. None of them were paying me a lick of attention. I couldn't have hoped for better. I stood up quickly, moving as fast as I could across the wooden floors in my high heels. If I'd had any bloody common sense during my planning stage, I would have taken them off.

Someone grabbed me, and I turned slightly, which only allowed them to firm up their grip. It was the glasses guy. Adrenaline thrashed through me, and I pulled away from him, making a dash for the door. I fumbled with the latch, and then found myself wrenched away from it and falling. Everything seemed to go in slow motion as I crashed against the wooden floor, banging my head hard. I tried to roll away from him with all my might.

"Let me go!" I started screaming at him as he pinned me down. His face was dark with anger. The floorboards were hard against my back, and my wrists hurt like fuck from the force and strength of him.

"Don't fucking move," he said, his voice steely. He eased off a little, and pulled a small gun from somewhere, and aimed it at my head. My breath hitched and I froze. My lip trembled as I stared down the barrel of the gun. I could feel my heart race as the light glinted off the steel, and all I could see was my life passing before my eyes. My parents. Elsie. Luke. Friends. And my work.

I lifted my eyes to meet the jade ones framed in designer glasses. His gaze was cold, calculating, methodical. He was really going to kill me - I could read the intent in his eyes. This man on top of me was more than just dangerous. He was lethal. From the way he was looking at me now, I knew that he was a trained killer. There was no air of nervousness about him. He was so calm, collected, and confident. I didn't stand a chance.

And it was only then that I knew without a shadow of a doubt that I wasn't ready to die yet.

"Chase, no!" My original captor broke the stare between us. "Don't you dare shoot her on my floor!" He hauled the man off me, but I still didn't move. I wanted to, but I couldn't. Fear still had me paralyzed. I had only just started breathing again.

"What, River? Either she dies, or she agrees to our proposal. It's as simple as that." He pointed down at me, and I automatically flinched. "Look at her! Does she look like she's about to agree to anything we ask right now?"

I would if they agreed to spare my life. I could definitely be persuaded. Right now, I was in a compromised position, and I was fairly certain I would do anything. I mean, tonight I'd agreed to sleep with someone for money, could whatever they wanted me to do be worse?

The guy's gun was still aimed at me. "Move, and you die," he said with distain.

I wasn't moving. I was hardly even breathing. This was the second time I'd had a gun pointed at me tonight, and this time round I was more scared than the last time, but more from the determined look in his eye than anything else.

"She might actually agree if we just talked to her,"

the surfer guy said. I flicked my eyes towards him with curiosity. What he said caused the glasses guy to lift his focus from me, and pay attention to him.

"Yeah," I piped up. "What he said." My voice sounded choked up and raspy. I hated it. I sounded so weak and helpless.

Their glances flickered down to me, but then rested back on surfer guy, who lowered his phone and snapped an image of my face.

"How long?" Glasses guy asked.

Surfer guy looked at his phone intently. "Searching. Shouldn't be long."

"What's not long?" I asked. I couldn't help myself. I knew I really wasn't in the position to be demanding answers, but I was fumbling, and I had nothing to lose.

None of them spoke until the surfer dude smiled and pressed his screen a couple of times. "McKenna Carmichael. Date of birth, first February 1983. Organ Donor. No infringements on her license." He tapped a few more times. "Majored in History at Oxford University. Oh, with honours, congrats," he said, eyebrows raised. "Parents deceased."

The glasses guy nudged me with his foot. "So. McKenna." I stared right back at him, and noticed his hard gaze had softened. He lowered his gun. Without the weapon pointed at my head, he now seemed a tad more approachable. "Would you like to come and do a job with us?"

"A job," I responded. I didn't know what sort of proposition this was, and I was buggered if I was going to talk about a job offer while lying on the floor. "If you could be so kind as to help me up, then perhaps we can talk about it." My voice was laced with sarcasm, but right now I didn't care. This felt like a way out of my own demise.

They instantly hauled me up off the floor. "Thanks," I said quietly as I brushed myself off, and readjusted my dress. Annalise was going to kill me if she ever saw this dress again. It had scuff marks on it, and I could see water stains on the fabric from getting drenched in the shower earlier. I grimaced.

They were all watching me with curiosity, and I was once again beginning to feel very self-conscious. I cleared my throat, snapping them out of their trance. What the hell was up with these three?

"Come on, McKenna," my original captor said, gently guiding me back towards the seating area. "Have a seat, and we can talk." Once I was comfortable, he asked, "Would you like anything to drink?"

"How very civilised," I muttered. He looked down at me with amusement. I cleared my throat. "Er... yes please. Anything will do." The other two had sat down side by side on the sofa opposite me, the surfer guy looked very relaxed, and the other one looking frustrated. They were so completely out of place with each other.

A drink was handed to me. I looked down at the clear liquid over ice in the chic crystal tumbler. A slice of lemon was floating in it. I sniffed the drink before I took a sip. Tonic. I took a sip, and found that a good measure of gin had been added as well.

"McKenna, my name is River," my original captor said as he sat down in the chair beside me. "This is Chase," he said, hand extended to the good looking glasses guy. "And this is our tech-engineer, Gabe." He gestured towards the surfer. "I should probably apologise to you, first off, for not enlightening you to who we are. And secondly, for scaring you." He threw Chase a disapproving glance. "Now I know that you need money right now. It was kind of obvious when we were in the hotel room."

I sighed. I didn't know what to make of this lot. I had started the day hung-over with no option but to become a high class escort to pay Luke out. Now I was sitting with the men who had killed my client, once again discussing how I needed cash. I took a sip of my gin and tonic, and slowly nodded. "I'm kind of in a pickle," I admitted, biting my lip. "You killing my client kind of fucked up my plan."

River cleared his throat. "Ah, yes. Darren. Well... like you, we were trying to make money. Darren was a target. He wasn't a nice person, so you shouldn't get too teary about it." He sat back, and laced his light brown hands together and studied me for a moment. "You should probably know that we are professional contractors. Darren was part of a job for us. But more to the point we have a job booked over in Mexico, and we need someone to come with us. Preferably you. You fit the profile we've been looking for."

"Let me guess... It involves killing," I said, a little too shakily.

Gabe laughed. "No, actually, not this one."

"We have a number of different roles, and not all of them involve killing someone. A lot of the time, it's intelligence gathering."

"So now you're spies as well, are you?" My mind jumped to the James Bond stories which I had always loved, but somehow this bunch didn't exactly fit into that box. Okay, maybe River and Chase did, but Gabe? Definitely not.

Chase rolled his eyes, and sighed. "Yes, some of the time. We make money from taking a few people out when the price is right, and we also make money from infiltrating organisations and gathering intelligence. That's where you come in, if you're willing."

River leaned forward, his eyes trained directly on me. "We'll pay you four hundred thousand pounds if you accompany us to Mexico and help us do this job."

My breath caught in my throat. I looked down at the floor. And then I looked out the window towards the London sky. That was a lot of money. A huge amount. An amount that I really needed. I pursed my lips together. If I had that money, I could almost pay

Luke out for half the house and all the other additional costs that he'd dreamed up, and all it would take was this one small job. I swallowed. First prostitution, and now this. What the hell was wrong with me?

"Of course, this would be an all-expenses paid round trip. We just need to have you distract someone over there. Go on a few dates with him, entertain him a little if you like, while we work in the background to get the information we need."

My heart had begun to race. The money I had taken from Darren would help pay for Elsie's care until I had done the job. This was my ticket out to pay Luke off. "Entertain? How? Would I have to sleep with him?"

River shrugged. "In our line of work, we do what we must to get the job done." He drained the remainder of his glass. "Sometimes it means sleeping with people we don't want to. But I think you'll be perfect for this role." He turned to Chase. "Don't you think?"

Chase eyed me critically and slowly nodded with an audible sigh. "Yes. With a bit of work, I think she'll do."

"Wait. What?" I didn't know what to think, but that statement was erring on the edge of insult. "A little work? What the hell does that mean?"

Chase smiled. "It means, darling, that you need some work done before we can let you loose in

Mexico. First of all, your hair needs to be cut a lot shorter so you can wear wigs comfortably. Secondly." He leaned closer to me, staring into my eyes. "Yes, secondly, I think we should get you laser eye surgery. How bad are they?"

I swallowed, staring back at him. The cheek of him. I huffed, thinking about the expense of all this, but then I let it go. I had wanted laser surgery for a long time, but just never bothered to investigate it. "Bad enough for me to wear glasses or lenses permanently."

He nodded thoughtfully. "I thought so. You'll also need to get tanned up, and of course your wardrobe outfitted. Once all that has happened, we'll have another look at you."

"I haven't even agreed to anything yet," I snapped. I took a sip of my gin and tonic and pondered the proposal. They all sat there expectantly waiting for me to say something. As strange as this all was, they seemed to be quite certain that I would say yes. "So just to clarify, there won't be any killing. This is only information gathering, and you want me to be a nice little distraction for someone over there?"

"Yes," Gabe answered, his eyes smiling in amusement. "And Chase wants to give you a makeover."

"And either I do this, or you could kill me or pin Darren's murder on me." I looked pointedly at River as Gabe burst out laughing.

"Naturally, we would prefer you to join us."

"Of course you would," I commented. I realised that I had power with these guys. They wanted me for something, and that gave me room to negotiate. "If I do this, I'm not paying for this new wardrobe, or any of the surgery, or anything like that. This will be a free trip for me, with a pay day at the end of it."

"In a nutshell, yes," River answered, a slow smile spreading across his features. He gave a knowing glance to both Chase and Gabe, who both smiled back at him.

It was that moment that I saw something between the three of them. They were a team, all with the same objective to get me to go to Mexico with them. The only person I ever felt like I was part of a team with was Elsie. They had left me alive and basically kidnapped me tonight but for the most part they had been polite and courteous. I looked at Chase. Except for him wanting to kill me.

"When we come back from Mexico, I can walk away free?"

"Yes," Chase said, his smile was now gone and he was beginning to look impatient with me. "Does this mean you're agreeing to our terms?"

I was nodding before I even realised. "Yes, I think so." This was it. This was my ticket out of my complications with Luke. I looked down at the laptop bag stuffed with money at my feet. "But I keep the money from Darren."

"Deal," River said, grinning as he stood up. He helped me to my feet, and shook my hand. "Welcome to the team, Mack."

I raised my eyebrows. "Only my best friend Jax has ever called me that before." I smiled.

Instead of taking my hand, Gabe gave me a big bear hug. "Uh, thanks?" I uttered with surprise. That was the last thing I'd expected.

He gave me a wide grin. "I'm just pleased you made the right decision. Now, I bet I can get you in with a private surgeon for your eyes within a couple of days, and tomorrow, you'll be booked in at a spa for a full body cleanse, sunbed, and a haircut." Weirdly, I thought he actually looked ecstatically happy about this.

Chase stepped forward, his intense stare meeting mine as he clasped my hand. "We fly out in ten days. Get used to us, because from now on, you'll have one of us with you at all times." He looked up at River. "I'll drive Mack home, and stay with her tonight. We'll meet you at the Respire Spa first thing in the morning."

I swallowed and pursed my lips together. Chase scared the shit out of me. I would have preferred either River or Gabe to drive me home. "Wait. What? You're staying at my place?"

"Is that a problem?" he asked.

I thought I could hear amusement in his voice, but he looked deadly serious. I slowly shook my head.

"Uh, no?"

He smiled. "Good then. Welcome to the team."

THE END

Enter Mack's world in TIJUANA NIGHTS, the action packed thriller, and the first book of Leigh K. Hunt's new Night's Series.

An Action Thriller Novel of The Nights Series

Tijuana Nights

Leigh K. Hunt

Dedication

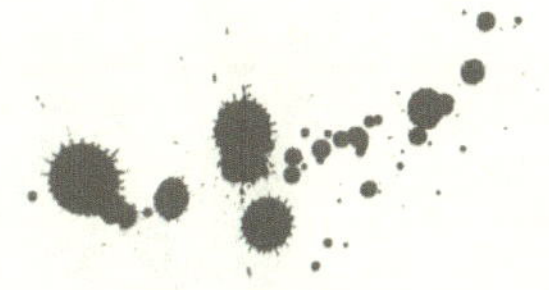

This book is dedicated to my husband, Michael.

You are my rock, and more often than not (or that I would like to admit) – my voice of reason.
Thank you for always listening and being there, even if I do cause you a few eye rolls. x

ACKNOWLEDGMENTS

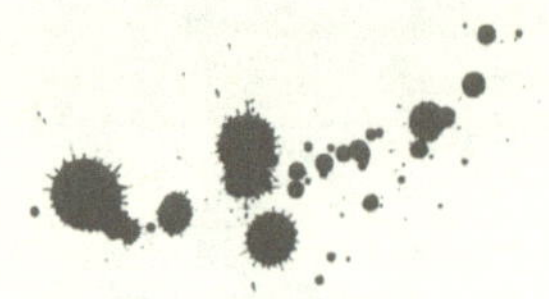

Writing a book is a lot like pulling teeth some of the time. At other times, it's amazing. But I wouldn't have been able to wrench this book together without an incredible team around me.

Abby, my daughter – thank you for your continuous two-year-old endurance – you are tenacious beyond your years, and thank you for letting Mummy get some good night's sleep. You're always making me laugh, even when I'm frustrated. I love you more than anything in this world. You help me keep it real.

My super-duper-amazeballs Editor and friend, Cassie Hart. Oh my – where the hell would I be without you? Need I really say more? You are my friend, my confidante, and you have been the most amazing trusted partner in this project... I doubt I could have done it with anyone else.

Evald Subasic and Nicola-Kiri Smith, for grounding me during the final planning stages of this book. Our dream-up sessions dedicated to talking

Cartel murder techniques were totally awesome, and you helped me find some diamonds in the rough. Even when I was flailing about.

Melissa Pearl, T.G. Ayer, J.C Hart, and Richard Parry. You have all been published before, which helped illuminate the way forward for me. Thank you for listening to my writer-woes, and just encouraging me to get this book done. Your feedback during my drafting and continuous and unwavering support fills my heart with a lot of love. You all inspire me.

Steve Clement, Penny Epel, and Breanna Glass for your extraordinary brainstorming session regarding Cartel names! I was stressing out, and you guys absolutely came to the rescue!

A big shout out to my proof-readers, Adele Woolley and Erin Travers, and my lovely team of beta-readers! Your feedback and confidence in this book was incredible!

And finally - the biggest acknowledgement is to my family. Thank you for believing in me. Thank you for always being there. And thank you for always encouraging me to pursue my dreams.

1

I kicked my high heels off under the courtyard table at the Little Havana bar in Tijuana, and sparked up a Marlboro Light, savouring the inhalation of the smoke. I kept telling myself I was going to give up, but it's really not the time. Especially not today. Adrenaline still coursed through me, and my hands shook as I lifted the margarita to my lips and took a sip. I swore as I spilled a few drops. I had to contain myself and calm the fuck down.

But who could calm down when they have just seen their plane blown to dust? I should, in reality, have been on my way to Los Angeles, before catching a connecting flight home to London. But I missed my flight, and then when I got to the airport, I stood by and watched the plane explode into a million pieces just after take-off.

And somehow, deep down... I knew that explosion was meant for me.

Tijuana was hot, and dusty, and I'd thoroughly had enough. I wanted to go home to England, sort out a few things, and settle back into my life as a historian, writing historical reports, and losing myself in the labyrinth of archives around Europe. The last place I wanted to be was stuck in Tijuana, in designer clothes, knowing that I'm up to my neck in shit. I stubbed my cigarette out, and had another sip of margarita, savouring every moment of the taste, in an effort to centre myself. I knew that I had to call River and ask for his help.

I rummaged through my handbag, pulling things out and dumping them on the table as I tried to find the business card with River's numbers on it. In the process I grasped my iPhone, my finger traced the bullet hole through the middle as I drew it from my bag and slowly exhaled.

My iPhone was the last luxurious thing I had got myself. I had bought it the day that I found Luke screwing my best friend in our bed and I threw him out. I never would have spent that sort of money if I'd known he was going to demand half of everything I owned. I bit my lip as I turned it over in my hand. Many people consider phones to be their 'life-savers'...

but usually that's just a figure of speech. No one actually believes their phone will literally save their life. But I do - I'm living proof. The bullet that killed my phone made me move; if I hadn't, the next bullet would have been in my head.

I found River's card and stood, leaving my shoes under the table as I walked barefoot into the dim bar.

Dredging up my limited Spanish skills I approached the bar, “Dónde está el teléfono?” I painfully asked.

After a frustrated look of confusion, the barman finally pointed the phone out to me. Looking down at the card in my hand I read the words - Mergers and Acquisitions. I grimaced. More like Murders and Executions. I picked up the phone, and dialled River's mobile number. After two rings he picked up.

"It's me," I said quietly, watching the barman across the room as he polished glasses. There were no other patrons apart from me. Not surprising really considering it was still morning.

"You're alive." River’s voice echoed with relief down the phone. "Where the hell are you?"

I smiled. "Little Havana Bar."

"I'll be there shortly."

He hung up on me, and I looked at the phone in disbelief. It's not the first time he'd done it, but I thought he would at least be a bit more polite. Particularly considering he’s British. Rolling my eyes, I hung the receiver up, and on my way back to my table, stopped by the bar and ordered another drink. I knew I wouldn't be able to drive legally after this, but who gave a shit about legalities in Mexico?

Twenty minutes later, I spotted River making his way through the dark bar, and out into the courtyard. As always, my heart raced when I saw him. From what I had gathered, River used to work for the British MI6 or some other covert organisation. He was trained as an assassin by a professional government outfit of some kind. If truth be known, I didn't really want to know the exact details.

I couldn't tell what nationality he was, as he looked like he was of mixed descent. He was from England - that I could tell from his middle-upper class accent - and almost African looking, but then he could have been Mediterranean, or maybe even Middle Eastern. River's colouring allowed him to fit in perfectly in places like Tijuana. He always maintained a professional composure, always dressed immaculately. Today, he was in a white shirt, casually open at the collar, and wore designer jeans despite the heat. I couldn't read his caramel-coloured eyes as they were hidden behind the aviator sunglasses that he always wore. Automatically I reached for the last of my margarita.

River sat down at my table, and smiled across at me. "I've spent the last hour wondering where the hell you were. Gabe hacked the passenger manifesto, and we discovered that you never boarded Flight 474 to

LA." He picked up my iPhone, and put his little finger through the hole. "Looks like you caught a lucky break, Mack. Very lucky." He put the phone down, removed his glasses, and lifted his gaze to mine. “What happened?”

I drew in a deep lungful of air as the explosion of the plane replayed in my mind. I didn’t know where to start. I ran my hands through my hair nervously. A part of me didn’t want to breathe a word of what had happened in this godforsaken city. Another part knew that he needed to know.

“Mack?”

“Yeah. Okay. Well, I woke up late this morning, God knows why; maybe because my phone was shot to shit and my alarm doesn’t work anymore. Anyway, I hadn’t finished packing properly, so I kind of just threw a few things together, and arranged for the hotel to send the rest of my gear back home.” I looked up at River, and saw that he was shaking his head in disapproval. “What?”

He smiled. “Rule number one. Never trust anybody - especially if they can be paid off for information.”

I wanted to tell him he could go fuck his rules, but thought better of it. It was not the time to pick a fight with an assassin. Instead, I frowned at him and shrugged. “Yeah, whatever. Anyway,” I continued. “Then my useless piece-of-shit car took ages to start, and when the engine finally ticked over and I hit the road, there was an accident, and I got stuck in traffic. Seriously, I tried to make that flight, I really did. I even took back roads through this shithole to try and get to the airport faster." I lit another cigarette, and slowly blew the smoke out into the sun-drenched courtyard. "The check-in lady informed me that I, "Rachel White", had missed the flight, but that I was more than welcome to watch it take off."

So I had. And I watched it explode mid-air. A huge white burst of light engulfed it, and I saw it before I heard or felt it. There were a hundred and fifty odd people on that plane, and I was meant to be one of them.

River reached across the table and grabbed my free hand. His fingers felt warm and steady against my clammy, shaky ones. "You need to settle down. I know you should have been on that plane. Now, Gabe has been checking the manifesto, and you're right. No one else on that flight, that we can tell, had any affiliation with the cartel, or even anything else remotely shady." He slowly smiled. "You are in good company, Mack. We'll protect you. We got you into this mess... we can help you get out of it."

The barman walked out of the bar, laden with two more drinks. I was really not going to be able to drive. I looked down at the Tag Hauer watch that River and Chase had given me, and noted that it wasn't even mid-morning. If my mother was still alive she would be kicking my backside to Timbuktu and back again for drinking before five o'clock.

"So, let me guess. You know who blew up my plane?"

River leaned back in his seat and laughed. "I like you, Mack. You're direct and to the point. It's damn refreshing. To answer your question, yes. We have our suspicions that the destroy order on the plane may have come from Carmen Amaro."

My guts sank. That was the same bitch that had shot my phone. The same bitch that was married to my mark. The same mark that bought me out to this fucking country. I wanted to scream. River could see my anger in my eyes. He smiled, infuriating me even more.

"What?" I snapped.

He shook his head, amusement evident on his features. "You've changed a lot since the first night I met you. You don't even seem that fazed by the fact that it's Carmen who is after you. Before, well, who knows? You would have probably been a little unstable about the whole situation."

I wasn't listening. I was too busy thinking about the best way to get revenge on her. Not only had she shot up my favourite phone, but now in the process of trying to kill me again, she had ended up killing a hundred and fifty innocent people instead. What the hell was her problem? I could see River still talking to me, but all noise was swallowed by the sound of my inner voice. I wanted her to die a very slow and morbid death.

No. I had to stop thinking like that. I was just as bad as her if I retaliated like that. Okay. Not quite as bad. I wouldn't go off and kill a plane load of people because I'm a jealous, psychotic bitch. I'd like to think I have more class and style than her.

I looked up at River. "For God's sake," I muttered. He was a contract killer - there was no reason why he couldn't take her out for me. I wouldn't even have to watch. If I couldn't run, and I couldn't hide, and I couldn't get home to England at the moment, then surely I should inadvertently rid the world of a terrible person.

"River?"

He looked at me blankly, and then shook his head. "No, Mack. No."

"What? You don't even know what I'm going to say."

"You don't have to say it. It's written all over your face." He sighed, and looked me directly in the eyes. "I'm not going to kill Carmen for you. Bottom line."

Damn. I was never good at playing poker, and it seemed that River could read me like an open book. "Why not?"

"Because I'm not about to screw up an entire information gathering operation all because you're letting your emotions get in the way."

Oh, I could feel it. I was about to explode under the pressure that was building up inside me.

"Emotions?" I said, dangerously quiet. "Are you for fucking real? This is the second time she's tried to kill me."

He laid his hand on mine, and his eyes softened. "Mack. Compose yourself. I understand, you know. I do. I get it. I've been the target of a few people myself. But you're not going to make this better by getting all emotional about it. You need a clear head. If you don't have a clear head, you get killed. Rule number two."

More. Fucking. Rules. But I knew he was right. I took a deep breath. This wasn't going to go away, but I knew he would help me. His phone started ringing, and he released my hand to answer it, keeping his impenetrable gaze on me the whole time.

"Gabe." He smiled at me, and I felt myself begin to relax again. I reached for another cigarette and the last of my third margarita as he gave short responses on the phone. Gabe is the tech-guy in their operation. Apparently he was some kid-genius hacker they pulled out of Langley when he was seventeen. Gabe is the biggest geek I have ever met, and that's saying something considering my academic background. But he's not your typical geek. He looks like a pot-smoking surfer, but then again, maybe that's his cover whenever they're on an operation. Gabe can hack into any system in the world and cover his tracks. I've watched him build fake databases, create new identities, leave false trails, and shift money without leaving a single trace that it was ever there. And I haven't even been hanging out with these guys for very long.

The sound of River dropping his phone on the table snapped me out of my daydream. "We're wanted," he stated, eyeing up my lit cigarette. "Finish up. Gabe has organised your gear from the hotel to be delivered out to my place. We're having a team meeting."

Handling alcohol has never been one of my strong points, and as we walked to the car park outside the Little Havana Bar, I felt slightly woozy. Fresh air, heat from the midday sun, and tequila really doesn't mix too well, and I questioned what the hell was wrong with these Mexican people, considering that from what I had witnessed, a big part of their culture is founded on drinking.

"You can't keep using that car," River said, disturbing my thoughts.

I slowed to a stop and turned. "What?"

"You can't keep using that car. Carmen will track it."

"What? You're trying to get rid of my car but yet you won't kill Carmen for me?"

"I'm not going to kill Carmen, you can do that." River smirked. "Besides, you might be one of the team, but you'll never survive here without us. Cars come and go."

I threw my arms into the air. "Well if I can't use this one, where am I going to get a new one from? Jack it?"

River snorted with amusement. "I would like to see you try. No, you can use mine until we get you another one." He held his hand out to me. "Come on, pass me your phone."

Baffled I rummaged around in my bag, and pulled out the iPhone.

He glanced at it. "You don't need this anymore." And then I watched my beautiful bullet-holed phone go sailing through the air towards an open dumpster.

"Are you shitting me?"

River shrugged. "What? You've got enough junk in that handbag without adding a dead phone to it. We'll get you a new one."

"You just threw my phone out!"

"Take your wig off as well," he ordered deadpan. "That needs to go. You're too recognisable in this town now that you've been out and about with Javier."

I swallowed, and started unpinning the wig from my head. Tears pricked at my eyes as the events of the morning came crashing back to the surface. I silently handed him my wig and car-keys without looking at him, and leaned against his car, crossing my arms in front of my chest.

River unlocked the rental car boot. He pulled my small suitcase out, and much to my horror, dropped the keys inside the boot as he slammed it shut. "I'm assuming you didn't need anything else out of the car? No spare iPhones floating about?" Eyebrows raised, he waited for a response with a glint of amusement in his eyes.

Since Luke had left me I had become a very independent woman. But here was this guy trying to look after me and take control. I swallowed my frustration. I knew he was just trying to help.

I sniffed, and swiped at my eyes, giving him a watery smile. "My lucky dagger?"

River burst into laughter. "I have a spare one you can use."

I rolled my eyes. "Is there anything you don't have?"

"Not that I'm aware of." He smiled. "C'mon, let's get out of here." He pulled his keys out of his pocket, and unlocked his truck. "The sooner this is over and done with, the sooner we can get you back to England."

I climbed into the big black Range Rover, and onto the cool leather seats. My hair was damp with perspiration from the Tijuana heat, and undoubtedly from the stress of almost dying again, and I wondered how the hell I signed up for this life. I'm a qualified historian, not some covert operative interfering with Mexican cartel business. I knew that River would protect me. I was just being silly. "I never understood why you needed such a big truck. Doesn't it draw attention to you?"

"No," he answered drily. "There are plenty of 'big trucks' around this region, if you hadn't noticed. It's one of the ways the cartels move their product. Luckily for me, I never seem to get stopped." He dropped his phone into its cradle, and pressed a button. "Chase," he said, his tone firm.

"Dialling," the phone responded.

Chase. Panic welled within me. I just knew that there was so much hiding behind those intelligent eyes of his. I couldn't tell if he was a good guy or a bad guy. "Why are you ringing Chase?"

River smiled. "Because he's the one that pays the bills." He took the phone off speaker, and lifted the mobile to his ear.

Chase is a different story to both River and Gabe. Chase is scary as hell. I don't know where he comes from, but he can put on any accent he wanted. I have the distinct feeling that he has always been an assassin, although I don't know for sure. His natural accent is definitely English. It sounds refined, but I don't think he grew up anywhere with the same level of class as River. Chase looks a million dollars at all times; everything designer. He's clean-cut, well spoken, with high chiselled cheekbones and vibrant blue eyes that he often hides behind glasses or different coloured contacts so that he's not so memorable. If I were going to pick any word in the world to describe him it would be 'tailor made.'

River once told me that Chase was extremely

accurate at reading people and the situation around him, which made him a handy asset to have on the team. Perhaps that was why he made me nervous. I constantly wondered if he was assessing me.

"... yeah, I've got her. She seems to think that she can do over Carmen Amaro." I looked up at River, instantly snapping back into reality.

"Roger that. See you soon." He ended the call with a press of a button and turned to me, his smile infectious, though, considering the circumstances, I should have been crying. But I wasn't.

We started to head towards the coast area. I had been to River's Tijuana house a number of times before. If truth be known, it was more like a mansion, by my standards, anyway. The first time we went there was a defining moment, where I really understood that being an assassin must pay seriously well. His house was huge and intimidating; I felt more at home in more intimate spaces.

I went to reach for my phone to check for any messages, when I suddenly remembered that River had thrown it out. It was a dead and useless phone anyway, but with it missing, I felt as though I had lost some sort of appendage. "I can't believe you threw my phone out," I said sullenly. "You could have given me some bloody warning."

"Out with the old and in with the new, Mack. If you roll with me, that's how it is."

I put my palm against my forehead and leaned

back, closing my eyes. "You have got to be kidding. I don't even want to roll with you. You guys are the ones who got me into this position in the bloody first place."

River snorted with laughter. "If I hadn't found you when I did, you wouldn't have nearly as much dignity as you do right this very minute. You were trying to whore yourself, I saved your arse. You should count yourself lucky that I took time out of my day for you."

I could feel a headache coming on from the direction this conversation was taking. "You should be lucky that I happened to need the money. Now I just want to go home."

River shook his head. "No sweet pea... you're damn lucky we have the money you need." He was focused on driving in the Tijuana traffic. "We'll get you home, don't you worry about that. But just remember that this was originally a business deal. You held up your end of the deal, and we promised you would go home safely." He paused and took a deep breath, "Now in the meantime, we just need to make sure nothing goes wrong."

"You think I'm going to do something wrong?"

He shook his head, "It's not you I'm worried about. It's Carmen. She's unpredictable, and so is the Cartel."

I glanced over at River, wondering if I should light a cigarette, but with the mood he was in now he'd almost certainly throw me out on the side of the road somewhere. The only other time he had ever let me have a cigarette in his car was the night I first met him.

Instead of killing me when he'd the opportunity, he'd let me live, and then taken a chance on me by offering me a better paying job. I could come to Mexico with his team, and do just one small job for them. Be a sexual distraction to one of the El Diablo Cartel leaders. Before I knew it, they cut my hair to a close crop so I could wear wigs, sent me off for laser surgery on my eyes, thrown me in a sunbed for a few sessions to give my English skin a few shades of colour, and dressed me in designer clothes. The attitude I seemed to be developing now has only been rearing its head since the night I met the team.

It was all too much; today, the past month. I knew that if I didn't close my eyes and sleep, I was in danger of throwing up from the motion of the car. I absolutely regretted drinking far too many early morning margaritas.

I woke to the sensation of salty air tickling at my senses. We rounded the top of the tree lined driveway to River's place, and pulled up in front of a low lying house overlooking the Mexican coast. River stopped the car and turned off the engine. "Listen. I will do whatever is in my power to assist you with Carmen. However, new information has come in, and I strongly suspect it has to do with Javier Amaro. So let's just play this one by ear, shall we? Our pay check will have everything to do with Javier, therefore he's the priority. Carmen's just a bonus if you can get to her. Okay?" I undid my seatbelt, and gave him a watery smile. "Okay."

2

When I woke a few hours later in one of River's guest rooms, I found that my clothes had been hung up in the wardrobe and I sighed with relief. After a shower, I felt thoroughly alive again, and more mentally prepared to deal with whatever was coming.

Despite the fact that it never got very cold here, River had the fire roaring by the time I walked into the living room. With the bi-folds wide open to make the room more bearable and the sea breeze ruffling white gauzy drapes, it made a far prettier scene than you'd ever expect to find in the lair of a contract killer.

Chase was stretched out on one of the sofas with a book propped up on his knees, and a glass of wine on the coffee table beside him. "I hear you've severely pissed Carmen Amaro off." Chase directed both the words, and his calculating blue eyes, at me. My breath caught slightly under his gaze. I nodded and sat down on the opposite sofa. Some people are just so good looking, that they made you feel completely inferior when you're near them. Yeah... Chase was like that for me. Was I attracted to him? Hell yes. But I didn't have a chance in hell with à man like him, I didn't even know if I wanted a chance. If anything I was scared shitless of him, yet found him intriguing at the same time.

He had his contact lenses in this evening. It made him even more good looking than normal. I swallowed as Chase smiled. "Yes, well, some days are better than others, eh? I guess we always knew this could happen." He closed his book, and turned his full attention to me. "And now you want revenge?"

I froze. Revenge? I shook my head slowly. "No... not revenge. I just don't want to get killed. Carmen seems to have a death wish for me, and from what I've heard, she'll do anything to achieve her goals. She's nuts."

Chase threw his head back and laughed. "You don't get to be a cartel wife just for looking pretty, Mack. I'm sure she has a few more assets behind her than that. Watch your back."

"Leave her alone, Chase," River interrupted, as he walked in carrying a tray with several crystal tumblers on it and a bottle of tequila. "She's had a shitty day."

I smiled gratefully at him as he lowered a tray

onto the coffee table. "That's an understatement," I muttered. River poured tequila over ice into four crystal tumblers, and handed a glass to Chase. When he passed one to me, I accepted it hesitantly. Alcohol was the last thing I needed right now, but I didn't have to drink it if I didn't want to.

Chase smirked as I eyed up the golden liquid suspiciously. "This tequila is nothing like the revolting stuff we get at home. This is pure and untainted. Try it." He raised his perfectly manicured eyebrow as he waited.

"What the hell," I muttered, and took a generous sip. Subtle warmth spread through me as I swallowed. Chase was right. Unlike the crap back home, this tasted mellow, cooled by the ice in the glass. I found myself taking another sip. "That's actually quite refreshing."

River laughed. "Yes, it is. You know, the Aztecs used to make their own form of tequila called 'octli'. The people from this region have been distilling the blue agave plant for hundreds and hundreds of years. Believe me – if it tasted as awful as it does from those cheap bottles we get in England, they would never have continued to drink it."

"River is quite right. There is only so much of a culture you can experience outside of a country. If we had never brought you out here, you would have continued to think that everyone in Mexico wore sombreros, lived on nachos, and drank cheap firewater tequila. As you have discovered - this country has so much more to offer."

"Yeah... a body count." I smiled, amused at my own wit. I had a feeling there was still a load of margarita in my system, and the tequila was just waking it up again.

River burst out laughing. "That too. The cartels have a lot to do with that though. Speaking of which - where the hell is Gabe?"

"Here," Gabe called from the doorway. He eyed up the glasses in our hands, and glanced down at the laptop he was carrying with him with disgust. "What? Ya'll started without me?"

I pursed my lips with guilt. We should have waited, and I felt bad on Chase and River's behalf. I liked Gabe. He was nice. I couldn't understand what sort of potential he saw in these two, but the relationship seemed to work. He plonked himself down beside me, put his laptop on the floor at his feet, and reached for a glass.

"So," Gabe started, his American lilt muffled by the glass at his lips. He took a long sip and put the glass down, "We have a completely new set of instructions, should we choose to do it." He shrugged. "Kind of a big job though. It's not going to be easy, to say the least."

Chase's eyes lit up with cunningness. "What do you mean? What's the job?" He swung his long legs off the sofa, and leaned forward with anticipation.

Gabe sighed. "Well..." He took another sip of his drink. "It's another directive from the clients. Apparently our little information gathering expedition has paid off somewhat."

He turned his focus back to his drink, and I really considered throttling Gabe, and throwing his fricking glass out the window. I'd had a no-good very-bad day, and the last thing I wanted was to listen to him playing games. I could see the others thinking the same thing. "Gabe," I said with impatience. "Come on. What's the job?"

"It looks as though the information we gathered was mainly structural, giving our clients full records of most of the higher ranking employees of the El Diablo Cartel. The hits are for eleven of those employees."

"Eleven," Chase muttered. His eyes met River's across the room, eyebrows raised. "That's one hell of a hit."

I didn't need to be a professional hit man to know that this was a huge job. Eleven people dying at the hands of Chase and River seemed insane. Although, from the little I knew of the Cartels, it wouldn't make that much of a dent in their numbers.

I couldn't help myself, I had to ask. "Is Carmen on the list?"

Gabe shook his head. "She's too high up the food chain... these guys are from, what do you call it? Middle management, I guess, for want of a better word."

River shrugged. "Payment terms?"

"Proof of death, the usual. They'll pay us two million a head, plus a bonus if the job is done within a certain timeframe."

"Two million?" I whispered "Seriously?" That would pay off some of the major debt that Luke had left me with, even if I only whacked one of them.

Chase smirked, and shook his head slowly with amusement. "Mack, you're not trained. Don't even think about it."

"She can train with me," River said quietly. "She needs the money, you know that."

My eyes went wide and my mouth dry as I glanced at River. Kill someone? Holy shit, I didn't know if I was ready for that just yet. I couldn't even use a gun properly, let alone think about blowing some random guy's head off. "Train me?"

"Yes, Mack. Train you. You need to learn some skills if you're with us - especially for your own protection. You want to kill Carmen, right?"

I nodded mutely as I dropped my gaze to the floor, unsure of what I wanted. My heart raced. Was I actually that kind of person? I guess I had to be. I knew that to get Carmen off my back it was going to take something more than an academic education and a pretty face. It was going to take some hard skills; skills that she had, and that I hadn't acquired... yet. Actually, it was kind of a thrilling feeling. I looked from Gabe who was looking at me with encouragement, to River, and then to Chase. They all looked at me as if they had complete faith.

"Well, then I guess you'd better learn, eh?" Chase snorted, and raised his glass to me. Holy shit. I really wasn't prepared for this.

"So – you want the list or not?" Gabe interrupted.

"Yes, Chase and I will take five each, and if Mack's got the skills to assist us by then, she can help us with the eleventh."

"Me?" It came out like a squeak, and I immediately drank back the remaining liquid in the glass. I stood unsteadily, and sought out my cigarettes in the handbag at my feet. "I need a fag. A lot to process."

Both River and Chase watched me cross the room, making me feel even more self-conscious. I stepped out onto the terrace under the starry night and lit up. I inhaled, the warm night air mixed with the cigarette smoke, which immediately went to my head and started to calm my nerves.

I could hear them still talking inside. Eleven people? Gabe called them middle management. But why wouldn't you kill the people at the top of the Cartel first? There must be some sort of grand master strategy, but I was buggered if I knew what.

I could hear the others discussing people and their marks locations. Part of me felt sick. Logically, I knew that these people were really bad people, but there was just so much death. Then again, I knew they had probably all killed innocent people themselves and they worked for Carmen and I knew she deserved to die...

After all, she and her staff had just basically murdered a plane-load of people.

———✷———

When I woke the next morning to River shaking my shoulder, I was feeling rather worse for wear. I'd had only three hours sleep, and felt like I had been at an all-night rave, not sitting around talking. I was just pleased that I'd had the common sense to stop drinking halfway through the night.

River looked as though he'd slept 12 hours at some luxurious resort, and was bright-eyed and far too bushy-tailed for my liking. He shook his keys at me, shoved some sort of ridiculously healthy, green smoothie onto the bedside table, "Come on - up you get. Things to do, people to see."

I groaned, throwing my arm over my face in protest, "Five more minutes," I murmured, feeling the drifts of sleep starting to pull at me.

Moments later I heard the curtains getting ripped back on their rails, and I opened my eyes to glare at him. "You have fifteen minutes to get ready, Mack." He tapped his watch, "If you go back to sleep, I'm taking you out in your pyjamas."

I rolled my eyes, and swung my legs over the side

of the bed. After a few seconds, the door closed behind him and I was alone. I looked over at the green smoothie, and my stomach went queasy just from the sight.

Once I had showered and dressed and finally walked into the living room twenty minutes later, he silently handed me a wig to wear along with a pair of huge sunglasses.

I didn't like being out in public, despite being behind the tinted windows of the car. Not only did I hate sunlight right now, but River was busy taking photographs of houses and the different people associated with his marks, and I was the designated driver. We were parked outside an enormous house with a large fence line, and electronic gates. I imagined there would be guards somewhere in the gardens or along the perimeter who wouldn't have an issue shooting us point-blank. "How bullet-proof is this thing?"

River lowered the camera, and sniggered. "It's not. You're just going to have to drive fast if we get into trouble."

I raised my eyebrows; he had a lot of naïve faith in my driving skills. I returned my gaze to the road in front of us, where not one single other car moved. I wondered if it was always like this, or if it was just the time of day. "So, how are you going to get into the house to kill her, maestro?"

"I'm not. I'm going to get Regina to come to me."

River looked back at the house through the gates. “It’s not impossible to get in there. Actually, I would say it’s rather easy. However, it’s better if no one knows you’re there. Regina is heavily guarded, so I’m going to hook up with her at a bar she frequents, and get to her that way.” He looked down at his iPad, fingers scrolling across the screen. “And, according to the information we recovered she’ll be out tonight or tomorrow night, and we can catch up with her then.”

“Tonight?” Anxiety filled me. I swallowed. “So soon?” I was going to totally screw this up. I had never watched anyone die. Well, actually, that wasn’t true. I had, technically, seen my parents die, but I couldn’t remember it. The psychologists said I might get the memory back. Might not too.

“Yes, tonight. Listen, Mack, you are on ops with me. To learn this trade, you need to live it. I need to show you exactly how it’s done in real life situations. Kinda like being thrown in the deep end.” He put the camera back in the case at his feet. “Now, let’s head back towards the city - there are a couple of other people we need to check on the way home. Then tonight, I expect to see you dressed to kill.”

Oh great, now came the fun.

3

When I looked in the mirror, I hardly recognised myself; dressed in a low-cut, black, slinky dress, my nails sparkled, and once again, I was wearing a wig that'd undoubtedly annoy the hell out of me later. This one was a short, dark bob, which made me look a bit like Cleopatra. My skin was thick with makeup, and I wondered where the hell River and Chase learned how to do this. This was one area I didn't feel completely out of my depth in. I could do my own makeup - usually in subtle hues and tones, low key, but River and Chase had really outdone themselves enhancing my features. Apparently they're masters of disguise.

I paced the terraced area of River's house, puffing

away on a cigarette. River wouldn't let me have a drink to calm my nerves, and I totally hated him for it. I needed something to settle my stomach, and the cigarette wasn't cutting it.

I tensed up as Chase stepped out behind me. I could tell it was him because his expensive cologne wrapped around my senses in the evening air.

"Are you ready, Mack?"

I shook my head. "Hell no. I don't think I'll ever be ready for this." I wanted him to reassure me, tell me that I could do this. But from what I knew of him, there was no way he would.

"You'll deal with it. We all do."

And there it was. Mr Compassionate. I flicked my cigarette into the darkness and followed him back inside. He was going out on a different mission tonight, with Gabe. The team had decided to eliminate the bigger fish first, so that when the cartel realised that a hit had been taken out on their people, they would have a harder time hiding the others. So while we dealt with Regina, Chase and Gabe were taking out Regina's boss.

Half an hour later, River pulled the car up in a dark alleyway, and the nerves hit me hard. Not only were my palms sweating, I was also perspiring in all sorts of unimaginable places. Strapped to my inner leg was a small sheathed dagger River had given me. How on earth I was going to reach it in a hurry in this dress was beyond me. I'd probably fall over in these bloody six-inch heels trying to get it out.

"Stop fidgeting," River muttered, as he helped me out of the truck.

"I shouldn't be here," I whispered, shaking.

River pushed me against the truck, firmly gripping my bare arms, and leaned towards me. His gaze locked with mine, and I stilled. "You can do this, Mack. You can. You just need to suck up all those feelings you have right now, and project them away from you. You will do this with me. You're not going to die. I'll make sure of that, okay? Now, you're going to act like my lover in there tonight, and we're going to pull this off. We're a team."

As I looked up at him through the darkness I could see a little grin playing on his mouth, and I smiled, exhaling my pent up breath. "Okay, I can do this."

"You can have one drink when we get inside to calm your nerves - then we get down to business," he said as he put his hand at the small of my back and manoeuvred me towards the club.

My skin tingled under his touch and heat perfused my cheeks. I was so pleased it was dark and no one could see me. It was awkward enough for me to play River's girlfriend, but I did what he said and tried to channel my nervousness toward a positive light to relax into my role. When we got out to the street, I was amazed at how many people were milling about drinking and dancing, and seemingly having a jolly good time.

River smiled at me, linking his fingers between mine as we entered the club. "Welcome to the life, baby."

His hand felt steady in mine as he guided me through throngs of people. I had always imagined that after the Middle-Eastern terrorist attacks in the USA that the Tijuana nightlife had basically shut down because everyone was lying low. How wrong I was. This was a niche market. There were hundreds of people in the dimly lit club, all having a fabulous time, but I knew that one gunshot would turn the place into an all-out killing spree.

We made our way to the bar where the alcohol and God only knew what else flowed freely. River ordered us a margarita each, and we found ourselves a seat in a booth.

"There are a number of exclusive back rooms in this place. That's where she'll be."

River didn't have to tell me who 'she' was. Regina Navarro, the target. Regina is one of the few females in charge of logistics for the El Diablo Cartel. Apparently she's considered anally-retentive about details and coordinating people, and was generally a hellish bitch.

I curled my leg around River's, playing the part of his girlfriend. I wondered where on earth Carmen was tonight. No doubt, she would have checked the same manifesto as Gabe, and realised that I hadn't been on that plane. It was only a matter of time before she made her next move. The music in the club electrified something within me, and I felt like some sort of secret agent, waiting and watching. I shivered with anticipation as the adrenaline started to kick in while I scanned the crowd. When I glanced at River, I saw him subtly doing the same. This was a game, and it was thrilling to see it starting to unfold.

He leaned towards me, pretending to nuzzle my neck. "I've spotted her already," he whispered into my ear. He patted my leg. "Come on, it's time for you to follow her to the bathroom." He stood, and extended his hand towards to me. I threw back my margarita, hoping it would give me some Dutch courage. I adjusted my dress, and took off through the crowd towards the bathroom.

The former beauty queen was talking to two people outside the bathroom, and I waited discreetly until I saw her walk through the door. The bathrooms were disgusting. Well, they were okay looking in the décor sense, but the mess was horrific. There were women everywhere.

I angled my way towards the shared vanity, and rummaged around my clutch for some lippy and eyeliner, taking my time reapplying it, and checking it over. Regina came out of one of the stalls, sniffing. I almost forgot myself and asked her if she was alright, until I saw the dusting of white powder against her nose. She was stunning, better than the grainy photo

I'd seen in her file. That photo really didn't do her justice. She washed her hands, and started to reapply her own makeup wiping away the remnants of the cocaine as she went. She caught my gaze in the reflection, eyes amused and eyebrow raised, and I immediately thought I'd been made. I knew I was just being overly sensitive. There was no way this woman would know who I was. Not looking the way I did, anyway.

Another stunning looking woman sidled up to her, speaking quietly into her ear, Regina just nodded silently, continuing her business, and I pretended to ignore her. As soon as I heard Regina snap her compact shut, I scrambled to casually get the contents of my clutch back together again, and followed her out of the bathroom.

River's eyes latched on me as I exited the bathroom, and I brushed my forehead with one finger to indicate to him that there was only one person accompanying her. I didn't see him, but I knew he saw me. I made my way back to the bar, and asked for a glass of water. My heart pounded in time with the bass in the club. I leaned against the bar, and watched the rest of the crowd.

That's when I saw River dancing with Regina, and I narrowed my eyes towards them. I was supposed to act like the jealous girlfriend and cause a disturbance, but to my disgust, I actually was feeling jealous. It wasn't because she was with River. It was the way she was so open about her sexiness, and her desire for him. It created intensity in the way they danced together. Regina was truly enjoying him with her hip grinding Latino dance moves. If we were back in England, that sort of dirty, raw dancing would be totally unacceptable. But here... it was magical. I think it was the way he held her, or maybe the sensual way they moved in sync together. Seeing them like that woke something up within me. I wished someone would move with me like that. Anyone. I put my water glass back on the bar, and I made my way towards River.

I knew that her dance moves and attraction to River were probably amplified by the cocaine in her system, but I still needed to act like River's pissed off girlfriend in public. River caught my eye, and I could see the amusement in them. The next thing I knew, I'd been swept into the arms of an awfully buff and good-looking Mexican man, part of Regina's security detail from outside the bathroom.

"You speak English, yes?" he whispered into my ear, clutching me close. I felt myself fall into step with him, and nod. "Good." He smiled. "Your boyfriend is a very good looking man, no?"

I smiled and nodded, trying to keep up with him while also watching Regina with River. This was a deliberate intercept so that Regina could get her hands on my supposed boyfriend. He had seen me making a beeline towards them, and had interrupted me. Shit. Talk about fucking up my plans.

"I'm sure you could get a good looking man like him any day though." The security guy swung me out into the dance floor, and I laughed, playing along with him.

"Flattery will get you everywhere." I smiled up at him. "You aren't so bad yourself." I laughed coyly. "Not a bad dancer, either." I winked.

He slowly smiled down at me. "Oh, you haven't seen anything yet."

He dipped me towards the floor, and I wondered how the hell my wish had just come true. I mean, I had wanted a man to dance with me like that, I just hadn't expected it to be so soon. And even though I was in a crap-load of danger, and technically on a mission, I was enjoying it.

Alarm streaked through me as I felt him slide his hand up my leg. I straightened, and shook my head. "Oh no you don't, mister. That sort of hand action is strictly reserved for the 'boyfriend'." I lightly pushed him away. Something caught my eye behind him, and I saw River getting pulled away from the dance floor. "Fuck," I breathed. I looked up at the security guy, and leaned over to kiss him on the cheek. "Thank you for the dance, Amigo. I have to go." I patted his chest affectionately and turned away to make my way through the crowd, following River's path.

"Wait," he said grabbing my arm gently, he raised eyebrow at me, expectant. "How about a drink?"

I shook my head. "I've already had too much tonight as it is. I think I need to go home."

"Another time, perhaps," he smiled with a wink, and disappeared into the crowd.

I turned to try and see if I could spot either River or Regina, but they had disappeared. I wracked my brain. The last time I had seen them, they were moving towards the back of the club. As I made my way closer, I passed another security guy who was distracted by something on his phone and therefore didn't give me a second glance, and found a long hallway with a number of doors leading off.

I was sure that they would be behind one of them. I just had to find the right one. Regina, the saucy bitch. I walked along the corridor wondering which one to choose first when I saw River's leather jacket hanging on the outside of one. I breathed a sigh of relief, thanking the gods that I didn't have to go barging through every single one trying to find them.

I lifted River's jacket, checked the corridor to make sure I was all clear, and then stepped into the darkened room. I could see them writhing on the settee, and I felt an empty pit of nausea well within my stomach. This was it. This is what River was waiting for. The air was thick and smelled sort of sweet from whatever air-freshener they used, making me feel faint. My mouth ran dry as I mentally flicked through all the potential scenarios of how to approach this. They weren't having sex yet, that I could tell, but damn, Regina was close to having her way with him.

She spoke Spanish in undertones, and he responded just as quickly. I hardly understood a word of it. It was actually the second most awkward situation I have ever been in, coming in close behind catching Luke sleeping with my best friend. I knew that now was the time to cause the distraction, and I would do it the same way I did with Luke. I walked towards them, my heels clacking against the wooden floor, and ripped Regina off River. "What the fuck?!" I shouted.

Regina's eyes sparked with anger. The Spanish rolling off her tongue completely baffled me, but I understood precisely what she said. I saw and heard much of the same thing when I ripped Nicole away from Luke that fateful day.

Regina started advancing on me, and my hand twitched against my thigh, itching for the dagger. She was just about to take a swing at me, when I saw something silvery flash behind her. River came up at her shoulder, looked me in the eyes, and wrapped a wire around her neck. Her body was drawn against him as he tightened the wire.

I couldn't look away.

She struggled and thrashed, her bulging eyes locked accusingly on mine. Her movements were jerky as she tried her hardest to get out of River's steady hold. She was panicking. I could see it in her wild eyes. River heaved against the wire, and they both crashed to the floor. Moments later, her eyes closed, and she was still. I let out a long breath I hadn't realised I still held. I felt mentally numb, and I uncurled my clenched fists, only then realising that my nails had been digging into my palms. I rubbed my hands as I watched River stand up, brush himself off, and take a photo of Regina's body on his phone. So calm, so cool.

I had literally just watched the life drain out of somebody. I couldn't believe how quickly it had all happened. I scrambled to sort out my thoughts and to try understand how River could do that so ruthlessly to someone he'd just been getting intimate with.

River grabbed my arm, pulling me towards him. "Come on, Mack. We need to go. Now."

Even as we walked towards the ensuite attached to the room to escape out the window, I couldn't help but glance back half a dozen times at Regina's lifeless body.

4

"I'm heading over to the States today. There are two targets there that we need to hit," Chase said to us over brunch the next day. His words reminded me that he and Gabe went out on a hit last night too. I thought about asking them how it went, but on reflection of my own night, I just really didn't want to know.

I didn't feel like eating, but I could feel River observing me closely, which forced me to have a few bites of my huevos con chorizo. Actually, it was delicious, but I just couldn't stop thinking about Regina's eyes on me as she died. I had dreamt about her all night, and when I wasn't dreaming, I was awake analysing every moment of it.

"Who are they?" I asked Chase.

"Osiel Ramirez, the main US distributer, and his right hand man, Alicio Mendoza. They're all going to be on high alert now that Regina has been eliminated as well. Alicio is a nasty piece of work. It's going to take a couple of days to recon both jobs, and then get it done."

"Aren't they all nasty?"

Chase shrugged. "There are different levels of nastiness. Both Osiel and Alicio are very bad men. Alicio, in particular. He's in charge of body disposal across the border. He has a huge team of people, and a million different ways to kill and hide the evidence."

"Acid," River mumbled between bites. "His favourite disposal method is acid."

Acid? I wondered if he meant that he gets them high on LSD first or if he actually meant real acid. Chase burst into laughter at my expression. "What?"

"Years ago, before Alicio climbed the ranks of the El Diablo Cartel, he used to be known as the 'acid-man'. He's been on our radar for years...there was a time when I considered recruiting him into our operation. In the end I decided I probably couldn't pay him enough."

"Thank God." River grimaced. "He's a loose cannon. We would have all been dead by lunchtime if he didn't like the way we did things."

Yeah... not exactly the polite conversation I was used to having over breakfast. But not exactly normal circumstances either. I didn't want to think about bodies in acid any more than I wanted to think about Regina. I was already having a hard enough time talking to River this morning.

"So... Mack, how did you go last night?" Gabe asked.

I studied my cup of coffee for a moment or two before answering him. How did I go? I shrugged. "Me? I don't know. River did all the work."

River reached over and rested his hand on my forearm "She was brilliant, actually. Didn't miss a beat." I met his latte-coloured eyes, and he smiled. "She played her role perfectly. Even when she was diverted by one of Regina's security guards she just played along. It was a stellar performance." He patted my arm reassuringly. "She may need some more training climbing out bathroom windows though."

"I was wearing high-heels!" I said indignantly. "For God's sake, you should try it some time."

Chase laughed. "Oh believe me - he has."

"You what? Really?" I turned to River. "Are you for real? High-heels?"

Chase shook with laughter as River stared daggers at him.

"It was for a job," he said through gritted teeth. "I was playing a transvestite to get to a mark who happened to have a little fetish for them."

I actually felt my jaw drop, and River blushed. "You hooked up with a tranny?"

Gabe burst out laughing. "Oh yes he did. And then he garrotted him."

Garrotted... "That's what you did last night, wasn't it?"

River nodded. "Yes. I was sorely tempted to shoot her, but I couldn't do it. I didn't want to use a gun because blood goes everywhere. Garrotting is a much tidier way to kill. She got a bit personal with me."

I raised my eyebrow. "Personal? I'll say. Was that before or after you almost shagged her?"

Chase choked on his coffee with a splutter, and shook his head with amusement. "Boy do you have a lot to learn, cupcake," he said. "We get close to our marks, and then we take them out. Long range kills have less risk, but there is always a chance that you could miss or fail to kill. Getting in closer to our marks ensures that we do our job properly... I guess it's also a point of pride in our line of work. We're contracted for jobs because they know that we get in close, use our skills, and get out. That is the nature of this business."

"Sometimes we just shoot them long range though," Gabe said with a hint of a smile. "I mean, I don't, but they do."

River lifted his napkin to his mouth, and then placed it down beside his plate. "Speaking of which... Mack. You and I are going to take out Filipo Olivas today."

The name rang a bell from our planning session

the other night. "He's the finance guy, right?"

Chase nodded. "Yeah, that's him. Shady fuck." When Chase swore he sounded rather eloquent. I wanted to learn to swear with the same finesse.

Gabe brought up a photo of Filipo on his iPad, and slid it across the dining table to me.

For some reason I imagined that Filipo would be like any other finance person out there in the world. Suited up, narcissistic personality, you know, the usual type. After all, I had lived with Luke who was in finance for seven years. But Filipo looked different. He was slick, in his thirties, but not only that - judging from the glint in his eye, he was dangerous. "He's not a normal finance geek, is he?"

River shook his head. "Far from it. He wouldn't be in the cartel if he was. But we better get cracking if we're going to do this job today." He pushed his chair out from the table. "I'm taking you downstairs." He turned to Chase. "Keep me posted on the situation in the US. I imagine they're going to start panicking soon with two members down already."

River had a secret room in his house; completely enclosed in steel, with a spiral staircase that wound its way down into an artillery room. The stuff I never knew. There were guns and other weapons everywhere down there, in cabinets, behind steel mesh cupboards, and even though it was damn hot outside, all I felt was cold. This room was designed to house killing machines.

“So, this is how you put a sniper rifle together,” River said as he laid five different pieces on the steel topped table between us.

I was confused just looking at everything. I had no idea which bit went where, but I was thoroughly enthralled by the mechanical process of it.

"There are a number of things that you need to consider before taking a shot. Disturbance and wind speed are the two main ones you need to be aware of. Also, if the target is moving, that’s another consideration. You need to watch, analyse, and predict where they are going to be before you take the shot. We’ll do some target practice another day so you can get a feel for it.”

“What about gravity?”

River chuckled. “Yes, that too. Gravity has an effect on the shot, the further the distance the more you’ll need to adjust a little to account for that.” River’s gaze hardened. “You must not hesitate. Once you decide to take the shot, you’re in the moment for real. You also have to have a sure way to get out, just in case you’re spotted. You need to remember that every shot is a kill-shot. You can’t just take pot-shots at people. It doesn’t work like that. Being a sniper is an art-form.”

I swallowed. “Kill shot... right.” More killing. Again, I suddenly wondered how the hell I managed to get myself into these situations.

River reached out and grabbed my shoulder reassuringly. "You're only watching at this stage, Mack. I'm preparing you for what may come with Carmen. You cannot let her have the upper hand with you. This training I'm giving you? It's stuff that took me years to learn. So far, you're handling it exceptionally well."

I snorted. "Well, I'm pleased someone has faith... I haven't tried to put one of those gun-thingees together yet."

I may not have ever put a 'gun-thingee' together before, but down in that basement, River made me practise until my fingers went numb, and then when we got up to the rooftop across from Filipo's office, he handed me the sniper case. With shaking hands, I pieced the weapon together while River watched my every move.

From the safety of the rooftop I watched Filipo leave his office through the sights. Filipo looked exactly like his photo. He walked with a self-assured gait, wore a sharp looking suit, with sunglasses on which were a lot like River's aviator ones. This guy was clean cut, tall, and suave. From the way he snapped at his phone, I was guessing he didn't tolerate simple minds, and I couldn't even hear what he was saying. His body language was saying it all for him.

We watched him walk towards the bank, the same run he did every single day at 4.30pm.

"Okay, now that we're ready with the rifle, we need to make sure our timing is dead on."

"No pun intended, right?" I smiled, gritting my teeth against the last heat of the day. We were technically in autumn at the moment, but since we had been here it had been warm and dry. An Indian summer. In half an hour the sun would go down, and we would be trying to do this in the dark if we didn't get on with it now.

River smirked. "No. No pun. Anyway, from Gabe's intel, we know Filipo comes back to the office at 5.00pm each day, opens a bottle of wine, and waits for his mistress to arrive. That there is our window of opportunity, before the mistress arrives."

"Before the mistress arrives..." I repeat as I lifted the binoculars to my eyes and looked into his office. It was pristine. An elegant dark wooden desk sat adjacent to the large window; bookcases lined the walls behind, with carefully placed ornaments, photos, and a few books on the shelves. I could see the leather arm of a chair or sofa on the other side of the office. It was an office that Luke would have loved. I cast the thought from my mind with a shake of my head. He was the last person I needed to think of right now.

"That's right. And when we kill him, you and I are going to pack up as fast as we can, and get down that stairwell and back to the car before the authorities even know he's dead. Okay?"

I nodded. Down on the street, I spied Filipo making his way back towards his office. "He's coming," I said in a hushed tone to River. I put the binoculars down, and wiped my hands on my pants. It was too freaking hot, sweat poured off me in buckets, and I started to feel like we were going to get caught.

That's when I saw the woman walk into Filipo's office. "Shit," I muttered, lifting the binoculars. "We got company." Filipo walked in close behind her, and threw her against the closed door to ravish her. "And it looks like he likes it rough," I added. I heard River snort, and immediately blushed, refusing to believe those words had actually come out of my mouth. "I said that out loud, didn't I?"

"Oh, yes you did," he said beside me, his voice laced with quiet amusement. I heard him sigh, and ready the rifle. "Looks like we may have to take them both out. Then it won't look so targeted, but more like a random kill."

Surprise filled me, but I kept my eyes firmly planted against the binoculars. "I thought Chase said you guys weren't savages."

"Chase isn't, but he can't speak for me." River chuckled. "I do what I need to get the job done quickly and effectively... I don't leave witnesses."

I looked over at him. "You don't look too savage to me. Not today, anyway." He flashed me a grin, and peered back through the scope. Witnesses. I was a witness to one of his kills. And he had let me live. I guess I should count myself damn lucky that he hadn't taken me out at the time. I was about to remark on this sudden insight, when he nudged me, drawing my attention.

"I'm not quite as vicious as him," he muttered, referring to Filipo. "Oh, here we go."

I lifted the binoculars back to my eyes and peered over the parapet towards the office once more. "Jeepers. They are getting right into it, aren't they?" And then River's phone rang. "Ignore it?"

"No can do," River answered. "It's Gabe."

I heard him answer, but kept my eyes on the couple. I felt sorry for the woman. She didn't need to die in all this just because she was shagging the wrong man. I heard River swear softly, and turned to him. He had his eyes firmly fixed on me, and I felt my blood run cold. Something was wrong. He would tell me in due course, I was sure. I turned my binoculars back, trying to clear my head. I noticed that the woman was no longer in the room. I double-checked the room quickly to make sure she wasn't on the floor somewhere, but I couldn't see her anywhere. I reached out and slapped River on the arm to get his attention. "River, she's gone," I said in a loud whisper.

"Hold tight, Gabe," he said down the phone as he placed it on the roof. He cocked the gun once again, eye to the scope. "Good work, Mack." Then he took the shot.

I was astonished at how easy it was. One moment Filipo was standing there pouring wine into a glass, and then next he fell on the desk, a bullet to the head. Adrenaline thrashed through me. I could see blood seeping over the paperwork, and the wine bottle rolled and fell to the floor. With the amount of blood and everything else, I was sure that half of his head was probably scattered on the desk. It felt as though everything was happening in slow motion. I gripped the binoculars tightly, keeping my eye on the room. She was going to walk back in, I just knew it.

"Mack, we have to go."

"Yep, just one moment." I breathed, keeping my eyes securely on the door.

He grabbed my arm, pulling the binoculars away from me. "No. We need to go now. All hell is about to break lose, and we need to get out of here."

I saw the concern for me in his eyes. Was he worried about my apparent morbid curiosity? Or was there something else? I heard the scream come from the building loud and clear. I immediately turned with my binoculars. The mistress was in there, on her knees, screaming her head off. And she was looking directly at me, standing there like a meerkat watching her. She knew it was me, or that I at least had something to do with it. My stomach plummeted, and I tried to swallow the guilt. By the time I turned back, River had already packed up the rifle, and was keeping low as he shuffled across the roof. I was quick to follow him.

Once we got into the stairwell, he really picked up the pace and he all but flew down them. Adrenaline and fear coursed through me, allowing me follow just as quickly. I felt as though I could run a million miles. By the time we got outside, and ran down a back alleyway away from Filipo's building, I could already hear sirens coming in our direction. We jumped into River's truck, and he threw the rifle case into the backseat, only just missing my head as he did.

"You saved a life today, Mack," he said quietly as he started up the engine. "Well done. I would have taken her out."

Once again, numbness started to take over my senses. "Why?"

River shook his head. "I don't like witnesses."

We pulled out of the alleyway, and I looked down the road behind us. I could see a few police cars race across an intersection, lights flashing and sirens wailing. "What about them?"

"What about them? The El Diablo Cartel owns most of the cops in this town anyway. They're not going to do anything to us." He checked his phone. "Not yet, anyway."

We joined the rest of the traffic, and I replayed the image of Filipo falling onto his desk. My heart pounded at the memory of all the blood and bits everywhere. It was a very quick death. "That was quite a humane way to die, really, wasn't it?"

"I like to think so. I trained as a sniper, and to be honest, regardless of what was said earlier - it's my preferred method of killing. Doesn't always happen that way though, not every situation is suitable for it. Killing up close and personal requires a certain level of skill. Sniper shooting is almost lazy in comparison."

I was silent for a few moments as I thought about River and his precise concentration up on that roofline, and then I remembered the phone call. "Hey, what did Gabe want?"

River looked over at me. "It's Carmen. She's discovered that you weren't on the plane." He paused and sighed. "And she's put a price on your head."

5

My blood ran cold. “How much?” I croaked.

River reached over and grabbed my trembling hand. “Ten million US. She wants you caught and dead. It’s a large enough amount that it gives everyone in Mexico an incentive to hunt you down.”

“Oh my God.” I suddenly couldn’t get enough oxygen. I opened the window, inhaling the warm Tijuana air, but it didn’t feel like enough. “I can’t breathe,” I whispered.

River turned on the air-conditioning full blast, and handed me a bottle of water. “Drink,” he ordered. “You’re hyperventilating. The water will help you regulate your oxygen.”

Fuck the water, I thought. Instead, I reached down to the bag at my feet, and before River could even utter a word of protest, I lit a cigarette. He coughed and spluttered in mock protest, but I didn't give a shit. I now had a dollar value on my life.

After a few puffs, I started to feel a bit better, if only slightly.

"Mack, they don't know your real identity yet. All they have is Rachel White's details. We'll sort something out - like getting Gabe to get you a new passport and name."

"Rachel White." I took another puff. Small blessings.

When we got back to River's house, Gabe was in a panic. Something was going on with border control into the States, and Chase had been held up, meaning that Gabe's set up over there was now in a mess.

"Everyone is looking for a blue-eyed blonde haired woman, going by the name of Rachel White. The border is a flaming mess. They're pulling women out of cars to prevent them going across the border - even if they aren't blonde. I wouldn't be surprised if this turns into some sort of international incident. It's holding up Chase, and he's not going to get to Alicio Mendoza in time - so he'll be delayed another day over there."

My breath left me. "Rachel White is being hunted," I whispered. My head snapped up. "What the hell is going to happen to those women at the border?"

Gabe shrugged. "I guess they'll double check

passports and other supporting identification and let them go. I can't imagine they'll detain many."

River passed me a glass of wine, and I collapsed onto the sofa. He turned the fire on, even though my shaking was only from my nerves. So I lay back, sipped my wine and watched the flames, only partially listening to River and Gabe talk shop. My thoughts were more on how long it would take for Carmen and her team to figure out that Rachel White didn't exist.

"No, it's not just on her head, it's payment on the delivery of her physical head."

"So I guess that means we can't fake it then," River murmured.

I sat up alert, and turned towards Gabe and River. "What?"

Gabe ran his hands through his long surfer locks with frustration. "Carmen wants your physical head delivered as proof of death, and then she will hand over the payment to the successful person."

I felt sick. At this rate, the bitch would have me dead before the week was out. My only consolation was that she was hunting for Rachel White, and not McKenna Carmichael. Tears sprang to my eyes. I wasn't ready to die. Now it wasn't just her hunting me, it was anyone who wanted to take my life for a shitload of money – and it was becoming increasingly clear to me that the number of people who might want to take her up on that offer was higher than I'd have ever imagined before.

If I died, there would be no one to take care of my aunt, who was living in an aged-care facility. She had taken over my guardianship when my parents died when I was twelve. She was also the same loving woman who signed over her house to me when she went into care. If Luke hadn't been trying to take my aunt's house off me, I wouldn't be here at all, nor would I have tried to prostitute myself to make the money to pay him out.

I slugged back the rest of the wine, and slammed the glass down on the coffee table. I needed something stronger.

I crossed the room to River's booze cabinet, and extracted the tequila, muttering obscenities about 'fucking Luke' as I poured a decent portion into a crystal tumbler. I had to get out of this fucking country alive, for God's sake. I couldn't die here. I didn't want the light from my eyes to go the same way as Regina's. I had now seen death up close and personal. I didn't want to have the first-hand experience of being assassinated just yet.

I just wanted to wake up when all this was over.

The tequila burned my throat as I sculled it back, but I didn't care. Something had to give here, and I'd be damned if it was my life. Alcohol it was.

I put the glass down hard on the sideboard, and poured myself another. I felt River move up behind me, and I forced myself to turn and face him. "I'm going to die, soon, aren't I?"

He shrugged. "Who knows? You could die of alcohol poisoning tonight if you don't slow down."

I couldn't help it. I smiled. "Yeah well. I would prefer that option to being hunted down like a wild bull and slaughtered." I took a sip from the glass, and leaned back against the sideboard, feeling lightheaded.

He put his hands on my shoulders to steady me, and looked me in the eyes. "Mack, I know this is hard. Trust me when I say this - I've been in your position before. But you need to fight. That's why I am taking you out on observations with me, so you can learn. I'm not going to let that upstart bitch take your head. Not yet anyway." A smile played on his lips, and I was captivated by his reassuring words. They inspired some sort of confidence in me. Or perhaps that was the tequila burning through my system. Right now it didn't really matter which.

I felt myself nod, and looked down at the floor. I took a deep breath and looked back up at his unwavering gaze on me. "I guess you'd better start teaching me more then." And with that thought, I disappeared out onto the terrace to light another cigarette, wishing it was something strong enough to make me forget everything I had seen and heard in this godforsaken country.

Hangovers sucked. It was still dark outside, but as

I groped around for my glass, I could tell that dawn wasn't too far away. I drained my water, and went to find some orange juice. I never dreamed properly when I had a large intake of alcohol, but it didn't stop me last night from dreaming about my aging aunt being tortured by that cracked cartel bitch.

When River and Chase told me about this job in Mexico, I hadn't even hesitated in saying yes. I guess I had been attracted to the riskier side of it, and also the money talked a hell of an argument. Never did I imagine that it would end up like this. All I was supposed to do was become a sort of extra-curricular fascination for Javier Amaro to play with for a while. I didn't even sleep with him, but I did have the 'pleasure' of accompanying him to a few places publically, and 'enjoying' his company. And while I was out with Javier, Gabe, Chase, and River were extracting information from Javier's computer systems on the El Diablo Cartel's operations.

Everything was running smoothly until Carmen, Javier's esteemed beauty queen wife, discovered I was on the scene, and interrupted our dinner one night when I was at one of his apartments in the city. I had never considered myself beautiful, but for some reason River and Chase thought that I would be the perfect distraction for Javier. But when I compared myself to Carmen, I had nothing on her. She was stunning. She had dark, calculating eyes, long flowing locks, a body of an hourglass, enhanced breasts, and a backside to match. Her skin was flawless, and she had big pouty lips. Apparently she had claimed some beauty queen title a few years ago, and damn, she probably still could.

Javier was smooth. He was good looking, fortyish, and for a cartel leader, he was surprisingly tender when I was around. I couldn't imagine why he would get into the 'business' as he didn't seem like that sort of person, although I knew the whole thing had to be a front.

But it was the way he turned on Carmen as she pulled out a gun, that was the thing that had scared me the most. When she let off a shot in my direction – the same bullet that went through my phone – that was the moment he threw her across the room, as if she were as light as a ragdoll. I ran. The last thing I saw of Carmen was her crumpled form on the floor in a heap, gun at her side, while her husband had his raw, blazing-violent, eyes on me as I disappeared from the apartment. That reality was far different from the one I now faced in River's house.

I reached the kitchen, and rummaged through the fridge, wading through all the healthy food that River and the team loved, and pulled out the orange juice. As I was pouring the juice into my glass, I heard a scuffle. I froze. A number of things coursed through me in that one moment. One: Someone was breaking into the house. Two: Carmen had found me. Three: I needed to run and hide. And four: Contrary to everything I'd just thought, I'd best go and check it out. I deliberated for a second on my options, before hearing another noise, which jolted me into action.

I picked up a large sandstone sculpture from the shelf near the door and tiptoed out of the kitchen, and down the dark hallway. I never realised just how squeaky some of River's floor boards were until I was trying to be quiet. I winced every time I stood on one, thinking someone would hear me. Then I started worrying that someone would hear my breath as I crept through the dark, so I held it as best I could.

I heard a grunt and a groan, and my head turned sharply towards the noise. It was coming from behind one of the many doorways that led off the passage. I crossed the hall, and leaned my ear to the door. There was another jarring thump, and I sprang back, readying my soapstone sculpture.

Something came over me, and I knew that I had to step through that door as opposed to hiding. Every hair on my body was standing on end as I reached for the door-handle. I leapt through the doorway, and froze. The room was flooded with light, and River had Gabe firmly on his back on a gymnasium floor. River's eyes cut to mine, and then to the sculpture in my hand. He started laughing.

I could see my reflection in the mirrors lining the room, and suddenly I saw what River saw. I looked like a right fool standing there, hair dishevelled, panting from holding my breath, with a wild look in my eye, and to top it all off - in my pyjamas - readying myself for a fight with only a sculpture as my weapon. A giggle escaped me, and before I knew it, Gabe began laughing too.

"You all right there, Mack?" Gabe coughed. "You look like you've seen a ghost."

I shrugged as River said, "Ghost hunting, more like it." I shrugged again, and put the sculpture down on the floor beside the door. "Actually, Mack," he added, "you did pick a good weapon. That thing would totally knock someone out if you got your aim right."

Gabe nodded. "Yep. Head crushing even." Then he burst out laughing again, but I ignored him.

"What the hell are you two up to anyway? Isn't it too early for this sort of thing?"

River shook his head. "It's dawn." He released Gabriel from his hold on the floor, and pointed up at the high windows. He was right. The sky was pink from the approaching dawn. "We train most mornings starting at six. You're more than welcome to join us if you want to. God knows you need it."

I couldn't argue there, but gave him a pointed glare anyway.

"Think of it this way, Mack," Gabe started as he got up and stretched. "If you're prepared for a bitch fight now, then you won't hesitate as much when it comes to engaging with Carmen."

Carmen. It all came back to her, didn't it? I sighed. They had a point. As always.

I crossed the room towards them, and put my hands on my hips. "Okay. You've convinced me. When do we start then?"

River smiled coyly at me. "Right now." And with that, he dropped into a crouch, and swept my legs out from under me with one quick sweep of his foot.

I landed hard on the mat, and felt all of my breath escape me. I was sharply reminded that I had a bit of a hangover, and this was definitely not one of my brightest decisions.

"Lesson number one: Keep moving. If you stand still you're going to get taken out."

"Noted. Keep moving."

River helped me up, and brushed some imaginary dust off my shoulder. "Lesson number two: Hand to hand fighting is dirty. Some people thrive on it, others use weapons. But always keep moving, and learn to get down and dirty too."

“Well, if you two are going to be training this morning, I’m going to shower, and check what Chase is up to.” Gabe smiled at me and winked. “Best of luck.”

Oh boy.

When I hobbled into the kitchen a couple of hours later, I felt bruised, battered, yet somehow invigorated. The hangover seemed like a distant memory, and I was buzzed. River had put a set of boxing mitts on my hands, and had me sparring with him, and forcing me to do all sorts of unsightly things like crunches, press-ups, and stretches.

I had never really been fanatical about exercise, but I could now understand the thrill behind it. Right now, I felt relaxed and focused, and I was starving. Gabe was sitting at the dining table with a hot cup of coffee and his headphones on as he stared intently at his laptop screen. I walked up behind him, and lightly placed my hand on his shoulder. He jumped about a million miles into the air, and ripped his headphones off.

"Jesus Christ," he snapped as he glared at me. "You gave me a hell of a fright." He patted the seat next to him. "But now that you're here, sit. I have something to show you." He handed me the headphones, fiddled with the computer mouse for a second, and moved the laptop to in front of me. "Watch." He pressed play on a video.

I raised my eyebrows in question when I saw the clip was of a beauty pageant. "What the hell, Gabe?"

"Watch." He grinned as he disappeared into the kitchen. I turned my focus back to the screen, and I felt my breath catch in my throat. It was footage of Carmen Amaro, back when she was about eighteen. Well... Carmen Quintero, as displayed on the screen. The name Quintero was familiar, but I had no idea where from.

'And what's one thing you would like to do with

your life, Carmen?'

I snorted. The questions they asked were ridiculous, but I continued watching, thanking Gabe as he passed me a freshly made cup of coffee.

She paused before she answered and smiled shyly at the audience. 'I would like to study medicine and work in countries that need medical assistance.'

I practically spat out the coffee I had just taken a sip of. "Medicine?" I muttered, "Are you fucking kidding me?"

Gabe smiled. "Keep watching."

'And what draws you to that profession?'

'I want to help people in need. There is so much suffering out there... I feel that I could contribute a lot to helping those who can't help themselves.' She sighed, 'I think being a doctor is a very noble profession.' When she finished her sentence, she smiled brightly at the host. 'It may not achieve the ultimate outcome of world peace, but it will certainly contribute to peace in some people's lives.'

I snorted with mirth and pressed pause on the clip. "Is this for real?" I asked Gabe.

He grinned. "One hundred percent. You know...some people believe that was her winning statement - about not achieving world peace, but helping people with their peace."

I shook my head in disbelief and looked back at the frozen image on the screen. The girl in the video clip seemed so young and innocent and nice. I was having a hard time comparing her to the same woman who blew up a freaking plane all because I was supposed to be on it.

'So tell me, Carmen,' the host continued. 'What is your definition of success?'

She looked thoughtful for a moment as she considered the question. 'A job well done," she answered smiling. 'I'm one of those people that when I set my mind to doing something, I like to make sure it's done properly and done well.'

My smirk froze on my features. This was some serious insight into the woman that was hunting me - unless all of this pageant rubbish was bullshit. A job well done... At the moment, I was just a job to her. And she was willing to pay through the teeth to kill me.

'Who or what inspires you the most, Carmen?'

'Mother Teresa. She is a truly selfless soul who helps all those that she can. One day, should I ever reach the same level of achievement as her, I would like to be recognised for it just as she has been. She is an inspiration to all of the women of this world in terms of strength, dedication, and love.'

Mother Teresa, I snorted. But then as I contained myself I thought about what else she'd said. A woman of strength, dedication, and love. If Carmen was anything, I guess I had to admit that she had all of those qualities ingrained in her. Love for Javier, strength... well; maybe just strength. Strength to be a cartel wife, perhaps? And dedication? I wasn't sure about that one, but she was certainly dedicated to killing me, so I guess she had that too. As for being recognised and likened to Mother Teresa - well... I doubt that would ever happen.

The YouTube clip ended with a load of audience clapping and the host thanking Carmen for 'the lovely social chat'. Social, my arse.

I took the headphones off, and turned to Gabe. "She really knows how to turn it on, doesn't she?"

Gabe laughed as he slid the laptop back to him. "That she does. She won that pageant, and within weeks, she married Javier Amaro. Didn't take her long to become a cartel mother, that's for sure."

I blew out the breath I was holding. "But she must have been so young."

Gabe nodded and slurped on his coffee. "She was. I think she was eighteen when they married. Javier was second in command of the El Diablo Cartel back then, and twelve years older than her. Not too much of an age gap, but Carmen must have seen something in him. Or... he offered her the world."

My mind thought to the millions of horribly ugly men out there with trophy wives, and I shuddered. At least Javier wasn't one of those men – she'd done well in that department. I drained the rest of my coffee, and sat in comfortable silence at the table with my head relaxed on my arms as Gabe typed away on his computer. Then he let out a low whistle that caught my attention.

"What?" I asked.

He shook his head. "I don't know if you want to know, actually."

Immediately I was curious. He yelled out to River, who came to the dining table moments later.

"What's up?"

"Take a look at this," Gabe said as he turned the screen towards River. River bent down to read the screen more closely, and then he straightened as his eyes cut directly to mine. I got that damn awful sinking feeling of dread again, the same feeling I got when he found out that Carmen was hunting me.

"What?" I said, but it came out more like a hoarse whisper.

He shook his head, sighed, and turned the screen to face me. It was the headline that really caught my attention: Twelve Caucasian Women Decapitated in Tijuana - and Counting.

My hand flew to my mouth, bile instantly rising to greet my throat. "Oh my god," I whispered. I looked up at River, who was staring out of the window behind me. "They're just killing anyone, aren't they?"

River shook his head. "No. They're not. Gabe, pull up the police files on the dead women." Gabe started typing away again on his laptop, and River turned to me. "I guess we'll find out shortly, but I think Carmen and whoever else saw you with Javier has probably put out Rachel White's profile to their contacts. There is a hell of a lot of money banking on your beheading, Mack. A lot of people are going to die in the process."

"Got it," Gabe said a few moments later. He blew out another whistle, and turned the laptop around. I was completely mesmerised by the group of images on the screen. The women varied in their ages, but they did have two similarities. They all had long blonde hair and blue eyes. My hands ran through my own hair, and I winced. As part of the job, both Chase and River had convinced me to cut off my long hair to a close crop, in order to make wearing wigs and disguises easier. I always wore a long blonde wig whenever I was with Javier, as Gabe said from Javier's internet surfing history, being a blonde would be most attractive to him.

I felt sick. I had to make sure I kept a wig on at all times from now on, and not a blonde one. Bile was no longer just starting to rise to my mouth; I could now taste the coffee I had just swallowed, mixed with stomach acid. My jaw stiffened, and my mouth started watering. I was going to be sick. I leapt up from the table, hand over mouth, and ran to the bathroom. I collapsed at the toilet, stuck my head over the rim, and heaved.

When I finished throwing up, I leaned back to rest my head on the edge of the bath. Tears streamed down my face as I thought about all those innocent women caught up in the middle of this. They all had lives, people who loved them, had their own families.

Now because of me, they were dead.

This was a mess.

River knocked on the bathroom door, and let himself in. He paused when he saw me sitting on the floor, and then made his way over and sat down beside me. "It's not your fault," he said quietly. "This is Carmen's doing. Had she said something like 'bring her alive so I can confirm' then they wouldn't be dead. But she didn't, she said 'bring me her head'. Carmen is a ruthless killer, Mack, never forget that. The Cartel do not care about human life. Humans are a means to an end, and they will use people however they see fit until they are no longer useful."

I sniffed, and wiped the tears away from my eyes with the palms of my hands. "But they all died because of me." My breathing was erratic from crying, and I tried to steady it. "They died because I didn't."

6

After River coerced me out of the bathroom, I decided that I needed to get extremely clued up as to what the El Diablo Cartel was really about, and who they were, starting with Alicio Mendoza. Gabe had pulled up all sorts of information for me, and I sat on the couch with River's iPad, scanning through it.

I knew that those in the cartels were bad news, but I never really understood just how bad they were until all those women were beheaded because they looked like me.

They were hunting me out, and just the thought of it made me shiver.

River said that border control would probably start turning away women coming into Mexico if they resembled 'Rachel White', for their own protection. And then he told me that the El Diablo Cartel also basically owned the police and border security anyway. I'd figured that if they had an ulterior motive, it was to stop flooding the area with blue-eyed blondes, and narrow the killing field down.

I pushed my thoughts back to Alicio's profile photo. Alicio was dark, greasy looking, and very close to balding. He had bad taste in clothing, and if I didn't know any better, judging by the shiny sweat-sheen in his photos, he had a bad body odour problem. Photos of his three children, all young, and clutching at their mother's skirts, came up on the screen. I peered at the mother, Alicio's wife, more closely. She was a gentle looking woman, but there was something sad and forlorn in her dark eyes. I couldn't imagine what on earth would have possessed her to marry a man like Alicio.

I opened up some of the files, and found legal documents about his wife trying to leave him under the premise of rape and abuse. My mouth went dry as an amateur shot video shot through a grimy window opened up of a brightly lit kitchen. My eyes were riveted to the screen as the sound of crackly cries came through the speakers. I swallowed hard. The wife ran into the kitchen, closely followed by Alicio. She stumbled, just about whacking her head on the counter, but managed to miss. Alicio shouted in muffled Spanish at her. I watched as he lifted his sobbing wife from the floor, and backhanded her across the face. She hit the bench facedown with a thud. Disbelief and anger ripped through me. I felt bile begin to rise from my stomach and into my throat. And even more so when I realised what he was going to do. He lifted her skirts, and rammed himself into her.

I stopped the video, bile reaching to mouth, and I took a deep breath to help swallow it down. Tears were streaming down my face. I looked around River's living room, bathed in warm sunlight, tried to centre myself. I couldn't watch any more. He was a diabolical and evil man. I sniffed, and wiped my tears away, pleased that I had never suffered anything like that. My heart went out to his wife. I hoped that she wasn't in the crossfire when it came to the point of Alicio's demise.

More video footage was sitting in the folder, but I hesitated to open it. I swallowed the awful taste in my mouth, and opened another one. This was shot inside some sort of caged area. Looking at it closer, I could see people inside the cages. "Oh no," I murmured. Alicio came on screen, talking to the camera. He walked over to one of the cage doors, opened it up, and ripped a blonde teenage girl out through the cage door. She was white with fear, and whispering her pleas. Some of the words met my ears, and I could tell she was American. I skipped the video a bit, and saw the horrific images of the girl unconscious and her face covered in blood, lying on a concrete floor. Anger flared in me. I skipped forward a bit again, and found the images of Alicio raping her.

I stopped the video, shocked.

In Gabe's notes, he'd written that most of the time the hostages don't escape with their lives, but that they were held so that their other family member would do their bidding, whether they were scientists, traffickers, or the like. Gabe's notes also showed that the drug industry was a lot bigger than I had ever imagined. They explored every means possible to export their product into the US, and also to other countries if they could. The US was their biggest market though. I swallowed thinking of all the drugs on the streets there, addicting and influencing young minds.

Looking back at the photo of Alicio made me want to be sick again, but I did my best to compartmentalise it. He was the man that had been entrusted by the cartel to look after these hostages, and he had raped and abused them, in the same way as he treated his wife. Then once they were no longer of use to the Cartel, he disposed of them. I knew that shortly Alicio's life would be over, at the hands of Chase, and for some reason that gave me a little solace.

"You finished yet?" River asked from the living room doorway. I knew that he had some surveillance stuff planned for us.

I shook my head. I didn't think I'd ever finish reading the pile of files that Gabe has transferred for me. There was so much information, an overwhelming amount.

"Well, if you don't feel like reading or watching anything else, you can go get yourself ready, and hop in the car. Car - not truck. Dress nicely, high heels and a dress if you can manage that. Oh, and a dark wig. We're off to socialise."

Something about the way River winked at me with a cheeky grin sent butterflies soaring within me. I knew that this was not just having a lovely glass of wine on the terrace or anything. He wanted me for a job.

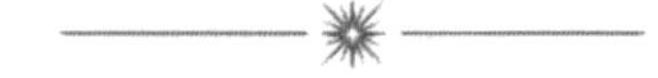

Dusky pink light lit the inside of River's sleek black Mercedes. If anyone took any notice of River in this country, they would probably think that he was one of the El Diablo Cartel from the cars he drove and the confidence that he exuded.

I felt damn awkward in a dress, like it was too short. I tugged self-consciously at the chiffon fabric of the skirt to encourage it further down my leg, and each time, I heard a chuckle come from River's side of the car.

He rested his hand on mine. "Calm down and relax Mack. Nothing is going to happen to you when I'm around. Just stick close to me tonight and you'll be fine." He squeezed my hand reassuringly before moving it back to the steering wheel.

I pursed my lips, and glanced at him out of the corner of my eye. He looked good in a tux, even if he was wearing a not-quite-traditional steel grey shirt under the black jacket. I licked my lips, and returned my eyes to the road. We were on the outskirts of Tijuana city now, and the darkness of the night was finally starting to drown out the dusky light.

The houses here were so different to those in England, especially in the poorer areas. They looked more like tin shacks with mismatched, multi-coloured roofs, as opposed to actual liveable dwellings. I could see children running, soccer balls being kicked along the dirty streets as they probably went home to have their dinner and go to bed. Bed sounded like a damn good option right about now.

When we entered the central business district, people flocked on the streets. Some of them dressed particularly well - like River and me - some casual, out for a good night. Some women were cheap and dirty looking in see-through clothing that left little to the imagination. I assumed they were looking for their night's 'work'.

River pulled the car down a side alley and slowed to a stop, turning to me. "Before we go inside, I want you to be packing."

"Packing?" I repeat, searching his eyes. Oh god. He wanted me armed. I swallowed. He opened up the centre console and pulled out a black belt with two parts, ribbon thin, and held it to me. It had a small gun attached to it. I gave him a look of disbelief as I took it from his hands. I stared down at it. “Um, where exactly do you expect me to hide this?" I said as I looked down at my dress. It looked like something out of a bondage and discipline book.

"Give it here." He took it from my hands. "Now, un-belt yourself and hitch up your dress to your waist."

I froze. "Couldn't we have done this at home?"

He shrugged “I’m sorry. We could have, but it’s not exactly a comfortable thing to have strapped between your legs. I thought this would be easier. Now get on with it - we need to go inside."

I swallowed. All my self-consciousness went out the window as I heard the urgency in his words, and I shuffled in an unlady-like fashion to get my dress up to my waist. River's hands were cool against my skin as he clipped the belt around my waist and the other part around my upper thigh. I pursed my lips, and my breath hitched slightly as his fingers lightly brushed the skin of my inner thigh as he deftly tightened the thigh ribbon. River started the engine again, and we took off around the corner. The gun sat frigid against the warm skin of my leg, and I rearranged the dress before River pulled the car up in front of a large building with a red carpet rolled out the front and turned to me with a reassuring smile.

I got out the car. It felt awkward, and I was about to readjust myself when River came around to my side of the car and took my arm in his. He paused a moment to hand the keys to a valet boy, and got a ticket in return. And then we were off. Showtime.

"Relax, Mack, you look good." He interlaced his fingers with mine as we walked confidently up the steps to the doorman. "Lucero Marquez," he said confidently.

We waited while the doorman looked the name up, and when he nodded his confirmation, we were ushered inside. We followed the rest of the people in, and found ourselves inside a lavish ballroom.

"Wow," I muttered under my breath. "I am so not dressed for this." But then as I looked around, I saw most of the other women were in clothing that they could move in, much like me. Then I saw that the dancing wasn't your traditional English Ball type; it was Latino. A thrill raced up my spine, and I couldn't help but grin up at River. "Wow," I said again.

He grinned, and squeezed my hand. "I thought you'd like it." He tugged me forward, and we stepped towards the dance floor.

Naturally, I worried about the gun strapped to my thigh and the possibility of it going off. Damn, I hoped River was careful.

He swung me out onto the dance floor with the crowd, and I felt the rhythm of the music throb through me, and my feet fell into time with his.

"Lovely," he whispered in my ear. "Now, we're here to observe Nicandro Valdez. He's a political player, works for the Cartel. He's also our next mark." He swung me out, and my eyes scanned the crowd of people. "I'll show you an image of him in a moment when we go up to the bar for a drink. There may also be other people here you'll recognise, and it's possible that Javier will be here."

My stomach dropped, and an icy chill flooded through my veins. "Carmen?" I whispered.

"No." River smiled. "Not tonight. I have it on good authority that she will be thoroughly distracted."

I pulled back at looked into River's amused eyes. "Whose authority?"

"Gabe's." River's eyes twinkled. "He's off to keep her company tonight."

"Gabe?" I mouthed, looking up at River as he grinned down at me. "My god," I whispered. "How?"

River's lip curled in amusement. "Turns out that Carmen has a certain liking for Caucasian men... and when her husband has other plans, she uses a service that provides them for her. Gabe hacked in, and got himself a date for tonight."

I shook my head with disbelief, and couldn't wipe the gleeful smile from my face. “Is he going to kill her?”

“No, not likely. He'll just keep her out of our hair for the evening,” River answered.

“He's going to sleep with her?”

"Whatever it takes to get the job done," River murmured. "Now, come get a drink. We need to mingle." He led me off the dance floor, and we walked over to check his jacket, then made our way through the groups of people milling around the bar.

River ordered two glasses of champagne, and passed me one.

He leaned against the bar, and a little towards me. "Now, back to Nicandro, he's standing over there next to the woman in the red dress." He kind of gestured with his glass giving direction to a tall, handsome man across the bar.

I raised my eyebrows at River, and took a sip of my drink, sweeping my eyes back towards Nicandro. He didn't 'look' like a bad man, but I guessed he was probably a right royal arsehole like the rest of the El Diablo Cartel. Nicandro was smooth, and radiated confidence. I imagined he could probably sell ice to an Eskimo if he put his mind to it. "What did you say he did again?"

"Strategic Communications. He's the man behind the politicians, the police, and any other official, both here and in the States." River smiled. "Quite the charmer isn't he?"

I nodded dumbly, mulling over what River had said and kept an eye on Nicandro. He was the man behind everyone official, meaning he was also the man that probably paid everyone off to turn a blind eye to the Cartel's activities.

It made me angry that the Cartel were never held accountable for any of the awful and inhumane things that they did, like kill a dozen beautiful, innocent women. And this Nicandro was one of the reasons for it.

I sank the rest of the champagne and handed my glass to River, who looked at me in surprise. "Another?"

River spoke to the barman and handed me another glass of champagne. I took it, and wrapped my fingers around the stem. I needed a cigarette. River said that we were here to observe the man and watch from afar. Well, I didn't feel like watching from afar. I felt like wrapping my hands around the smarmy prick's neck and throttling him. Unconsciously, I took a step toward Nicando.

River placed his hand firmly on my arm before I could move any closer. "Steady on, Mack. We are just doing a bit of observation on him."

I turned to River. "I need a fag and some air. Where's the nearest exit."

He led me around the bar towards a set of double doors that opened out onto a terrace. We stepped out into the warm evening air, and I passed River my drink so that I could open my clutch and look for the silver cigarette case. I snapped it open, pulled out a fag, lifted it to my lips, and lit it with the matching slender silver zippo.

I felt River's eyes on me, and turned to him.

"Thanks," I muttered as he passed me my drink. We walked across the terrace to the balcony, and looked down into the courtyard below.

"It's a beautiful evening," River commented as he leaned against the stone balcony and watched the people dancing inside.

Now that the nicotine was entering my bloodstream, I had calmed down a little. "It is." I smiled. I reached up and slightly adjusted the wig on my head. I could feel one of the pins digging into my scalp. Once again, I was wearing the Cleopatra-styled wig, the same one that I had worn to the club, as per River's direction. It looked good with the dress, I had to admit.

"It looks fine." River reassured me as he looked down at his empty glass. "I'm going to go and get another drink. Are you going to be okay out here for a few minutes?"

I nod. "Of course." I watched him disappear into the crowd of people, and turned to look out over the terrace. River was right. It was a gorgeous night. I could see stars twinkling through the haze, and I closed my eyes, enjoying the small breeze on the air. Doing reconnaissance wasn't such a bad thing, even if we were reconning a nasty piece of work.

"Don't I know you from somewhere?"

The deep voice startled me, and my eyes flew open to find a man standing beside me. I wanted to kick myself for not hearing him sidle up beside me.

River would kick my arse if he knew. I looked up at the stranger, and recognition flared in his eyes, and I imagined the same was in mine. It was the man I danced with at the bar the night Regina was killed; her security detail.

Jesus H. Christ. I forced a smile and tried to calm down. "Yes, I believe we danced once," I said charmingly. Surely he knew I had something to do with Regina's death... surely.

He smiled. "Yes we did. Interesting that we bump into each other like this. Do you come to political balls often?"

His eyes searched mine, and something in them made my skin crawl. "No, I don't. This was a bit of a surprise for me," I said honestly.

He grinned. "You still have your boyfriend?"

I couldn't help it, I laughed. "Yes, I do."

He took a sip from his drink, and sighed. "Too bad." He grinned. "I'd like to dance with you again tonight," he added. "That's if your boyfriend doesn't mind too much?"

I took a puff of the cigarette as I considered my response. I knew what River would do. He would go along with it to maintain his cover. I dismissed his comment with a wave of my hand. "Sure," I found myself saying. "I'd love to."

He held his hand out to me. "My name is Alvarez," he said, eyes smiling down at me as he assessed me.

I reached out and shook his hand. "Ciara," I

responded, remembering my new alias. For some unknown reason, Gabe was fond of giving us names that represented colours or anything to do with colours. Ciara meant 'black one' or something obscure like that. I thought the name suited the wig I was wearing.

"Ciara? What a lovely name. Where are you from?"

I dropped my cigarette into the ashtray at my feet, and looked up at him. "England, actually. Could you not tell?"

Alvarez laughed, shrugging. "No. All you English speaking people sound similar... well, to me anyway."

"But your English is very good," I commented.

"Yes. The woman who raised me was English speaking, she thought it was a good idea to raise me bi-lingual. 'Better work opportunities', she used to say."

I watched him curiously, noting the distant look in his eyes. "The woman who 'raised you'?"

He turned to me and smiled. "Yes. I believe you would call her a Governess?"

Sudden clarity. "Ah," I said. "You sound as though you miss her. Is she not around anymore?"

"No, she's not," he said sharply, with a bitter note to his voice. He then turned to me, his eyes softening. "Forgive me for my bluntness. She died a few years ago."

"Oh, I'm sorry to hear that." I tried to smile at him,

but fear coursed through me. This was an awkward conversation, and I wanted to know more than anything how she died. I pushed my fear away, and put my hand on his arm. "Come on then, let's have a dance."

I could feel River's eyes on me before I saw him as I walked back into the ballroom. He was standing near the woman in red, and near Nicandro who was talking to an older man. River flashed me a smile, and turned his focus back to his companion. I knew he had my back should I need him.

Alvarez held me close, and I hoped like hell he couldn't hear or feel my heart thumping inside my chest. And that he wouldn't get handsy and discover the gun.

"To dance is a way of communication," Alvarez murmured in my ear.

I swallowed. "Really? And what, pray tell, am I telling you right now?"

He laughed. "That you need more dancing lessons." He swung me away, and then back into his arms. "You need to relax." He grabbed my hips. "Loosen up. Dancing should never be restricted. In Latin-America, dancing is the one place where we can truly be ourselves."

I pursed my lips together, not sure what on earth to say. Alvarez was a big, strong man, with hard features. A part of me was scared of him, but another part felt thrilled by the way he handled me. "Right," I said. "Loosen up."

"Yes. Look around the room...notice the women. Look at how they are free as they dance. They do not let their minds restrict their bodies. They move to the music and with their dance partners."

He was right. About both the women, and their freedom. I was green with envy. I wanted to move like that, but while I was in the arms of Alvarez, I couldn't help but feel self-conscious and reserved. Something told me that he knew I had something to do with Regina's death, but then when he looked down at me, I wasn't sure. I wondered if he knew Carmen and Javier, or if he was just a security buff around these parts. He had an air of authority about him though that made me question what his real role was.

"Mujer hermosa," Alvarez whispered in my ear.

I smiled. "What does that mean?"

He laughed. "Looks like you need to brush up on your Spanish as well. It means that I think you are a beautiful woman."

I couldn't help it - I blushed, and he bent down and kissed me lightly on the cheek. "Thank you," I said.

It was at that moment that River intervened. "Ciara," he said quietly. "May I have the next dance?" River smiled down at me, and then held his hand out to Alvarez. "I am Lucero, and I don't believe we've met."

"Alvarez," he responded, and then turned to me.

He handed me a business card. "I would love to talk with you more."

I took the card, and slipped it into my clutch, and nodded. "Of course. I'll call you."

He smiled, his eyes flicking towards River's momentarily. "If you like - I can give you some dance lessons, and then the next time you are at one of these functions you'll dazzle everyone not only with your beauty, but with your communication."

I smiled. "That would be lovely."

As Alvarez left the dance floor my eyes followed him until he disappeared into the crowd and River took my hand in his. "Do you know who that man was?" he asked quietly as we started to dance.

"Yes - I think so. He was on Regina's security detail. He danced with me that night as well."

River pulled back and smiled down at me. I thought for a minute he was going to ruffle my hair affectionately, but he didn't. "No, that is Alvarez Rico. He may have been with Regina the other night, but he was probably more of a companion than on her detail. He's one of the men on our list, and he's head of Security for the cartel."

I actually felt adrenaline kick in. My throat felt tight, and I fought the urge to run. He was on the hit list. "Oh my god," I whispered.

River winked at me. "And, apparently he likes you... so guess who's going to have a dancing date with him soon?"

7

"If you stand still or move in any sort of pattern, Mack, you're going to get hit. The first rule of fighting is to always keep moving. Fighting is gritty work. If you enter into a fight, you're going to get hit - there are no two ways about it."

I pulled my foot back into a fighting stance, just as River had shown me, and stared him down.

"Now hit the bag, and hit it hard."

I did as he told me, and as my boxing glove connected with the bag, I felt a jarring reverberation up my arm and winced. The bag hardly moved.

River grabbed my shoulders. "Now, what happened just then?"

"I hit the bag?" I shook my arm out, trying to loosen it up and stop the pain.

He shook his head. "No. You bitch-slapped the

bag. I want you to really HIT the bag. When you hit something, you follow through with your whole body. You don't just slap the bag around - you smash your glove through the bag. Now–" He stood there, hands on hips. "Do it again."

I grunted, and returned to my pose. River turned the music up with the small remote in his hand. "Go, Mack. Put your body into it. Through the bag."

I had no idea what the hell he was talking about, and it was far too early in the damn morning to start arguing. I swung my arm out as I got closer to the bag and connected with it. This time, it didn't hurt as much.

"Good, getting there. Get up close and personal with the bag, Mack, and imagine you're pushing it as you punch."

I did, and the bag swung away from me. And then it swung back and hit me in the chest, throwing me backwards onto my arse. As I sat there on the floor, River's laughter met my ears. So did someone else's whoop of amusement. I turned and saw Chase standing at the doorway, amusement evident on his face. I bit my lip in embarrassment, closed my eyes, and lay back on the floor. Typical fucking timing. I could feel the blush crawling up my neck to my face, and knew that it would be in full force by the time I opened my eyes.

"When did you get back?" I heard River ask.

"A few hours ago. I ended up driving back down."

"Mission accomplished?"

I opened my eyes to see Chase shake his head. "Not really. Yes, Osiel Ramirez is done, but Alicio Mendoza is here now, so I followed him back." He looked down at me with amusement, and extended his hand.

My stomach exploded with fluttering as my fingers wrapped around his, and I had to take a deep breath as he effortlessly lifted me to my feet. "Thank you."

Chase smiled, his aqua eyes locking with mine. "You're welcome. So..." He raised an eyebrow at River. "You're teaching her how to box?"

River laughed. "Not really. More teaching her a few self-defence moves just in case she needs them."

What? I put my hands on my hips. "I thought you were teaching me how to fight?"

Chase put his hand on my bare arm, and I felt my skin tingle. "Mack, he is teaching you, but let me tell you, it takes years for someone to become an advanced fighter. And they can still lose." He glanced at River "So what he's teaching you? It's probably enough to get you out of a situation and then run. That would be my advice anyway."

"And that's what I'm doing," River commented. "You're going to have to learn how to get yourself out of a compromising situation, and then run."

I looked between the both of them. "Or I could just shoot my way out."

Chase laughed. "You could indeed." He looked at River. "Mind if I take her off your hands for a while? I think she should come and train with me for the morning." He smiled. My pulse raced.

"Be my guest." River chuckled.

Chase took me down towards his bedroom, and my nerves went wild. "What are we doing?" I asked, choking the question out.

He smiled coyly at me. "Well - I'm going to get changed into something a bit more comfortable, and then I thought we would go and see a little scenery."

We walked into his bedroom, a suite just as lavish as my own.

"Take a seat," he said as he disappeared into his closet. He pulled a couple of things out, and walked through to the bathroom. I could see his reflection of the mirror as he stripped his top off. My mouth went dry, and I turned away, trying to become interested in something else. Anything else.

Moments later, he emerged dressed in shorts, t-shirt, and running shoes. "Oh dear God," I muttered under my breath. I picked up a design magazine and started leafing through the pages. I wasn't paying attention to the pages as I turned them. I was more curious as to why Chase had design magazines. I thought he would be more into men's health magazines, or maybe even some of the luxury goods magazines, given the way he dressed. This design magazine showed him in a different light.

"What?" he asked, as he transferred his glasses for contact lenses.

He'd just caught me gazing at him, but I hadn't really been ogling, thank God - I was just watching him more out of curiosity, "Nothing."

"So, I read River's entire file when I got in. You two have been busy. Nicandro and Alvarez at the ball, huh?"

"Huh," I murmured. "Yeah." I looked up at him. "Was Gabe back when you got home?" I asked, suddenly remembering that Gabe had spent the evening with Carmen.

Chase grinned. "No. I picked him up on my way through." He walked towards the door and then turned back to me. "You coming?"

I jumped up after him, and he took me down the hallway, and out towards the back of the house. We went down a set of stairs, and Chase opened a door out to a small terraced garden area. "I like it out here," he commented. "I thought River was mad when he first bought this place, but we needed a base in Central America, so it was ideal really."

"So where are we going now?" I eyed the stone pathway in front of us.

"For a run," he said with a grin as he stretched. Oh my god. Before I knew it, he had started jogging down the pathway, and I was scrambling to catch up. I hated running. I was never very good at sports, and athletics had proven to be embarrassing moment after embarrassing moment for me during school. In the sprints I would trip over my shoelaces, I would crash through hurdles, and don't even get me started on the high-jumps they used to make us do. That was probably one of the core reasons why I chose a profession where very little movement was required. Yes, being an historian required me to rifle through archives, and hang out in libraries, and every now and then I went to an historical site - but the majority of the time I was sitting on my arse writing. It was the way I liked it.

We ran down the hill and out towards the coast. The downhill part wasn't so bad, but once we hit the flat area, my lungs started to burn, and I was quickly regretting the number of cigarettes I had smoked lately.

Chase ran effortlessly without even breaking into a sweat. For all I knew, he did this every day. I didn't want to do this for much longer. Chase noticed that I was starting to lag behind him, and slowed down a little to allow me to catch up. Once I reached him, I bent over and gulped for air for a few moments. "Jesus," I wheezed. "Are you trying to kill me?"

He leant back against a fence and watched me with a grin. "You need to get in training. That's all there is to it. So, for the next few days I'm going to bring you out running every morning until you've built a bit of stamina up. Then you can resume your self-defence fight training with River." He sighed a little. "And then... depending on how you go, I'll start teaching you some more finesse around your fight moves."

"Whatever," I grumbled.

He started walking. "Come on - we'll take it slowly from here to give you a break, and then we'll pick it up again."

Taking it 'slowly' didn't really cut it for me. My heart was still thumping in my chest, and I would have loved for someone to drive down the road and pick me up right now, but I knew that wasn't going to happen. I reluctantly followed after him, and fell into step.

"I need to track Alicio Mendoza today, if you'd like to come with me."

I stayed silent as images of the man flashed up in my mind, and I swallowed.

"Come on, Mack." Chase slapped my upper arm lightly. "This will do you good."

"Yeah...right." I didn't want to meet Mendoza any time soon not knowing how violent he was. "Do you have any idea where he might be?"

Chase smiled. "Possibly. I was getting Gabe to look at a few things for me this morning, so hopefully he's come up with something."

The Mexican morning heat was starting to get to me, and I seriously wanted a drink, anything liquid would do. We reached the coast, and made our way down the sand dune area to the beach. The tide was out, and the sand stretched for miles in front of us towards the States. The sea breeze cooled me down significantly, but I had an overwhelming desire to jump in the water and cool down properly. I was never much of a swimmer when I was younger either.

"I've been meaning to ask you," Chase said once we reached the water's edge.

I turned to him. "What's that?"

"How are you coping with all of this ... stuff?" His sharp eyes scrutinised me, and I turned back to the sea.

I shrugged. "I don't know. It's all going so fast. I have this crazy psycho woman who wants to kill me, and the chance of me getting out of Mexico alive is kinda dwindling..." I took a deep breath. I refused to cry in front of Chase. "And then there is all this other rubbish happening, which appears to be keeping me thoroughly distracted. I've never really seen anyone die before, you know. Well... apparently I saw my parents die, but my mind has kind of blocked that trauma out. Not like now," I added, the images of both Regina and Filipo as they died flashed through my mind.

Chase put a hand on my shoulder. "I've never really had the pleasure of being as innocent as you, Mack. My first kill was my abusive step-father when I was eleven years old."

I turned to him wide-eyed, shocked that one; he was telling me something about himself, which was pretty damn rare, and two; about his step-father. "You killed him?"

Chase nodded, the breeze ruffling his hair and he stared out towards the ocean. "It was an accident, actually. But they still put me into a penitentiary system for boys. I haven't seen my mother since. I looked her up a few times over the years, and I've seen her from a distance, but never engaged with her."

He kicked at the sand with his shoes for a bit, and I stayed silent.

"She never protected me from him. That was her one job, and she failed." He ran his hands through his hair. "I understood how she had failed me as a child... more so once I was in the system. All of the other boys in there had been failed by their parents as well at some point or another. A group of us started training in martial arts as a way to protect ourselves in the future. I vowed never to allow anyone have that sort of power over me ever again."

I sucked in a breath. "And then what?"

Chase shrugged and smiled at me. "I was recruited. I trained incredibly hard, won a lot of competitions, and then one day my teacher came to me and introduced me to another man, Archer. He said that he required a diversion." He paused. "I guess a bit like how we recruited you, actually." He smiled. "Anyway, he needed a boy with my fighting skill. I was thrown into a competition ring of street fighters - all bigger and older than me. I should have lost that day, and in a way, I did. I lost my innocence... the very same innocence that you're still trying to hold onto."

"You killed someone?"

Chase took a deep breath. "Yes, but not in the ring. After the competition, I went searching for Archer, and found him upstairs in a standoff with another man. Archer wasn't in good shape at all, and for some reason - I liked him. If I understood anything about being in a youth penitentiary, it was that teamwork and trust were crucial to achieving any goal. So I intervened. Somehow, I managed to throw the best kick in my career, and I kicked Archer's opponent backwards. He fell against a big window, and he went through it." Chase went quiet for a moment. "Don't get me wrong. I knew what I was doing. I was a trained fighter, and I knew the power behind the kick. But I also knew that Archer probably wasn't going to leave that room alive if I didn't do something to protect him."

"Wow," I murmured. "That was a hell of a thing to do for someone you didn't really know."

Chase turned to me, his eyes cutting directly to mine. "I did my job. Archer paid me a hefty sum of money after that, and I joined his business. You see... Archer was a contract killer. What I didn't know at the time was that he was also very sick, dying of cancer. He hid it well from me. In a way, Archer became the father that I never really had, and I craved his approval."

"You trained under him," I commented.

Chase nodded. "Yes I did. I soaked up everything he taught me. When Archer died two years later, I was seventeen, and the sole inheritor of his estate. I never wanted anything from him but for him to teach me. Instead, he gave me a whole new life, but in the same breath - it was a life where I took others."

We started walking back towards the sand dunes, towards the house. "So what happened after you lost him?"

Chase shrugged. "I don't know. I was pretty depressed, but I eventually turned back to martial arts training, and re-centred myself. If martial art gives you anything, it's centring. I booked myself a holiday to Tokyo on my first fake passport, and trained under an Aikido master for two years. I lived and breathed everything that the old man taught me, and then before I turned twenty, I decided that it was time to come home."

We paused at the edge of the dunes, and Chase let me climb up them first. After a few fumbles and clumsy moments, I managed to get to the top, and as I caught my breath, I turned to watch him effortlessly scale them behind me.

I held out my hand for him to step up the last bit. "Thanks." He grinned. "So I went home... and I started recruiting. I actually got two of the boys who I was in the youth penitentiary with to join me. But they were young. I had seen so much that they hadn't, and the divide between us became evident. After a while, they left me to go partying, and hook up with women." Chase smirked at the memory. "And once again I was on my own. So I linked up with two of Archer's old contacts, and I ran about with them for a little while. Eventually, I started to make my own contacts, but business was slow. People don't want to employ an amateur assassin. They want to contract professionals. So I knew that while the few kills I had would keep food on the table for a while, I needed to up my game."

We crossed the road, and made our way towards the house. I was utterly enthralled by Chase's story. I knew deep down that Chase wasn't such a bad person. Yes, he killed people for money, but it was the only profession he knew. He hadn't come from a good loving family like I had. He'd came from the streets.

"River actually found me, in the end. I was a job for him. MI6 didn't want people running about interfering with their missions, so they had a crackdown on the assassins based in England. River was one of the spies in the team." Chase smiled as he remembered. "You know, he's a few years older than me. But he took a liking to me. Between us, a bond formed. River saw that I needed a more professional approach, and he took it upon himself to give that to me. I had the money and collateral from Archer's estate behind me - River had the technical knowledge. He retired from MI6, and joined me. We've been working together now for more than ten years and never once have I questioned his judgement or his skills."

I smiled. "He's your best friend," I commented. Any fool could see how close those two were. They never did anything without consulting the other. I knew that the first time that I saw them in a room together. That was the night River let me live. And the reason I was here now.

I looked up at Chase, who quirked his lip as his eye caught mine. "Yes, River is my best friend. So is Gabe. We are an elite, professional team, and we get the job done." He blew out a slow breath. "Most of the time, our marks don't even know that we're there. I feel it's more humane that way."

I snorted. "Yeah, well... whatever helps you sleep at night, sweetheart," I muttered.

Chase laughed. "Death is death. Luckily for us, we don't do death unless we get paid well for it. Gone are the days where I would take jobs just for the money. Now I choose what I want to do."

We reached the gate at the bottom of River's property, and started up the little pathway that we'd run down earlier. "So, if you earn so much, then why not retire?" I thought of the sheer amount of money they were being paid to take out the El Diablo Cartel members.

Chase nodded. "Yes. It pays well. River, Gabe, and I have all made our retirement fund, and it's been put aside and locked down. When the time comes that one of us want out of this business, we've decided that we'll close up shop. But we're not ready for that step in our lives yet."

"Wow," I commented, stunned by the commitment they had to each other.

Chase laughed. "That's the nature of the business, though, Mack. To quote Alexandre Dumas, 'All for one, one for all.'" As we reached the small courtyard area, he added, "And after rising from nothing... I wouldn't have it any other way. Would you?"

"So, tell me - how was Carmen last night?" I asked Gabe as soon as I walked into the dining room with a fresh cup of coffee. Gabe was looking a little worse for wear, but I refused to feel sorry for him.

"I did it for you, you know."

I shook my head. "Don't use me as your excuse. So, how was she?"

"I didn't sleep with her, if that's what you're implying. She loaded me with tequila and tried to get into my pants a few times, but she was constantly interrupted. Thank god," he muttered.

"Interrupted? By whom?" River asked as he joined the conversation. He gave me a small smirk. I was still slightly annoyed at him about the whole 'self-defence' thing.

Gabe sighed and took a sip of his coffee. "By

special deliveries." His eyes flicked to mine, and I was immediately overcome by the sinking feeling of dread.

"What sort?"

Gabe shook his head. "Ugh. Heads, actually. Three more were delivered to Carmen last night." Gabe scrubbed his hands through his hair, and his eyes found mine again. "Don't look at me like that, Mack, I didn't have anything to do with it. I saw one, and the whole thing was so revolting I had to force myself not to throw up. Carmen, though," he exhaled loudly, "she's septic about Rachel White."

My mouth went dry, and I could feel the fear rising within me. Three more heads? That meant that there were another three bodies out there somewhere. A part of me wanted to know who those women were, but the other part wished that I could just hide in a hole somewhere and forget about this whole ordeal.

I stood up and reached for my cigarettes. Once I was out in the sun on the patio overlooking the coast, I started to think. I had to get out of fucking Mexico. These people weren't going to stop until they found me. I couldn't get near Carmen even if I wanted to right now, and if I got close to her, I would probably be dead within moments.

"They haven't found you yet," Chase said as he stepped behind me. "Remember what I said earlier? All for one, and one for all. We're not going to let her kill you."

I turned on my heel and stared at him. "But

technically I'm not employed by you. You have no loyalty to me. When you really look at it, I'm just in hiding with you at the moment. What the fuck am I supposed to do? I need to get out of here."

Chase shook his head. "There is nowhere in the world where they can't find you. They have contacts on every continent, in every country - you're going to have to wait it out with us until we finish this job. I will help you hunt Carmen down, and protect you in the process. And you'll get your cut for the ones you take down yourself." He inhaled deeply. "But this is your fight, Mack. She's not on our list, and we won't get paid for her demise. But it will give you your life back."

I took a long drag on my cigarette, and stayed silent. He was right. I had to somehow confront this issue. Not just an issue, either. The fucking woman was going around murdering other people who looked like me. "I need this to stop," I whispered.

Chase put his hands on my shoulders. "And eventually it will. Right now we have a job to do, and while she's not a target, it's intimately connected to Carmen Amaro. The more we kill, the more we take down her defences. You need to wait it out. Learn."

I slowly nodded; Chase made sense.

"Listen. River's going to track Alicio Mendoza today for me. But Nicandro is at home, and I think you and I should go and pay him a visit. Right now, he's not feeling so well from the ball last night. River slipped him a roofie. I want you in his apartment when he wakes."

"Me?"

Chase laughed and ruffled my hair. "Yes. I want him to think he slept with you last night. That way you can thoroughly distract him for a little while, so I can make sure he ingests some Ricin."

"And how exactly are you going to do that? Isn't that like rat poison or something?"

"No. No it's not - it's extracted from castor beans. Thoroughly toxic." Chase frowned. "Takes a while for it to take effect on the body too, so you'll be well and truly out of the way by the time it does."

I liked the sound of that. Of not being there when he died, that was. Then my heart sank. "Does this mean I have to get dressed up again?"

Chase's eye lit with mischievousness. "Only for a little while."

I was in the black dress and wig from last night, buckled up in the car waiting for Chase to get in. He was talking intently to both River and Gabe as I watched. There was something about Chase's smooth exterior, dangerous smile, and quiet demeanour that really had me confused.

I had never in my life met someone as good looking as him. While my tummy flip-flopped all over the place whenever I was in close proximity to him, I knew that he was hands off. He did his job, and he got out. I questioned whether or not that went for his relationships as well. But he had shown me a different side of himself this morning - a side that I quite liked. I could almost see myself being with him in the future. Visions of Chase naked swam into my mind, and I blushed.

Now was not time to think about that.

He opened the car door, and slid behind the wheel. "You all good?" he asked.

I blushed again, and turned away from him. "Fine," I said shortly. "Get in, get the job done, and get out, right?"

"Mmm," he said as he reversed the car out. "That's the general gist of it."

Once we hit the road, Chase turned on some music. Like all of their cars, this one was black as well. I wondered if they ever drove any other colour. In England, I drove a bright red Mini Cooper, my favourite kind. Luke bought it for me for our five year anniversary. I loved that car more than anything - and it was yet another asset Luke was threatening to take away if I didn't pay him out.

I sat quietly, listening to the smooth beats playing. Not my usual sort of music, but it was very relaxing. It was jazz, but it had this gorgeous Spanish mix to it - a tango style I wouldn't have thought would go with jazz. Chase drummed his fingers against the steering wheel as he drove.

He was dressed in his normal top-to-bottom designer clothes. I now knew how he afforded such luxuries. My research career never would have allowed me to have anything even remotely designer. Now I was in a different world - a world of assassinations, beheadings, the super-filthy rich, those who wanted money and power - and were ruthless enough to get it. I still felt as though I didn't know enough about the Cartel to fully understand the dynamics, but the more I read, the more it soaked in. I just had to wonder who had ordered all the hits that River, Chase, and Gabe were doing.

I leaned forward and turned down the music a little. "Chase?"

He looked at me, and my stomach flipped a little. "Yeah?"

"Who are we working for again? It's another Cartel, right? Why are they getting us to do their dirty work?"

Chase pursed his lips a little before answering. "It's a directive from the Santa Muerte Cartel. I believe they want access to the Tijuana and USA borders, and the El Diablo Cartel is hindering that."

My blood ran cold. "You mean to say we're helping another Cartel to smuggle drugs into the States?"

"That is a part of their operation, yes. I'm doing it for different reasons. A part of me is doing this for you. Had your plane not been blown to shit, I wouldn't have stayed here. Instead, I thought that this would help you resolve your issues with Carmen."

I blew out the breath I was holding. "You guys stayed because of me?"

"Yes."

"Because you got me into this mess?"

Chase smiled and shrugged. "That, and also...because I like you. You fit well with our team. And I don't say that about just anyone."

"Just how many people have you had on your team before?"

Chase shrugged. "A few. None were quite as pretty as you though." I felt a blush crawl up my face, and turned my face to the window so that he wouldn't see my embarrassment. We were driving through a fairly swanky part of the city. I hadn't been in this area before. Low lying sleek apartment buildings surrounded us, and Chase started to slow the car.

Chase looked out the windscreen at a glass building, and pointed. "That's his building right there," he said. We found a park and got out of the car. I wanted nothing more than to have a cigarette right now. My nerves were starting to get to me.

"Which one's his?"

"Top floor," Chase said as he took my arm. "Come on, beautiful. You have a role to play."

Chase took two seconds with a small pick and the flick of his wrist, and he had Nicandro's apartment door unlocked.

He paused as he listened for any sign of movement before stepping through. "Take your dress off," he instructed.

I didn't have the nerve to start an argument with him right then, so I did as I was instructed, undoing the side zip, and letting it fall to the floor.

His eyes raked over my body and I shivered, immediately remembering the naked thoughts I had of him earlier. "Now your heels," he whispered.

I bent over, and undid the small buckles on my shoes with shaking fingers. I wished he didn't have to see me standing there in my underwear. It was unnerving.

He gave me a small smile when I stood up. "Now just relax, and go and get into bed with him." Before I turned to leave him standing at the door, he ruffled up my hair slightly. "Good, go."

The apartment was all wooden floors, and full height windows, every surface was glossy lacquer. It reminded me of something out of the magazine in Chase's room. I crept through the apartment until I heard the sound of snoring. I snuck into Nicandro's room, and slid between the sheets, and faced the door. I tried to relax as much as I could. Chase peeped around the doorframe and winked.

This was my worst nightmare.

I tried to amuse myself with thoughts of flying home and paying Luke out and getting my house back into tip top shape. I really wanted to see my aunt, and

I imagined what it would be like to pay her care fees a full year in advance. All I had to do was make it home. There was no place like home, there was no place like home. My new mantra.

Nicandro rolled over towards me. I turned towards him. He was completely naked beneath the sheet. "Oh my god," I whispered. What the hell was I doing here?

As he lifted his arm over his head, I saw that he had a panther tattooed on the side of his ribcage. It didn't look like a normal tattoo though. It was red, and looked as though it was indented into his skin, making me desperately want to touch it - to trace it with my fingers. I wondered what the cat meant. Perhaps it was something stupid he did when he was younger. I tucked my hands beneath the pillow, which reeked of his cologne, and waited.

That was when he opened his eyes and looked at me. I wasn't expecting it. In fact, I almost jumped. Nicandro pushed himself half up, and as he took in the sight of me in his bed between his crisp white sheets, his eyes got wider.

I knew I should say something, but I had frozen in place.

Nicandro sighed, and put his head back on the pillow. He murmured something in Spanish, and I thought that was the best time to clarify I didn't speak the language.

"I'm sorry, I'm English," I said quietly.

"Oh, of course," Nicandro said, running his hand through his hair. "I was wondering what happened last night. I do not remember any of it."

I smiled. "So you don't remember me then?" I traced the muscles on his arm. "Because I certainly remember you." I didn't know where that came from, but I had a feeling he would like it.

"Who are you?" He rubbed his eyes. "You are very beautiful, but who are you?"

I chewed my bottom lip, and gave a little frown. "I'm Ciara. You really don't remember?"

Nicandro looked at me baffled, and shook his head. "Not really." He sat up, and rubbed his eyes again. Then he groaned. "I need water. And aspirin. Would you mind?"

I had no idea what effect taking a roofie had, as I had never been subjected to it, but this guy looked like he was in pain. I almost felt sorry for him.

I slid out from the sheets, and knew without looking back that he was watching my arse in my black lacy underwear. I left the room, and made my way towards the kitchen, hoping like hell I would find whatever I needed in there. I opened a few cupboards and felt Chase slide up silently beside me. He handed me an aspirin, and I filled up a glass of water to drop it into.

Chase held my arm back though and used an eye dropper to drip some liquid Ricin into the water. It didn't seem like enough in my opinion. I doubted only a few drops would kill someone. But I dropped the pill into the water to dissolve, and slowly walked back to the bedroom.

"So was it a memorable evening?" Nicandro asked me as I entered. He was sitting up against some pillows, the sheet only covering his lower half, leaving washboard abs bare. He had no other markings on his body apart from the cat.

Forcing a smile, I nodded. "Yes. It was." I winked at him and handed him the glass of medicated water.

"Good."

I watched as he drank it back in one go. "Are you all right?"

He nodded as he put the glass on his side table and picked up his phone to check his messages.

"I should probably go," I said quietly.

"What if I'm not done with you yet?"

I swallowed, trying to push my fear down. I lay back against the pillows, in a suggestive pose. "Well then, you better make it fast," I whispered. "Or I'm going to run late."

He grinned. "You'll be as late as I want you to be."

Oh boy. At the rate Nicandro was going, I wasn't going to have much of a choice. I hoped that Chase would get his backside into gear and help me out here.

As Nicandro grinned at me, I saw his jaw tense and his eyes fill with agony. He released my knickers, and pulled away, shaking his head. "I'm sorry," he muttered, clutching at his abdomen. "I don't feel so good."

I sat up as he grimaced again, and then he stood, shook his head, and ran from the room to the ensuite. He closed the door, and I could hear him trying to throw up. Now was the best time to make my exit.

I turned and saw Chase beckoning me from the doorway. "Come on," he mouthed as he crossed the room and picked up Nicandro's glass.

"Nicandro, I think I'm going to go ..." I called out.

There was a few moments silence before I heard him groan, "Okay."

I didn't need to be told a second time. I leapt out of his bed, adjusting my underwear back into correct position before following Chase out. He helped me into my dress, and I carried my shoes.

We stepped into the elevator and I turned to Chase, about to ask him about the Ricin contamination and the glass. But Chase shook his head, and lifted his finger to his lips. I quickly shut my mouth, and turned to face the door. He slipped the glass into my handbag before we reached the ground floor.

When the elevator reached the bottom, it dinged and the doors parted.

That was when I saw Alvarez standing there waiting for the elevator to arrive. My gut dropped a million miles per hour when his steady gaze met mine.

"Ciara," he said, stepping forward and kissing me lightly on the cheek. "We must stop running into each other like this." He smiled.

"I know, funny isn't it?" I stammered. I suddenly remembered Chase standing beside me, "Oh, I'm sorry. This is..."

"Davin," Chase said holding his hand out. "Her brother."

"Davin," Alvarez repeated as he shook his hand. "Alvarez. Ciara and I keep bumping into each other. This is what..." He wiggled his eyebrows at me. "Our third serendipitous meeting?"

I forced a laugh to my lips. "Yes. Most unusual." I put my arm through Chase's. "Anyway, we're running late. We have a lunch meeting."

Alvarez frowned at me. "Lunch? But you're still dressed in what you wore last night."

Shit. I desperately wanted to head-slap myself for that blunder. "Yes, I'm off home to change now, actually. Hence why we're running late. I dressed in the first thing I saw this morning so I could come and pick up my brother."

Alvarez smiled. "Well don't forget to call me. We have a dancing date to attend to."

I shook my head. "Of course not. I'll give you a call tomorrow and we can sort something out."

He leaned down and kissed me on the cheek again. "Lovely to see you again." As he straightened, he said to Chase, "And nice to meet you as well."

"Likewise," Chase said with his usual confident composure.

Alvarez stepped into the elevator, and as the doors closed, Chase tugged me out of the apartment complex doors, and across the road to the car. I had a feeling that Alvarez would be watching our car if he got to a window fast enough. The thought of it sent shivers down my spine, and I forced myself not to look up at the building as Chase nudged me towards the driver's seat to maintain our cover.

I started the car up, and carefully pulled out of the park. Chase told me to drive straight ahead. I hated driving in Tijuana, hated it with the rental they first got me, and I still hated it now. The drivers were erratic, there was loads of traffic heading to the border, and everyone seemed more impatient than was necessary.

Both River and Chase were much more composed when driving in this city.

"That was close, Mack," Chase said quietly from the passenger's seat. "With Alvarez, I mean."

I nodded, still too nervous about the whole meeting to say anything.

"Chances are he could be going up to meet with Nicandro. We don't know."

I shook my head, keeping an eye on the road in front of us.

Chase pulled out his phone, and dialled a number. "Gabe. Everything is set up; you should be able to link through now." There was a pause as Gabe responded. "Yes. Three of them. Also - we just bumped into Alvarez when we were leaving the building. You better check to see if he's meeting with Nicandro."

My throat closed at the thought, and my hands gripped the steering wheel. Alvarez would know that I didn't leave with Nicandro last night, and if Nicandro told him about waking up with me, it would open a whole new can of worms that I really didn't want to deal with right now.

I swore, and thumped the wheel.

Chase looked over at me in surprise, eyebrows raised. "What? You forget something?"

"No... Just thinking, that's all." I sighed when Chase didn't say anything. "Okay, I'm just hoping like hell that Nicandro keeps his mouth shut about me if he is meeting with Alvarez. I'm pretty sure Alvarez watched me leave the ball with River last night. He'll know something is up if he discovers that I apparently slept with Nicandro."

Chase patted my leg gently, causing the butterflies inside me to return to their dance routine, and I swallowed.

"If anything happens, we'll try and cover you."

"Damn straight," I muttered. I threw my hands up at the traffic in front of us, "Now, where the fuck am I supposed to be going here?"

While I had been in the bed with Nicandro, Chase had set up pinhole cameras around the apartment which Gabe could tap into. So, by the time we got home, Gabe was watching every movement of Nicandro's closely. So I knew that after we saw Alvarez, he had gone up to Nicandro's, who had told Alvarez he thought he had food poisoning. Thankfully, without even mentioning me, he sent Alvarez away and said that he would call him later.

Apparently, because Ricin has a delayed reaction, sometimes it could take a while for the person to die. Chase assured me that he had poisoned a number of other things in the kitchen as well, so if Nicandro ate, or drank the water in the kettle, he would poison himself even more.

I needed something to do, which was why I was in my room, flicking that business card through my fingers. As if I didn't have enough to worry about with Carmen hunting me down, now I was worried about Alvarez trying to meet with me.

I needed to do more research. That's what I needed. I always felt better if I knew more about the subject worrying me. So research on Alvarez was probably the best diversion I could have right now.

I pulled myself up into sitting position on the sofa and looked around, wondering where to start. My room was a freaking mess due to the constant clothing changes and unscheduled trips out. The life that Chase, River, and Gabe lived was on the edge. Anything could happen at any time, and they were ready for it. I wasn't. I liked everything to be planned out meticulously in advance.

So I changed tack and decided to clean up my room before I went and delved into research. I couldn't think properly when everything was in a state of chaos.

I fished my iPod out of my suitcase, and docked it into the sound system. Drum and Bass started pounding around the room, and instantly I felt my dark mood starting to lift. I separated my dirty laundry from my clean, and took it down to put it in the machine. The rest of the house was quiet, but my room was thick with noise. I loved it.

I was surprised that River didn't have staff in this house, but then he probably had trust issues, so that wouldn't work. He was the one who said that anyone could be bought with enough money. And he was right. With the right connections and wads of cash, you could.

I hung clothing up in the wardrobe, and stacked shoes neatly side by side. The stuff that River and Chase had bought me was all designer, and beautiful. I guess I needed to look the part in any situation. Since they had paid me to come to Mexico and they were currently protecting my sorry arse, I was sort of living on their terms.

When I finished sorting out my clothing, I walked

into the bathroom and took in that state of chaos. I put my make-up away in draws, my toothbrush in the holder, and tidied up the bottles in the shower. I picked up the wet bath towel, and other used towels, and together with the sheets from my bed, I took those down to launder as well once my clothes were finished. I was starting to feel much better about the world.

I shut the music off in my room, and went to find Gabe, who would be able to supply all of the files I needed on Alvarez.

Only the house was empty. They had all disappeared. I looked out the kitchen window and saw that two of the cars were missing.

"Bugger," I muttered. I stood there with my hands on the bench for a few moments before I turned around and rifled through the fridge for a glass of chilled juice. With drink in hand, I retrieved the cigarettes from my bag and stepped outside into the afternoon sun, to light up. I decided that I was going to savour a few moments peace while I could.

I sat down on one of the deckchairs, lowered my sunglasses over my eyes, and inhaled deeply. It was heaven.

The sun was hot as it beat down on me, but I didn't care. I felt safe. Chances were that it was going to burn my fair English skin to a crisp, but that didn't bother me too much either. I wanted to have a little more natural colour by the time I went back to

England, and there was really only one way to achieve that. At least lying in the sun wasn't exerting.

I really needed to write to my aunt and let her know how my 'trip/holiday' was going. She would worry if she didn't hear from me soon; especially as I should have been back in England by now.

I walked into the coolness of the house and over to Gabe's iPad. I keyed in his security code, and logged into my email.

I hadn't checked it in ages, and I blew a sigh of frustration when I saw a message sitting in there from Luke from a week ago.

McKenna,

We need to talk. And we can hardly do that if you're flitting off around the world somewhere and won't even respond to my emails.

We agreed that you would buy my half of the house off me, and so far I haven't seen a penny. Where are you anyway? You know that you can't run from your problems. And you can't run from me.

Call me when you get this email.

Luke.

I wanted to scream. Actually, more than that - I wanted to bash the shit out of Gabe's iPad for delivering the email to me. "Fucker," I growled. Who the fuck did he think he was? It was MY house. Elsie had transferred the family home into my name when she started to get sick, for god's sake. I gritted my teeth. She would be utterly horrified if she knew what Luke was up to.

He'd fucked my best friend, was reaming me for half the value of the house, had forced me into the sex industry, which in turn had me whisked away by assassins, and now I had a giant fucking bounty on my head - all because he was an arsehole. To put it plainly - he fucked me seven ways from Sunday.

I was no longer going to be emotionally controlled or abused by a man - not now, and not ever again. But now Luke wanted to fucking talk. Again. I wasn't going to talk to him until I got back to England. If we were going to talk, it was going to be on my terms.

I exhaled a sigh, shook my head to clear it, and returned to checking my emails.

There was another email amongst the junk that I opened, from Theodore Olsen. I had no idea who that was, but I opened it anyway.

He was a lawyer.

"Oh god," I muttered.

Dear Ms Carmichael,

It has come to our attention that you have not been in contact with Mr Luke Sommers for an extended period of time.

Mr Sommers has charged us with the collection of 460,000 pounds, the current level of debt owing for the house in East Dulwich, London, the

2010 Mini Cooper S that he states he bought you, as well as 96,000 pounds in joint assets and financial support he has given you during the last six years, in which you only earned minimal amounts.

We understand that you are currently out of the country. However, it is still imperative that we speak with you.

If you do not want this matter to go before the Courts, then please contact us by the 31st October, and we can have a discussion.

Yours sincerely,
Theodore Olsen
Solicitor

I looked at the date on the screen. Today was the 29th October. I had two days to get back to them. I just didn't know what to say.

8

I felt as though this was just the beginning of the end. Temporarily foregoing the email, I was going to write to my aunt's carers, I stormed off to my bedroom, rifled through the drawers and wardrobe, and found some clothes to work out in. I just couldn't write the email to Elsie's carers when I was in a foul mood. I had to somehow get this rubbish out of my system.

I stomped my way down to the training room, and started smashing the shit out of the boxing bag. With each hit, I imagined Luke's smarmy face on the receiving end. After a while, I started to feel buggered, and a bit better. If I was really being honest - I was actually enjoying myself. Perspiration poured from my head, and ran down my body, but I just kept going. I remembered what River had said about punching through the bag, and that the hit doesn't just end at impact. And the harder I worked, the more I threw my body and weight behind it, and the more the bag swung. I even managed to get into a rhythm of dodging when it swung back at me. Practice was definitely helping my technique, and what was even better was that there was no one there to critique me. It was just me and the bag.

I thought that target practice with a gun would probably work wonders as well, but I highly doubted that River would allow me to do that in my current state of mind.

I just couldn't believe that after all this Luke still had power over me and my emotions. As an accountant, he already had the 'arsehole' streak in him. I just never really imagined I would be on the receiving end of it. I punched the bag again.

And the cheek of him involving lawyers!

I grabbed the bag as it swung back at me, and leaned against it. I refused to cry. I didn't want that bastard having any more of my tears.

If I was going to cry, it was for those poor women who had lost their lives because of me. It was for their families and friends. And I guess also for myself. I was getting deeper and deeper into a dire situation, and right now, I had no way out of it.

I sat down on the floor, and lay back like a starfish, waiting for my heart to regulate after my physical exertion.

I started making a list of stuff that I had to do in my head as I stared up at the ceiling, littered with halogen lights.

1. Contact my lawyer, and see if there was any way we could delay the whole potential court thing until I got back. I had the money - well - River and Chase had it. Well, most of it.

2. Pay Luke back a shitload of money.

3. Get my arse out of Mexico, preferably alive. If that meant killing Carmen, then so be it. I didn't really want to kill anyone, but at least if she was dead then it would go some way towards me feeling better about all of those women who'd died because of me.

4. Have a holiday. I really needed a break, without any drama. God knows how I would pay for it, but hopefully my lawyer could work out some way to maybe bring the 'Luke Debt Level' down a bit so I could disappear somewhere and have some time out.

Chase walked through the door of the training room, and stopped when he saw me.

"I've been looking for you everywhere," he said, crossing the room towards me.

I didn't want him to see me like this. I was all red faced, puffy, and my body was soaked in sweat. I needed to hit the shower, and wash all of the negativity off me.

But that wasn't going to happen.

Chase sat down beside me. He was wearing long

shorts, and a white linen shirt with the sleeves rolled up which showed his tanned forearms. He obviously had contacts in, and his hair looked as though it had been a bit compressed by a hat. I mentally licked my lips as I looked back at his muscly forearms, one of which was sporting a Rolex. I closed my eyes.

"What?" I mumbled. "What do you want?"

"It's just you and me here tonight. Gabe is off to meet with Carmen again... seems she likes him." Chase laughed. "And River is tracking Alicio Mendoza for me."

Poor Gabe. "Ugh," I said, opening my eyes and rising up on my elbows. "You do realise that she's going to try her best to sleep with Gabe, don't you?"

Chase shrugged. "Yeah. Probably. But we've all slept with people we didn't want to for the sake of the job. Besides... if Carmen is occupied with him, then she's not thinking about you, now, is she?"

I stayed silent. He had a point.

Chase got to his feet, and extended a hand to me. "So, my lady, what would you like for dinner?"

When I walked out of my bedroom, after having a long shower and scrubbing all signs of stress and exertion from my body, I found the dining room lit up like something out of a fairy tale. Candles were everywhere, the fireplace was blazing away, and chilled wine sat on the table with two glasses ready.

There were two places set with silver cutlery, and linen napkins.

I turned to find Chase leaning against the doorframe, confidently smiling at me.

"Is this some sort of special occasion?" I asked.

He shook his head. "Not really. Some days just need it though, right?" He held a finger up in the air. "Be right back."

I nodded, turning back to survey the room. He'd obviously gone to a lot of effort. The ambience was gorgeous. I never could have pulled off anything like this in my house in England. I didn't have near the amount of candle holders, nor a real dining room. And my silver cutlery was badly in need of a polish.

Chase nudged my arm when he came back in, and handed me an icy margarita. "River said you're quite partial to these." He smiled.

"Thanks," I murmured, taking a sip. Icy coolness mixed with the tang of lemon, tequila, and salt slithered down my throat, and I smiled, savouring the taste.

"Good?"

I laughed. "Yes. But seriously." I waved my hand around the room. "I feel underdressed for this," I commented, looking down at my lightweight wrap dress and bare feet.

"Not at all," Chase said warmly. "I told you - this isn't a special occasion, I just wanted to have a little fun."

This is what he classed as fun? New light started to dawn on me as I considered him. "Well, it's certainly something."

"Just relax, Mack. Please. We have the night to ourselves. No jobs, no other stressors, really. And we are both in good company." He eyed me suspiciously. "I think?"

I couldn't help it, I laughed. I pushed away any thoughts of Luke or Carmen, or even Alvarez from my mind, and hit Chase playfully on the arm. "Good company, indeed."

"Good. Now, go and have a cigarette or something. Dinner is about an hour away. Sit down, put your feet up, and relax a little. I'm going to put on some music, and enjoy my drink."

He walked from the dining room into the living area, and fiddled with the sound system. Chase was so confident in any environment.

I couldn't help but compare Gabe, Chase, and River to Luke. Luke was an uptight, constantly strung-out workaholic, who had always obsessed about money. Really, it shouldn't be a surprise that he was being a prick about me paying him out. For all I knew he'd probably kept a spreadsheet about how much I had spent over the years while he was the main income earner.

I lit a cigarette and stepped outside onto the terrace. Luke had always come home to a clean and loving house though, not to mention most of the time he had home cooked meals made by yours truly. It wasn't as if he couldn't afford to keep me. But obviously he preferred to keep Nicole more.

When it came to River, Chase, and Gabe - they were all so different in comparison. They lived well, killed well, and they relaxed in the moments when they could. Like now, with Chase.

I heard music start up in the living area, and Chase stepped out into the night air with me, carrying both of our drinks. The music was more up my alley than the jazzy Latino stuff he was playing earlier. I felt myself starting to move a bit to the music, and Chase laughed.

"I knew you were a partier from way back," he mused as he eyed me.

I smiled, and licked my lips. "I was known to visit places like Ibiza in my youth. But to be honest, I prefer my own company. Doesn't mean I don't listen to music though," I added.

"Yeah?" Chase chuckled. "Tell me, what's your favourite music?"

"Drum and Bass," I said without missing a beat. Surprise filled Chase's features, and I laughed. "Don't act so shocked! You'd be surprised to discover how much writing and research can be done with music playing. I love it."

"You're right, I would be surprised. You are an anomaly, Mack."

I shook my head. "No. I'm just plain old boring.

No anomaly here." I stubbed my cigarette out, and Chase took my hand, leading me back inside. My nerves tripped and stumbled over themselves, as he led me to the sofa, his leg brushing against mine as we sat.

"Actually, I beg to differ," he stated. "There is nothing boring or plain about you. Why do you think we asked you out here?"

I shrugged. "I was a good distraction?"

He threw back his head and laughed. "No. No, that's not it." He chuckled some more, and then leaned forward and tucked some of my hair behind my ear. I stilled, breath hitched, and stared at him. "It was because River saw a rare fire in you. There you were, trying to make ends meet, any way you could, and you were prepared to put yourself out there. While you couldn't see it for yourself, we could."

He was sitting close to me, and I didn't know what to make of him. "Really?"

Chase nodded. "Yes. River saw it, I saw it, and Gabe saw it. There is something special about you. And look at you now. You are lovely and tall, your skin is getting a bit of sun - as opposed to all of that conditioned air and artificial light you've been under for years, and you no longer hide behind your glasses."

I shrugged off his comments. "I'm an historian, Chase, I'm supposed to be like that."

He leaned back, and relaxed into the sofa cushions. "Not all people are cut out to be stereotypes." He took a sip of his drink, looking thoughtful, and then turned his piercing blue gaze to lock with mine.

I stared at him. I didn't know what to say in response. "And on that note," he said after a few moments of silence, "I need to go check on dinner."

I watched as he stood and made his way to the kitchen. I'd come to realise that Chase was nothing like I had imagined. I had always been a bit wary of his smooth good looks and persona, but now, I wasn't so much.

There was a lot more depth to this man whom I hardly knew. A deeper level of loyalty than I guessed was there. I had the impression when I first met him that he was all about business, and nothing else. It couldn't be further from the truth though. He was sensitive, had built his business from the ground up, and he had lost a lot in his life. If anyone was going to understand my situation, it was Chase.

I drained my margarita, and nestled back into the soft cushions of the sofa, closing my eyes. This truly was relaxing. Dinner being cooked, I was being plied with booze, and then there was the company. My stomach somersaulted, and I smiled.

I realised I actually liked Chase.

Nothing would ever happen between us though. Especially not at the moment; I was running from a mad woman, and had my own issues to deal with - Luke in particular. There was no way I could even entertain the idea of getting into a relationship at the moment. Ugh. And apparently Alvarez needed dealing with as well.

Chase sat back down, the movement caused me to open my eyes and watch him. He held out a wrapped present to me.

"For you," he stated.

I gave him a wary look. "What on earth for? It's not my birthday."

Chase grinned. "Go on ... open it."

I sat up properly, and started to undo the yellow ribbon. When that fell away, I carefully undid the purple wrapping paper. Peeling back the paper, I saw a cheery oak box with the Apple logo on it. "Oh my god," I muttered. "You didn't."

"I did." He laughed. "And it's all yours. Latest generation iPhone 5. A Gold Elite."

I almost choked as I opened the box and pulled the phone out. "Oh my god, Chase, this is 24 carat gold." I turned the phone over in my hands. "What on earth compelled you to get me this?"

He shrugged. "I got it as a replacement for your phone while I was in the States. Gabe cloned your old phone, so it's already loaded with all your apps, contacts, music and photos." He ran his hand through his hair almost nervously. "They didn't have a bullet-proof model in stock, so I went for the gold one instead. So... do you like it?"

Then I did something completely unlike me. I

threw myself on him, wrapped my arms around his neck, and I kissed him. I pulled back. "Thank you." I stilled at the closeness of us, and then realised what I'd done. Chase was rigid as he stared at me. I started to move off him, mumbling. "I'm sorry, that was uncalled for."

He grabbed my arm, and pulled me back onto his lap. "You're welcome." He smiled.

I stopped breathing as his lips inched closer. His mouth met mine, and time stood still. The kiss was slow, deliberate, precise. Like everything he did.

Chase's phone started to ring, and I pulled away from him, jarred back into reality. Chase smiled, his eyes dilating as they met mine. "Ignore it," he whispered as he pulled me towards him again.

But then I thought of River and Gabe somewhere out there in trouble, and I shook my head. "No. You better answer it." I slid off his lap, my heart thundering as Chase pulled the phone from his pocket.

"Yes?" Chase answered.

I looked down at the new phone sitting in my palm and turned it on. I couldn't believe that I had kissed him, or that he'd kissed me. What the hell was going on? I was short of air, and I didn't want to look at him. I shouldn't have done that. No... WE shouldn't have done that. If anything happened between us, it would just complicate life so much more than it already was.

"You're where?"

Chase was dangerously quiet, and fear sliced through me. I didn't know who it was, but it sounded like trouble.

"Okay. Sit tight, I'll figure something out."

He hung up the phone and turned to me. "Shit," he muttered. "Gabe's down in Cabo San Lucas. He said Carmen flew him down there to her holiday home."

"What? That's miles away isn't it?"

Chase nodded, and drummed his phone against his leg as he stared off into space. "It is."

He stood up and swore again, and then he walked towards the kitchen. "Dinner's cancelled. Go get ready; we'll have to intercept River."

It couldn't have happened at a worse moment. Not only was I starving, but the last thing I felt like doing was going out in the middle of the night on a rescue mission.

Chase's personality had instantly switched into business mode as he blew out the candles in the dining room and turned dinner off on the stove. A part of me desperately wanted to take some food with us, but instead I was jostled towards my room, and told to dress in 'comfortable clothing'.

So I did. Cargo pants, a racer backed t-shirt, and a leather jacket. As I was slipping some shoes onto my feet, Chase walked in and assessed me.

"Wig," he instructed, passing me the glossy red one. I shoved my short blonde hair up into it, and pinned it down. I looked in the mirror, and noticed that the red did wonders for my complexion. Chase was right; I had managed to get a little natural colour on my skin.

Chase moved behind me, pushing my hair to the side, and gently kissed me beneath the ear. I felt my knees starting to go, and I leaned back against him. "I'm sorry we have to do this," he whispered, sending shivers through me. He looked into my eyes in the reflection of the mirror. "But the team comes first." He straightened, and passed me a hair tie. "Tie it back off your face, and meet me in the car in ten minutes. River's expecting us."

I looked at his retreating figure in the mirrors reflection, and sighed. I had no idea how long we were going to be, so after I tied up the long red hair in a ponytail, I turned and grabbed a couple of things like my iPod and wallet, and stuffed them into my backpack.

Then I went to the kitchen and pulled a couple of bits of fruit from the bowl, and some nacho chips from the cupboard. I was hungry, and I guessed that Chase probably would be as well.

As I reached the car outside, I realised that I'd forgotten my cigarettes, and dumped my backpack to dash back inside. I met Chase as he was coming out the door, his arm loaded with two guns, a bag full of grenades and god knew what else, and a sniper case. I paused momentarily to let him pass then ran through the door. The air in the house smelt like blown out candle wicks, and I once again threw a forlorn look towards the kitchen. I snatched up my cigarettes and lighter, and locked the house behind me. Chase had loaded whatever artillery we needed into the back of the car, and started the engine as I got in beside him.

As we raced down the driveway in to the darkness of the night I asked, "Just how far away is Cabo San Lucas?"

Chase shrugged, and threw me a wary glance "More than a thousand miles, I think. I know it takes a couple of days to drive there."

"Ah fuck," I muttered. "That's not good. I take it we're not driving then?"

"No." He thumped the wheel with frustration. "Silly bitch," he muttered. "Why the hell did she have to take him there?"

I didn't answer. Instead, I lit a cigarette. Chase didn't even bat an eyelid as I did so, and I wouldn't have cared if he did. We slowed as we entered a warehouse district, and Chase switched the headlights off. He unlocked the car doors, and we waited in the silent darkness.

His fingers laced between mine. "I'm sorry about this evening," he whispered. "I'll make it up to you." He suddenly let my hand go, as a shadow reached the car, and River threw the back door open. I flicked my cigarette out the window before he could start complaining, and met Chase's gaze.

"Airport," River instructed.

I felt my breath quicken. The last time I'd been at the airport, my plane had exploded mid-air.

"Red suits you, Mack," River said from the back seat.

I smiled. "Thanks."

The drive to the airport took hardly any time at all. River instructed us to drive around to the private aero club area. When we got out, he jogged over towards a private hanger, and walked through the door. Chase passed me a bag, while he carried the guns, and the sniper case.

"Follow me," he instructed. I did as I was told, apprehension filling me.

We stepped into the brilliant white light of the hanger. A plane sat there with a pilot waiting for us to board. I let out a slow whistle. "You're telling me you guys have had this the whole time we've been here, and you didn't think to fly me out of this godforsaken country?"

Chase gave me a wary look. "We'll all fly out once the job is done. Until then, this is for work purposes."

Business is business. I blew out a sigh of frustration, climbed up the retractable steps, and found myself a spot to sit.

I watched as River and Chase climbed on-board

and sat either side of the plane in front of me. Chase pulled Gabe's iPad from his bag, and the pilot started it up.

I couldn't believe these guys had a private plane at their disposal. It was my way out of this fucking country, and they had failed to mention it. I looked out the window as the plane rolled out of the now dark hanger onto the runway. I waited a few moments as we took off, and once we were in the air, I pulled out my new phone, turning it over in my hand. Chase turned around and smiled at me, causing me to swallow hard. I averted my eyes back to my phone, and unlocked it, assuming it was fine since Chase had Gabe's iPad already on.

I opened up the photos that Gabe had transferred for me, and immediately wished I hadn't. There were a million pics of me and Luke, of my aunt, Jax - my other best friend - and of me and Nicole. Those memories were ones I really didn't want to recall right now.

I had asked myself a million times what I'd done to make Luke cheat on me and then leave me high and dry the way he did, but I couldn't come up with a single reason. Sometimes I wondered if it was because I was so focused on being an historian, and delving into research. Other times I thought it was because I didn't make enough money. And then I thought that perhaps I just wasn't attractive enough. I probably didn't look after myself quite as well as Nicole. Doing my hair and nails or having constant facials or even joining the gym hadn't really been a priority for me. Not like with her.

Had I known if these things were the triggers that caused him to leave, would I have changed them? Probably not.

My mind flicked to how I had caught them in our bed, and I couldn't help but wonder if it was because I wasn't adventurous in bed. I was the first person to admit that I was a bit of a missionary girl when it came to sex. I felt like I was acting, or not really comfortable when I did anything else. Like I was a fake. I still couldn't forgive him for what he did though. And I couldn't forgive Nicole either.

I sighed, and backed up all the photos to my cloud account, and then I hit delete on all photos of me with Luke and Nicole. I only kept the photos of Jax and my gorgeous but doddery Aunt Elsie.

I leaned back in the seat, and watched Chase and River talking. Every time I thought of Chase kissing me, I couldn't help but smile. But then if I wasn't a demon in bed, what the hell was he going to see in me? I couldn't keep Luke interested, which meant I definitely wasn't good enough for Chase. He could have any woman in the world, and for some unknown reason he'd kissed me.

I tormented myself with the memory of his lips on mine until I fell asleep, knowing that it probably wouldn't happen again.

I dreamt of Luke chasing me through the cobbled streets of London while I was trying to shop. He stalked me through department stores, telling me that I couldn't afford to buy this or that because I owed him. And as I ran, blockades barred me at every turn with teams of lawyers and bobbies threatening to take me to court and arrest me.

Only I didn't know what they were arresting me for, but they kept repeating the same thing in unison: 'McKenna Carmichael, you're under arrest.'

I woke to someone shaking me gently, and as I opened my eyes, I found Chase looking at me with worry. I sat up, and realised we were still on the plane. I felt something wet on my face, and realised to my horror that I had been drooling.

Chase smiled at me. "We're here."

I looked around. River was no longer on board, and it was just us. I flushed at his close proximity, and licked my lips. "Where to now?" I asked, hoarsely.

To my amusement, he unbuckled my seatbelt, and grabbed my hand to pull me to my feet. Before I knew it, we were standing all too close again. I took a step back and smiled at him but avoided eye contact, just about tripping over my seat in the process.

Chase reached out to steady me, grinning mischievously. "We've been tracking Gabe's phone, and we have a location. River's getting us a rental car."

I gripped my bag so tightly, it turned my knuckles white. This was an opportunity to kill Carmen, but I wasn't ready. Not even in the slightest. "How far away is he?"

Chase shook his head. "Not far, I don't think. Out on the coast. Looks like a big house, with a little security. Gabe's last message said that there were a few of the El Diablo Cartel there with Carmen." He saw my panic stricken face. "You'll be fine, Mack. We're going to get in, get Gabe out, and then go home." He rubbed my shoulders. "Just stick with me." He pushed loose strands of hair out of my face, and stared down into my eyes. "River's right. Red does suit you."

Speechless and flabbergasted, I watched as he walked away from me, flashing me a grin over his shoulder as he stepped out of the plane. The burn on my face flared back to life as I picked up my bag and followed him.

I checked my watch and noted that it was close to midnight. It had taken us a couple of hours to get here. Chase was right. Fucking miles away from Tijuana.

I got into the backseat of the Mercedes River had rented, and to my surprise, Chase got in beside me instead of the front. He laced his fingers through my trembling hands as we rode in the darkness. I didn't want to be here. It had been a month since I came to Mexico, and I longed to be home in England surrounded by the comfort of my own things. I didn't want to be in close proximity to Carmen, not at all. I couldn't help but wonder what the hell would happen if she saw me.

Could I run? My mouth was dry from anxiety, and I reached into my bag to retrieve my water bottle. I dismissed the running idea, after recalling my casual jog with Chase. I didn't fare so well on that, so what on earth made me think I could possibly outrun Carmen or any one of her support staff?

Chase passed me a hand gun, complete with silencer, and I looked at it in my hand, and it was a hell of a lot bigger than the one River had strapped to my inner leg. I had never even shot a gun before. "The cartridge is fully loaded. Look after it and only use it if you have to." He smiled. "It's my favourite type of weapon."

I cringed. I had to remember that Chase was a trained, very professional killer. I looked at the gun in my hands, and I wondered how many lives it had taken. I had no idea if I would be able to protect myself with it, but I guess that if it came down to it, I had to try.

"The safety's on though, so you'll have to remember to flick that off before you fire," River said from the driver's seat.

I met his gaze in the rear-vision mirror, and nodded. I bit my bottom lip as I tried to figure out where to put the gun.

"You'll be fine, Mack," River reassured me. "Stay in the shadows, and try not to be seen. If that means hiding the entire time we're there, then so be it."

I continued chewing on my bottom lip, and gazed out at the houses we were passing, illuminated only by the street lamps. No one else was on the road apart from us. Every now and then I could see the moonlight flickering across the water out on the bay.

It was such a picturesque place by night; I bet it would be dazzling by daylight.

"It's beautiful here," I said softly.

"Beautiful yes... and deadly," Chase spoke quietly. "While this place is a bit of a neutral zone for the cartels, it still doesn't stop them from shooting one another if they can."

"But it's so silent. Not like Tijuana at all."

"All the more reason for everyone to stay in their houses at night. Most people around these parts know not to go out, or stop their car unless it's an emergency. It's not safe here. There are many who will mug, kill, and do whatever they can to get ahead in life."

I couldn't see a soul out there. I guess that there was safety in numbers sometimes.

River took a left, slowed the car, and we went down a winding hill towards the bay. Chase started up the iPad again, and I saw a map on the bright screen. Then a number of flashing dots on the page.

"What are the dots?"

Chase pointed to a blue one. "That's Gabe." He moved his finger across to a cluster of other dots.

"And those three there are you, me, and River." I could see us closing in on Gabe's location as we drove. It was fascinating.

I looked out again at the empty streets as we wove through them. All of the houses were enormous, and sat safe and securely nestled behind guarded, electronic gates. I guessed Carmen's would probably be of a similar ilk. Which bought me to my next question.

"What's the plan for getting Gabe out?"

"We're going to create a nice little diversion," River responded. "Then hopefully amidst the chaos, he'll have the opportunity to leave."

"That's it?" I commented. "Seems rather simple doesn't it?"

"Sometimes the simplest plans are the best."

I couldn't argue with that logic. River pulled the car over under an overhanging tree so that it wasn't too open to prying eyes. Chase reached for my hand and gave it a squeeze. My heart was hammering in my chest. I so did not want to be here right now, and nor did I think I was going to be helpful at all in this little operation. Especially with Carmen out there on the loose.

"You ready?" Chase asked me quietly.

"No," I said, my voice tight. I couldn't help it. I had lumps in my throat, adrenaline was starting to pound through me, and I felt like I was going to throw up. Different scenarios were running through my head at a million miles an hour and I kept thinking what if we all got separated and they left me here?

"You'll make sure I'm with you when you go back to Tijuana, right?" I asked in a small voice.

"Yes," he said, leaning over to gently peck me on the lips. His scent enraptured my senses, and suddenly I wanted more. I wanted to be safe and secure with him somewhere, out of danger. But would this be what it was always like with him? I had to wonder. He let go of my hand as he got out of the car, shocking me back to reality. He looked at me through the car door. "We'll leave the car unlocked. You can stay here if you want to, or you can come."

I looked around the dark street, and immediately decided that I didn't want to be here on my own, not knowing what was going down.

"I'm coming."

The house was a few doors down the street. River glanced at Gabe's dot his phone. I was wondering if my new phone could do something as cool as that when Chase clarified it for me. "All of our phones are linked so that we can always find each other. Your phone has the same."

"Oh," I whispered.

When we reached the property, River darted ahead, leaving me alone with Chase.

"Now for the diversion," Chase murmured.

Even though the night was warm, I felt cold. I rubbed my arms through the leather jacket I was wearing, the gun digging into my flesh in the process.

Chase reached for the gun, and snapped something back on it. "Just turned the safety off, Mack. You're free to use it as you see fit. Just don't shoot one of us in the process."

I nodded, afraid my teeth were going to chatter if I spoke. We waited silently in the dark for a few moments, and then I heard something foreign. At the far end of the property, the night lit up like fireworks, and the ground rumbled beneath our feet. Then my ears rang as mortar and stone splintered and blasted apart.

"Holy shit." I sank to the ground. "What the fuck was that?"

"The diversion. A grenade," Chase said. "Get ready. Stick close to me."

Alarms started ringing, and people were yelling. But they were running towards the house in the opposite direction from the front gate. Chase was doing something to the keypad on the front gates by holding a device over it. Suddenly the gate clanged loudly as the bolts unlocked, and it started opening outwards. I looked at Chase in surprise, and he gave me a knowing smile back. I got a bit of a fright when I saw River silently approaching out of the corner of my eye.

He grabbed my arm and started pulling me through the gates. "Come on," he whispered. "Time to get into position."

I swallowed, and dogged his steps as silently as I could. I was getting the jitters. I had no idea how long these things took, but already this seemed to be taking forever.

"How long?"

River smiled. "As long as it takes."

I cringed. That could seem like forever in such close proximity to the woman who wanted my head.

"Gabe could be in a compromising position. Don't worry, Carmen will leave him to his own devices so she can be head of command shortly, and he'll be free to go." Chase was smiling from ear to ear, and I realised then that he loved this sort of drama.

Carmen. Head of command. If I didn't watch it, I really was going to be sick soon. Thank god I didn't have anything in my tummy to heave up.

Chase pulled me behind some trees down the side of the house, and I watched River disappear ahead of us. "Quiet," he whispered.

I forced myself to control my nervous breathing. Armed men ran out of one of the house doors, and straight past us.

"Amateurs," Chase muttered. Then he pulled me forward, and we stood behind the next set of trees. We were so close to the house now, I could see people through the windows.

"God, how many people are in there?"

Chase assessed them critically from the safety of darkness. "Who knows? Gabe did warn us that she had a contingent of cartel members here."

I swallowed. "Oh boy."

"Brace yourself," Chase whispered. And I did. But I braced myself against him. I heard another grenade blast on the opposite boundary.

"Where the hell is he?"

Chase pointed to the roof. "Up there. He can throw grenades a good distance from heights." He suddenly clamped his hand over my mouth before I could respond as all hell broke loose inside.

Carmen came into view, and I felt myself suck in a breath through Chase's hand. He realised, and loosened his grip on me. "Sorry," he whispered almost inaudibly.

I watched Carmen issue orders to people around her as she stood in a negligee, baring her long bronze legs and leaving little else to the imagination. I couldn't believe that all these people knew that she was cheating on her husband - their boss! And yet, Javier either didn't know, or he cared too little to do anything about it. And then as I watched her take command, I realised that she was a natural born leader. I always had the impression that she was just a cartel wife, and that was why Javier courting me was so offensive to her status and rank within the cartel.

It appeared that I was wrong. Watching her now, it was damn clear that she was the boss. There were no two ways about it.

"I need to get closer," Chase whispered. "Do you

want to stay here, or are you coming with me?"

I gave him a quick nod to say I was coming, and followed him from the bushes. We ran quickly up the pathway alongside the house, towards the back. Chase found an open window and inched it silently open to climb through it.

I swung my leg over. I knew this wasn't a good idea, but there was no way I was staying out there in the garden by myself. I watched Chase check the hallway outside the room, and then he shone his phone around the room we were standing in. It looked like a small, unused sitting room. There were a couple of older styled sofas, a bookshelf lining the back, and a TV mounted on the wall. If I didn't know any better, I would say it looked like a man cave, but for someone much, much older.

Chase sent a text to Gabe explaining where we were. I hoped that was the end of it and we could get out of here as soon as possible.

Another explosion rocked the house, this one much closer. I pursed my lips. The last thing we needed was for River to blow the shit out of us. Chase signalled to me to get down behind the large couch. I didn't question or argue - it was common sense in case somebody walked in and found us.

I knelt beside him and rested my head on the floor. I sat there quietly until something foreign greeted my senses. Muffled sounds came through the floorboards, and I strained to hear properly through the vibrations of the people running around in the house. And then I heard something that sounded like a whimper.

I moved my head into a better position and listened closer. It wasn't just one whimper. It was a whole lot of whimpering and crying. Right beneath us.

Alarm swept through me and my blood ran cold. There were people down there. I suddenly looked up at Chase. "Can you hear that?"

His gaze met mine, and he lowered his head to the floor for a few moments.

He lifted his head again, and then put it back to the floor. "There are people down there," he murmured. "Women, by the sounds of it."

"Oh my god." I tried to keep my voice down. "What if they aren't meant to be here?"

Chase shook his head. "I'm not sure, Mack. They could be anyone."

I lowered my head back to the floorboards, and as I listened, I could make out some of the words. "They're speaking English." I sat up again and looked at him. "Chase. I don't think they're meant to be here."

He pursed his lips at me, and looked at his watch. "Our operation is to get Gabe out."

I stared at Chase incredulously. "But what if these people need us?" Panic started to well within me. Nothing about this was good. I dropped my ear to the floor again. 'Please help us,' I heard someone say.

"We have to get them out," I whispered. "They're asking for help."

I saw doubt creep across his features, and then he shook his head. "We don't know what we'd be getting ourselves into. I don't want to compromise the mission."

Frustration ripped through me.

Right then, the door burst open, and Chase and I both knelt silently to the floor.

"Chase?" A whisper came through the darkness.

Gabe.

Chase sat up, and peeked over the sofa. "Gabe," he spoke softly. "Are you ready to go yet?"

"Yeah."

I had my head pressed to the floorboards once again. They were crying and whimpering. Obviously these people needed our help. I didn't know what to do, but I wanted to do something. Chase grabbed my arm.

"Come on, Mack. We have to go."

Another blast ruptured somewhere, and I heard the house groan. I looked at Chase in alarm. "He's going to bring the house down."

Chase shrugged. "Possibly."

"There are a bunch of people down there that it will fall on!" I looked between Chase and Gabe.

Gabe sighed. "Yes. We have to go."

Chase heaved me up off the floor, and we made our way towards the window. People were really running around the property now, I could smell smoke and it plumed in through the windows of the house.

Chase sent a message to River, and before I knew it, we were going out the window. "Go to the trees," Chase instructed. I didn't need to be told twice. As soon as my feet hit the ground, I was running.

We reached the shrubbery, and knelt down to let it cover us. And then I had an idea. "Chase, do you have any grenades on you?"

He nodded, and lifted his finger to his lips, which made me go still. People ran past up the path in the direction we'd just come from. Rapid gun fire erupted from somewhere, and I prayed that River was all right. It was also a stark reminder of the gun I still held tightly in my hand.

"I'll throw a grenade in the general direction of those people as we leave, and they may have a chance of getting out," Chase whispered in my ear. "But when I do, we're going to have to run for our lives, because people are going to be swarming the area as soon as it happens."

I gave Chase a silent nod of thanks. He somehow knew what I was thinking. At least we had tried something. If they were hostages, I hoped they survived.

A message came through on Gabe's phone. "River's out near the road," Chase whispered. As we stood, Chase threw a grenade high over his head with all of his might. "Run," he ordered.

Gabe and I raced through the bushes and out onto the pathway. I heard Chase behind us, then the explosion rocketed through the air. And then I could hear nothing but my own breathing as I ran for my life down the dark pathway, trying not to tread on Gabe's heels.

A big man suddenly stepped out on the path in front of us, and we skidded to a stop. And then he fell in front of me. I looked down at him stunned, and saw he had a bullet-hole, precisely between his eyes.

Chase grabbed me. "Come on," he urged.

We continued to run towards the entrance. The Mercedes pulled up at the gates, and Chase threw me into the backseat with him, and Gabe somehow managed to make it into the front. River pulled the car away, the doors still open. Gunfire ripped through the night, and I heard a series of bullets hit the car.

As River gained control of the vehicle, both Gabe and Chase managed to pull their doors closed.

"That was fucking close," River shouted at us.

Close. "Oh my god," I moaned. River threw the car around a few bends and Chase and I were thrown around the backseat.

"Are you all right?" Chase asked me.

"No," I answered. "No I'm not." I pulled myself into a seated position, and tried to inhale deeply to calm myself down. "I think I'm going to throw up," I commented. I leaned against my door, head against the cool glass. And then the window started winding down. I leaned my head out of the speeding car, gulping in oxygen.

Chase pulled me in once he was sure I wasn't going to be sick, and wound my window up. "Best you don't lean out for too long," he said quietly. "It's not good practice to hang out of windows."

I shook my head and rolled my eyes. The motion was making me feel ill. Gabe passed me some water from the front seat.

"Thanks," I said gratefully. I uncapped it, and drank half of the bottle down.

"We're going to have to make a hasty exit when we get to the airport," River said to Gabe. "Set it up."

"We can't go," I said. "What about all those people back there?"

"What people?" River's eyes cut to me in the rear-vision mirror.

Gabe groaned. "The people." He sighed. "She's talking about all the women they have trafficked in. That was why Carmen flew us down there in the first place. A shipment of women came in through Cabo san Lucas."

"Human trafficking?"

Gabe nodded. "Yeah, that. Carmen flew in to inspect them. They're all women, collected from around the place. You know... south. Anyway, they are all undergoing breast implant surgery tomorrow for the cartel to insert bags of pure heroin, and then they'll be sent north across the border."

"Jesus Christ," I spluttered. "You're not serious?"

Gabe turned to me. "Deadly."

I started trembling. I had effectively sent those women to their death. They would be cut open in less than hygienic circumstances, given a heroin boob job, and then trafficked to the States. I wound down my window again, this time I really was going to throw up. My stomach heaved, but little other than water came out.

After a few moments of bringing up bile, I started to gain control of my stomach again and I pulled myself back into the car. Chase handed me the water bottle, and I drank the rest.

"This is a nightmare," I whispered.

Chase lay a hand on my knee reassuringly. "You're having an adrenaline crash. Most people get it in a milder form, but then again, most people don't go on an all out rescue mission like we just did."

"That's what you call this?" I choked. "An adrenaline crash?" After I said it, I seemed to recall that often people got emotional and threw up when they had an adrenaline surge, but I couldn't recall where on earth I'd heard that. I wound up the window, and sat back in my seat properly and was quiet for a few moments. "I think I need my bed."

And it wasn't like I had the luxury of putting it off either.

9

When I woke, I found myself in bed at River's house, fully clothed. I vaguely remembered getting off the flight back to Tijuana, and getting into the car. However, I didn't remember making it from the car to my bed. I took a wild guess and assumed that River and Chase had transported me.

Curious about the time, I looked at my watch, and was startled to see that it was after two in the afternoon. "Oh god," I muttered. I threw the covers off, and rolled to a stand. At least they had the decency to remove my shoes before putting me under the covers.

I stumbled into the shower, and soaked myself for far too long under the falling water. It felt good to wash away all of the shit from last night. I couldn't believe that we'd been on a whirlwind trip down to Cabo San Lucas, and basically blown up a house to get

Gabe out. And I couldn't believe that Carmen was importing women to fill their cup size with heroin. The thought of the whole operation made me sick. Transporting drugs inside somebody's breasts was sick. The fact that Carmen was the person behind the operation was even worse considering she was a woman. If anything, I would have expected a woman to be against that sort of inhumane act. It just showed how cold hearted Carmen really was.

When I eventually got out and towelled myself dry, I got my underwear on, and decided to tie a sarong around myself as opposed to getting fully dressed. I had a sneaking feeling that it wouldn't be too long before I was seeking the solace of my bed and clean sheets again. I thanked my lucky stars that I had washed it all yesterday. There was something special about clean sheets. I knew that if I ever won the lottery - I would have them put on my bed every day.

I saw my new gold iPhone sitting on my bedside table, and a grin spread across my face. I picked it up, checked it for any messages. There were a couple from Jax asking if everything was okay with my holiday. I responded saying that everything was fabulous and that we would have a good catch up when I got back, and tucked the phone into my bra strap. I missed Jax and her eccentric French ways, and I longed to tell her all my woes. Part of me wanted to ask what the situation was like back home with Annalise, Jax's friend and Escort Services boss, but I had left in such a rush, that I also didn't want to know. But it was best if Jax didn't worry about me, or else she would be on the first flight out here. I was dying for a cigarette and a cup of coffee, so I left the sanctuary of my room in search of the good stuff.

I wandered into the kitchen, and found Chase leaning against the bench, dressed in shorts, a white shirt, and a very nice pair of glasses. I automatically caught my breath, and I felt my face flare up. Memories of the previous evening assaulted my senses, and I paused to contain myself.

"Afternoon," he said warmly. He turned around, opened a cupboard, and passed me a cup.

I smiled shyly at him, and accepted the cup. "Thanks," I mumbled.

As I turned to the coffee pot, I felt him move beside me. "So... did you sleep well?"

I nodded. "Yeah. Not bad." I wondered what on earth else I should say. "Did you?" I enquired.

He smiled down at me. "It could have been better."

I froze, wondering what the hell he was implying, and if he was referencing anything to me or us in particular. "Always the case. The others up yet?"

"Of course. Those two can survive on hardly any sleep at all. I was more concerned about you though. You feeling okay?"

I thought of those women trapped in Carmen's basement, and felt anger well within me. Without meaning to, I rounded on him. "Not really, actually. Chase... we left those people there to fend for themselves."

He nodded slowly. "I know."

"And what if some of them died because of us? Whether they managed to get out or not. What that bitch is doing to them is completely fucking inhumane. I can't believe that even someone as sadistic as her would have the audacity to cut women open all for the sake of drug trafficking. We should have got them out."

Chase pursed his lips, and gazed at me silently.

I felt myself swallow as I met his eyes. "Sorry."

"You finished yet?"

I shrank back from him, crossed my arms, and stared out the kitchen window.

"Mack. Our mission was to get Gabe out. We don't usually deviate from the mission, or else things can start to go terribly wrong. I know that you're compassionate, and you care. But when we're not all on the same page, people get hurt. What would you do if we managed to save all those people - god knows how - we weren't set up for those logistics - but can you even imagine what it would be like if we lost any one of us in the process?"

I pursed my lips together, forcing the lump in my throat down. This was all too real.

"I'm serious." He exhaled with a sigh. "Do you have any idea what they would do to any one of us if we were captured? They would torture us, find out who we are, and because of the damage we've done to their cartel already - they would probably kidnap and murder all of our loved ones in the process. That's how ruthless they are, Mack, and that's probably an understatement."

I couldn't help it. Tears fell from my eyes, and I sniffed. Chase wrapped his big, strong arms around me, and I found myself embracing him back, sniffing and silently crying against his shoulder. "I'm sorry," I whispered. "I guess I just didn't understand the reasons behind your decision."

He kissed me lightly on the head and pulled back.

Gabe walked in humming along with his headphones carrying his dirty dishes, his eyes widened as he saw us. Then he saw my red cheeks and puffy eyes, stopped, and pulled his headphones off. "Erm... did I just interrupt a lover's quarrel or something?"

My eyes cut directly to Chase, and he looked back at me in alarm.

"Just kidding!" Gabe laughed "Geez. You people take me far too seriously sometimes."

I suddenly remembered to breathe. Chase patted me on the arm, and I picked up my coffee to take a slurp from it.

"Mack's still a little upset from last night," Chase told Gabe.

Gabe chuckled. "Women, eh?"

Chase rolled his eyes, throwing his hands up in

the air with feigned frustration. "Women."

"I need a fag," I muttered, carrying my coffee from the kitchen and into the living room. I found my backpack on the table behind the sofa, and fished out my pack of cigarettes, only to find it empty. I walked back to the kitchen needing to ask if we could go and get some more, but I walked right into what looked like to be an argument between Chase and Gabe.

"Errr.... lover's quarrel?" I commented.

Chase gave Gabe a thunderous warning look, and then stalked past me.

Gabe shrugged at me, muttering about how Chase couldn't take a joke. I swallowed, leaving my question for later. If they weren't going to help me get a new pack of cigarettes, I was happy to take a car and help myself.

I grabbed the keys to the car that Chase had been driving, and hopped behind the wheel. I drove down the driveway, and out onto the road. This was the first time I'd been by myself since all the issues with Carmen had begun. There was an old gas station a few miles down the road that we often drove past, so I headed for that.

I was heady with freedom for finally having some form of control over something, and it felt good.

This was what it would feel like once I got out of here and back to England. I would be able to drive down the road in a car I loved, and hopefully, fingers crossed, have my debt to Luke paid off. I pulled the car into the gas station, and walked inside.

The place was dusty and grimy. I couldn't understand how River managed to keep his house so damn pristine in this climate, as opposed to this run down gas station, with filthy shelving and little stock. A woman stood behind the counter looking bored, reading a magazine.

"Un paquete de Marlboro cigarrillos light, por favor?" I stumbled through my request with my usual crappy Spanish, and handed her some cash, hoping it was enough.

She silently handed me the packet, and watched me as I retreated from the store.

An older truck pulled in as I reached mine, and the man behind the wheel slowly got out, keeping his eyes fixated on me as I sat down behind the wheel. He stood there watching me as I pulled out, and turned around on the road back towards River's place.

I kept glancing in the rear-vision mirror as I drove down the road, he stood there the whole time watching my car retreat from sight. A shiver ran down me. "Creep," I muttered. I turned on the stereo, and Chase's music started playing.

A few moments later, I noticed that the truck had sped up behind me. I slowed down, and tried to wave him past, but he was pulling in.

Panic ripped through me. I didn't know this

person, and I had heard and witnessed far too much during my stay in Mexico to think he wasn't after something.

I swallowed, planting my foot on the accelerator, propelling the car forward. My hands felt clammy as they gripped the steering wheel. I kept an eye on the truck, but before long, he was right up my arse again.

"It's okay, Mack, it's okay." I tried to reassure myself, but I was lying. I reached for my phone and dialled Chase.

"Where are you?" he said immediately.

My eyes were almost a permanent fixture on the truck behind me, and I was only glancing at the road ahead. "Um, I don't know. I'm on the main road."

"For God's sake, Mack, what the hell are you doing?"

"Well... errr... right now, I'm being followed." Even I heard the tremor in my voice.

There was a pause. "Are you sure?"

"Pretty darn." I took a lungful of air and forced myself to analyse what was happening. "There is a driver in a truck right up my arse. I tried to pull over to let him pass, but he just pulled in behind me. Now... let's just say if I put my brakes on he'll be in my back seat."

"Keep driving. DO NOT come back to the house. You hear me?"

I cringed. "Yes?" I looked back in my rear-vision mirror. The driver was on the phone. "Fuck."

"What?"

"He's on the phone, Chase! Jesus Christ. Where should I go?"

"Just keep driving south. I'll track you and catch up." I hung up the call, and threw the phone on the passenger seat.

I watched as the truck sped up beside me. The driver was leering at me. I swore, and accelerated more, jumping forward. We sped past River's house, and I had no doubt that Chase probably heard us roar by.

Despite Chase's instruction, I almost felt like ripping on the handbrake, and going in the opposite direction towards Tijuana. At least there I could possibly lose this guy in amongst the streets.

But I didn't.

I kept going.

Every now and then, I would pass people who stopped and stared at the two vehicles speeding down the road. Civilisation was getting more and more remote, and soon it was only farm houses that I was passing. I hoped to God that Chase hurried the fuck up, or else I would be driving down to Cabo San Lucas.

The guy was back on his phone. My heart sank. I guessed that he'd recognised me and was yet another psycho that wanted to take my head off.

Never in my wildest dreams did I think I would be in a car chase. A year ago I had been blissfully happy in a relationship with a man I loved, doing a job I loved. Now I didn't really have a job, and a bunch of crazy Mexicans were out to kill me.

I opened the pack of cigarettes, and lit one. The truck had dropped back a little. I saw River's big black truck in the distance behind us, and relief flooded me. Help was on the way. "Finally!"

And then the driver was right up behind me again. A part of me felt like I was being herded. "Oh God, what if I am?" I whispered.

And I was. I could see a bunch of cars in the distance acting as a road block. I immediately picked up the phone. "Road block ahead," I said before Chase could even answer with pleasantries.

"Can you slow down?"

"I don't know." I took my foot off the accelerator a bit, but the truck just got closer. "I'm trying."

"Hang in there. We're not far behind you."

Hang in here? What did he think I was doing? Having a fucking tea-party? "If you're not here in time, what should I do?"

"Drive through. If you see a gap between the cars, aim for it."

"You're not serious?"

"Deadly. Do as I say, Mack, if you want to stay alive."

I hung up and saw River's truck getting closer and closer. They must have been seriously speeding. I clenched my jaw, and against all instincts, I started to slow my car down, forcing the truck to brake. And then he nudged me. Just. It was enough for me to force the car to leap away from him though. This guy was serious, he meant business.

And if he meant business, then so did I. I reached over, and unclipped the glove box. There wasn't a gun in there. I lifted up the centre console under my elbow, and found a little gun strapped into it. I pulled it out, and fumbled with it while I tried to check if it had any bullets in it. There were a few. Enough if I needed them.

The road block loomed as I drew closer. My heart raced. I couldn't see any gaps between the vehicles. "Fuck!" I pounded the steering wheel as River's truck pulled up behind the truck.

There were no road exits, not even any leading up to a farmhouse of any sort. I couldn't drive out onto the fields either due to a nasty, sizable ditch on both sides of the road.

I had to make a snap decision. Either I ploughed on through, with a high chance of severely damaging myself in the process, or I did something I should have already done.

I ripped the handbrake on.

The car spun out of control, but still continued its momentum towards the road block. I wasn't prepared for that. They never did that in the movies.

As I got closer, my eyes focussed on the group of men, all holding guns. I slammed on the brakes as hard as I could, and eventually the car slowed enough for me to gain enough control over it again. I planted my foot to the floor, and saw River and Chase right in front of me.

River was taking aim at the driver of the truck. He let off a few shots, and the truck veered off the road and into the ditch. They sped past me, Chase catching my eye to make sure I was all right.

While it was a relief, it wasn't enough. I now knew that no matter what happened, both River and Chase were about to get caught in a gun fight. And it was my fault.

I had to help them.

"This is bloody crazy." I pulled the car around, and drove up behind theirs. Chase pulled the truck broadside to the roadblock, and they both leapt out the other side, using the truck for protection.

Gun-fire cracked through the air. I stopped the car, and released the boot latch. I knew he would have more weaponry in there. I stuck close to the car as I slid to the back and looked in. And he did. I pulled out the sniper case, and quickly put it together. I got on the ground, and aimed under both of our cars at any feet I could see in the blockade. Then I fired. Amazingly, there wasn't much throwback when I fired. No wonder River preferred this method.

I missed a few times before a couple finally met their mark. I didn't have time to really think about River's instructions about wind factor or elevation or anything even remotely technical like that, I just went with my instincts.

When I ran out of bullets, I leapt to my feet, and threw the gun inside the boot. Then I saw the bag Chase was carrying with him last night nestled in the back corner.

"Holy shit," I muttered as I looked inside. There were a handful of grenades, and two Glocks. I was looking around the side of the boot lid to check on River and Chase when I heard something hit the car. Then I heard another one. A beam of light appeared through the boot lid, and then another. Something sparked on the ground a few feet away, and it eventually dawned on me that I was being fired at.

I ducked in behind the boot again, now fully aware that the boot was not going to stop any bullets coming through. “Stupid, Mack,” I muttered, wiping the sweat from my forehead. “Stupid.” I didn't know if I could run to get the bag to River and Chase without getting shot, but I had to try. I took one of the Glocks out and felt the weight of it in my palm. I ducked my head around the edge of the car again to look for my shooter. It was the bloody driver of the truck. Somehow, River hadn't killed him, and neither had crashing his car down the ditch.

I swore, braced myself, and let off a bullet in his general direction. The gun in my hand leapt in the air and narrowly missed my head from the throwback. I wasn’t prepared for that. Shooting a hand gun had always looked so simple! Clenching my teeth, I wrapped my other hand around the gun, and braced myself, letting off another couple of rounds in his direction. This time I was mentally prepared for the gun to kick, and it wasn't quite as bad. I knew my target would be scrambling along the ditch towards his friends at the blockade by now. I saw his arm waving out to someone, and I aimed again. I missed, and the dirt in the ditch flew.

I bit my lip. I now had a clear run towards River and Chase. I got as close as I could, and threw the bag of grenades far enough so that they could reach them.

I could see that Chase was telling me to go, but I was frozen to the spot. River's truck was going to be an absolute mess by the time this was over. So instead, I ran back and got behind the wheel of Chase's car and edged forward. I had to get them out of here.

A blast ripped through the air as River's grenade exploded. My ears were ringing, but I didn't hesitate. Gunfire still sounded loud and clear. Probably wasn't close enough. I threw open the passenger door and yelled to both River and Chase to get in.

It was well and truly time to get out of there. River launched another grenade in the blockade direction, and I stilled waiting for it to go off. But it didn't.

Before I knew it, both River and Chase were in the car, yelling at me to go.

As I turned the car around, River threw another

grenade - this time at his truck. I floored it. River's truck actually lifted off the ground with the blast and was thrown on its side.

"Damn," River yelled.

Chase looked at me. My heart was pounding so hard I thought I might have a heart attack. "That was a little too close!" Chase yelled at River.

I looked in the rear-view mirror. And then I saw another blast rock the blockade.

"Looks like they pulled the pin by accident," River grinned.

When we reached the house, I was exhausted, and my arm muscles hurt.

I switched the car off, and leant my head back against the rest. "God," I moaned. "How the hell did that happen?"

"Come on," River ordered. "We need to regroup and figure out how to get rid of this car."

Chase gave me a pointed look. "I actually liked this car."

"Sorry," I muttered as I followed them inside. Something inside me froze when I saw Chase's arm bleeding. I ran up to him. "Oh my god, Chase, you're bleeding."

He grunted. "Yeah. Nothing serious."

"He got clipped," River said, giving me a tired smile. "You're damn lucky we were here. Or else I have no doubt we'd be finding your body out there somewhere. Sans head." He poured himself a large a glass of water, and bought it into the dining room.

"I think you better tell us what happened," Chase prompted, as he opened up a medical kit and started laying implements out on the table.

He stripped off his shirt, and stood there cleaning his upper arm with an alcohol swab. I swallowed, not only from the ordeal I'd just put them through, but also because now Chase had been hurt. What made it worse was the lecture he'd given me before I left the house.

I told them about wanting cigarettes, and then how when I left the gas station the truck guy stood there watching me leave.

"That's when you should have called us," Chase commented. "No. No. In fact - you should have just let one of us go and get your bloody cigarettes for you. Obviously when it comes to you, smoking has more than one way to kill you."

"What the hell were you thinking, Mack?" River huffed. "You could have got us killed. I mean, Chase got shot as it was."

"It's just a graze," Chase muttered.

River shook his head. "I don't care. It could have been a whole lot worse than it was." He pointed his finger at me, and I automatically flinched. "You. You took one of the cars, didn't let us know where you were going, and you didn't even wear a bloody wig."

"River..." Chase warned.

I gritted my teeth together. He was right. It was reckless of me to just go off and do my own thing. And now Chase was hurt. I looked up at him as he was dressing the bullet wound, and stood to help.

"Sit down," River growled. "He's fine."

I did as I was told and looked down at the table.

"So, in future, you'll know that instead of going out on your own, you'll sit tight until one of us can accompany you. You were a sitting duck out there, Mack. You gave us a hell of a scare."

I swallowed. I didn't want to cry in front of these two. I had well and truly fucked up.

"These rules we've placed are for your own protection," Chase said quietly. "Don't break them, or you could get killed. It's as simple as that."

I pursed my lips together. They were mad with me. And I could totally understand why. "I had no idea anything like that would happen," I whispered. I put my head in my hands. "I'm so sorry."

"Mack. It's okay," River said with a sigh. "Shit happens, we get it. The unexpected always happens in our line of work. We're used to it."

I shook my head. "It still doesn't make it right."

"No, but next time you'll know better."

Chase finished bandaging up his arm, and swallowed a couple of painkillers with the remains of River's water. He then leaned on the table. "Now that's sorted–" He nodded at his arm. "–we're going to have to get a new fleet of cars."

River sighed. "Yes. And we need to get rid of yours."

I groaned and looked at Chase. "I'm sorry about your car," I said in a quiet voice.

To my surprise, he laughed. "Don't apologise to me - it's his car that was destroyed."

I looked down at the table. "Sorry about that, too," I added.

Gabe came into the dining room with his laptop, and shook his head at me. "Can't let you out anywhere, can we?"

I gave him a stricken look, not knowing what to say.

He tutted at me and smiled. "Well, you're all still alive, so that's something, isn't it?" He put his computer down. "So. New cars, yes?"

"Yes," Chase answered.

I wondered how much new cars would cost, and a pit of dread settled within me. "I'll pay for them," I said without thinking.

River laughed. "Darling - you have enough debt on your hands. This is the nature of our work. It's covered."

Gabe looked up at River. "Did you leave anything in the Range Rover?"

"Nothing important," he answered. "My identification stuff in there is for Roderick Brown."

Gabe sighed. "Well, there goes that alias." He

pottered around with his computer for a few moments while we sat quietly. "So, now we have another problem to add to the growing list... Nicandro is dead from the Ricin poisoning, congrats Chase and Mack... however, I've gone back through the footage from his apartment, and it looks like he finally died last night while we were down in Cabo San Lucas."

"So what's the problem then?" I asked when the others groaned.

"The cameras," Chase answered. "We were meant to get back into the apartment as soon as Nicandro died and retrieve them."

"Can't we do that now?"

Gabe shook his head. "Now the place is crawling with cartel members and police." He sighed. "Actually, someone has already found one of them. I cut the live feed as soon as I could... I just have to hope that they don't have the technology to trace the signal back to us."

"Ah shit," River muttered. "Surely not. They're pretty archaic down here."

Chase shook his head. "Some might be. But remember the cartel employs a crap-load of scientists to build all sorts of advanced methods for trafficking. There is no reason why they can't do the same thing for this." He gestured at the computer, and stood to look out the window, his back to us, hands on his hips.

I didn't have to be an amateur to know that this

was a bad situation to be in. My eyes kept flitting towards Chase. He was now rubbing his eyes with frustration as he tried to figure out the next move.

He turned around. "Where are we at with Alicio Mendoza?" he asked River.

River shrugged. "No sign of him at any of the usual cartel spots. Are you sure he crossed the border?"

Chase nodded. "Positive. I followed him over. He's here somewhere."

"We'll find him," Gabe chipped in.

I was pretty sure after hearing all sorts of shit about the man that I didn't want to have anything to do with finding him. "Do I have to tag along or can I have some assassination time out?"

"You'll be with me or Gabe. River's going to keep tracking him. Slippery little prick," he muttered. "Okay. Plan of action. River - work with Gabe to see if you can find any electronic trace of him. La chica—" He pointed his thumb in my direction. "—and I will take the remaining two cars and destroy them. And in the process, we'll acquire two more."

Chica? Are you kidding me? I threw him a dirty look.

"Don't look at me like that." He smiled. "Go get changed and wigged up. We're outta here as soon as you're ready."

"Wear the red one." Gabe chuckled.

I rolled my eyes. It sounded like I didn't have a

choice in the matter.

"Hang on one moment," River interrupted as I started to stand. "You also need to set up a dancing date with Alvarez."

"Shit," I muttered. I had completely forgotten about that. "I can't dance, River. You know that even better than the rest of the Mexican community who saw me on the dance floor."

"I don't care. Make the date, and in the meantime Chase can teach you the basics."

My eyes flicked to Chase who was watching me intently. My stomach flipped, and I felt short of air just thinking about it. "Okay," I said in a small voice.

River passed me his phone. "Here. Use it." He looked at Gabe. "Number?"

Gabe reeled off a string of numbers, and I dialled them.

Two rings later, and Alvarez answered. "Alvarez? This is Ciara Merle. From the other night?"

"So finally you ring me. I have been waiting patiently beside the phone this whole time." He chuckled. He was teasing me, and yet I still panicked.

I forced a laugh to my lips. "Sorry. Got caught up with... family stuff. Listen - about those dancing lessons... are you free sometime tomorrow?"

I could feel three sets of eyes on me as I talked, so I turned away with embarrassment. There was no way I could concentrate while they all stared at me.

"Tomorrow? Sure. What time is good for you? I

can probably clear my diary to fit around you."

Gack. I cringed and refrained from sighing. This would have been easier if he'd just named a time and a place. "How about four?" I suggested.

"Perfect, and then we'll do dinner afterward," Alvarez agreed. "Have you got transport? If not, I'm happy to come and pick you up?"

"No no," I said quickly. "I have a car. Where should we meet?" This whole conversation was just plain bloody awkward. It would have been a complete disaster if I was actually attracted to him.

"My place," he said. He gave me his address, and I hung up the phone. "I need a fag," I muttered as I threw River his phone. I looked pointedly at Chase. "Then I'll go and get ready."

Great, I thought as I lit up, now I had a date with a dude who would kill me for breakfast if he actually knew who I was.

An hour later we were browsing through the car lots. We had abandoned the cars in town, unlocked, with the keys left in them. It felt like a total waste in my opinion, but Chase had said that whoever looked closely at River's plates would be able to trace them back to the original dealership, and see that two other cars were bought that same day.

I guessed that he was being extra cautious. And then he clarified that if the truck driver had managed to get the plate of the car I was driving, and tell anyone about it, then it was a foregone conclusion that they would check that as well... and sooner or later they would be tracked back to us and on someone's watch list.

That was a point I couldn't argue with.

I ran my hand over the gun-metal grey paint of a particularly nice Mustang. It was an American muscle car that I would love to drive one day... would be even better if I could drive one in the States. I would feel like a character in Thelma and Louise, only I would never be as careless as to drive it over a cliff.

"You've got good taste in cars," Chase commented as he walked up beside me. "I used to own one of these."

I hated to ask but I had to. "What happened to it?"

Chase shrugged. "Gave it away."

I shook my head. "So no throwing it over a cliff or anything, then?"

He looked at me blankly. "Not lately," he responded. He turned around. "Come on," he called over his shoulder. "We got a couple of cars to drive home."

We weaved in amongst the cars in the dealership, and eventually reached a man holding some paperwork in a file, and keys in the other hand.

He didn't look happy with Chase. Or maybe he didn't look happy with me. He was a short stocky man, with a bushy moustache. It made it hard to tell if he was smiling or not, especially since he was wearing reflective sunglasses.

Chase spoke a few words in Spanish to him, and he replied with something to do with him being a gringo. I studied him hard.

I don't think he liked selling these cars to Chase, but he eventually handed over the keys and the paperwork. Chase handed me one set, and pointed to the far end of the yard. "Just beep the central locking, and you'll eventually come across it."

"Righto," I muttered. Wasn't the first time I'd had to do something like that.

I made my way in the general direction Chase pointed me, clicking the little remote as I went. And then I saw it.

It was a Dodge. A nice, sleek, dark grey one. As I got closer, I saw that it was the Charger model.

I sighed, and smiled. I was going to get to drive good old American muscle... just not in America.

Chase jogged up to me, and handed me a memory stick that he'd pulled from the car that we'd just ditched. "Music... just for you." He smiled at me, and then over at the car. "You like?"

I nodded, grinning. "Definitely."

"Good. Be careful on your way home. I'll follow you. Oh." He turned around and smiled at me. "This one has more horsepower than my last car, so be careful."

I opened up the car door. "It's not about the

horsepower," I said suavely as I lowered myself into the seat. "It's how you drive it."

10

Gabe and River had gone out to try and retrieve the cameras from Nicandro's apartment before any more of them were found. River had been muttering about shooting anyone if they were there to enable easy retrieval. Sounded anything but easy to me... and here Chase and I were again, alone in the house. He stood just across from me, with his hands on his hips.

"You need to step towards me, Mack. I can't teach you how to dance if we're four feet apart."

I pursed my lips and edged closer to him. This was going to be embarrassing. It was bad enough having River know how awful I was at dancing, let alone now having to show Chase.

His eyes pierced mine as I moved closer. "That's

better," he said gruffly, closing the distance between us. He'd made me change into a dress for our dancing lessons. When I had protested, he cut me off saying that it was better I learnt to dance in proper attire than in my gym gear.

"Now, put your left hand on my shoulder," he instructed, "and your right hand in mine."

I did as I was told, willing myself to calm down as he held me close to him.

He smiled. "Okay, now that you're in position, it's important to remember to keep your back straight. Keep your head held high, and put your shoulders back."

I smirked. "You want me to put my chest out, right?"

He laughed. "Yes, if that's how you want to put it."

"But you're not that crass?"

"No. Now, don't ever look down at your feet. That's a sign of someone who doesn't know what they're doing. Even if you screw it up, you just realign yourself with the music and your partner, and fall back into step - okay?"

I nodded.

He gave me a shake. "Relax, Mack, this is supposed to be fun. Stop being so rigid."

I bit my lip, trying to relax my arms a bit. "Just give me the damn instructions and let's get this over and done with."

"Since I'm teaching you to Salsa, you need to

remember that most of your body movement comes from your hips."

My face flared, and I swallowed hard.

"I'm serious. Keep your upper body stiff, and sway your hips from side to side. You'll get into a rhythm once the music is on. Okay?" He watched intently while I tried to sway from side to side. I felt like a fool. After a while he stopped me. "Just slow down. You're jiggling a bit like a Hawaiian." He dropped his hands to my hips, putting slow pressure on the left one, to make me move to the right, and then his hand on the right, making me move to the left. "Loosen your hips up, and try and use a slow, fluid motion to start with."

He looked up at me, and smiled.

A burning sensation hit my cheeks. I couldn't believe that he was teaching me how to dance, and he had his hands on my hips making me sway to an imaginary beat. If I didn't feel self-conscious before, I sure did now.

My mouth was dry, and every time his eye caught mine or he was too close to me, I would feel my heart miss a beat.

"Don't be afraid of me, Mack."

I hesitated. "I'm not."

He stepped back and looked at me. "You are. I'm not here to judge you; I'm here to teach you. But you need to let me do that, or you're still going to dance stiffly."

I felt short of oxygen just looking at him, and I

lowered my gaze. He moved closer to me. "Look at me," he said quietly.

I lifted my head; his fingers brushed my neck as they made their way up to my chin. He leaned forward, and I forgot to breathe. "I just have to get this out of the way," he murmured as his lips sought mine.

My lips parted and I breathed him in. Energy sparked between us as our lips touched and the kiss deepened. I couldn't think straight. All of the stress, worry, and anxiety I'd felt brewing over the past few months seemed to drop away, and I instinctively started to wrap myself around him. My hand ran over the light stubble on his jawline, and traced its way down his neck and shoulder.

If I was honest with myself, it was probably the best kiss I had ever been party to. There was just something between us that seemed to be in rhythm.

Unlike my dancing skills.

I broke the kiss, and put my hand against his chest. "What was that for?" I whispered.

He smiled, and kissed me lightly again. "No reason. I just wanted you to relax."

I rolled my eyes. "Do you say that to all the girls?"

Chase pulled back from me, his eyes deadly serious. "There are no other girls, Mack."

"I think you better keep teaching me how to dance," I said after a few moments. Men that looked like him usually had a flock trailing after them. He was the first person to say that he would do anything to get the job done, and if he lived by the same philosophy that Gabe had with Carmen - I had no doubt that there were other women.

He obviously saw the doubt on my face, and blew out a breath. "So, that's how it's going to be is it?"

I met his gaze. "Yes." He knew that I was pulling away from him. I didn't want to be just another notch on his bedpost, so to speak. Besides... a relationship between us complicated things. Don't get me wrong. I wanted him. Especially after that kiss, but I just knew that everything would be so utterly different between us if anything more happened. At least this way, we could try to pretend we had a normal working relationship.

He nodded. "We'll come back to that later. In the meantime, step towards me, assume the standard position, and let's get down to business."

I went to bed that night with Chase on my mind. I don't know what it was, but something was there. He'd said he wanted to talk about it, but the geeky, introverted part of me just wanted to bury my head in the sand.

I had to admit, the dancing was fun. Once the music had started, I actually found myself getting into a groove that I'd never experienced before. Every now and then the reflections of us in the mirrors lining the training room would catch my eye and it would give me warm fuzzies.

Chase was an anomaly to me. He was so different to every person I'd ever met. He was full of intrigue, and yet was open and honest about things when it suited him. But he was also deadly in every sense of the word.

Oh, and that Dodge Charger he let me drive? Wow. I had to get myself one of those. If I managed to survive. Just the sound of the engine made me understand why men are so obsessed with cars. It was loud and powerful, and the way it hugged the roads as I drove to River's made me feel really safe. Like I was untouchable.

I guess it was how Chase made me feel; as though Carmen couldn't touch me when I was with him. Perhaps there was a future there... perhaps not. Perhaps he would forget all about me as soon as this job was over and we all went back to England. Perhaps I was the 'job' for him right now. Still, I went to sleep with memories of his lips meeting mine.

Eight hours later, after a heavy sleep, I woke to someone shaking me. I opened my eyes lazily, and found Chase standing beside my bed with a lopsided grin on his face.

There was something funny about the way he looked at me. Then I realised that his eyes were almost black with dilation. Or maybe that was the dim light. Whatever it was, it made me shiver with something. Excitement?

I shook my head. "I'm sleeping."

"No you're not. We have a job to do."

"What job?" I lay back and put my arm over my face.

"Jandro Ramon." He tugged my arm off my face, and interlinked his fingers with mine, pulling me up and out from the sheets. He sucked in a breath, raking his eyes over my body.

That was the moment I remembered I only had my knickers on. "Ah fuck," I muttered, grabbing at the sheet, and trying to wrap it around myself with little coordination. I looked up at Chase, frustrated. "Out!"

He backed up, still watching me. When he reached the door, he put his hand on the handle, turned back to me and paused. He looked as though he was fighting some internal battle. "Jandro can wait," he said quietly as he crossed the room towards me.

I froze. He took my face gently in his hands, and kissed me with such intent, I was utterly breathless when he pulled away. But I didn't stop him. There was no way my mind or body was going to let that happen. Every cell in my body screamed with need.

And then all of a sudden, I was wrapping my arms around his neck, seeking more. I felt as though I couldn't get enough of him, and didn't even protest when he lifted me onto the bed. He pulled back, looking down at me, his gaze locked on mine, filled with desire. I sensed a shiver of anticipation rip through me as I drank in the shape of his lips, his jawline. "This would be pretty inappropriate," I whispered as he lowered those delectable lips towards me.

"I know," he exhaled the words as his lips met mine.

Everything about Chase enthralled me as he slowly kissed his way down my neck. Luke had never kissed me like this.

"I want you," I murmured.

"I know." He chuckled between kisses.

Well that wasn't the definitive response I wanted to hear, but it did amuse me.

And then his phone started buzzing.

Chase pulled away from me, and the air flooding the space between us suddenly felt cold. His eyes locked on mine the entire time he was listening down the phone.

"We'll be there in five," he said, hanging up. He slowly edged his way towards me again, and I smiled. "You're going to be the death of me one day," he whispered as he kissed me once again. He started pulling away. "But right now you and I have somewhere to be."

"Jandro," I commented.

He backed up off the bed. "Go get dressed in whatever. You don't need to wig up, and you don't have time for a shower. You're not going to need it anyway."

I gave him a curious look. I didn't know if he had just complimented me, or if there was some other meaning behind his words.

I wrapped the sheet around me, and walked to the wardrobe. I fished out a tight pair of track-pants, a sports bra, and a zip up sweatshirt, and then disappeared into the bathroom to get dressed. Chase was still in the room when I walked back in.

Before we reached the door, he pushed me gently to the wall and kissed me again. I was just pleased that I managed to quickly brush my morning breath away.

"For the record? I want you too."

11

Gabe drove the big Dodge truck that Chase got yesterday. It was a damn nice truck, but I definitely preferred the Charger. Chase had said that River always had trucks if he could help it, or sports cars. Gabe generally preferred the smaller cars; he was more than enchanted when he found out I drove a Mini.

Chase said he liked to drive anything with power, hence the Dodge Charger. I had to agree with him. That car was like sex on wheels. There was something thrilling, dangerous, about a car with loads of horsepower. The Dodge truck had a similar feeling about it too, but I preferred being lower to the road.

Gabe was talking to Chase in the front seat.

When we got home, he was going to start the upload of the kills to the database that he ran, and then hopefully we would see some money come in for each kill to date. He had been tracking the police as well, and apparently there had almost been an all-out war down in Cabo San Lucas after we left. According to the reports, Carmen had issued a directive to attack one of the other Cartel houses there because she assumed it was them who attacked her.

I was interested, but I also didn't want to know. Gabe confirmed that Carmen had flown back to Tijuana last night under the directive of her husband. Apparently she had texted Gabe when she landed, wondering where the hell he had got to amongst the chaos of River blowing holes all through her garden.

Just the thought of her made me cringe. I still couldn't believe what she was doing to those poor women. It made me feel sick. It was just so inhumane. I hated to think what she would do to me if she ever found me alive.

"Mack?"

"Yeah?" I answered Gabe.

"Are you ready for a bit of fun?"

I shrugged. It was too damn early in the morning. I mean, for god's sake, it was still dark. "No... probably not. It's too early."

"This will wake you up." He chuckled.

Sadistic bastard, I thought irritably. "So what is it that we're doing?" I was probably irritable because of

Chase and the way he made me feel. Just thinking about him made me tongue tied.

"We're going for a swim," Chase answered.

"You're kidding me, right?"

"Hell no!" Gabe whooped. "I should probably say that this is my favourite assassination method. It's epic."

We pulled up at a gate of a secluded estate, and Gabe put his device over the electronic keypad, much like I had seen Chase doing the other night down in Cabo San Lucas. The gates clicked open and swung inward. We drove in through the dark grounds with our lights off, and Gabe parked the car under some trees near a big stone wall. "Gear's in the back," he said quietly to Chase. "Go suit up, and I'll check the doors."

I got out of the car with Chase, and he opened up the back. He handed me a very thin black wetsuit to put on. I stripped off my jacket and track-pants, and pulled the wetsuit on as quickly as I could. I didn't want to be caught out here in the dark by someone I didn't know whilst standing in my underwear. By the time I turned back to Chase, he was already zipping himself up. He grabbed a hood, and told me to put it on. I did as I was told, and found it strangely bizarre that it had a black mesh that covered my face. I sat in the back of the car while trying to pull my boots on. The boots weren't like normal boots that I had seen surfers wear. They were wide at my toes, liked webbed feet. But they felt comfortable and roomy.

Chase silently handed me a slim-line dive tank. He helped me get it on my back, and strapped it on before he did his own. I noticed how lightweight it was, and how it hugged my back. He wrapped a heavy belt around me, and connected a small breathing apparatus to the tank, which then clipped around my neck, so that I could easily reach it through the mesh front of my hood.

Gabe came silently around the car and spoke in a whispered voice to us, "Okay, you're all set to go," he confirmed. "Go through the back door around there, and you'll see the pool dead ahead. It won't be long before Jandro gets up for his morning training session. The guards are all asleep, and I've pumped some amyl nitrate through the ventilation system of the guard's quarters, so they'll wake pretty dopey."

Chase nodded. "Good work." He grabbed my hand. "Come on," he instructed. We followed the path that Gabe had given us, and slipped in through a door in the stone wall. We stood in a pump house that was hot and steamy. "Now, when we get in the water, we are going to stay stationary until Jandro gets in."

"Won't he see us?"

Chase shook his head, and pointed through a glass door at the end of the room. I walked over, and looked out at the enormous pool. Then I noticed something incredibly unusual. "It's black?"

Chase smiled beneath the gauze. "Yes. And that's

why we have black suits on. Sometimes the best assassination is the one when they don't even know you were there."

We walked through the glass door, and as I watched Chase slip silently into the water, I saw a large blade glinting on his belt.

I slid into the pool after him, trying to be quiet, but I still made a bit of a splash. Looked like I wasn't graceful at this either.

"You ready?"

I shrugged. "I don't know, Chase. What am I even doing here?"

He gave me a slow smile in the dim light and moved closer towards me. "We've never done a job together, I wanted you to see me at work and this is safe way to do it. This is a different and very covert way to kill someone. You never know when you might need to do something like this." He leaned even closer to me, "You look gorgeous dressed up like a sleepy platypus."

I pursed my lips in amusement, forcing a giggle down.

"You ready yet?" He put his hand up to my covered face, and brushed it lightly down my cheek, causing me to shiver with the explosion of memories from earlier when he'd touched me.

I took a deep breath and nodded, not trusting myself to speak, and put my mouth piece in. We dove to the bottom of the pool. It was a strange sensation sitting there at the bottom of the pool with Chase. I had never been diving before, and I definitely couldn't imagine what it would be like in actual open water or the sea. I thought that would scare the crap out of me. In a pool with no predators, it all seemed a little easier.

I looked over at Chase, who was facing the surface. He pointed and I looked up to see that some lights had been turned on. Chase checked his watch, and held his arm out so I could see the face. We had been in the water for more than fifteen minutes already. I wondered how long our tanks could give us oxygen for. That was something I didn't particularly want to think about right now. I guessed Chase would make us surface before anything like that happened.

Jandro dived into the pool right at that moment, and my heart began to race. I watched with anticipation as he did lengths, just waiting for him to see us.

Chase moved languidly across the bottom, out towards the middle. Jandro took that moment when he was above me at the water's edge to take a break. I held my breath as his feet dangled down about a metre above me. I looked out in the water, and almost couldn't see Chase anymore - just a faint outline. It was strange not being able to communicate during this. It was so different to all of the other jobs I had been out on with River where he would give me a step by step instruction of what was happening. It was at a time like this one when I desperately wished I had ESP with Chase so I could at least understand what was going on in his head.

Jandro dipped down in the water, and I shrank back without making much movement. I really did not want him to accidentally touch me. That would blow this whole operation out of the water, literally. The place would become a state of havoc.

Jandro took off through the water in a backstroke, and I watched intently. Chase sprang up from the bottom and met him in the middle of the pool. I couldn't quite see properly, so I swam closer. Chase wrapped his gloved hands around Jandro's neck, and squeezed. Jandro struggled in the water, but since Chase was crushing his windpipe, I doubted whether Jandro could even breathe, let alone shout out. Chase wrapped his body tightly around Jandro, and continued to hold his neck with his forearm.

It felt like it took forever for the struggling to stop. When it did, Chase twisted Jandro's head, and I thought I heard a slight crack through the water, but really I had probably imagined it. Then he let the body go.

I didn't know what it was, but I felt like crying. Something about that kill was just so personal. We were all sharing the same pool, and Chase had taken Jandro's life with his bare hands. There hadn't been much of a fight once Chase had wrapped himself around Jandro.

I wondered how long it would take for the guards to find him. If I had learnt anything this morning, it was that Chase was a serious pro. He was a professional killer in every sense of the word. I had seen River kill, and didn't really bat an eyelid... but when it came to him... well. When it came to him, it was an art form, and he didn't even use the knife. I had thought this might get bloody and brutal, but it hadn't. It was clean, and almost natural. I was officially in awe of his skills. It made me want him even more than before. He was sexy, and dangerous, and that ramped up my emotional connection to him even more. He was exciting.

Chase dived down to me, and pointed to the other end of the pool. We swam towards it, surfaced, and climbed out. I took the apparatus from my mouth, and Chase grabbed my hand. "Come on," he whispered. "Time to run."

He led me through the pool's filter room, and out the back. Gabe had towels at the ready when we reached the car. I didn't bother changing, and neither did Chase. We just got in silently, and Gabe drove out the gates.

I sat there numbly, wondering what the hell had just happened. "Wow...." I muttered. I heard Gabe chuckle from the front seat. "Just wow."

"Pretty up close and personal, isn't it?" Gabe said. "The first time I ever saw that, I was probably feeling the same as you are now. And you know what the best part is?"

I shook my head. "What?"

"Nobody even knows you were there."

And that was the moment when I wondered if I could do a similar sort of stunt on Carmen. "Does Carmen have a pool?"

12

I was dressed and ready to go meet Alvarez. River had taken it upon himself to do my makeup while telling me about killing some woman named Beila, who was another Cartel member on the list.

I reached up to his face, and tentatively ran my fingers gently down the scratches on his face. "You're a mess," I said, my voice quiet.

He nodded. "I garrotted her – like with Regina. She was quite nasty, and a heck of a lot stronger than she looked." His eyes met mine. "But enough about that. I'm assuming you and Chase have managed to sort something out between you?"

Colour flared to my face, and I looked down at the floor, biting my lip.

"Look, Mack. Right from the first night we met

you, there was obvious tension between you and him..." He smiled. "I'm just pleased that it's positive tension now."

I snorted, remembering. "He wanted to kill me."

"He did," River agreed, "But it's been obvious to both me and Gabe for a while now that our best friend was falling for you. And rightly so. You're a beautiful, smart woman. I consider you like a sister. Don't ever forget that. Especially not tonight when you're with Alvarez. Use those skills you have, and your wit and looks to your advantage. It doesn't matter if you can't dance. Alvarez likes you for a reason."

I laughed, relieved that the tension was dissolved. "Are you saying that my dance moves aren't attractive?"

River smirked, his eyes laughing with amusement. "I'm saying that if Alvarez only liked women for their dancing skills - yeah - he could probably do better than you." He brushed some hair away from my face tenderly, and leaned forward to lightly kiss me on the cheek. I could feel a warm sensation of trust surround me from him. He really did consider me part of his family. I felt accepted. I stood and wrapped my arms around him, embracing as a smile lit my face.

"You're all good, Mack. Now, go knock him dead with your dance moves."

I was damn nervous about going to Alvarez's place. But I guess it had to be done.

When River finally let me go, I ran straight into Chase in the hallway. He gripped both my shoulders. "Slow down, tiger," he commented with a smirk. "I was just coming to see if you were ready to go."

I hesitantly nodded. "Sort of."

He smiled down at me. "Good. If you're ready to go, I'll take you there. I want to keep watch on the place and be your back up in case anything goes wrong."

My mouth went dry. "What could go wrong?" I squeaked.

Chase shrugged. "Anything really... I may have to take him out while you're there. You'll be fine though. I've got your back. Now..." he smiled. "Go get your bag or whatever it is you need. I'll be out in the car."

I ran straight to my room, glancing at my watch. "Bloody River," I muttered as I threw a few things into my handbag.

I heard a knock at the door, and Gabe poked his head around it. "I have something for you before you go," he said, grinning. He walked over to me, and pinned one of the most beautiful brooches I had ever seen to the strap of my dress.

"That's gorgeous," I commented as I ran my fingers over it.

Gabe nodded. "It sure is. It has a camera and microphone in it, so you're linked up to us here and on our mobiles. Just in case..."

I sighed, of course it was. "Honestly - what could

go wrong? Chase is all worried about it, and now you..." I watched Gabe closely, but he wouldn't meet my eye. "Is there something you're not telling me about Alvarez?"

He shook his head. "Go." He shooed me out the door. "You're running late."

Damn it, he was right. I picked up my bag, and ran out to the car. It rumbled to life as soon as I closed the door, and I settled into the soft red leather seats. Chase put some music on, and I noticed that it was from the USB stick he handed to me the other day which I'd never got around to plugging in.

Drum and Bass sounded throughout the car, and I turned to Chase in surprise. "You have this?"

He smiled. "I've been known to listen to a variety of music. But I remembered what you said the other day about how this was your favourite sort, so I loaded some."

I smiled, letting the music and the vibrations from the car's engine wrap around my senses. I closed my eyes, and realised that I could smell Chase's cologne as well. I didn't want to go to Alvarez's house. I wanted to stay here listening to amazing music in this car, and hang out with a man I really liked who made me feel safe.

But that wasn't going to happen.

Chase grabbed my hand, and I opened my eyes to look at him. "You're going to do great," he said.

I smiled lazily at him. "I would prefer to stay here

with you."

"I know." He laughed. "Believe me when I say this - I would like nothing more than for you to hang out here with me as well. But you have a job to do."

That was the thing about Chase. He was just so damn focused on his work, our work, and what we had to do in order to make it all happen.

I then wondered why he was really here with me.

"Do you have an ulterior motive, Chase?"

"When? Now?"

I nodded.

"When it comes to you, Mack, all my motives are ulterior."

I laughed. "Gee, well that clarifies things. No ... I mean ... Are you going to take Alvarez out while I'm there?"

He shrugged. "Depends."

"On what?"

"On what his ulterior motives are, for one."

I rolled my eyes. "Oh come on, Chase. You know what his ulterior motives are. You know he's going to try his best to get me into bed with him. I'm not going in blind, you know."

Chase pursed his lips together, and kept his eyes on the road. "And how are you going to handle that, then?"

I sighed. "I have no idea. I'll figure that out at the time." I glanced at him. I could tell he was angry from the set of his jaw, and the way he refused to look at me. I could feel something simmering beneath his surface. “How are you going to handle it?” I asked, almost inaudibly.

He exhaled. "Well, just know that I will have a gun trained on him as much as I can, so if you ever need my help, you just give me the signal."

Great. Now I was never going to be able to relax. It was bad enough knowing that Alvarez was in the El Diablo Cartel, let alone that he liked me, was going dance with me, but now I knew that Chase would be aiming at him the entire time. I was already nervous enough!

Chase started to slow the car down as we turned a corner into a dusty but tree lined street. He pulled up in front of a walled complex, and showed me the gate. "Go ring the buzzer and you'll find him."

I looked at Chase, and he finally met my eye. "What are you going to do now?"

He gave me a tired smile. "I'll find a tree and perch up there for a while. Go." He leaned over and opened my door.

He was so close, I could smell the shampoo residue in his hair, and the raw scent of him mixed with expensive cologne. He paused, and I froze.

"Now?" I whispered.

"Yes." He was just inches away from me.

"Okay," I said, my tone breathy.

He put his hand on the back of my seat, and kissed me. "You look beautiful, Mack." He smiled slowly. "Seriously."

My heart stuttered. "Thanks."

I had to leave. It was too intense, and I needed to mentally prepare myself for Alvarez. I gave him a quick peck on the corner of his mouth. "Take care," I whispered as I got out of the car.

I waited at the gate to be buzzed in, glancing over my shoulder at Chase before I walked through. The garden was pristine and manicured, with a heap of trees. It was obvious that Alvarez had gardeners come in and do the work, as I doubted he would have the time to do it himself.

I walked up the pathway to a modest sized house. He opened the front door before I reached it.

"Ciara." He exhaled with a light sigh, kissing me lightly on the cheek. "How lovely to see you."

I smiled. "Likewise," I said as I followed him into the foyer. There was a small table displaying a large arrangement of blooming flowers, and I stopped to smell them.

Alvarez smiled as he watched me. "Ah, I see you have an appreciation for the more beautiful things in life."

"Mmmm," I responded.

He touched my bare elbow. "Come through to the kitchen."

I followed him through a set of double doors, and stepped into an expansive kitchen full of light. "Nice place," I said genuinely.

"Thank you." He smiled as he pulled two glasses from a large rack that sat above the bar area. "Wine?"

I nodded, looking around. There was a dining nook at the far end of the kitchen, with French doors that opened onto a bricked patio area. Seating was placed out there with large bright cushions, for people enjoy the garden.

"This house belonged to my parents. It was one of their smaller properties. I moved in when I was eighteen." He shrugged. "And I guess I never really left."

I smiled. "Your parents had good taste." I perched on one of the barstools, and took my glass of white from him.

"Yes, I thought so." He laughed. "I do feel at home here, I must admit."

"What sort of work did your parents do?"

He took a sip of his wine before answering me. "Oh, imports and exports. You know - that sort of thing."

Oh boy, I thought. I fixed a smile on my face. "Looks like it was a lucrative business," I commented. "My parents were fairly boring. My dad was an accountant, and my mother was a housewife."

He laughed. "I'm sure they were more interesting than just that. Tell me - what do you do Ciara?"

"Me?" I took a sip of wine and gave him a small smile. "I'm a historian."

"A historian? Well I would never have guessed it."

He chuckled. "You don't look like one."

"Really? Well obviously I love Egyptian history." I patted my Cleopatra styled hair. "Mostly I research early civilisations, human migration, and war history."

Alvarez paused, looking thoughtful for a few moments. "And what brings you here to Mexico?"

I shrugged. "Holiday mainly. My brother, Davin? You met him the other day."

Alvarez nodded.

"Anyway, he's working here at the moment. Lucero and I decided to come out for a holiday. We were meant to be travelling down to Brazil, and spending some time in Rio de Janeiro, but that hasn't exactly panned out."

"Why is that?"

I shrugged, and played with the stem of my wine glass. "Davin has him working at the moment."

"Tell me, what line of work is your brother in?"

I had to think of the answer for a second. "Mergers and acquisitions, mainly. He's working with some companies here while they expand. That's why we were at the ball the other night. I think Davin and Lucero are trying to get some political influencers on-board with them."

Alvarez chuckled. "Aren't we all," he said, taking a sip of wine, amusement dancing in his eyes.

"So, now that you know all about me - what about you?" I asked. "What sort of work do you do?"

"I have a security company," he said simply.

"Yeah?"

He nodded. "I provide security to all sorts of people. Dignitaries, politicians, and so on. Anyone who wants to pay me."

"Do you do it all by yourself?"

He laughed. "No, no, Ciara. I have a large team that work for me. Surely you have noticed how dangerous Mexico is while you have been here?"

I nodded. "Sort of. I haven't been exposed too much since I've been here, but I hear and read things through the news."

"And yet you chose to come here," he said good naturedly.

The more I looked at Alvarez, with his laughing eyes, the harder time I had believing he was a member of the El Diablo Cartel. He just seemed so genuine and real. He wasn't pretentious at all like Javier was. He didn't seem power hungry or money driven. And he lived in modest but nice surroundings. He just didn't fit the profile.

"Do you mind if I have a cigarette?" I asked, pointing out to the garden.

He shook his head. "Not at all. Come." He walked over to the French doors. "Enjoy my little piece of paradise."

As I lit a cigarette, I peered out towards the garden and lowered my sunglasses over my eyes. I didn't want Alvarez following my line of sight as I looked in the branches of the trees, wondering where

Chase was.

I couldn't see him. Alvarez was still talking to me about the garden, and how his mother planted most of it. He liked to keep the garden in the same condition she always left it in, with the plants she loved.

"I'm not exactly... how do you say it? Green handed?"

"Fingered. Green-fingered," I clarified with a giggle.

He laughed. "That too."

"Guess you really love your mother then, huh?"

He nodded. "Of course. Everyone loves their mother. But mine passed on some years ago. Now I celebrate her life with a garden she loved."

See, now after a statement like that, I was actually questioning whether or not this guy had enough badness in his heart to even consider joining a cartel. Maybe he was just on Regina's security detail, or maybe he was at the ball protecting someone. Maybe... just maybe... we had the wrong Intel on this guy. He was too genuine and kind hearted.

"Well it's a beautiful celebration," I admired.

Alvarez turned to me, smiling. "Are you able to stay for dinner, Ciara?"

I swallowed, and looked shyly up at him. "Yes?" I found a place to stub my cigarette out without making too much of a mess since he was so proud of his garden and all. "I guess so. I'm not exactly expected home any time soon. Both Lucero and Davin are meeting with people."

Alvarez clapped his hands together. "Wonderful."

I followed him inside to his kitchen, where I put my half-empty wine glass on the counter. I perched on a barstool, while he used an intercom. He was speaking in fast Spanish, but I heard my name mentioned.

When he finished, he walked across and leaned on the counter. "Are you hungry now?"

I shrugged. "Yes, I guess so. It's been a long day." Damn right it had. Starting with a ridiculously early wakeup call from Chase wanting to go for a swim. I rubbed the back of my neck, only just realising how tired I actually was.

Alvarez looked at me with sympathy in his eyes. “Tell you what,” he said as he walked around the counter. “Why don’t you go and relax in the lounge–” He picked up my glass of wine– “and dinner will be here shortly. We can dance later.”

I paused. “Here shortly?”

He laughed. “I don’t cook much. I don’t have the time, so I have someone here who cooks for me.”

“Here in the house?”

He shook his head. “No - there is a cottage out the back where they live. It’s just you and me here.”

And Chase... somewhere out in the trees apparently. I sighed as I considered Alvarez’ offer. Relaxing actually sounded pretty good. I gave him my hand, and got off the barstool. "Relaxing and dinner sounds lovely."

He led me through to his living room, where an enormous sixty-odd inch TV was mounted on the wall. Leather sofas with chaises sat in front of it, and the large bar was surrounded by an extensive DVD collection on the back wall. This was most definitely a man-pad. I walked over to the DVD collection, and brushed my fingers along the spines as he stood back and watched me. A load of them were in Spanish, but there were a few blockbusters in English.

"You like films?"

I nodded. "Yeah. I love them. Stories I can experience in a couple of hours."

He turned on the TV to show a range of video camera shots of the house and surrounding areas. I pushed down my panic, thinking of Chase. "Gosh," I choked out. "That's a lot of cameras."

Alvarez smiled over at me. "Yes, Well, I am in the security business, and my home is my testing place." He changed the channel, and an old black and white movie came on. He patted the leather upholstery. "Come sit down." I did as I was told, and he handed me the remote. "Just make yourself at home. I'll be back shortly - just going to check on dinner."

He left me in front of the TV. Something told me that if he had cameras everywhere outside, he probably had them inside as well. I didn't want to look around though, just in case I spotted one. It was better that I acted completely normal. I didn't even want to check my phone, just in case there was a message on there. I knew how effective Gabe's cameras were, and how he could zoom in on the minutest detail.

I unexpectedly remembered the brooch I was wearing and gently fingered it; but again, I knew that it would probably look weird to someone if I suddenly started talking to it. Instead I left it alone, and examined the remote. I pressed down a channel, and a movie was playing that I recognised: The Sound of Music. I took a sip of my wine, and settled back into the sofa, listening to Maria sing her heart out on a hilltop with a bunch of children.

I suddenly woke up, fumbling around for my phone. Someone had covered me in a blanket. The room was dark, and it took a few moments for me to orientate myself. I was still in Alvarez's living room.

"Holy shit," I muttered. I found my phone tucked into my bra where I had last left it, and looked at the time. "Fuck," I swore. I had been asleep for hours. I suddenly wondered why Chase hadn't come and got me out already. One of my shoes had fallen to the floor during my slumber, and I fumbled as I put it on.

I could hear voices and I froze. I looked over to the double sliding doors, and could see light shining under from the kitchen. My heart raced. I had no idea who was there. I didn't know what to do. I questioned whether I should sneak out or not, but then changed my mind. It would be too suspicious if I did.

I put my head in my hands, and thanked my lucky stars that I always pinned my wigs nice and securely to my head. I brushed the hair a bit through my fingers, and tried to make myself look at least a little bit presentable. My dress was slightly skewed when I stood up, and I straightened that out before I crept across the plush carpets towards the double sliding doors.

Two male voices were behind the door, one I recognised. Unfortunately, they weren't speaking in English, so I could hardly understand a thing they were saying.

I really didn't want to open the doors and be exposed to god knew what. So I crossed back to the other side of the room, and hissed into the brooch. "Get me out of here." I just had to hope and pray that they would be listening at the other end of it. "It's now or never," I murmured to myself in the dark.

I crossed the room noisily, and when I had almost reached the doors, I heard the conversation stop on the other side. I slid the doors open, blinking in the bright light.

"Ciara," Alvarez said warmly.

I took in the sight of him, half undressed, with only a plush white towel wrapped around his waist. The first thing I noticed was that the man was incredibly well built. The second thing was that there were extensive tattoos covered one side of his body, all the way from below his navel up to his left pec. His hair was damp, so I made an educated guess that either he had been for a shower or a swim. Another man was sitting at the counter with his back turned to me. Two beers were open between them.

Alvarez gestured me into the room. "Come in, come in," he smiled. "This is my friend Jose." He gestured.

I smiled, and held out my hand. As the man looked up at me standing there, I suddenly recognised him. I had just come face to face with Alicio Mendoza.

13

Alicio looked at me and took my hand. I tried to settle my raging thoughts into a sea of calmness, but it was hard to do that when I was holding the hand of a killer who disposed of bodies in vats of acid.

"Nice to meet you," I said. I could hear the tremor in my voice, but he didn't show any signs of hearing it.

"You too," he said in thick English.

Just then, my phone rang, and I fished it out of my bra, much to Alvarez's amusement.

"Hello?"

"Ciara," River's voice came down the phone. Relief swept through me.

"Hi." I said tightly.

"Where are you?" I could tell he was asking me this just in case they could hear my conversation.

"I'm still at Alvarez's place." I chewed on my lip. "I'll head home soon."

Alvarez was watching me, but Alicio was ignoring me, and slugging back his beer.

"Make sure you are," River answered. "We have an early start in the morning."

"See you soon." I hung up the phone, and smiled with a shrug at Alvarez. "I guess we have to postpone our dancing lesson to another day, then?"

He shrugged, and looked down at his beer. "Yes, we'll do that." He looked forlorn, and I felt sorry for him until I remembered that Alicio Mendoza was sitting across from him.

Alvarez picked up my purse from the counter and handed it to me. As he lifted his arm, I saw something I recognised inked on him. It was another panther, almost identical to the one on Nicandro's body. I paused, and Alvarez saw me looking at him.

"Sorry," I muttered, embarrassed.

Alvarez laughed. "No, no, look all you like."

"It's just..." I semi-stuttered, whilst trying to compose myself. "The work you've had done... it's very tasteful." I wasn't lying when I said it. I'm not a big fan of tattoos, but a lot of his looked like they were from the Aztec culture. That appealed to my historian side. I was curious.

He shrugged, still amused by me. "One day I'll tell

you what it all means."

I grinned. "Deal." I opened up my purse and dropped my phone inside. "I'll call you?"

"Please." He smiled.

If it weren't for the fact that he had a cold-blooded killer sitting in his kitchen, I would have thought he was one of the nicest men I'd ever met.

He touched my elbow. "I'll walk you out." But he wasn't looking at me when he said it - he was looking at Mendoza. I saw a sort of fierceness in his eyes that I had never seen before. It was almost as if he were protective if me.

"Thanks." I turned to Alicio. "Nice to meet you, Jose."

His eyes met mine, and he gave me a slow smile that crept down my body with appreciation. Before he could say anything, Alvarez was shuffling me out the door.

"Sorry about my friend..." Alvarez said quietly when we stepped into the night air and out of earshot. "He doesn't get out much."

I smiled up at Alvarez. "And I'm sorry for falling asleep on you," I said changing the subject. "It can't have been much fun."

He shrugged. "No bother. You obviously needed it." He moved closer to me, leant over and kissed me gently on the cheek.

I froze. "I did," I whispered. I was faced with his pecs.

And then he lifted my chin so that I looked him straight in the eyes, and kissed me again, his lips crushing mine. There was absolutely no doubt in my mind what he wanted. I pulled away from him and shook my head. "I'm sorry. I better go."

I started walking towards the gate.

"Ciara," he called out.

I turned to look at him standing there, bathed in moonlight. "Yeah?"

"Please take care of yourself."

I nodded. "Of course." I laughed lightly, and gave him a little wave. "I'll call you."

I pressed the gate release button, and closed it behind me. I walked down the road to the parked Dodge Charger, unlocked it with the set of keys Chase had given me, and climbed behind the driver's wheel. I knew that Alvarez would probably have his cameras trained on the car, so I started the engine with a press of the button, did a U-turn, and started driving down the road. Five hundred yards down the road, a shadow leapt down from a wall, and ran out across the road in front of me.

I recognised Chase, and slowed the car down while unlocking the doors. He hopped into the passenger seat beside me.

“Alicio Mendoza,” I said as soon as he closed the door. “He was there. In Alvarez’s house.”

“Yeah, I know. I saw him. That was why I couldn’t take Alvarez out. There were a heck of a lot more people from the cartel on that property as well. Seems that Alvarez has a few people living there with him."

I shook my head. "But I didn't see anyone else. Are you sure?"

"Positive, Mack. I was up a tree. You fell asleep. People came and went while you were out to it. Alicio came from the other house on the property. Obviously, this is where he has been hiding out since he got here, which explains why we couldn't find him."

"He scared me... there was just... I dunno. Something about him. He's not like Alvarez who is charming. He's dark." My voice was quiet. I looked over at him, and groaned. Chase looked exhausted. "Oh god, Chase, I'm sorry. You must have been stuck up that tree for ages."

"It doesn't matter." He brushed my comment off. "You're fine, I'm fine, everyone's fine."

"Yeah," I agreed. "Everyone's fine." I leant over, rifling around for my purse. All I succeeded in doing though was grabbing at Chase's leg.

"Settle down, Tiger." He laughed. "If you want me that bad, you should have started a little higher up."

I blushed in the darkness of the car. "I was trying to find my purse," I responded through gritted teeth. "Stop being so bloody presumptuous."

"No harm in trying." He chuckled as he handed me a cigarette and the lighter from my purse.

I lit it, and wound the window down. "Don't you

mind me smoking in your car?"

He shrugged. "There are times when I have to smoke while on the job. So, no, not really."

"And here I was thinking it was because you liked me," I joked.

Silence met me from the passenger seat, and I looked over at him. His expression was unreadable.

"Pull over," he said quietly.

I pulled the car over, thinking that he wanted to drive or something. I undid my seatbelt, but he grabbed my arm.

"Mack." He switched the light on overhead, and turned my chin so that I was facing him. His eyes searched mine. "I do like you." His voice was a whisper. "Very much."

I pulled back from him, and took a puff from the cigarette in my hand. I blew the smoke out slowly, but my heart raced.

"Shit," he muttered. Then he reached for my brooch, and fiddled with the back of it for a second. "There," he muttered. "It's off. Jesus." He sighed, shaking his head. "There's never any bloody privacy in this line of work."

I pointed at the brooch, and then looked at Chase. "They were listening?"

He shrugged. "Who knows. Possibly." He licked his lips, and turned back towards me. "So... have you got anything to say?"

I shook my head slowly. "Not really." I was too

sober for this conversation. I was better having chats like this once I'd had a few glasses of wine. "No..."

"Well, let me tell you something then. I haven't had a relationship... not a real one anyway," he corrected, "not for six years. But when you came along I started to see a different sort of future."

I looked at him in surprise. "What?"

He sighed, running his hands through his hair. "I told you, Mack, I saw something unique in you. You may not see it, but you are genuine, kind-hearted, determined, bold, and yet you've just been fucked over by your Ex so your confidence is shot to hell."

I pursed my lips, refused to look at him, and stared dead ahead. He was right. My confidence was shot to hell. I didn't know if it had ever really been there. It all seemed like a façade while I was with Luke.

He linked his fingers through those of my free hand.

"But you were such an arse when we first met... and then when we got out here, you were an even bigger arsehole. What the hell was that about?" I asked.

He sighed. "I'm always like that. I'm sorry... I treat people..." He paused. "I don't know. I guess I throw up barriers with people until I get to know them."

I shook my head, and threw my cigarette out the window. Then I turned to him. Something inside me flip-flopped when his gaze met mine. "You were so cold and arrogant... it was such a change when you finally started talking to me normally." I shrugged. "I just don't know what to make of you, Chase."

"Why?"

I shrugged and let go of his hand. "I think we have a connection, but I don't know if that's enough. Besides, I could be dead in a week. We just don't know."

He shook his head. "No you won't. You know how I know?"

I just looked at him.

"Because," he continued, "You have one of the best assassination teams in the world behind you, and we won't let you get hurt."

I shook my head. "You can't guarantee that."

He took a deep breath and paused. "I don't have a problem tracking her down and killing her now if you like. But River thinks you should do it yourself." He reached for my hand again, and I let him take it. "And you know what? I think he's right. You'll never have inner peace unless you do it yourself."

I exhaled the breath I was holding.

"In the meantime ... let me love you."

My resolve crumbled, and I reached for him.

14

I woke up tangled in my sheets, smiling. I never woke up smiling ... but today I did. I had put the stern word on Chase in the car, and told him that if we were going to head towards a relationship, then we needed to take it slowly. He'd been out of the relationship game a long time, and I hadn't been out long enough.

I knew it was my head talking, not my heart ... but after a speech like the one he gave me, I just couldn't help it. I don't know many people who could have resisted that.

I untangled myself from the sheet, and shot through the shower.

Dressed in my training clothes, I felt energised. It was because of him. I, for one, couldn't help but smile.

I was even smiling at my reflection as I brushed my teeth. I took extra care applying minimal make up before I even left my room, which was something I never would have done in the past. And I smelled great, perfumed in my favourite Ralph Lauren scent. Another thing I wouldn't ever have done unless I was attending some sort of party. I actually felt more alive and ready to take on the world than ever before.

I bounced out to the kitchen and poured myself coffee from the freshly brewed pot. I could hear the others in the training room working out and doing whatever it was that they were so inclined to do at this early hour of the morning.

I took my coffee outside in the morning air, lit a cigarette, and sat down on the lounger. The sun wasn't quite up yet, but it was lovely and warm. It was going to be another stunning Mexican day.

Nothing could dampen my mood. Even the thought of Carmen hunting me down wasn't worrying me. It was amazing.

I opened emails on my phone, and started deleting the junk. Then I saw another email from Luke's lawyers.

"Bugger," I muttered as I opened it.

Dear Miss Carmichael,

On the 25 October, we wrote to you in regard to our concerns surrounding the debt you owe our client, Luke Sommers. In that correspondence, we asked that you get in touch with us by close of business, October 30th.

It has since been one working day from that date, and we have yet to hear from you.

As previously advised, this matter will be going to the courts. We will give you until the 1st November to respond to this notification, or this matter will go before a judge.

I look forward to hearing from you.

Yours sincerely,

Theodore Olsen

Solicitor

"Shit," I swore darkly. "Shit, shit, shit." I exited out of my email, and looked at the date on my phone. 1st November. I put my hands in my hair, and closed my eyes. This was a nightmare. I had meant to email him back, but suddenly everything had snowballed out of control. I should have just done it then and there, but I needed time to try and gather my thoughts. "Idiot," I muttered, slapping my head. How could I have been so stupid as to not respond? Just when life seemed on top of the world with Chase, that arsehole Luke and his legal team had to bring it crashing back down.

I threw my cigarette into the ashtray beside the door, and stomped inside. I didn't have a choice now. I had to ask Chase, River, and Gabe for help.

What a way to put a damper on my new relationship with Chase. "God," I whispered. The sooner Luke was out of my fucking life, the better. He was an arsehole, and I so didn't need his shit right now.

It was so bloody ballsy of him to involve lawyers, especially when it came down to the fact that my aunt had signed her house over to me - not both of us. He knew I was going to fold. Luke was using what I held most precious to me - a stable home - against me. All for the sake of fucking money. Luke still had power over me. And that made me angry. I made myself angry with the fact that I was reacting this way. I should have just dealt with it straight away. How could I forget?

If he was here right now, I would shoot him myself.

But he wasn't ... and when I thought about it, I doubted I could shoot him, either. As much as I hated Luke at the moment, I didn't actually want him to die. Maybe I just wanted to hit him.

Chase walked into the kitchen, soaked in perspiration, as I was rinsing and scrubbing the shit out of my cup while I thought about Luke and what the hell I was going to do. This was my fault as well.

He sidled up to me, and kissed me on my neck. I felt myself go weak at the knees, and I turned to him, a smile creeping back onto my features. "Good morning," I said as my lips met his.

He eyed up the cup curiously as he kissed me back. "What did it do to you?"

I looked down at it, and put it on the bench. "Um." I bit my lip. "Actually ... I have a bit of a favour to ask. Not a bit of one, I guess it's a big one."

"Anything." He grinned as he leaned in to kiss me again. "Anything you like."

I rolled my eyes. "Well..." I gently pushed him away, and stepped back slightly. I ran my hands through my hair again. "It's just that I have been receiving some correspondence from Luke. Actually, not him, per se... His lawyer." I swallowed. I didn't want to ask Chase for help, but I was stuck between a rock and a hard place.

Chase's mouth was set in a hard line. "What do you need, Mack?"

I couldn't look at him. I blew out a breath I didn't even know I was holding. "I need to pay him, or else this is going to court. And if it goes to court..." I leaned down on the counter with my head in my hands. "If it goes to court, they are probably going to question why I'm 'holidaying' in Mexico while I owe him a shitload of money."

"How much?"

"Almost six hundred thousand," I muttered. "Half my house, and living expenses incurred from the care of my aunt and me, apparently."

Chase crossed his arms, and looked at me thoughtfully. "How much have you already got?"

I shrugged. "I don't know. You guys paid me four hundred thousand for the initial job out here. So there is that, minus the debt I have already paid on my credit cards and the care costs for Elsie. So there is probably–" I paused and counted it up in my head. "I don't know... maybe three hundred and fifty odd left?"

Chase nodded, and stayed quiet for a few moments. He crossed the kitchen to me, putting his hands reassuringly on my arms. "Listen. I understand what a bind this has you in ... I'll tell you what. You pay Luke what you have, and I will top up the remaining amount out of my personal account."

"But–"

"No, Mack. I'm serious. But you'll have to do a few things in return for me. I'm not doing this for nothing."

I nodded, but stayed quiet. I didn't want to be indebted to him, but I didn't want him to change his mind either.

"You'll accompany and assist me on at least three more jobs. But on the third, I want you to do the job yourself."

'Me?" I squeaked. I got the shakes just thinking about killing someone. I didn't know if I could willingly take someone's life without really knowing why.

But these people were bad people. I knew that. If I took a life on this job, I would probably be saving thousands of countless other innocent lives in the process. That was really the only justification I could come up with. I looked at him and saw the intensity in his eyes as he watched me process it. I nodded. "Okay. It's a deal." I held out my hand for him to shake, but instead, he moved closer and kissed me. Intensely. Passionately.

"Deal," he murmured.

15

Gabe uploaded a bunch of photos of the kills to his database while I watched over his shoulder. He was such a demon on the computer, and he was so fast! I didn't know how he could operate that quickly, but he did.

When he had finished, he logged into my accounts, and did the transfer to Luke's accounts. True to his word, Chase had wired the money into mine, and it was all sitting there, ready to go.

"God," I groaned when it was done. There was only a few thousand left in my account. I was going to be doubly screwed by the time we got back to England if I couldn't make the kill Chase wanted me to. A few thousand was definitely not going to cover the next quarterly instalment for my aunt's care.

I emailed both the lawyer and Luke at the same time, and said that the money had been wired through in full, and that there was to be no further communication to me from either of them. I never ever wanted to see or hear from Luke again. He had right royally fucked me in every way possible, and I was cutting him off. As far as I was concerned, this was done and dusted. Luke was damn lucky I had Chase to back me up.

I rested my head on the table. I had no job to go back to, and no money. I was right back to square one. But at least I was free of that arsehole.

When I looked up, I saw images of the bodies on screen from the kills on the screen. Weirdly, looking at those images now, I felt quite detached from the whole operation. Each of those bodies was a pay cheque. One of the future bodies would be my pay cheque according to Chase. I had to make that kill.

"Impressive, isn't it?" Gabe commented. "We've got seven more to go, and then we're out of here."

River came into the dining room at that moment, and sat down. "How are we going?" he asked Gabe.

Gabe nodded. "Good. I was just saying we have seven more to go. I've uploaded the images through to the client, and I guess we're going to start seeing some money shortly."

River nodded. "Good." He turned his focus to me. "You all right, Mack?"

"Yeah, I guess so."

River gave me a knowing smile. "You know - we can help you out when we get back if you want. He'll never be a problem again. Free of charge," he added.

I shook my head. "No. No way. It doesn't matter how pissed I am at him right now, he's not really that bad."

He shrugged. "Your decision."

I smiled. "Thanks anyway. It's nice to know you have my back if I need it."

"You're part of the family now, Mack. You'd do the same for us."

"Damn right I would." I grinned.

River slapped the table. "Ah...yes... I forgot the reason why I came in here in the first place. Chase asked if you could go and see him. He's in his room."

Just at the mention of his name, my heart skipped a beat. "Thanks," I mumbled, as I stood from the table.

As I left the room I overheard Gabe say. "Are they...um...?"

I grinned, not stopping to hear the answer.

I found Chase a few moments later. He was lying on his bed, reading a book, glasses slightly askew as if he'd been lying on them.

"Hi," I said shyly.

"Hi, yourself," he responded with a grin. I took in his dark hair, chiselled cheek bones, and bright aqua-coloured eyes. I guess I just couldn't believe that a man of his calibre could possibly see something in me.

I bit my lip as I stood there, unsure of what to say or do. "Um, thank you for your help," I said quietly. "Gabe helped me transfer the funds through to Luke."

Chase nodded with a lazy smile, and patted the bed next to him. "Any time ... Come sit."

I crossed the room to sit down beside him. He stretched out, and looked at me. "I think," he said slowly, "that this guy, Luke, probably won't stop just there. He could come back again..."

I inhaled. "God, I hope not." I shook my head. "I really hope not."

Chase tucked a strand of hair behind my ear. "I'm just warning you. From what I know of him ... which is a lot because Gabe did a background check on him ... it seems he has done this sort of thing before."

I looked at Chase sharply. "What? What do you mean?"

Chase shrugged. "You should get Gabe to give you the files so you can read through them yourself. But Luke did have a biggish settlement about seven odd years ago ... and it looked like a relationship settlement. Did he ever say anything?"

I tried to think back to when Luke and I were first dating, but I couldn't remember a time when he mentioned any settlement. He had come out of a relationship with a woman named Eliza, but apparently she'd left him. I shook my head. "I don't remember anything like that."

"Hmmm," Chase said, his eyes fixed on mine. "Well, whatever happens... we can sort it out later." He smiled, and pulled me on top of him. "Plenty of time for that," he murmured, his eyes fixed on my lips.

I felt a shiver ripple through me, and my stomach exploded with butterflies. "Hopefully." I let him pull me down for a kiss. He suddenly flipped me onto my back, and was on top of me in an instant. I felt a thrill go through me, and I laughed. "Is that all you asked me in for?"

He shook his head with a cheeky smile on his face. "No ..." He slowly kissed me, his breathing becoming ragged. I could tell he was holding back. And I loved it. It was like savouring dessert. "I had other plans, too."

I laughed, and gently pushed him away from me. "I can tell!"

He rolled off to the side, and got comfy, holding his head up with one hand, leaving the other one to rove across my body. "Oh, don't you worry," he whispered. "I have plenty of plans for you and me." He cleared his throat. "Starting with..." He leaned down and kissed me, his hand brushing over the curve of my breast. "That." His hand trailed down and caressed my side, and he gently pushed me under him again, leaning down to kiss my breasts. "And then there's this," he murmured. Before I knew it, he had unbuttoned my shirt, exposing my bra.

"Quite clever, aren't you?" I teased.

“I am.” He laughed as he started to sit up. “But now, we should probably go out and do some work for the day.”

"What? You're not going to finish what you started?" I gestured at myself.

"Plenty of time for that later." He winked as he pulled me up. "Come on. Get yourself sorted. We have to go and meet a woman named Paulina."

I gave him a sidelong look, and slid off the bed. "Paulina?"

"Yes," he said, “We have a job to do.” I groaned. I wanted nothing more than to stay put and snuggle up with Chase. This day had been taxing already with having to sort Luke's stuff out. "Can't we just stay here?"

He smiled, leaned over and kissed me just below my ear. "Another time, perhaps." He stood and turned to me, giving me an assessing look. "Red haired wig, I think. And dress in something smart but casual."

I rolled my eyes. "Bloody hell," I grumbled.

He tapped my backside playfully as I swept past him and out of the room and up the hall to my own. I closed the door with a silly grin on my face, crossed to my wardrobe, and looked at it thoughtfully. I settled on keeping my white shirt on, but upgraded my pants to skinny jeans. I slipped high-heels on, and walked into my bathroom.

I brushed my hair, and fixed the red wig to my scalp. Once it was on nice and tightly, I leaned on the hand-basin, and stared at myself in the mirror, blowing out a deep breath that fogged my reflection in the glass.

I couldn't believe that I had become so accustomed to being out on kill jobs; I no longer batted an eyelid when I was instructed to get ready. I didn't know how I had finally come to this reality, but the life I was currently living... well it had its thrills that went along with the kills.

The targets weren't good people though. I didn't know if that meant they deserved to die, but it was better than letting them carry on with doing what they were doing and destroying innocent lives.

I put on a little bit of make-up, and then deemed myself ready to go out in public.

I grabbed my leather jacket, even though I didn't really need it, and a handbag that held my precious gold phone, my cigarettes, and Ciara's identification.

I met Chase in the dining room, sitting down with River and Gabe.

River was about to head out on a job too... some woman named Paz. I had no idea what sort of name 'Paz' was, but it sounded butch to me.

"There are a lot of women involved in this organisation, aren't there?"

Gabe smiled. "Yes. There are. The cartel backs beauty queens, and primes them for employment. Once they win their titles, they're recruited properly into the cartel. Some of them climb to high places fast

... others don't." He shrugged and turned the screen in front of him to face me. "This is Paz," he stated. "She was Miss Venezuela five years ago."

The woman on the screen was definitely beautiful. But then as I looked closer, I saw something very different. She had a large scar that ran from near her ear, down over her cheek bone, almost to the corner of her mouth. Her eyes were cold and hard, and she looked like as much of a hard-arse as I'd predicted. "That's a hell of a scar."

River nodded. "Sure is. According to her medical records and police statement, her face was cut open by her father not long after she won her title and moved up here."

I pursed my lips thoughtfully. "Maybe he didn't like her new line of work."

"Dead right," Gabe said, turning the screen back towards him. "Her father is actually the cocaine exporter for the El Diablo Cartel. It looked as though Paz's twin brother was the one being primed to step into the El Diablo Cartel to be the main contact for the export. Paz was recruited instead."

I shook my head. It was all so political, yet so brutal.

Ten minutes later, Chase and I were in the car driving towards Tijuana. "So, what's the plan with this Paulina woman then?"

Chase smiled at me, linking his fingers between mine. "Paulina? I predict that she's probably going to commit suicide."

"Suicide? Really?"

He nodded. "Yeah. Paulina is quite depressed at the moment. We're going to go and pay our condolences, and hopefully slip her something to help make her more comfortable. River was tracking her last night. Apparently she drank herself into a very public and sorry state. River took her home, and ended up putting her to bed."

I had to laugh. "While you were stuck up a tree and I was asleep on the job?"

He grinned. "Precisely. Anyway," he continued, "her partner was recently found dead, and she announced last night to everyone in the bar that she couldn't live without him. That's why suicide is going to be the ruling kill today."

My heart went out to her. "He died? How?"

Chase turned to me. "You know how, Mack. It was Nicandro."

My stomach plummeted. "Oh my God." I thought of Nicandro under the sheets with me, and I grimaced. "But he was so willing to cheat on her with me," I muttered. She obviously loved him; I had to wonder if it was unrequited.

Chase was focussed on the road ahead of us, but squeezed my hand. "Apparently that was quite the norm for him." He gave me a fleeting smile. "If what Paulina said last night was true, Nicandro was pulling away from her anyway, and Paulina was trying to trap him back into the relationship by trying to get pregnant."

"Oldest trick in the book," I muttered darkly. I hated women like that, who didn't have enough dignity to get up and walk away. And then I thought about my recent situation with Luke. Never once had I considered having children with him. He was never the 'Daddy' type. I hadn't even seen a wedding in our future.

I shook my head. Perhaps deep down I already knew that Luke wasn't going to stick around, but yet I'd kept playing happy families with him anyway.

Chase pulled the car over in a quiet street lined with shorter apartment buildings. There were hardly any cars parked on the roadside, as they were probably all hidden away in underground residential parking.

I grabbed Chase's arm just before he got out of the car. "Wait a second," I said as he turned back at me surprised. "What role does this woman play in the El Diablo Cartel? Surely we're not killing her only because of Nicandro?"

"No." Chase smiled. "Paulina is Nicandro's second in command... she's now leading Strategic Relations, managing all of the political influences of the cartel, and the military control."

"They worked together?"

"Yeah. And we always knew that once Nicandro died she was primed and ready to step in immediately."

I got out of the car. "Wow," I muttered, falling into step with Chase as we crossed the road. I couldn't imagine ever having that much power or the political savvy to manage a job like that. "And she was in love with him?"

"Appears so." He smiled. "Follow my lead, chica. We're going in there to pay our condolences, slip her something, and then get out again."

We stepped into the elevator and rode three floors up to the penthouse apartment. Chase knocked on the door, and a maid answered.

"Estamos aquí para ver Paulina Silva."

The maid looked at Chase curiously and asked who they were. From what I could understand from my poor Spanish, he said that we were here to give Paulina our condolences.

The maid turned on her heel abruptly, and we followed her inside to the foyer. "We'll wait here," Chase said putting his hand on my arm to stop me from following the maid right into the apartment.

“There's no security or anything,” I whispered, my heart beating fast with nervousness.

“Probably no need.” Chase's hand lingered for a few moments before it made its way down to the small of my back and settled there.

The maid returned a moment later. "Sígueme," she instructed, and we trailed after her. The apartment was gorgeous and expansive, with floor to ceiling glass. It was furnished with expensive pieces of artwork, sheer flowing curtains, rugs, and exceptionally tasteful furniture. This woman lived in the epitome of opulence.

When we were shown into the sitting room, we found a beautiful woman in there, lying back on a French chaise. I recognised her as the same woman who was dressed in red at the ball, hanging off Nicandro's arm. But this morning she had red, puffy eyes, and she was dressed only in a flimsy white dressing gown, giving me the impression that she'd just got out of bed.

"Señora mía," Chase said respectfully. "Mi nombre es Davin, y esta es mi hermana Ciara. Yo era un viejo amigo de Nicandro."

Her eyebrows rose up at the mention of me, and I assumed Chase had introduced us.

"You are English, no?" Her accent was thick, but her English was very clear.

Chase nodded. "Yes." I could almost sense the relief from him that he didn't need to speak Spanish anymore.

"So, you worked with Nicandro?"

Chase shook his head. "No. I met him when he was in America, and we kept in contact over the years."

She nodded, her eyes misting over. "So you have heard the bad news..." She trailed off, and sniffed.

Chase gestured for me to sit on one of the cream

covered seats, and he sat down on the other. "Yes," he said quietly. "He spoke most fondly of you, and so I thought we should pay our respects."

"Ha!" She laughed. "He was a great one for fondness," she said sarcastically. She then waved her hand. "I'm sorry. I apologise. As you can tell, I am feeling... how do you say it? A bit under the weather?" She pulled out a tissue and dabbed delicately at her nose and eyes.

Chase smiled warmly at her. "You have had a rough time," he said, his voice caring. "Nicandro was a good man, Ms Silva."

She nodded, her dyed blonde ringlets bouncing limply around her features. "Yes. Yes he was." She sighed. "I have been trying to organise his funeral, actually. Very stressful," she whispered. "He has only been gone a few days, and I miss him."

As she reached for a tissue, I saw just how hard she was taking Nicandro's death. Guilt licked at the edges of my empathy for this woman... and then I quashed it. This was Nicandro's partner in crime. They both 'managed' the police and the politicians. They were both responsible for public relations, for information, and they both technically worked for Javier and Carmen. God only knew what sort of damage they had done over the years.

"I love your hair, Ciara..." Paulina said, instantly drawing me back to reality. "Is that your natural colouring?"

I shook my head. "No. I get it coloured." I fingered the long dark red tresses between my fingers. "But thank you." I smiled.

"Did you also know my Nicandro?"

"No. I had only ever heard about him from Davin."

She shrugged. "He would have liked you," she said simply.

The maid came back in, and brought with her a tray laden with coffee and cups. Paulina dismissed her from the room, and turned to cast her eye appreciatively over Chase. "So tell me, Davin, what other business brings you to Mexico?"

Chase gave her a winning smile. "The usual," he said flippantly. "Contacts, friends, and loved ones."

Paulina poured the coffee into the cups, and turned her sharp brown eyes back to Chase. "Contacts? You wish to build further relationships, yes?"

He nodded, and I watched Paulina smile.

"Well perhaps I can assist you with that." She winked.

It suddenly dawned on me that despite the fact that the supposed love of her life wasn't even in the ground yet, she was hitting on Chase. I almost bristled. In fact I did bristle slightly... I just hoped that she didn't notice.

Her eyes turned to me. "And do you accompany your brother often on business, Ciara?"

I wasn't sure how to respond. "Sometimes," I

answered thoughtfully. "But only when he goes to interesting places."

Paulina tinkled with laughter, and then lay back on the chaise as if she had exerted herself too much.

Chase immediately crossed to her. "Are you all right?"

She opened her eyes and turned her gaze back towards him. "I'm a little lightheaded."

He checked her temperature with the back of his hand against her forehead. "Can I get you anything?" His voice was full of concern. "If you want, we can come back and visit later."

She shook her head. "No, no. I like the company." She smiled lazily at him. "It is lonely when I am by myself."

Chase smiled down at her. "We'll stay a little longer then. Now, would you like a glass of water or anything?"

She smiled. "Such a gentleman ... Water would be lovely." Chase turned and started walking from the room. "And ask Amora for my medication as well, please?"

She turned back to me once Chase had left the room. "Your brother is a very handsome man. Is he married?"

I shook my head.

"Many women?"

Again I shook my head and smiled. "Not lately."

She nodded, her features lighting up. "Good."

I felt sick just thinking about the possibility of them together, but I knew that this was all an act for Chase. A ruse to get her to like him, to trust him.

Chase returned a few moments later carrying a large glass of water. He also had a small porcelain dish in his hand, containing a number of tablets. He passed her the dish, and without even looking at the pills, she dropped them down her throat and gulped back some water.

Chase grabbed her hand. "I'm sorry, Paulina, I've had a call and we must go. I would love to catch up with you later though if you're free?"

Paulina smiled, captivated by his attention. "How about dinner?"

Chase chuckled, and kissed her gently on the cheek. "I'll pick you up at eight."

Paulina wiggled her fingers at him as we let ourselves out of the apartment.

Once we got down to the car, and my heart rate had semi-regulated again, I turned to Chase. "Are you really going to have dinner with that woman?"

Chase laughed and started the engine. "God no. Ghastly. She'll be dead by then."

"She will?" I thought back to the medication Chase had given her. "I would highly doubt a few tablets of paracetamol are going to do much to her, Chase."

Chase shrugged, pulling the car out onto the road. "No, but the cyanide will."

16

“How was she?” River asked as soon as we walked through the door. I still couldn't believe that Chase had slipped her cyanide. I never would have thought to do something like that.

"She was sad..." I responded. "For a while anyway, until she started eyeing up Chase."

River laughed. "She was a bit like that last night too. One minute she was talking about not being able to live without Nicandro, and the next, she was groping my leg. It was about that time that I decided she should probably go home and sleep it all off."

"Guess it wasn't just the alcohol talking then." I laughed. I felt a sense of seriousness wash over me suddenly as I thought about that woman. "She was pretty upset though, to begin with. I could feel her pain, and I had to keep reminding myself that she's not a good person."

River shrugged, and put some of his paperwork down on the coffee table. "No, she wasn't. And if it makes you feel any better, she's the one encouraging the police to turn a blind eye to all of the blonde beheadings."

I stared at him, a calmness settling over me. "She is?"

River raised his eyebrows at me. "Yes. But now she is no longer our problem." He patted the paperwork beside him, and I caught a glimpse of profile pictures, and a heap of other writing surrounding them.

"What's that?"

"Possibly the next job that we'll take on. I don't know." He blew out a breath. "I need to run over it with Chase before we make a call on it."

A part of me itched to see what sort of people they were, and if they were bad enough to kill, but then I didn't want to know. Beyond Mexico, this wasn't going to be my life. I was going to head home to England, spend some time with my aunt, and settle back into a normal life. Without Luke.

"So..." River crossed his legs at the ankles and watched me carefully. “Alicio Mendoza is hiding out at Alvarez’s place. I was wondering why we couldn’t find a sign of him anywhere. How was that coming face to face with him?”

“Kind of scary,” I admitted. “He doesn’t look like a

very nice person on paper - but in the flesh ... he made my skin crawl."

River grimaced. "Well, his reputation does precede him. I'm glad we never got him on board with our operation. It could have been messy. We'll catch up to him when we plan the hit on Alvarez. Now that we know where he is - that will make it easier." He changed the subject, "So I found Osvaldo Corona this morning."

I looked at him blankly. "Corona who?"

River laughed at the confused look I gave him. "Yes, Corona. Like the beer. It's actually a very common last name around these parts. He was on our original list. He's the head of exports for the El Diablo Cartel. He's loading a big shipment as we speak."

"And?"

"And you and Chase need to come with me on the job. Osvaldo is a slippery prick at the best of times, and there will also be a few staff there."

Another job, already. I nodded slowly. "Does Chase know?" I looked towards the hallway. Chase had gone for a shower as soon as we got in. He had suggested that I join him, but I still felt a little odd about jumping in the shower with him, we'd barely hit second base.

"I'll text him about it once I spot Osvaldo."

I slapped my hands on my knees. "So I guess this means I need to go get ready, yeah? When are we leaving?"

"You're fine as you are, Mack. We'll leave once we're ready. I need you to come and help me down in the artillery room though."

It was a statement rather than a question. I stood and followed him to the hatch of the artillery room, then descended the spiral stairs. It was dark and cool down there, and to be quite frank, a relief from the constant Mexican heat.

River picked up two black bags, and hefted them up onto the steel table. "Go through those, and tell me what ones you like."

I hesitated before peering in. They were loaded with hand guns. I almost groaned, but forced myself to stop. River obviously needed my help with this job, or else he wouldn't be making me do this. I started pulling out the guns slowly, handling them, and then placing them carefully down on the table. I pulled out two small silver versions of Chase's Glocks, and gripped them in my hands. They actually felt quite comfortable. I looked at the writing etched into the sides of them: Smith & Wesson.

River looked up at me right at that moment. "You like those?"

I shrugged, and gave him a small nod.

He gave me an approving look. "Good choice. Small, light, can hold a cartridge." He reached over and took one from me. "And these ones even have a laser sight so it's easier to see where you're aiming." He turned the laser on, and pointed it around the room for me to see.

He handed back the gun. "Let me see if I can find the cartridges for those guns, and then they're all yours."

He was giving me guns? "To keep?"

River gave me a small smile. "Yes, to keep. You need to have your weapon of choice. I think you should probably be carrying at all times from now on. Especially since you've now met Alicio Mendoza."

I felt sick just at the mention of his name. "So are you going to give me any gun training with these?" I turned the guns over in my hands, eying them up.

River grinned. "Yes. Now, actually. I don't want you being unprepared. You may have shot a gun before, but a little training will go a long way."

I bit my lip, and looked up at him. He seemed to have faith that I could actually use these. "So, where are we going to train then?"

River lifted up two long black tubes from the table, and screwed them into each of the weapons. "Out in the garden. I don't have a gun range here, but with these silencers on, we'll be fine just as long as you can aim straight."

I cringed. That was something I could not guarantee.

On the way back to the house an hour later, River stopped and turned to me. "You should probably start watching Carmen if you can." He gave me a tired smile. "Get Gabe to track her accounts for you and you'll know where she's likely to go."

"Is that how you normally do it?"

River smiled. "It's one option. Usually the first anyway." He shrugged. "Electronic tracking is the easiest way. Everybody leaves digital footprints."

"Except me, at the moment." I laughed. "Well ... not since I've been here with you guys, anyway."

River gave me a knowing smile. "You would be surprised. Didn't you transfer a heap of money this morning to your Ex? Someone would be able to track that you're in Mexico from that transaction."

I didn't want to know. It gave me the creeps that someone could track me like that. But I did kind of want to know what Luke was up to. I wondered if I should have a look at that file that Chase was talking about earlier to see if I could glean any new information.

We walked back into the house and down to the artillery room, putting our guns down on the bench. I watched as River reloaded cartridges and pottered about. The more I thought about Luke... the more I realised that I just didn't care anymore. He had his money, and hopefully I would never hear from him again.

River started zipping up the gun bag, and I jumped off the stool I was perched on. He handed me a small box along with both my new guns. I looked down at the box with confusion. Damn it was heavy. "What's this?"

River winked at me. "Bullets."

Oh what a dumb-arse, I smiled. That was kinda obvious.

"Come on," River said as he started to climb the stairs. "Let's get going."

When River stopped the car I found we were back in the warehousing district where we had picked him up from the night we had to go and rescue Gabe.

"The warehouse is five hundred metres in that direction." River pointed, and both Chase and I looked. There were a number of cars parked along the road, and a bunch of warehouses that all looked the same.

"I'll take your word for it." Chase grinned. He turned to look at me sitting in the backseat of the car. "Stick close to us. This could get messy."

Once again I felt myself tense with anxiety, and I nodded mutely, hoping that he couldn't read my mind. They had already told me that there would probably be a few people there.

I wasn't sure that a gunfight was something I really wanted to get involved in, but I guess I had to know how to handle myself in one. Not that assassination was a career option for me, but I thought a new skill in survival probably wouldn't hurt, well, unless it killed me.

I followed River and Chase down the road. They both had slim line backpacks on, fully loaded with further ammunition. River had found a double gun halter for me, and now I had two guns nestled in the small of my back, hidden beneath my jacket. It was too damn hot to be wearing a jacket, but I sucked it up. This would all be over soon, one way or another. This was nuts though. I was supposed to be either running from Carmen, or killing her, but not any of this crap.

I wanted a drink, and not just water. A cold margarita would have gone down nicely at that point. That was what I was going to do once we got back to River's. Have a drink, put my feet up, and imagine that I was anywhere but here.

We reached a fully fenced area, and I saw a two storied warehouse to my right. There were a few cars parked here, but not as many as I imagined. One car stuck out like dog's balls to me though. A sleek, black Maserati. I had seen that car before.

River put his hand on my arm firmly. "Carmen's here."

My heart actually stalled. As I looked at the Maserati, memories flooded me. It was the same car that was parked outside Javier's apartment the night Carmen just about shot me. "Fuck," I whispered, giving both River and Chase a panicked look. I shook my head. "I'm not ready."

River shook his head at me. "You have to be. It's either your life or hers. That's all you have to remember."

"Right, mine or hers." I pursed my lips together. This whole situation wasn't exactly ideal. Now I really needed a drink. Every instinct inside me screamed to turn back and run as fast and as far away as I could.

River and Chase walked through the open gates, and down the side of the building. My eyes traced the patterns in the corrugated iron exterior of the building, suddenly fascinated by all the rusted patches. I would have thought that the Cartel had more than enough money to fix the place up. It looked like a slum warehouse rather than a centre of operations for drug exports. There was an open door, and a pallet that acted as a step up to it.

The alley smelt like urine, and hot rubber. I assumed that this was a regular ablution area for the workers to pee into the long grass that lined the fence. "Dirty bloody Mexicans," I muttered. Both Chase and River were watching through the doorway, and I seemed to just be an extra pair of hands. I could hear a few voices inside, but not many.

When I turned my attention back to the warehouse, I saw that they had slipped inside, and I instantly moved to follow them. Large trucks were inside. I felt small in comparison to them.

"This is the large shipment I told you about," River said quietly to Chase. "They've been bringing it all up from Columbia, moulding it, and exporting from here."

"Moulding it?" I asked in a harsh whisper. "Moulding what exactly?"

"Cocaine," Chase muttered. The look he gave me told me to shut up and pay attention. I looked around and saw the most beautiful white sculptures sitting on pallets at the back of each truck. They were works of art.

The historian inside me yearned to just roam free and examine them from every angle, but now was most definitely not the time. I heard a door slam, and lifted my eyes to the upper offices overlooking the warehouse. I sharply inhaled in as I recognised Carmen walking down the steps speaking in rapid Spanish to two large men trailing behind her. She was gesturing like she was pissed about something.

She was too far away for me to even begin to try and understand a word. Chase pushed me against the truck out of sight with him and River, and we waited for them to pass.

A part of me didn't want her to leave. I think I was secretly hoping that either River or Chase would take her out, but they didn't. No, they were still leaving that up to me. Bless, I thought with sarcasm.

We started to move through the warehouse, stopping every now and then when we heard voices. As I got near to one of the sculptures, I stopped to take a closer look. It was remarkable. Before me stood a nude woman with curls falling over her face. I wouldn't have minded her standing in my garden at home. Where on earth did they get pieces like this? Pristine white, smooth, and because of this I wondered if they were fakes. So far on my travels in Mexico, I had discovered that there were a lot of very good fakes of well-known brands in this region. I wondered if this was just another example.

"It's cocaine," River whispered as he stood right behind me.

I turned to him, hand paused in mid-reach to touch the piece and run my fingers over the smooth stone surface of her clasped fingers. "What is?"

"This artwork. It's been moulded out of cocaine. They'll break it down once they cross the border."

My mouth dropped open. "This?" I pointed to the sculpture.

River gave me a silent nod.

I looked back at it, closer, but there was no way on earth I could tell that it was made out of an illicit drug. It looked like stone.

River tugged my arm, telling me to get a move on. I quietly followed them, but soon found myself getting distracted by another sculpture. Forgetting where I was, I crossed over to it. It was a replica of David. And it was stunning.

As I admired the detail in in, I turned to River seeing that he had stopped to watch me. "Can I have it?" I mouthed at him. Both he and Chase smiled at me.

Then I heard a shout. “Détente!”

I swung around, and saw three men running towards me from the open doors of the warehouse. "Shit," I muttered.

One of them approached me, his face covered in tattoos. He looked damn scary. I wasn't sure what to do. I had the option of pulling a gun on him, but by the looks of the men behind him carrying their AK-47's, it wasn't going to happen.

“Quién eres?”

I shook my head. "English?"

He spat on the ground, and I grimaced. Then after a moment, he leered at me. "I asked who you were." His accent was thick, and he smelt damn awful, sour as though he'd needed a shower for weeks.

Now I was in the shit. I didn't know what name to give him. So I turned on the charm in hopes that it would save my hide. I gave him my biggest smile. "Am I not supposed to be in here?"

He shook his head and leaned closer to me, his liquid brown eyes meeting mine before working their way down my body. I felt like squirming beneath his gaze, but I didn't.

"These sculptures are just so stunning," I commented. “I saw them, and just knew I had to get a closer look."

He gave me an assessing look, and grabbed my arm roughly. "Who are you? A dirty little cop?"

I swallowed, my fear threatening to brim to the surface and show. "No. No I'm not. I'm an art collector."

He narrowed his eyes, and looked closer at me. "An art collector," he mused. I got the distinct impression that he didn't believe me for one second.

Hell, I didn't believe me, but I nodded as convincingly as I could.

He wasn't letting go of my arm. "And how did you get in here?"

I swallowed and hesitated. Again, I didn't know how to answer him. I knew I should have been coming up with some sort of cover story while I'd been stalling, but a part of me was still hoping that he'd let me go. The longer I stood there with him, the less likely I felt that was to happen.

This could turn to shit, very fast. I glanced up at the other men standing there, but they weren't paying us too much attention... well, they were curious, but they didn't think I was a threat. They had even let their guns drop to their sides.

I pointed in the direction of the side door. "Through there."

He instantly clicked his fingers at the men, and they took off. I wondered where the hell River and Chase were at, and why the hell they hadn't helped me out a little already.

"So you just walk through any open door, not even knowing where you are?"

I grimaced, partly because of my cock and bull-crap story, and partly because of the smell of him. This was not going the way I planned. I hoped that he was just going to let me go, but I didn't think that was going to happen, no matter how innocent I looked. Or hoped I looked.

"Yeah." I choked. "I'm sorry, I didn't realise."

He leered at me, and roughly grabbed my arm, hauling me towards the back of the warehouse. "Well, now you will understand the consequences of walking into private property."

Despite my tripping and stumbling, which much to my horror, I wasn't faking, I was still taking in my surroundings in the dim light of the warehouse. I could see all sorts of different contraptions that I had never seen before. Some were different types of tools, others looked like machinery. If I were to guess I would say that they were constructing the sculptures inside the warehouse.

We stopped at a metal bench, and he threw me against it. I cried out in pain as it lanced down my back. Now I was fucking mad. This was not going the way I had intended. Playing innocent and nice obviously wasn't working for me.

He looked me directly in the eyes, and released my arm. "I have men all over this place that will shoot you on sight. Run, and you're as good as dead."

He stepped back, assessing me once again. Sweat ran down my back, not only from the heat, but from the stress. My mind raced. River and Chase still hadn't shown their faces, and I was beginning to question what the fuck they were waiting for.

"Do you know what we do to pretty girls like you?"

"What?" I whispered, looking down at the concrete ground.

He smirked. "We teach them lessons..." I wanted to correct his crappy English, but he stepped closer to me, running a grubby finger over the curve of my breast. I stopped breathing. I understood every intention he had for me; it was written all over his face. That was not going to happen. Not in a million years.

He pushed me hard against the bench again, almost crippling me in the process, but he wrenched me up and started unzipping his fly. My breath caught with dread as he leered with delight at me, grabbing at my jeans to try and yank them down. I held onto my belt-loops with all my might, until he pincered his hand into my wrist, hitting a nerve, forcing me to let go. Before I knew it, his rough hands had managed to pull my jeans down. White hot fear pummelled my senses as he stepped back to survey me and pull his cock out. I moved a little. Guns dug into my back, and I instantly reached around for one. There was no way I was going to be raped or killed by him, and if River and Chase weren't going to help me out, I was going to help myself. I took aim, and pulled the trigger.

17

All hell broke loose. It was my hell. I had missed. Sort of. I shot his ear off. He lunged for me, screaming. I'm not entirely sure what he was shouting. It sounded incomprehensible. I tried to get away, but he caught my arm and grappled me back down to the bench. I was pinned by him, his bloody ear dripping on my face. I looked sideways, repelled by the stench of his breath and what I suspected was rotting teeth, and saw my gun lying about six feet from me.

"I will tie you to this bench and fuck you 'til you scream for me to kill you, and then you will die a very slow death," he said through gritted teeth. I didn't doubt it, not if this guy had anything to do with it. He released one of my arms and began to get off me, reaching for some rope to restrain me with. It was the opening I was looking for. This guy wasn't too smart. It gave me enough time to reach around and grab the second gun from my back.

He was still kind of on top of me. When he saw the second gun, his eyes went wide as I pulled the trigger. I let lose a bunch of rounds into his body, and he slumped back on top of me. There was blood everywhere and I couldn't breathe. His dead weight was too heavy, and I felt like I was being crushed and suffocated at the same time. I struggled to get him off me, yelling for help. River and Chase both came into view instantly, and hauled the body off me, rolling him to one side.

River picked me up as if I weighed nothing and planted me back onto my unsteady feet, pulling me behind a truck that was parked close by. I stared down at the body a few feet away as I struggled to pull my jeans up properly. I couldn't tell how many bullets I had used because there was so much damn blood everywhere. I grimaced, feeling the still warm and sticky liquid all over my clothing, rapidly growing cold. I swallowed, tears threatened to come.

"Look at me, Mack," River instructed, clicking his fingers in front of my face. I did as I was told, breathing hard. "Focus. We still have a job to do," he said softly.

I shook my head, trying to clear the bloody mess from my thoughts. "The others," I whispered, looking around the warehouse.

"Have been disposed of," River said quietly. "Now, follow me."

I strained to slow my breathing down and calm myself at the same time, and nodded silently. I couldn't believe that I'd just killed somebody, even if it was in self-defence. My body tingled with fear, dread, and something along the lines of exhilaration. We moved silently around the truck, and I noticed that Chase had disappeared somewhere. As we rounded a corner, I saw the guy's mobile phone lying on the ground. I looked closer at the screen, and saw that a call was openly connected. I tugged at River's arm, pointing to it.

River gave it an assessing look, and then stomped on it with his boot. By the time I looked back at the phone, the screen was mangled and dark. "I suspect we'll have company shortly." He bent over and picked something up, turning towards me. He handed me my gun, causing me to smile.

My thoughts went to the roadblock we had faced, and I pursed my lips. This was not ideal. A shadow caught my eye as I looked out across the warehouse. I saw Chase on the other side, making his way towards the back. I looked up at the office, wondering where exactly this chap, Osvaldo, was, and why the hell he hadn't come out to investigate the earlier commotion.

Echoes of shouts from the front of the warehouse alerted us that we were soon to have more unwanted company. As I met River's steady gaze, he shoved me towards the metal staircase. Reluctantly, I began to climb, Chase following me, and River bringing up the rear. When we reached the top, Chase put me in a darkish corner so I was partly obscured by some metal framing.

I watched the scene below us unfold. The warehouse was suddenly swarming with a bunch of people, all shouting in Spanish. They came across the body of the guy I'd shot, and new orders were given to some of the men. Some of them started towards the trucks, climbing in the back, obviously searching for someone, or checking their stock. Once they jumped out the back, a driver got into the front, and they started the engine and left the warehouse.

I could see Chase carefully scrutinising the man who was giving instructions, a dark glint in his eye. He mouthed something to River that I didn't understand, and I saw River acknowledge him with a quick nod.

River then raised his gun, aimed it precisely at the man, and fired. He dropped dead instantly. I didn't see the full shot because of my vantage point, but I did see a huge amount of blood splatter hit a number of the pure white sculptures behind him. My mouth went dry as a swarm of men suddenly started looking around the warehouse for the shooter, and I sank back as far as I could behind the warehouse framework. I looked over towards Chase, but he had disappeared. I assumed he'd slipped into the office since he was quite close to the door that we had seen Carmen come out of earlier.

River signalled for me to follow Chase, and I didn't hesitate. I ran. Behind me, I could hear River opening fire on the floor below. Bullets pelted into the walls and pinged off the framework around me, but I didn't stop. Adrenaline pounded through my veins, forcing me to move. As I reached the door, Chase grasped my arm and pulled me through, slamming the door shut behind me.

"This is not my idea of fun." I breathed heavily, his hands steady on my shoulders.

"You're doing well," he whispered. "Come on, we have to find Osvaldo."

I looked behind him and saw a relatively short hallway with three doors leading off it. Chase pointed to one. "Toilets." Then to another, "Storage and server room... and that–" He pointed to the third, "I assume is the main office."

I swallowed, fear reigning. "So I guess we're trapped."

Chase frowned. "Observant. Only way is forward, Mack. Let's get going."

I stayed behind him as we moved silently down the corridor, with one gun drawn, and the other tucked into my holster at the small of my back. I could still hear shots being fired in the warehouse area, and bizarrely, it reassured me that River was still alive.

We edged closer to the door and Chase stopped,

lifting his finger to his lips. His eyes twinkled with mischief, and I realised that this was the part he really got a thrill out of. Me? Not so much. I just wanted to make it out of here alive, and I knew my best chance of that was with either Chase or River.

Chase silently turned the handle, and slipped into the room, leaving me standing there. I could hear shouts from the warehouse, and more gunfire. I imagined that the warehouse was going to be a total mess, and I couldn't help but worry about River. Even if he was a commando type dude, he still wasn't invincible.

I looked back at the door, and slid through the opening.

The room was empty. Of people, that is. There were a number of desks with computer systems set up on them. The place looked like a completely different building compared to the warehouse downstairs. If I was going to call it anything, I would say it looked corporate, in a rustic sort of way. Companies paid designers shitloads to achieve this sort of look with exposed pipes, wooden floors, and halogen pendant lights over each desk. I looked at Chase, who was eying up the room critically. He caught my eye, and gave a quick shake of his head, warning me not to speak. I understood, loud and clear. He thought that someone else was in here.

I could see another room off to the side, and when I moved closer, I saw that it was an industrial kitchen set up, complete with a couple of sofas and a high table with stools. I heard something move, and our attention immediately snapped to the area where the sound came from.

There was definitely someone else in this room.

Chase dropped to the floor, and looked around the room under the desks. He aimed his gun, and let off a round. I heard a squeak and a groan and tried to identify where the noise had come from. Someone was on the other side of the room, over by the window.

I waited till Chase stood before moving slowly towards it. My heart thudded violently in my chest, and I was holding my breath as I focused. I didn't want to trip over anything as I made my way across the room, nor did I want to make a sound. This was multitasking at its finest as I held the gun out in front of me with both hands.

Chase dropped to the floor once again and shot at a desk. Wood splintered from the impact, and so did a man. He scrambled out from under the desk, eyes wide, as he sharply looked up at us.

"Nice to meet you, Osvaldo," Chase said looking directly at him.

Osvaldo shook his head. "Do I know you?"

Chase gave him a cold smile "Does that matter?"

Osvaldo turned his attention to me. "But I do know you," he said as he looked me over. "Yes ..." He mused.

I watched him, my lips pursed. He was right. He did know me; as Rachel White. I looked down at him. He was stocky looking, clean, his corporate white shirt marred by the bright red blood seeping from the gun wound to his arm. The last time I had seen him he had two women flanking him when he met with Javier in a private club. I was, naturally, Javier's companion that night. Most of what had been said I hadn't understood as they spoke Spanish, and I was more distracted by the finger that Javier had been trailing up my bare thigh.

"You look different, Rachel," Osvaldo said, amusement lacing his tone. He looked pointedly at my hair and licked his lips. "Red suits you."

"Thanks," I muttered. Osvaldo had been pleasant the last time I met him. He still maintained that air about him, despite the situation.

A scuffle in the hallway diverted our attention, giving Osvaldo the chance he needed. He stood up and launched himself at Chase. Chase reacted instantly, turning to deflect the blow. The pair of them crashed into the desk. I didn't know what to do, but I knew I had to do something. I don't know why Chase hadn't just shot him to begin with.

Gun shots sounded from the hallway, and I heard a thud. I turned to the door, and raised my weapon, preparing to defend us against whatever came through that door. I was not going to die in this fucking dirty, old warehouse. Granted, I knew I might not have a choice in the matter, but I could only try. Something hit the door, and my finger landed on the trigger ready and waiting. Out of the corner of my eye, Chase was still grappling Osvaldo. They were fairly evenly matched, while Osvaldo was shorter than Chase, he was stockier.

Something thudded against the office door again, causing me to flinch and redirect my attention back to it. The worst thing was that I had no idea what or who was going to come through that door. Or even when. The anticipation was killing me. The sounds of a struggle met my ears, and I frowned. My reasoning told me that River was out there, or else we would have cartel members through those doors in seconds.

"What do you want from me?" Osvaldo exhaled hard, as Chase reached for him again.

I saw Chase shake his head. "Not much."

"I'll cut you a deal." I heard Osvaldo say. "Anything you want."

Chase sneered at him. "A deal? The only deal I'll make is that if you stop being difficult, I'll make this as quick and painless as possible."

A part of me believed it, but the other part of me didn't. I could tell Chase was damn frustrated and more than pissed off. He had dark scratch marks down his neck from where Osvaldo had tried to throttle him, and he was covered in blood. I did a quick assessment, and deduced it wasn't his, but Osvaldo's, from the bullet wound. Someone fired a gun just outside the room, and my heart raced. My hands were clammy from gripping the gun so tightly, but I didn't dare let go to momentarily wipe them.

River burst through the door, his eyes met mine. Relief flooded me, and I relaxed my grip on the gun. He took in the scene before him instantly, and raised his weapon. He let off a bullet, and the big plate glass window behind us shattered. The sound of tinkling glass raining down on me made me move quickly away from the window. River crossed the room in about three strides, throwing Chase out of the way; he picked up Osvaldo as if he weighed nothing.

Osvaldo started screaming obscenities in Spanish, River just shook his head. And then he threw him out the broken window. Everything in that moment seemed to slow. I hesitated then I took a couple of slow steps towards the window. Air rushed in at us from the Tijuana winds, ruffling my hair. But that wasn't what I paying attention to. I was looking down at Osvaldo's body impaled on the tall steel fence that surrounded the perimeter of the warehouse. Several steel rods were protruding from his body, growing in size as Osvaldo's lifeless body slid down them. Blood pooled on the dusty ground as it dripped from him. My hand flew to my mouth, and my eyes were wide as I looked at River standing there, silent and still.

His eyes were dark, not just from the violence and bloodlust, but also from anger. It was a side I had never seen in him before. Usually he was relaxed in every situation, went with the flow. Even as we destroyed Carmen's house, he had been fine, light-hearted almost. This time it was different.

He turned around and saw Chase sitting up on the floor. He reached down, and extended a hand to assist him. As Chase saw the end result out the window, he shook his head. "What a fucking mess."

I bit my lip, exhaustion flooded my system as I let go of the breath I had been unconsciously holding. "What now?"

Both Chase and River looked over at me, almost surprised that I was there.

"We go home," River muttered. "We clean up." He looked over to Chase, "And then I think we make plans to get out of this place."

Chase ran his hands through his hair, and nodded his agreement. "Time to really go home."

"To England?" I asked. I felt stupid, but I had to clarify. When Chase gave me a curt nod, my heart leapt. This was the best news I'd had since we came to Mexico. I glanced back at Osvaldo, and grimaced. This trip to Mexico had been the worst trip of my life. I would like nothing more than to just go and jump on that private jet that the team had and get out of this bloody country. The more I looked at Chase and River, the more I saw the stress and worry they had been harbouring. This job was taking its toll on them. I had been so damn consumed with my own problems with Carmen, and paying Luke out – I hadn't really stopped to consider them.

I followed them from the room, keeping close just in case River had accidentally left someone alive out there. We stepped out onto the metal walkway, and I took in the sight before me. There were bodies everywhere - at least twenty of them. Blood and God only knows what else had splattered against the cocaine sculptures, making the vista a stark and gory reality. A lot of people had died today, and I was partly at fault. If I hadn't stopped to look more closely at the sculpture of David, my assailant never would have made that phone call. I couldn't believe that River, who was normally such a gentle soul, could have caused so much bloodshed and damage.

Chase tugged at my sleeve "Come on. There could be more people coming, and we need to get out of here."

He was right. I followed him down the metal staircase, my shoes clunking with each step, and my hand trailing blood on the railing. As I looked out over the warehouse, the air was thick with white powdered dust from the bullets hitting the cocaine sculptures, and instinctively, I held my breath. Stepping over bodies on the warehouse floor, we took the side door we'd come in through, and went out into the fresh air and sunlight. I felt tainted and dirty. The blood on my shirt was no longer sticky, but drying hard. I wanted nothing more than to get home to River's, shower, and throw these clothes out, never to see them again.

18

Water thudded against my skin, washing away the death from the day. It felt good standing under the hot water, just leaning against the tiled wall and letting it pummel me. I couldn't help but think about all the blood on the sculptures that had been shot to bits, all the bodies that were scattered about the warehouse.

River certainly was a dark horse underneath that relaxed exterior of his. He had managed to kill just about everyone in that building today, but not without a few scrapes of his own. He'd been shot in the side of his abdomen. It was only a graze, but that didn't mean it didn't hurt. He could move fine, and operate normally. But it had still pissed him off. Chase said he'd hesitated with Osvaldo. In hindsight, he knew that he should have just shot him as soon as he had the chance, but a sinister side of him wanted to play with Osvaldo. I could understand why. Osvaldo had been a smug bastard, even when facing his own death. He actually thought that someone would save his hide. I guessed that the last person he expected to walk through the door was River.

Shouts from my bedroom bought me back to the present and I pushed off from the wall, and shutting the water off. Chase burst through the bathroom door, and I tried to cover myself up. "What the hell?" I yelled, shocked by the interruption.

He shook his head, and threw my towel at me. "We have to go. NOW!"

"What? Why?"

"GET MOVING. We have the Cartel almost on our doorstep." Chase left the bathroom, and I stood dumbstruck. "You have thirty seconds," he yelled through the closed door.

I kicked into action, pulling on my clean underwear as fast as I could. It wasn't easy since I didn't have time to dry myself off. I looked down at the sundress I had picked out to wear with disdain. I wasn't going to be able to move fast enough in it. I flew out the bathroom door, and directly into the pathway of Chase, who was in my wardrobe throwing a few things into a bag. Pulling a sleeveless t-shirt over my head, I sought out a pair of track-pants, pulling them on as rapidly as I could. Chase nodded with approval, throwing me a pair of socks. I pulled them on, and found him passing me some training shoes and a hooded sweatshirt.

He pushed past me into the bathroom, and grabbed a couple of wigs from their stands, and swept the contents on top of my vanity unit into the bag. Grabbing my arm, we ran down the hallway to the training room. I caught sight of myself in the reflection of the mirrors, dishevelled, wet, but bright-eyed and focused. I might look like shit, but surprisingly, I had a clear head.

Chase ran to the cupboard, swung it open, and keyed something into a lit keypad. He slammed the cupboard shut, and pulled me over to one of the mirrors. It slid open. I felt my jaw drop, but couldn't utter a word before he was pulling me into the darkness. I turned around to see the panel silently glided back into place behind us. As my eyes adjusted, I realised it wasn't quite pitch black, like I originally believed. Tiny little lights dimly glowed, lighting the pathway ahead.

We ran. Jesus H Christ, did we fly down that hallway. We descended into the depths of the hill beneath the house, Chase gripping my hand tightly. Not once did I stumble. I saw a slither of electric lighting, and realised we were running towards it. Now that I had a destination, it just forced me to run harder. We burst through a doorway, and all but bowled Gabe and River over. Panting, I half bent over, trying to catch my breath. "What the hell is going on?"

"We're getting out of here." River grimaced. "Immediately."

As I slowly straightened, I finally took in our surroundings. Monitors lined the walls, and Gabe watched them intently. What I saw on those screens made my blood run cold. People with what looked like military grade weaponry were swarming the grounds and the house above us.

My mouth went dry. "Shit," I squeaked, looking up at River wide-eyed. It felt surreal. A couple of minutes ago I had been having a lovely time relaxing in the shower. Now I was holed up in some sort of bunker watching a really nasty home invasion.

River pursed his lips as he watched the monitors. "Wait," he said quietly to Gabe.

I frowned, confused. Chase put his arm around my shoulders, pulling me closer to him. "Go get in the car," he whispered in my ear, kissing me quickly just below my eye as he turned me away from the screens. Behind us, a big black truck sat gleaming in the neon light of the room. This place was a garage. Somehow I had missed that when we first entered the room. Chase handed me my bag with a grim smile on his face, and turned back to watch the screens with Gabe and River.

I walked over to the vehicle, and climbed into the back seat. The car smelt of brand new leather finishing. I turned around to watch what was happening. River gestured to Gabe, who nodded. I wondered what the hell they were waiting for.

And then I saw every single screen except for one light up like Guy Fawkes. One by one, the video feeds failed in rapid succession, and I heard a large rumble in the earth, and vibrations move the car. I gripped the door handle, hanging on for dear life, thinking we were having an earthquake, but it soon slowed. Gabe, River, and Chase all got into the car, River behind the wheel, Gabe riding shotgun, and Chase beside me.

"What ... what was that?" I asked in a quiet voice, as the car started slowly down another tunnel, headlights on. We came to a stop, and sat there in silence.

I thought perhaps they hadn't heard me. Then River responded as a garage door began to open in front of us. "That was my house blowing up," he said almost as quietly as me.

Chase reached over and grabbed my hand, linking his fingers between mine. I met his eyes and swallowed. That beautiful house. River's sanctuary. Gone. I bit my lip. A part of me wanted to cry. "How?" My voice was a whisper, but River met my eyes in the rear-view mirror.

"The house was rigged with C4. Once we could see that the majority of those people were inside, we blew it."

I stared at him. "C4?"

Gabe looked at me, without any of the humour that usually laced his features. "Yes. As in the plastic explosive. We rig all our houses just in case we're compromised. It's a failsafe."

"Failsafe..." I whispered. As I processed that thought I came to the conclusion that these guys were erring on the side of nuts. I mean, they rigged their houses? Therefore blowing all of their possessions sky high as well as the men inside?

The car started moving again, exiting through the garage door, and River pulled out into the setting sunlight near the road. I turned back to look up at the house as we sped off. Fire and smoke marred the sky, and the acrid smell of it seeped into the car. "Where are we going to go now?" I asked, my voice quiet.

"To beat these fuckers," River said quietly from the driver's seat. I gaped at him, and when he met my eye in the rear vision mirror, he grimaced. "And then we're going home."

I saw Chase looking at me across the car, and I gave him a tired but emotional smile. I felt like crying, God knows why. I needed some sort of release.

No one spoke 'til we hit Tijuana city.

"Turn left here," Gabe directed. That brought me out of my daze, and I started to pay attention to where we were going. We were quite close to the US border, driving through a different warehousing area. I could see crappy housing that all looked the same lining the border into the distance. I never wanted to live in a place like this. I questioned whether or not that was from my experiences here, or whether I actually just didn't like the place. I couldn't really tell the difference at the moment, and nor did I want to try.

It was quite dark in the city now, and Gabe was still giving directions. Finally River pulled to a stop and parked the car under a large tree, giving us some cover. I could hear people somewhere. Muffled cries, shouting, and some cheering. It was as if they were watching a football game. It was a weird notion to consider, especially when we were as good as homeless here now, with nowhere to go. Everyone else carried on with their lives, while we had just been in a big shootout with cocaine sculptures, and blown a house up.

River and Chase got out and walked around to the back of the car, opening the boot. River passed bags to Chase, and lifted up the wheel housing. I strained to watch over the backseat. There was a lot of different shit in there; more grenades, guns, ammunition, something that looked suspiciously like a detonator. River handed me two small Glocks similar to the guns that I had used in the warehouse earlier. Chase opened my bag and pulled out my Cleopatra styled wig, throwing it to me. He then chucked a small clear packet of bobby-pins as well. I got to work immediately, blindly pinning the wig to my head. I had no idea how it looked or if it was even sitting straight but I did my best.

I turned to Gabe. "This look all right?"

Gabe looked up from his iPad, and gave me a quick nod of approval.

I slumped back in my seat and rifled through the bag for a change of clothing. "What exactly are we doing here, Gabe?" I noted that someone had also included my double gun holster as well, and dumped that on the seat beside me.

He gave me a cursory glance before he returned his attention to his screen. "River's pissed. No...scratch that. He's on the war path. He loved that house, and he's more than fucked off that they managed to trace us, which gives us the insight that they have more cards up their sleeves that we were prepared for." He blew out a big sigh, and looked up at me. His eyes were sad, and he looked tired.

"So... we just go in there and take them down?" I found some jeans, and switched into them in the back seat. I then shrugged off the sweatshirt, clipped the holster to me, and pulled on a leather jacket that Chase had packed.

Gabe shrugged. "I don't know. I'm not one of the action men around here." He shoved his thumb towards the direction of the boot. "They are. I do what I'm told." He jabbed a finger against the screen a couple of times, and then looked back up at me. "This time it's personal," he whispered. "They fucked with River directly, and now they're going to get what they deserve." Something beeped, drawing his attention back down to the device. "Fuck me," he muttered. "Damn. Damn, damn, damn." He put the iPad down while I looked at him questioning what the hell was going on.

Gabe got out of the front seat, and walked around the back to River and Chase. "They know who she is," he said quietly. I almost couldn't hear him, but when I saw their faces, my blood ran cold. Everything seemed to slow. They were talking about me. My mouth was dry, and I desperately needed to think - to figure out what this meant.

I quickly pulled on some boots without zipping them up, and got out of the car, lighting a cigarette.

"How?" River asked.

Gabe shrugged. "Looks like they ran facial recognition software on her and pulled some records. Driver's licence, an arrest from like twelve years ago, and passport information."

I walked up behind them, my hands shaking, and my skin tingling. "I was never charged," I muttered.

River looked sharply at me, and shook his head. "It no longer matters," he stated. "Gabe, wipe the records. Too late now of course, but we don't want any of that to come up in the future." He looked back at me. "You know what this means, right?"

I looked between him, Gabe, and then Chase. Slowly I shook my head.

"It means," Chase said softly, "that unless we deal with them, they will hunt down all of your friends and family, and use them against you until they get what they want."

I dropped the cigarette on the ground, and mashed it with my boot. "But they're in England."

"Doesn't mean they're untouchable," Gabe stated. "They will hunt every known associate down, and kill or torture them one by one until you come out of hiding. That is what these people do. No one is safe."

My mind flicked to Elsie, and my throat closed up. I didn't want anyone to hurt her, let alone look at her the wrong way. She was the sweetest and most caring woman I had ever known, and she had raised me as one of her own when I had lost my parents.

I pressed the heel of my hand against my forehead and gritted my teeth. I couldn't think clearly. This was all getting too damn complicated. I refused to cry. This was not the time. Anger flared inside of me. "What do we do now, then?" I asked through gritted teeth.

'We take 'em out," Chase said plainly. "Now."

I stared at him, wondering if I'd misheard, but from the way he looked at me, it was clear he was deadly serious.

My phone started ringing in my pocket, and I reached for it, giving the others a confused look. It was an unrecognised number, which wouldn't have been too hard, considering no one really knew this number except for the people standing around me. "Hello?"

"Ciara." Someone sighed deeply. I looked up at River in alarm.

"Yes?"

"It's Alvarez," he said. "We still haven't had our dancing date yet."

A part of me felt relieved to hear a friendly voice at the other end of the phone, but I also knew that I didn't give him my number. Hell, I didn't even know my number. As River moved closer to me to listen in on the call, I collected myself. "Lovely to hear from you," I said quietly. "You're right - we haven't."

Alvarez chuckled. "Been busy, have you?"

"Yeah, something like that."

"I have time now, if you're free?" he said suddenly. "Come meet me."

I gave River a panicked look, but he just silently nodded. "I just have to wrap something up, but you caught me on a good day," I answered. "Where should we meet? Your place?"

Alvarez laughed outright then. "No, no. I'm working late - so you can meet me here."

He gave me the address, and I repeated it back to him before ending the call.

"Fuck," River muttered.

"What?" Chase asked.

"He gave her the address of the warehouse we're about to go to." He blew out a sigh, as I stared at him.

"He knows, doesn't he?" I whispered, my heart racing.

"I would say so," River responded, gripping my shoulder with reassurance. "I guess all we can do now is what we came to do. Then we get to fly home."

I swallowed. "Can't we just go now?"

River moved in front of me, putting his other hand up on my shoulder, and looked me in the eye. "I know this is hard, Mack, but they will never, ever stop. There is nowhere in the world they can't find you. They have their hands in every pie. We need to finish this before they get to your friends and family...and before they eventually catch up with you."

I clutched my arms to my chest. I felt like I was going to faint. I avoided looking at him, and stared at the ground. "Can I stay in the car?" I asked in a small tight voice.

Chase stepped up behind me, his hand around the small of my back. "You will never have closure from this unless you do it yourself. It's better to see things with your own eyes, instead of constantly being haunted by it."

I turned to him. "I don't want to go in there. I have seen enough death and bloodshed today to last me a lifetime."

"And you will see a lot more if you don't help us end this."

I gnawed on my bottom lip as I considered his words. The gravity of the situation was quickly becoming a reality. I looked at the three men standing around me. Chase with his ability to quickly and accurately analyse every situation, his extreme emotional intelligence, and his ability to care deeply and yet kill with calculated precision. River, the role he'd played in getting me to come to Mexico and becoming my mentor, protector, and voice of Zen-reason. And then there was Gabe, the American hacking guru who moonlighted as a diversion for those he loved, and who was always quick for a light-hearted laugh. They all looked back at me now, their features solemn as I considered my options.

They had my back, I realised. Completely and utterly. They considered me one of their team, through and through. For the first time in a long time, I felt like I was part of a family. A family who looked out for each other. This team was built on friendship, trust... and something else. Comradeship. They went into situations to kill, and they came out alive because they trusted each other.

I wanted that. I wanted them to trust that I would make the right decision. If it weren't for them, I would have been dead a long time ago, probably beheaded, and a trophy on Carmen's mantel.

"Okay."

"Okay, what?"

"Okay – we go and do this," I clarified.

19

Climbing scaffolding wasn't something I ever thought I would have to do, but I guess there was a first time for everything. Thank God River and Chase both helped me up some of the trickier parts, or else I would have landed on my arse. Now we were standing on a rickety walkway that surrounded the roof of an enormous warehouse. I was already knackered from the day, and would've much preferred to put my feet up and have a glass of wine or something equally numbing.

There was a shitload of cars parked around the warehouse, and judging from the noise this was apparently the place to be. As we rubbed some of the grime off the skylights, and peered down below, every cell in my body froze as I took in the mayhem below.

This was no viewing of a football match game. “What the hell is going on,” I muttered, peering down through the dim and dusty light. I inhaled sharply as I recognised a couple of the people below us. Alicio and Alvarez. This was a cartel party, and what made it worse was that I had an official invite. I knew that invite was no accident.

“Initiation rituals of the Cartels usually involve murdering someone,” Chase whispered as he cleared off a patch in my skylight and looked down.

I examined the scene below me. There were men and women held captive, strung up in chains around the walls. They were alive by the looks of it. Some had thrown up, and I had no doubt that wasn’t the only mess made.

“The more brutal and skilled the person is, the better placed their position will be within the cartel.”

I could feel my mouth begin to water as I watched those people down there... but it was watering from the sudden urge to throw up. This was absolutely nothing like even the worst horror films I’d seen, or my worst nightmares. It was even more alarming. These people were about to be killed in front of an audience. That’s what the cheers were about that erupted every now and then. The rest of the cartel were fucking cheering them on.

“I can’t handle this.” A lump formed in my throat, tears ran down my cheeks as I forced myself to hold the contents of my guts in. "I can't be up here while innocent people are down there dying." I looked pleadingly at Chase. "Let's just go. Please."

Chase shook his head, and reached his arm out to steady me. "Take a deep breath, Mack," he instructed. "Close your eyes, and breathe in and out slowly. Re-centre yourself."

I opened one eye at him. "You sound just like River," I accused.

Chase gave me a lopsided smile. "Yeah, well - sometimes you pick up useful tips from people." He squeezed my arm. "Close your eyes and breathe."

I snapped my eyes shut and tried to concentrate. It was hard to do knowing what was going on beneath my feet, but I forced myself to focus. I'm going home soon, I'm going home soon, I chanted rhythmically in my head. I began to feel a bit more like myself after a few moments. I could feel Chase's warmth, and even though there were a bunch of people getting murdered below me, he made me feel safe.

By the time I opened my eyes, my shoulders had slumped forward. Did I feel any better? No, I didn't think so. There was absolutely nothing I could do about what was happening beneath us. I watched as Alicio instructed a young man, who I guessed would be about fifteen or sixteen years old. The boy walked up nervously to a pile of tools and weaponry on the ground.

"Just brace yourself," Chase whispered in my ear.

"This won't be pleasant."

Alicio's voice cut through the crowds chatter.

"Tonight we bear witness to Izel Ayala's family sacrifice to the Day of the Dead," Chase translated slowly for me, "and Izel will officially adopt us as his new family forever after." Cheers erupted from the crowd as Izel picked up a bloody chainsaw from the pile. I swallowed. I knew what was going to happen, and as much as I wanted to look away, I simply couldn't tear my eyes away from the scene below me.

A woman who was chained up against the wall was looking at Izel, tears in her eyes, shaking her head. I was rooted to the spot, eyes trained on her. They had similar facial features, and at best guess, I would say she was Izel's mother. My mouth went dry, as she spoke in rapid Spanish to him. I couldn't understand her, but I could feel that she was trying to talk him out of whatever he was about to do. It was his leer that made my breath catch.

Shocked disbelief swept over me as he started up the chainsaw. My tongue stuck to the roof of my mouth. The woman had closed her eyes, and I could see her lips moving quickly. I realised she was praying. She could have been praying for life, praying for mercy, or even praying for a quick death. Mostly, I imagined she was praying for her son - especially when she suddenly stopped speaking and looked at him with such love it almost broke me.

Chase grabbed my arm, and held on to me as the

chainsaw cut rapidly through her neck, releasing bloody splatters all over the other people chained up next to her. Her head dropped to the ground with such a thud; I could imagine the sickening sound of impact over the noise of the chainsaw. The crowd roared with blood-fever, and when Izel turned around to face the crowd, I saw it was all over him as well as he lifted the chainsaw victoriously above his head.

Feeling sick didn't even begin to describe the horror that filled me, seeping into every cell and pore within me. Alvarez stepped up to Izel, slapping him on the back in congratulations, and led him through the crowds, who in turn were giving their congratulations. If I leaned my head down low enough, I could see Alvarez leading Izel to a back room with glass frontage. "What's he doing?" I whispered to Chase.

"Probably marking. That's what the entire Cartel does."

"Marking?"

Chase smiled indulgently at me, even though he had a hard look in his eye. "Yeah. Tattooing. The El Diablo Cartel tattoo their sign, the Jaguar, to the lower ranking members, and they brand it with a hot iron onto the senior members."

Jaguars. Branding. Suddenly I knew why Nicandro's and Alvarez's cat tattoos looked different. They were branded, not inked. My attention was drawn to the scene below me once again as I heard

Alicio's voice ring out. He had another child standing beside him, but this one took me by surprise. A teenage girl stood poised and confident. There was none of the nervousness that I saw in Izel. I looked at Chase, who was staring intently down at them. "Is she...?"

Chase gave a grim nod. I realised that he didn't like this any more than I did.

Once again Alicio formally introduced her to the crowd, giving the same speech he had for Izel. This time I didn't need Chase to translate it for me. I already knew what he was going to say, and every part of it made me feel sick.

The girl picked up a knife, and inspected the sharpness of the blade. "Don't tell me she's going to cut a head off with that," I muttered. "That really would be sick."

Chase didn't say anything in response; he just continued watching silently and calmly. The girl walked over to a chained up teenage boy who was probably around the same age as her. The crowd roared as the boy spoke to her. "I think that's her brother," Chase whispered. The girl ripped open the boy's shirt, pulling the buttons off effortlessly, and began running the knife around some of the concave areas of his abdominals and chest area. "Shit," Chase muttered, sitting upright. He turned to look at me. "I don't think you should watch this."

I swallowed. "I get it. He's going to die, just like

the rest of those innocent people down there."

Chase shook his head and glanced down. I followed his gaze when I heard the screaming start. My eyes snapped back to Chase's. "She's skinning him?"

"Yes. Alive." The screams of the boy surrounded us, as they echoed around the warehouse. The crowd cheered her on, and even though I wasn't watching this, I could hear her progress on their tongues. I swallowed, wishing that this would be over, wishing that I could do something to help. But instead, I was on top of a roof, being protected by Chase, River and Gabe. Chase put his arm around me, holding me close. "Don't worry. He should pass out soon from the pain, and then maybe she might have mercy on him and make it a faster kill."

I bit my bottom lip as the boy's screams started to die down, and the crowd's noise swallowed it with their cheers. "I think we should get out of here," I said quietly. "I really don't think I can cope with this." I wrapped my arms tighter around Chase, wishing I was Dorothy and had the ability to just click my ruby-red slippers three times to take me home. Life wasn't like that. I understood why Chase, River and Gabe wanted to finish this once and for all, but this was not something I ever wanted to see or hear again.

Even though the night air was warm, something cold and hard had buried itself within me. This was not normal behaviour. Every single person inside that warehouse was psychopathic. These were the types of people we were told to stay away from at all costs while we grew up - and here I was with a crowd of them below my feet.

I had to do something. I couldn't just stand by and watch a bunch of innocent people dying horrifically for sport.

Wrapped in Chase's arms, I could hear the next announcement from Alicio. From Chase's arms, I eyed the crowd below. Another girl was standing in front of the tools spread around the floor, ready to choose. Her target was an old man with calm, kind eyes. Of all of the people chained up down there, he didn't look as though he was scared, or had even soiled himself in some way. He was stoic as he watched her approach him. She had a knife, but I could see that her hand was shaking, even from this distance. "She's not going to do it," I whispered to myself.

Chase looked sharply down at the scene, his eyes calculating every movement from her. He shook his head. "No. She may want the life of the cartels, but it seems that she hasn't yet lost the love she has for her old man."

I watched with fascination as tears ran down her young face, and she dropped the knife with a clatter to the concrete floor. As she turned towards the silent and stunned crowd, all I could see were warring emotions of love and remorse on her features. She shook her head.

Alvarez pushed his way through the crowd and addressed her. She held out her hands, crying. He then walked up to her, pulled out a Glock from a holster, and shot her point-blank, the back of head spraying out behind her onto her loved one. The man slowly lifted his eyes from the girl's body on the floor and met Alvarez's with such vehemence, my heart stopped. Another shot was let off, and the man's body slumped forwards into the chains. "No..." I whispered. "No..."

River walked up to us and started talking in hushed tones to Chase, but I didn't hear a word. I was too busy, my eyes fixed on the bodies of the old man and the girl. People undid the chains of the old man, letting his body fall to the floor next to hers. A few people dragged them off out of sight, no doubt to dump them into a pile with the rest of the people they'd murdered in there tonight. The girl had shown such strength in not killing the man, and she'd faced down the cartel - if only for a moment. To me, that was a stronger show of commitment and loyalty than publicly killing someone. The longer I stood up here with Chase, River and Gabe, the more people would die. I just didn't know if I could stand by and let that happen.

I pushed myself out of Chase's arms, and walked over to Gabe, whose lips were pursed in disgust and frustration as he peered through his own skylight.

"Gabe?"

He looked up at me, eyes hard and focused.

"Alvarez... when he was initiated into the Cartel - who did he kill?"

Gabe thought for a moment. "Well his parents were dead by that time. He has no siblings..." He thought for a moment. "That's right. I believe it was the nanny who raised him."

It was like a slap in the face. "Thanks," I murmured, my mind whirling back to the night I was officially introduced to him at the ball. The same woman who raised him and taught him English, one day hoping that he would be smart enough to get a good and decent job. Probably away from the cartel life. And he'd murdered her in cold blood. And then I remembered Chase's words earlier about how the more horrific the murder, the higher the position they got in the Cartel.

This was a man who wanted to get friendly with me. A man, that somewhere inside of him I had believed to be good. But in reality, he'd just invited me to a slaughter house to be strung up alongside the rest of those people down there. I knew that if it wasn't for Chase, River, and Gabe, I would have been dead a long time ago. I would never make it out of Mexico.

And if I wasn't going to make it out, I was going to go down with a hell of a fight.

20

Chase watched me curiously as I stood still, trying to figure out what to do. There had been enough innocent deaths since I had been in Mexico. All those beautiful women that Carmen had hunted down, hoping that each head brought to her was mine...the women that were used as drug mules, who would probably die across the borders from wherever they were sent...and the people in the warehouse below me. No one was holding the cartel accountable.

Sure, I didn't know if I was the right person to do it, but I would make a damn good start. I just couldn't believe this was happening, and why River, Chase, and Gabe were just standing by and watching it take place. The only way I could think of stopping the slaughter beneath us was to surprise them. Surely if that happened then they would at least postpone their initiation... right? Something told me that the captives now had a death warrant on their heads regardless.

Unless we took out all of the cartel members in the warehouse right now... then they might at least have a chance of survival. Me included. And as much as I loved and respected these men I was with, I didn't think waiting around on a roof was going to help us.

And in that moment, I made a completely irrational decision against all my better judgement. I pulled out the two Glocks from the small of my back, and shot through the skylights.

Glass splintered and shattered to the floor below, and while the mayhem started, I trained my sights on Alicio Mendoza first since he was the closest cartel member that I knew. He smiled as his eyes met mine, but it wasn't warm. It was cold. And I pulled the triggers, letting off a couple of rounds, before River and Chase both slammed into me, pulling me down onto the iron of the roof.

Shots rang out in the evening air around us. "What the hell are you doing?" River shouted at me. I struggled to get up, but they had me pinned.

"What you should have done ages ago." Heat flared in me, and I knew that we didn't have much time.

"She's right," Chase shouted to River over the noise. He pulled out a gun and a grenade from his jacket pocket. "She just took out Alicio Mendoza for us. Now's our chance to take the rest of these fuckers down."

River shook his head. "So be it." He extended his hand to me, helping me get up, and gave me a tired smile. "I hope you know what you're in for."

I shrugged. "I don't have a choice."

"No, you don't," he said to me just before I watched him fling himself through the shattered skylight, and onto a number of stacked wooden pallets before he expertly rolled off and joined the fray below.

I didn't have time to dither about now, but I also didn't exactly know what to do. I had basically called an all-out war on the El Diablo Cartel, on their turf, and I seriously wasn't qualified. Chase had already shot through the next skylight, and was taking calculated shots at people. I watched him shoot one of the innocents in the head, as they dangled from their chain, having been half gutted. It was the most humane thing to do. I was grateful that they wouldn't have to suffer any more than they did.

Out of the corner of my vision I saw something move on the roof. It wasn't Gabe, as he was in front of me. I turned to see an arm, reach up and over the warehouse roof parapet, gun in tow. "Shit," I muttered. I lifted up my gun, and took aim, releasing the trigger after a heartbeat. I missed. A face stared back at me as he raised his gun toward us. I fired off another shot, and it hit his arm, forcing his weapon to clatter onto the roofing iron. I ran across the roof, and took a sweeping kick at his neck, trying not to lose my balance. Gabe grabbed my arm, just before I accidentally killed myself. The man's young body was twitching on the ground below us, with his head and neck at an impossible angle.

Chase ran up to us on the roof. "We have to get off here. We need to get to River."

I didn't need to be told twice, but I also knew that once we were down on the ground, with the rest of the psychotic cartel members, we were fair game. I gave him a sharp nod, and picked my way over to the rickety scaffolding. Chase grabbed my hand as he caught up to me, causing me to grin, and making my heart flutter.

"Mack." The tone of his voice immediately told me to stop and pay attention. "Thank you."

I shook my head. "For what?"

He shrugged, suddenly looking shy. "For everything."

I spluttered. "I may have just signed our death warrant, and you're thanking me?"

"No, not for that. Thank you for being you, when you're with me."

I stared at him, speechless. My mouth was dry, and I licked my lips as his jade coloured eyes bore into mine. A shout from below broke the connection, and I turned my attention to the ground. Gunfire ripped through the air, and Chase pulled me to the rough roofing iron. Bullets pinged against metal.

"Thank God we weren't on the scaffold," Chase muttered. "They would have picked us off."

We shuffled towards the edge and peeked over. There were about thirty odd people down there, all looking up at the roof, watching, waiting, with a few of them taking pot shots at our general location.

"Move back," Chase murmured. "I'll get us out of this."

I didn't hesitate, but moved back towards Gabe. Chase took a grenade out of his pocket and pulled the pin. He waited a moment, and then threw it directly among the mass of people below. He covered both me and Gabe with his body as the explosion ripped through the air, and shook the building violently beneath us.

I heard screams, felt the heat from the blast and I hoped and prayed River wasn't anywhere near that.

"Come on," Chase said to us. "Coast is clear - we need to move."

We got to the scaffolding, and leapt onto it. I didn't even worry about the height or my safety as I made my way down as quickly as I could. I knew that both Chase and Gabe were fine, but I had the sudden urge to make sure River was still okay. Common sense told me that he was, because he was trained for this sort of covert combat. But I still had to make sure with my own eyes. People were scattering to the wind - getting into their cars and roaring out of the parking area towards the city. I grabbed both my guns, and crept along the building, taking shots at anyone that looked threatening.

I reached a door, and slowly opened it, waiting to be shot at, but nothing came. Chase and Gabe caught up to me. "Go," Chase ordered Gabe. "Get the car, and make sure we have an out." He grimaced. "If we get out."

Gabe gave him a quick nod. "See you soon." I watched him as he took off through the darkness towards the road, and I looked up at Chase, who was also watching Gabe's retreating figure. After a moment, he looked down at me and smiled. "Come on."

I tucked one gun into the holster, hoping that by using both hands on the one gun it would improve my aim.

Weapons at the ready, we made our way through the open door and into the darkness. Someone had shot the lights out, or flicked the switch, but judging by the amount of glass crunching under my boots, I guessed it was the former.

We made our way through another door and saw two figures struggling on top of a reclining dentist type chair. River was one of them, and when we slammed the door open, they sprang apart.

The other was Alvarez. He turned at looked at me, covered in blood, his lip split, and his clothing torn, revealing the tattoos covering this chest. My eyes fixed on the panther tattoo, and I just knew without a shadow of a doubt that it was the cartel brand. “Ciara,” he said as pleasantly as he could through ragged gasps. “How nice of you to finally join us.”

I shrugged. “Oh, you know me. I never turn down an invite,” I said flippantly through gritted teeth and forced smile.

Alvarez moved closer, causing Chase to bristle beside me, but I stood still. My eyes cut towards River’s, and I saw he was watching this exchange with curiosity. I knew what he would do in this situation. He would stand strong, and proud, but always at the ready. Having both of them in the room with me made me feel more confident.

“I had such high hopes for you, Ciara... or should I say Rachel? Or is it McKenna now?” Alvarez gave me a lazy grin as my stomach dropped. They knew all of my aliases, and I felt my confidence start to drop away.

“How long have you known?” My voice was quiet and wavering slightly.

Alvarez shrugged. “I have known you weren’t who you said you were since the night you slept on my sofa.”

I swallowed, and he raised his eyebrows with amusement.

“I also knew at the ball that something was off about you, but...” He mused for a moment. “I just couldn’t put my finger on it. I knew that the odds of you being in the same place as me on two occasions wasn't a coincidence. Have I mentioned that I don't believe in coincidences? And then of course, the next morning I saw you with your 'brother'." His eyes cut to Chase and then back to me. "And then I really knew you weren't who you said you were." He took another step closer. "So when you were at my house, I drugged you, and ran facial recognition software. Aquí está, McKenna Carmichael – a research historian based in the U.K. Both parents deceased."

I cleared my throat, narrowing my eyes at him. "Well. It seems you know everything about me then, huh?" I held my head high and glared at him. I was not going to let this thug get the better of me. He may have fooled me once, but he wouldn't again.

"Just about," Alvarez sneered. "Your boyfriend Luke is a charming young man, might I add. He's proven to be of spirit and cowardice while we have been holding him."

Luke? "You have Luke?" I clenched my jaw and tensed. I may have hated Luke, but this wasn't the fate he should have.

Alvarez looked at me with a coldness that caused my muscles to quiver. "Oh yes. Your aunt has been harder to track down, but we're not far away now." He scratched his chin thoughtfully as if he was trying to get a read on my reaction, and I cast my eyes to the ground. They had found my friends and family. This is what I had been afraid of. River, Chase, and Gabe had all warned me that this is what the Cartel did to those who went against them, but I guess I'd never thought they would do it to me.

I didn't know if I should take him seriously or whether he was just trying to wind me up. As I looked up at him, he lurched towards me, spinning me around, causing me to drop the gun in my hand as it whacked against the doorframe, and he wrapped his arm tightly around my neck. I felt the sharp blade nick my throat, forcing me to freeze. He pulled me backwards across the room, and I made a desperate attempt not to trip over anything that might cause the knife to bury deeper into my neck.

A bead of warmth dripped down my neck, and I knew that it was my blood. My lip trembled as I looked at both Chase and River, who were both staring wide-eyed back at me. Chase rearranged his features, and gave Alvarez a cold stare. He lifted his gun, and aimed it at Alvarez's head. "Really?" Chase said. "You still want to kill her even with both of us in the room?"

Alvarez laughed. "Trust me. All it takes is a little twist of my knife, and I'll slit her jugular. Nothing you can do after that, especially not in this country. Medical services here are under our directive and I doubt they'll respond."

I felt the warmth of his breath, tinged with the scent of alcohol, brushed against my neck. I couldn't believe I had been so stupid as to ever think that there was something good about him. He was just like the rest of the cartel. Cold. Callous. Cruel. I licked my lips, trying not to squirm. I took in my surroundings properly, wondering what I could do to get the hell out of this position. Tattooing tools were on the benches, the reclining dentist's chair, which I thought I could probably kick to create a distraction. But then I still had the issue of the knife at my neck.

I looked over to Chase, and he gave the slightest shake of his head at me. Confused I looked at him again, trying to decipher what the hell he was saying. He looked pointedly at the chair. He was telling me to stay still and not do anything rash. I inhaled deeply. I had to trust him. My arm throbbed with the sharp pain from when my forearm had hit the doorframe. The dribble of blood was now making its way down toward my cleavage. Unless it was sweat. I had no idea, and there was no way I could look down to see what it was anyway.

"You killed your nanny," I rasped to Alvarez.

He gave a light laugh. "My governess, and yes." He cleared his throat. "And I bet the morbid curiosity inside you wants to know how she died. Well, if truth be known, I skinned her alive. Much like what I could do to you right now if I chose. Afterwards, I cut out her organs." He paused, letting that little fact sink in.

I didn't feel well. I felt too hot all of a sudden, claustrophobic, like I couldn't get enough air.

"You remind me of her," he whispered in my ear.

"Strong-willed. She didn't even fall unconscious when I skinned her. She still cursed me for what I was doing, right to the bitter end without ever begging for her death. She didn't want to me to live the cartel life, but what could I do? It was in my blood. It was my legacy to follow in my parents' footsteps. She hindered that."

"She cared," I stated simply.

From where I was standing, I could just see the glint of light reflecting off my gun through the doorway. And then I remembered. The other gun was holstered at the small of my back. It was my option out as long as Alvarez stayed well and truly distracted.

Alvarez chuckled. "Yes. She did."

"If you kill Mack, you know you'll die anyway, don't you?" Chase stated. "I will shoot you if that knife gets any closer."

"Ah, yes. You take me for a fool. You see, I would never have done this without thinking this idea through. McKenna is my ticket out of here. I know that neither of you will endanger her life - you have both spent too much time protecting it so far."

I couldn't argue that point. They had. I pushed the panic down knowing my time was running out. I slowly dropped my arm, watching Chase's eyes as he followed the motion. He lifted his eyes to meet mine. I knew he knew. He wasn't giving me any signals to stop. I didn't know if this was going to work, and chances were that Alvarez could plunge the knife into my neck anyway. I made a movement to try and readjust the way I was standing, and Alvarez tightened his arm hold around my neck.

"You're going to take Mack as hostage?" River confirmed.

"I guess that would make sense," Chase added.

I repressed a smile, and pursed my lips together, knowing that they were both stalling Alvarez. I edged my hand up slowly, beneath my jacket, and felt the warm metal of the gun, as I tried to get a decent but slow hold on it in my left hand. Whatever happened, it was going to be an issue shooting with that hand, as I wasn't terribly coordinated with it - not like I was with my right. My fingers shook, and I tried to slow down and inhale some sense of calmness into myself.

The gun slid effortlessly from the holster, which in my humble opinion, was probably the only thing to actually go right this evening. I kept the gun close to my side, and used my leg as leverage to get a good grip on it. Both River and Chase's eyes cut to it, but then quickly focused back on Alvarez.

"Just let her go, Alvarez, and I'll make sure your death is quick," River said quietly. "If you take her, you will be running while we hunt you down. And then it will get messy."

Alvarez shook his head. "No. You killed the rest of them. I know it was you. Why should I give you what you want and make this easy for you? So you can get paid?" He spat. "No. Mack will be coming with me, and we'll disappear. Follow me if you like... but we all have an out if we need it." He leered at them. "You'll never ever find us."

Now was my moment. I raised the gun, pressing the metal against his ear. I squeezed my eyes shut and held my breath as I pulled the trigger, praying that there were still rounds in the magazine. It was too quick for him to even register what was happening. All I heard was the shot ringing in my ears. The knife dropped to the floor next to my foot, and Alvarez's arm went slack, which made me open my eyes. His knees buckled, and he slid to the ground behind me.

I looked at both River and Chase, stunned. "I got him?" I whispered, more to myself than to them. River's face broke into a smile, and Chase strode across the room towards me, gun still in his hand. I turned around and dropped my gaze as Chase reached my side. He put his arm around me, and I stepped into his warmth. Blood pooled on the floor at my feet, and I stepped back from it, swallowing my guilt. Alvarez had intended to kill me. I shot him in self-defence. To survive. I reached up to my neck, to feel my wound, and my hand came away, slick with blood.

I looked up at Chase, and then back at the blood on my hand. "Oh my God," I whispered.

Chase turned me slightly to look at it closer. "No...it's only a surface wound. It's not pumping out – he didn't hit an artery."

Relief spread through me at his words. The sound

of sirens in the distance bought reality crashing back around me. I swallowed. We were in a warehouse full of dead bodies, and possibly people still chained up against the wall alive. "We have to go."

River gave us a sharp nod. "Yes."

"We need to get those people out of here."

He pursed his lips in thought. "We should."

Chase shook his head. "Mack should go and meet Gabe - you and I will get those people out." He pulled out his mobile, and dialled Gabe, instructing him to come around and pick me up. I knew that there were probably still cartel members around, so I appreciated the thought.

"Go, Mack," Chase instructed. "Run. Gabe will be here in a minute, and we'll be out shortly."

I gave him a cursory smile, and a sharp nod, picking up my fallen gun on my way out of the room. As I exited the building, I saw the big black truck swing around in front of the warehouse, ran to the passenger door and threw myself in.

"Thanks for the pick-up." I said, short of breath, putting my seatbelt on.

"Thanks for being here," a woman said. The doors automatically locked around me. I looked up sharply at the driver, and froze. It wasn't Gabe. It was a stunning looking Latino woman with a ragged silvery scar on her cheek, running from her eye, and down to her jawline. Dread filled me as I recognised her from a photo I had seen earlier this morning. Paz. She snatched the guns out of my hands before I could react and threw them in the backseat, then lurched the vehicle into gear.

Just before I thought things couldn't get worse, I felt the cold steel of a gun press against the nape of my neck. "Lovely to see you again, McKenna Carmichael," I heard Carmen say from behind me.

My blood ran cold.

21

Having a dusty and grimy canvas bag shoved over one's head is not a pleasant experience. I didn't even want to know how many heads that bag had been on. The woman driving the car was throwing it about a bit, and since I couldn't see where we were going, it made me feel ill from the motion. Well, a combination of that and the terrifying situation I found myself in.

The vehicle turned onto a gravel driveway. I could hear stones beneath the wheels, and I felt the ruts and potholes shudder through the car. A few moments later the engine turned off, and almost immediately I was pulled, stumbling from the car, and shoved roughly forward.

We paused, and the sound of a garage door

rattled. I was shoved forward through a doorway, and found myself walking on wooden flooring. Handcuffs were clipped to one of my wrists, around something metal, and then attached to my other wrist. One of them whipped the bag off my head, and the blinding light of the room caused me to blink rapidly. I was facing a wall of mirrors, and looking down; I found I had been cuffed to a metal dance rail, running the length of the mirrored wall. This was a dance studio.

"Retrieve her phone, and anything else that's there," Carmen ordered Paz, while watching me with a cold stare. This was it. I knew that this was the end. I shook my head. I should have paid attention to the car as it pulled up. But really, I had only seen River's one once, and was hardly familiar with it. Besides, it was damn dark outside – and all black trucks look the same at night. I just couldn't believe my stupidity.

The woman patted me down, quickly finding the gold iPhone in my back pocket. I gave it a forlorn glance as she admired it, turning it over in her hand. I was rather attached to that phone. And not just because it was gold... but because Chase had given it to me. Not to mention, it tracked my location back to Gabe. I pursed my lips, watching Carmen snatch the phone, and take the SIM card out. She pulled a cigar cutter out of her pocket, and cut the SIM in half with a snap. There went my chance of Gabe ever tracking me.

I was on my own.

Paz was still turning the iPhone over in her hand. Deep down I had a feeling I was never going to see it again. I turned away from them, glancing at the rest of the room in the reflection of the mirror. An enormous fish tank lined the opposite wall, filled with watery vegetation, and what looked to be swarms of ugly fish. They reminded me of wasps or bees; something about them felt dangerous.

I heard a snort of amusement behind me, and I found Carmen watching me as I analysed the fish tank. "I see you have noticed Paz's... babies." She leered at me. "She brings them up from the south. I think the piranhas remind her of home. Beautiful but deadly."

My mouth went dry. I was being held hostage in a room with a tank full of piranhas? My heart rate leapt as I thought about that tank breaking. I had never seen a piranha before but I had heard plenty about them. I knew that they could strip a cow's body of flesh in about three seconds, and I guessed a human body in half that time.

Carmen was watching me with sadistic curiosity as I processed that information. I refused to look at her, keeping my eyes on the tank. "What do you want with me?"

She put her hands on her hips, her dark eyes glittered. "First of all, I want you to meet my dear husband." She spat the 'husband' out viciously, and I cringed. "Then... You and I are going to play a little game." She stepped closer to me, and trailed a long fingernail up my jeans, over my shirt, my breast, and up to my neck, where she dug her fingernail into the knife wound Alvarez had kindly given me, causing me to flinch backwards and into the mirror.

I swallowed. "What sort of game?"

Her hand dropped away. "One where you will be my patient, and I will be the doctor. I'm going to monitor your resistance to a variety of poisons." She smiled, and clapped her hands like a delighted toddler. "But first things first. Javier." She turned away, and snapped her fingers at Paz to get her attention away from my phone. "Ring Javier for me. We require his presence."

I hardly listened. My mind was still trained on the fact she wanted to experiment on me. I felt woozy, and desperately needed a drink of water, as if that could rebalance me. The world was starting to spin. The lighting was too harsh, the wooden floors were too loud with Carmen pacing them, and even just acknowledging the piranha fish tank was giving me the shakes.

I looked down at the handcuffs. They were so tight that they cut into my wrists every time I put any pressure on them. I watched Carmen and Paz walk through another door at the end of the room, talking quietly between themselves. They closed the door, and I found myself alone. The first time I had been alone since I was having a shower, after I almost got shot to hell in the cocaine export warehouse.

I looked at myself in the mirror. I was a complete mess. There was blood all over my clothing, my hair looked like I had been dragged through a thorn bush backwards, and I looked tired, like I'd had a hell of a bad day. And while it had been one of the longest and most intense days of my life, if felt like it had flashed right before my eyes. I shivered. I had almost died multiple times today... and now I was cuffed in a dance studio by an insane bitch who wanted to experiment on me.

Analysing the metal dance rail, I tried to see if there was any way I could possibly escape. I walked the length of the rail before a rail mount stopped me. I couldn't even attempt to unscrew it or anything, because of the cuffs restricting me.

A part of me was starting to accept the fact that I was fucked. Stuck under the same roof with a crazy, murderous woman and her evil sidekick, a place where no one knew where I was. This was not the sort of day I had expected. I had been hoping to kick my feet up with a drink in hand after being in the cocaine export warehouse. That was the plan. Then when River's house was blown to shit, I was hoping we would get on that plane out of here back home to England. I had hoped that I could eventually take my relationship with Chase to the next level. But now, finally, I was resigned to knowing that my life was drawing to a rapid close.

I slumped down to the wooden floor, with my hands hanging above my head. I watched the piranhas swimming calmly in the tank across the room. There was something about the movement that lulled me into a semi-relaxed state as my eyes fixated on it. I caught myself wondering who the hell would ever have an enclosed tank of piranhas in their house.

I never had fish when I was growing up. Mary Hope, my childhood friend, had a big tank of them when we were young. Huge, colourful tropical fish, all named after people in our class. I recall begging my parents for one, but after countless arguments, they decided that it would probably end up being them who looked after the fish and cleaned out the tank. Instead, they got me a cat. She was black as midnight, with a white crescent moon under her neck. I named her Mitzy. She was the only friend I had when my parents died. I took her to Elsie's with me, and had her until she died at the age of eighteen.

Tears pricked my eyes. She was a good cat. A really good friend. And I treasured her friendship and companionship even more when Mum and Dad died, as it reminded me of their patience, their common sense, and their good foresight to get me a real companion to play with – instead of just a bunch of fish that only swam around.

I could still hear Paz and Carmen talking behind the closed door. It sounded muffled, and the only reason I knew Carmen was upset was because of the pitched tone of her voice.

I had to wonder exactly what she was upset about though. Hadn't she got what she wanted? She could finally wipe me off the face of this earth once and for all – and even do the job herself, instead of paying the finder's fee she had out on my head. What the hell was she waiting for? I was sitting right there. I wanted to yell and scream at her through the door and really rile her up. Why make it as easy as possible for her, when she was going to kill me anyway? I might as well fuck her right off in the process, so that she knew I wasn't going down without a fight.

Stones crunched under tyres in the driveway. I heard a car-door slam, and held my breath, waiting to hear the garage door lift. I wasn't disappointed when moments later I heard the rattle. Blowing out a resigned sigh, I readjusted myself. I strongly doubted that this was my rescue party, if I even had one. There was always a slither of hope there though.

Javier walked calmly into the room, and his eyes instantly cut to mine. They assessed me from head to toe before he took a step toward me. I felt like a sitting duck, ready for slaughter. Was I scared? Yeah. A little bit. But I also knew that my death was inevitable. Right now, it was only a matter of time.

"Rachel." He exhaled my name once he reached me. Hearing him use my alias made me freeze. His finger traced my cuffed hands. "What has she done to you?"

I shook my head, too afraid to speak. Too afraid that I would lose my composure, and turn into an emotional, blubbering mess.

He shook his head sadly, and once again turned his brown eyes to mine. "Jealous wives never like girlfriends."

"Is that what I was?" My voice came out raspy, and almost pleading.

Javier smiled. "I would like to think so. You can imagine my disappointment though, when I found out it was your team killing off my men, and my business." His eyes hardened, and he stood up abruptly. My blood ran cold. I had seen that look in his eye the night Carmen just about shot me. "Now, I must go and deal with my wife."

I swallowed, watching him walk away towards the door, the heels of his designer leather shoes clicking against the polished wooden floors. Despite the clicking, I could still hear Carmen's muffled voice ebb and flow. I doubted that Javier's presence was going to calm her down much.

I slumped against the mirror once again and waited. Javier had left the door open as he spoke calmly, trying to find out exactly what Carmen was up to. Carmen stormed past him, and out towards me. "Look at her!" she shouted at him. "How could you love her, over me?"

"I never loved her, Carmen." Javier responded as if placating a child. "You should have killed her back at the warehouse instead of bringing her here. What were you hoping to achieve?"

I clenched my jaw, and tried to glare at Carmen. But movement behind Javier caught my attention. More to the point, the glint of something metallic. I opened my mouth to warn him, but no words came out as Paz slipped the needle into the side of Javier's neck, quickly and silently pumping the contents into his blood stream. Carmen watched with satisfaction as her husband slumped to the ground at her feet.

Her smile was cold when she looked back at me. Javier's eyes were open and watchful. I felt bile rise to my throat. "He can see and hear everything," Carmen said with quiet delight. "But this particular snake poison paralyses almost every muscle in his body." She looked up at Paz with a nod. "Lovely work."

Between them, they dragged Javier over to me, and Paz produced another pair of handcuffs from her back pocket, cuffing Javier into the same position as me.

"You're sick," I muttered.

Carmen's head snapped towards me, her eyes leering. "You think I'm sick? He's the one who cheated on me...with you. Of all people, he chose an ugly gringa." She shook her head, causing her mass of loose curls to sway about. She might consider me ugly because of my colouring or race, but I was just as smart and intelligent as she was.

"I think the question you should be asking is

'what do I have that you don't?'" I gave her a cold smile. "There must be something that he liked about me. Do you know what it was?"

I could see Paz visibly freeze as Carmen glared at me. "I have everything he needs." She paused, and glanced down at her husband, her eyes calculating. "He has told me for years that I am the only woman for him." She spat on the floor next to him. "He is a filthy liar."

"Don't think for a moment that I have been the only other woman Javier has had."

She gave me a conniving smile. "Oh, I don't. But the rest are all dead." She crouched down in front of me, lifting my chin so that I looked straight into her eyes. "It is you who has eluded me. And only because of your slutty ways, with your little toy boys who have protected you." She started laughing. "You thought I didn't know? I know all about you, McKenna. I have eyes everywhere."

"Not everywhere," I countered. "You have absolutely no idea what I am capable of."

She stood, placing her hands on her hips as she towered over me and Javier with her glare. "You? You are weak. You had no idea what you were getting mixed up in when you came to my homeland. You still have no idea."

I knew that I needed to keep her talking...that I needed to piss her off. Piss her off enough to do something irrational and stupid. "Still. Your husband wanted me. So what is it, Carmen, that I have, that you don't?" I stared up at the ex-beauty queen, willing her to come up with something that would surprise me.

"I have everything. He told me a thousand times. That is why I am his wife, and not just his mistress."

"No," I said, building my confidence. "Your husband liked being with me because he appreciates intelligent company. You see, Carmen – I'm smart. Far smarter than you. Your husband likes women with brains. That is why he chose me. Brains over beauty." I knew it wasn't the smartest thing I could have said, nor was it true, but I wanted to piss her off, and I knew that dismissing her gorgeous looks was one way to do it.

Sharp pain lanced through me from her slap, throwing my head back into the mirror. Everything turned a stark white. Glaring hot remnants of her touch were left on my cheek as my vision cleared, but I didn't bother to try and rub it.

"You have no idea what you're talking about. I have the brains, and I have the beauty. If I didn't, I wouldn't have been able to do all this." She gestured to both me and Javier. "You see, my father was a great man, and one of the reasons why this operation has run as smoothly as it has. Now that he is dead, my legacy is dead." She stared down at me, her dark eyes boring into mine.

"So you're having father/daughter issues, then?

That's what all this is about?"

Carmen laughed. "No, no, my dear. I'm pleased my father is gone. He basically sold me off to this prick." She threw a nod towards Javier. "All because of business. My father was one of the biggest suppliers of cocaine in Mexico. I was a business deal! But now that my father is dead, my brother has set up new connections with the Santa Muerte, and they have invited me in."

She put her hands on her hips, looking momentarily pleased with herself, but then her features twisted into something dark again as she looked back at me. "You have almost destroyed that agreement. You were meant to die, and your friends were supposed to wipe out this cartel, and therefore prove that I am a leader, deserving of a high position in the Santa Muerte."

My mouth was dry. It was hard to keep up with the ramblings of a crazy woman, but I was getting the distinct impression that this whole operation was a set up. My team had been set up. I had the overwhelming desire to rip my cuffs off, and smash her head into the mirror behind me. This whole situation was her fucking ambitious fault. She was the reason we had almost died multiple times is this bloody country. All because she wanted to switch allegiances. "I know you think this is a smart move," I said through gritted teeth. "But they will kill you as soon as you go over to their side."

"That's where you're wrong. I have the brains. I have always been the brains behind this entire operation. They need me." She turned to Javier, and toed his leg with her foot. "You will see," she said, more to him than to me. She turned on her heel, and stormed down past the glowing fish tank, and into the room beyond. She was shouting expletives at Paz. I had the distinct impression that her night was not going as planned.

22

Paz walked into the room, closing the door silently behind her. Her phone was pressed to her ear, as she spoke in hurried Spanish to the recipient. I watched her with curiosity. Even with the scarring on her face, she was still a stunning looking woman. I could tell she was irritated with Carmen, but she had been suppressing it well. Now that she was in a different room from Carmen, I could see it written all over her.

I looked at Javier. He was the core reason why I'd come to Mexico. Now he was in the same state as me. Well - I hadn't been drugged yet, but we were both cuffed to a rail. A part of me was wondering why the hell Carmen hadn't injected any of that stuff into me yet. Now that I knew her master plan, I knew that I was more than a liability.

Javier's eyes met mine, and I suppressed a shiver. Carmen's words came back to me, informing me that he could see and hear everything. I wondered what on earth he would do if he ever got free from this mess we were caught up in. Would he kill her? I would kill her. Or would he respect her even more now? Who knew what really made these Cartel guys tick.

Paz had stopped talking on the phone, and now stood in front of the enormous fish tank. She turned slowly and looked at me. "You killed my lover, you know?"

Bewilderment infused me. "What? Who did I kill?"

"Filipo. He was my lover. I saw you that day on the roof with your boyfriend," she sneered at me. "Carmen doesn't know it was you. But I saw you with my own eyes." She took a few steps in my direction, her hands on her hips. "He was my payday. He was going to get me out of here," she hissed. "But you screwed that up. Now he is dead, and I will probably be next."

"Why are you working for Carmen then?"

Paz shrugged. "Because I know which side my bread is buttered. She may actually take me to the Santa Muerte Cartel with her."

I shook my head with disbelief. "You can't be serious? Look what happened to her husband." I looked over at Javier. "She has no loyalty to him and she was married to him."

"He's a liar and a cheat," Paz stated simply. "You... well... your trip to Mexico has screwed up a lot of lives. But it won't for much longer. After what you did to Filipo? You deserve everything that's coming for you." She waved her hand in dismissal at me before I could respond, and turned back towards her fish tank. "Feeding time, babies?" she murmured, the sound of her voice carried over towards me.

I gritted my teeth. Something told me that feeding these fish didn't mean a sprinkle of fish food. Paz disappeared through the door, and after a moment, I could hear her moving around upstairs. I had to wonder exactly how big this place was. Something disturbed the waters of the fish tank. Bile rose to my throat as I recognised a human arm with the hand still attached. A leg was the next appendage to hit the water. I had wondered what the fish were waiting for. Another leg and an arm were dropped into the tank, and then a male torso. I thought I was going to faint. I guess 'getting fed to the fishes' wasn't just a Russian mafia term. Not now. Paz took it literally.

The fish moved as if they were one entity. They swarmed around the dead flesh, manoeuvring it, so they could get to more of their dinner. While I was disgusted, I was also fascinated. Javier was watching them too. He didn't look surprised, but in saying that, he couldn't move a muscle in his body, so it was pretty hard to express any emotion.

How the hell was I even in this situation? This wasn't reality. This wasn't what real people did. I was trapped in some sort of bizarre alternate reality.

I heard a car pull up, and my insides jumped with anticipation. It was probably more cartel members. I groaned. More cartel members, meant more of an audience for the ultimate demise that Carmen had planned for me. Without looking at us, Paz walked through the room, and straight out to the garage. I heard the garage door lift, and she spoke quietly with someone. The garage door rattled to a close, and they stepped into the room. My heart almost stopped as Gabe's gaze brushed over me.

"I see you have company," he said quietly to Paz.

She threw back her head with laughter. "Don't we always?"

He chuckled along with her, but as she turned away from him, his eyes once again cut to mine. My heart sank with the dawn of a new reality. Gabe was in on this. Somehow, he'd been turned. Carmen had got to him. I could see it. Hope of getting out of here alive was dwindling faster by the minute.

"I'm sorry." I heard a whisper.

My eyes snapped to Javier. "Did you just say something?"

I saw the smallest of nods.

"The poison is wearing off?"

"Sorry," he said once again, the words almost

indistinguishable.

I sighed. "It's all right, Javier." As if these things happened on an everyday basis. "Your wife is crazy, although I kind of knew that already." I blew out a sigh of regret. "I'm sorry too. If it wasn't for me, we probably wouldn't be in this mess, and you would still be living your married life in ignorant bliss."

A thought crossed my mind, thinking of Gabe in the next room. Why would he turn? What on earth would Carmen have that could compel him to go against his friendship with River and Chase? From what Chase had told me, they were completely and utterly loyal to each other. I swallowed as a tear slipped down my cheek. Anger and disappointment welled within me. Chase trusted him! River loved him like a brother. Why would he do that? I sniffed, and wiped my face on my arm. This was such a huge mess. What an end to my short life. I hadn't even really lived.

After a while, I could hear sounds of a sexual nature coming from the other room, and I looked over at Javier. He had his eyes on the door. I could see the shadow of a frown starting to form on his features. The thought of Gabe with that woman was starting to make me feel ill. What was he doing? He would probably be the next to die at Carmen's hand.

I hummed to myself, blocking the noises from the other room from my consciousness, while wondering what the time was. I had been awake for a long time, and I was actually starting to feel exhausted. Adrenaline alone was the only thing keeping me awake but it was now starting to wear off, and being replaced with heavy resignation and exhaustion.

Elsie crossed my mind. I missed her. I actually just wanted Elsie's cuddles right now. I wanted to smell the lavender scent of her clothing as she wrapped her arms around me, drawing me into her bosom. I swallowed, feeling tears spring to my eyes. If anything, I wished that I could at least say goodbye, and thank you for being the best substitute mother anyone could ever have hoped for. Peter Pan's word came to me then: Death would be an awfully big adventure. I swallowed hard. Tears sprang forth as I imagined Elsie holding me.

This was the hand I had been dealt. Life surrounded by the deaths of those I loved. Death was everyone's ultimate calling. I just didn't think it was quite my time yet.

I don't know when I fell asleep, but I dreamed of being wrapped in Elsie's arms on my childhood bed at home. I woke suddenly, pulled from my dream, disoriented, as something wet spattered on my face. My eyes flew open, but it was pitch black. A flash came from across the room, and a split second later, the mirror behind me splintered and shattered around me. Scrambling, I tried to get away as the glass came crashing down around me, tinkling as it hit the wooden floors. I still couldn't see a thing, and I was restrained by handcuffs to the rail. But damn, I could move when I had to, no matter how awkward it was.

Someone grabbed me from behind, and I thrashed out.

"Mack, it's us." River's voice echoed in my ear, and I froze.

"Get me out of here," I whispered. He was already working in my cuffs.

"Sorry, I don't have any bolt cutters on me, or this would be a lot faster." I couldn't see what he was doing, and I had no idea how he could see either, but none of that mattered right now. What mattered was that they were here. With me. Relief swept through me. Moments later, my hands came free from the tight cuffs. Instinctively, I rubbed my wrists. Blood began to flow properly again, making my hands throb.

"Javier?"

"Dead," River stated. He tugged me across the endless darkness of the room, and opened the door to the garage. Dim light shone through under the roller door.

"So dark," I whispered.

"Power's out," he responded. "Come on - we'll get you safely to the car, and then Chase can finish what we started."

Chase. His name was almost on my lips, before a scream interrupted my thoughts. Something crashed above us, and we both stopped short. River moved around me, and slammed his hand to the wall.

Instantly the garage door jumped in response, slowly lifting as it wound up. Light poured through the widening space, but was it wasn't blinding sunlight. It was early dawn light. A shiver ran through me. Freedom.

Another crash came from above us. I turned to look at River, and did a double take as I took in the goggles he was wearing. He pressed a set of keys into my hand. "Go. My truck is out there - wait for us. We won't be long."

I looked down at the set of keys, but before I could argue with him, he had already disappeared into the darkness. I stood there for a moment in the quiet air, feeling a deep sense of surrealism. The smidgeon of light was growing stronger as the sun began to rise over Mexico, but it was still a long way off before it actually broke through the darkness. Earlier I had been resigned to the fact that I was about to die. This, for some reason felt like I had been cheated. It was a weird and bizarre feeling.

I ran down the dark driveway, towards River's big black truck. I wanted to know what the time was, but Paz still had my bloody phone. If she was still alive. I wrenched the driver's door open, and switched on the engine. The time splashed up brightly on the display of the dash. Five in the morning. I groaned. It felt like I had been held for days, not mere hours.

I sat in the dark car. Everything felt quiet; too quiet. I couldn't help but worry that something had happened to River and Chase. I looked towards the buildings on the property. There was a modestly sized cartel house a fair distance away from the garage-dance-studio-piranha house. The garage side of the building looked like it could comfortably house an enormous long-haul truck. It made me wonder exactly what the purpose of the building was. But there was a second storey, with a large deck overlooking the driveway. It was strange, remote, and it felt ominous.

And then I saw a shadow.

Squinting my eyes to try and see with better focus, an old habit from before I had eye surgery, I peered up towards the second floor of the building. Someone was standing up there outside on the deck, back pressed against the wall so as to not be seen.

Something about the way the figure moved struck me as familiar. It definitely wasn't Chase or River, and I highly doubted it was Gabe. But it was hard to tell from this distance, and in this light. I watched as the figure climbed over the deck railing, crouched, and then hung from the deck, with about a six foot drop to the ground. My heart beat faster and I held my breath in anticipation. As they dropped to the ground, the hood from their jacket fell back and a mass of dark loose curls fell free.

Carmen.

I swallowed as I saw her start to run towards the driveway, heading for the road. There was no bloody way that woman was going to get away after everything she had done to me without us having words first. I reached for the glove compartment, finding an array of River's weaponry. I selected a handgun, which was a shitload bigger and heavier than the ones I had been using, but with the adrenaline that was rapidly coursing through me, I didn't care.

I turned over the trucks engine, keeping the headlights switched off, and took off after the figure running through the dark. While I was conscious of the noise levels of the engine, I was also aware that time was playing a huge factor. My focus was fine-tuned, and my target was in sight.

She turned when she heard the engine, her eyes wide. I wanted to swing the truck around in front of her path, and have the final say with her. I tried to go around her, and swing the vehicle around. She must have thought I just wanted to pass, because she side-stepped right when I was pulling the handbrake on to spin the truck, and the vehicle hit her with a sickening crack. It was as if suddenly everything moved in slow motion. I saw her head bounce off the bonnet of the truck and, slumping, she disappeared under my wheels. The truck screeched to a halt, and I sat there wondering what the hell had just happened.

"Oh my God," I whispered to no one but myself. My hands still gripped the steering wheel, my knuckles deadly white. I didn't know if she was still alive or not. I picked up the gun from my lap, and glanced in the rear-view mirror. I couldn't see her anywhere, which gave me no comfort whatsoever.

I inched my way out of the car in the stillness of the emerging morning light, my feet hitting the gravel as I went. I walked slowly around to the back of the vehicle, not wanting to know what I was going to see. In some ways, I would have much rather buried my head in the sand and lived in blissful ignorance. But I knew that if I didn't confirm with my own eyes, I would never know. River, Chase, and Gabe were right when they told me that. I had to know.

I knew she was dead as soon as I saw her. There was absolutely no doubt about it. Her skull had cracked open, and part of her face was severely impacted. I didn't remember running over her with the wheels, but everything seemed very blurry all of a sudden.

I collapsed onto my knees, ignoring the gravel digging into my knees and shins. Tears streamed down my face. I didn't know if the tears were from the sadness of taking another person's life, or if they were from relief. Whatever it was, it felt good to finally release some of the pent up emotion. My hands shook as I lifted them to wipe away the salty tears with the backs of my grubby hands.

"She was a bad person," I whispered. "She was a bad person." I swallowed, and breathed through my nose to try and calm myself. "It's okay, she was one of the rotten apples." I closed my eyes, replaying everything that had happened over the past twenty four hours. It had been a horrific rollercoaster of a ride. I sat up straight, and once again sucked in a lung full of air.

I heard the sound of footfalls on the gravel drive, and whipped my head around, gun raised, instantly scanning for the next danger to come at me. Three figures walked towards me. I squeezed my eyes shut, swallowing the next well of emotion that pounded through me, breathing deep through my nose again. Chase, River, and Gabe. They were all okay. Realisation hit me that Gabe must not have been a traitor. Visions of seeing Gabe and Chase arguing in the kitchen rose to my memory's surface, and I knew for sure that he was still on our team. He was just playing a role, one that Chase didn't like, but they had come for me. I pursed my lips together, and looked through teary-eyed vision down at Carmen.

All of this had been because of her. I had no idea how one woman could wreak so much havoc, but she had. In this moment, I felt a deep sense of remorse for her sweep through me. Carmen had lived a hard life. One that it seemed she hadn't chosen for herself. I knew that she was going to kill me, but it had been no different from any of her other killings. I was just the last loose end before her ascension into the Santa Muerte Cartel.

I never wanted to be forced into anything I didn't want to do. I never wanted to let someone else have that sort of power over me.

Arms wrapped around me, and hauled me to my unsteady feet. The scent of Chase's cologne encircled me. I was safe. I closed my eyes, letting him lead me away from Carmen. We stopped a few paces off, and he lifted my chin, staring into my eyes. "You scared me," he whispered.

I couldn't speak. All I could do was slightly shake my head, and stare back at him. His gaze softened and I felt my lip wobble. His arm wrapped around the back on my neck, pulling me towards him. His lips met mine briefly, before he encircled me into his arms, holding me tightly.

This is where I belonged. I found my voice. "Chase," I whispered. "Don't ever let me go."

"I won't, Mack. No matter what."

23

I sat staring out the window of the plane, deep in thought about my life, when something hit me. "What about Luke?"

River looked up from some paperwork he was reading, and put it down on his lap as he considered me. "What about him?"

I could see Gabe almost smile as he looked at his brightly lit computer screen, and if I wasn't so damn tired, that smile would have infuriated me. "I mean – what about Luke?! I don't want him to die, but Alvarez said that they had him."

River looked thoughtful for a moment, and nodded "They did have him. But not for long. While we were trying to find you, Chase put in a call to one of his contacts in London. Gabe ran a trace on Luke's mobile. And between us, they managed to find Luke," River paused and picked up his paperwork again, looking back down at it.

"But–"

"No, no." River shook his head keeping his eyes on the document. "Before you ask, Luke's fine. A bit knocked about, but alive."

Chase chose that moment to plonk himself down in the seat next to me, and I gave him a tired but relieved smile. "Did I just hear you talking about Luke?"

I nodded, fighting to stop the tears from filling my eyes. I was utterly relieved that Luke was actually okay. I didn't love him anymore, and I think that in my time of being held captive by Carmen, I had even forgiven him.

I swallowed as Chase's fingers laced with mine reassuringly. These guys were an amazing group of men.

I wished I could email Elsie and tell her I was on my way home, but that bought up the image of my phone slipping into Paz's pocket.

"What happened to Paz?" I asked.

"Fish-tank," Chase whispered.

I pursed my lips and gulped. For some reason, it felt like a fitting end. "I guess I'm going to need a new phone then..."

"Now that all the paperwork's done, we've been

paid." Gabe announced, looking across the table over his computer, causing me to snap my head up in attention. "All except for you, Mack," he looked pointedly at me.

I was about to utter some sort of expletive at him, when he held up his hand, making me hold my tongue.

"Just hang on a moment." He smiled. "You will be paid accordingly, but there are a few things to discuss first." He glanced at River beside him, who gave him a nod. Chase laced his fingers reassuringly between mine.

I wriggled in my seat. "What?"

Gabe cleared his throat. "While you were snoring your head off at the back of the plane before, we had a meeting. A discussion of sorts. You will receive payment for Carmen's kill, Alvarez's kill, and Alicio. But here's the catch."

I held my breath. Monetary numbers in the millions were stacking up in my head. That was a lot of money. A shitload of money. "What? Carmen? She was never on the hit list." I squeaked.

Gabe laughed. "She made the Santa Muerte hit list with Javier last night just before she took you. Orders came through while I was waiting in the car for you lot at the warehouse. She would have died anyway, but we thought we would take the opportunity for a payment as well as a rescue mission. That's why I was there. Two birds, one stone."

"How much was Carmen?"

"Five million U.S," River replied. "So was Javier."

"Anyway..." Gabe sighed "That's not what we want to talk about." He looked up at Chase, and threw his hands in the air. "Come on," he urged impatiently.

Chase squeezed my hand; his eyes glittering with amusement. "We'd like you to join our team," he said.

"You want me to what?" I looked from River to Gabe, and finally at Chase. "You want me to join your team? ...to become an assassin?"

"Yes," River said quietly. "It's what we do, and how we make a living ... a fairly decent one, might I add."

I licked my lips, and settled on chewing my bottom lip for a second. There was so much to think about. Chase being in the relationship mix was a completely different kettle of fish. I shrugged. "Are you sure?"

"Yes." River smiled with amusement. "We're sure."

I had the sudden urge to stand up and pace around, but I couldn't. We were on a goddamn plane, for Christ's sake, and Chase had me trapped against the window. "But I'm not like you guys," I said softly. "You guys are pros, and I am nowhere near that calibre."

Gabe laughed. "That doesn't matter. We are a team with different skill sets that complement each other. What? You think I'm the world's best assassin?" He snorted. "Hell no. But I'm teamed up with two guys who are."

Gabe had a point. I resumed chewing my lip, and gazed out the window at the clouds far below us, and analysed the frosting encasing the outside of the private jet. If there was one thing I had learned throughout this whole tip, it was that I never wanted to let anyone ever control me like Carmen had. If I took up with this team, I wanted it to be on my terms. "Okay, well, I have few questions before I make my decision: What if I eventually want out?"

"Tie up any loose ends, and you can go."

I looked at Gabe. "You're not going to go and blow my house up with C4 or anything like that are you?"

He laughed. "No. Not likely. Even if someone put a hit out on your head, I don't think I could do that to you. As River said, you tie up any loose ends with your kills, and you're free to take your money and go live whatever life you want."

"What money?" I asked.

Chase answered. "For each kill we make, we invest a certain percentage into the business. That pays for things like weapons, houses, cars, and planes – like the one we're currently flying in."

"What sort of percentage?"

"Fifteen percent of each kill goes into the business. If one of us ever wants to leave, nine percent of the business profit will be paid out on leaving. Six percent stays in. You already know that we three–" He pointed to himself, Gabe, and River. "–have agreed to close up shop once we decide to retire. You... well, you're different."

Gabe laid his hand over mine on the table. "You can choose to leave now. You can take your money, and go. Truly. But if you choose to come with us, then you'll have a hell of a ride. There are thrills and kills, and a lot of amazing experiences. Life will never be the same."

"If I come with you, whatever I've earned, the business will take a percentage now, won't it?" I actually didn't care. I just wanted to know all of the ins and outs before I signed up for anything.

"Yes," River replied. "That's why Gabe has held off on paying you. We wanted to see what you wanted to do."

I gazed around at the three of them. They had risked their lives for me, and taught me so much in such a short space of time. They had got me out of financial shit with Luke, rescued me from prostituting myself, and killed on behalf of me. In the very least, I owed them my friendship. And I also had a sneaking suspicion that Chase might be just a little bit in love with me.

Butterflies leapt in my tummy. "As long as I get to choose who I kill, then I'm in. I don't want to kill anyone who doesn't deserve it. If we research my targets and they have murdered multiple people, or terrorised a community, then I will do my job. But I'm not killing innocents. That's the bottom line."

Chase grinned, and pulled me in for a kiss, not caring that both River and Gabe were watching me with silly grins plastered on their faces. Fire swept through me, and my heart raced, not just from the kiss but from the agreement I had just made with them. Something about all this felt right.

"Welcome to the team," he whispered as he pulled away.

THE END

About the Author

Leigh K. Hunt is a reader, writer, mother, and wife from the Land of the Long White Cloud, otherwise known as Aotearoa, New Zealand. She has a weird obsession with books like Alice in Wonderland, Peter Pan, Pride & Prejudice, and adores Thrillers and Dystopian novels. To say that she lives in her own dreamy wonderland is an understatement.

As a child, her whole world was fantasy-based reality of tree huts, artistic endeavours, musical creations, and story inventions. She would only come back to the 'real world' to do the mundane things like feed the dog her broccoli or Brussel-sprouts under the dining table.

If Leigh could have one superpower in the whole wide world, it would be to have the ability to fold space and time, so that she could be anywhere, at any time. Leigh loves travelling with a fiery passion, and exploring foreign countries, delving into different cultures, and immersing herself with the people.

In her adult life, she works full time, is a mother to a

gorgeous but very lively three-year-old, and is married to her rock, Michael. She also has numerous mothers, fathers, and a couple of very special siblings who keep her grounded, despite her desire to permanently live inside her head.

To connect to Leigh, please visit her website:
www.leighkhunt.com or email her at:
leighkhunt.author@gmail.com

Love Music?
Each of Leigh's books are written to music - so discover the playlists on **Spotify** - just search for *Tijuana Nights* or *London Dusk*, and you will find them.

Subscribe to Leigh K. Hunt's Book Updates Newsletter, and you will be the first to know about any book news, new releases and giveaways.
Author Newsletter: http://eepurl.com/XpTuL

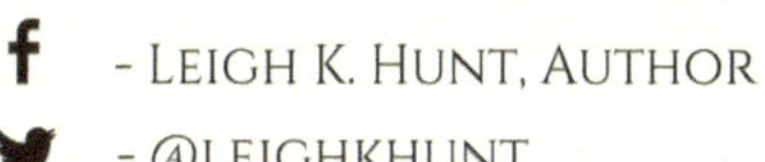

Other Works by Leigh K. Hunt

Venice Nights
The Nights Series

McKenna Carmichael has a new job in the beautiful country of Italy. This isn't a pleasure trip: she must eliminate her mark and get out.

Her target Luigi Donati is rich and handsome, and his fashion house leads charity work. But his dossier shows that's a front, hiding ties to where his real money comes from: slave labour.

Mack realises that not only is Luigi innocent, but someone else is intent on killing him. Thrown by doubt, Mack must choose her role in this Italian job – predator or protector.

Join Mack on her next thrilling adventure in Leigh K. Hunt's new Night's series.

Leigh's new thriller -
The Mediterranean Source
is coming soon....